Shadow Target

R.D. West

Shadow Target

For information contact :

R.D. West

rdwest@rd-west.com

First Edition

ISBN : 9798360153979

Also by R.D. West

SHADOW TARGET SERIES

SHADOW TARGET
HUNTER ELITE (COMING SOON)

We wouldn't be able to write without those who support us. We thank you for your encouragement and for being there for us.
To those that read our books, thank you for your support.

Preface

Shadow Target takes place in different locations throughout the United States. In the spirit of telling a compelling story, some aspects of the real towns and cities have been altered. Thank you for understanding the author's creative freedom.

Chapter 1

After pulling into the Sunshade Motel parking lot a shy past 10:00 p.m., Brad Jones navigated his inconspicuous, late model, black Toyota Corolla under the seedy motor inn's porte cochère. The office had its blinds tilted at a downward angle. A neon "No Vacancy" sign glowed brightly from the outside of the window; it washed out the darkness around the bushes near the entrance in a blood-red hue.

Inside, the desk clerk was nowhere to be seen, allowing Brad to pass by without detection. The parking lot was dotted with a wide variety of vehicles, ranging from poorly-cared-for clunkers to high-end, luxury sedans. Motels like Sunshade were a perfect spot for D.C.'s elite to frequent with their mistresses or call girls, not to mention the other nefarious dealings transpiring behind closed doors. Being located far from the capital and the prying eyes of city dwellers, the lodge was a breeding ground for the corrupt to conduct their business. That night was no different.

Brad swung the Corolla about and then backed into an open slot near the far edge of the motel's car lot. The headlights vanished a second later and the engine cut off. He removed the keys from the ignition and retrieved his phone from the cubby hole in the center console.

As he pressed the power button on the side of the device and then applied his thumbprint to the screen, Brad swept the front of the rooms facing the expanse of the motor inn's lot. Not a soul stirred outside. It was completely quiet.

Brad then diverted his gaze down at the screen. He studied the balding, middle-aged man's picture that stared back at him.

Frank Talbot was about as ordinary as they came; his features were plain and nondescript. He wore thick-rimmed, Coke bottle glasses and had a black mustache. His round head and double chin erased any sort of defined, chiseled features from his pasty, white complexion.

The words *"Sunshade Motel. Room 4B."* were printed under his image. That's all Brad had to go on, and all that he needed to complete his assignment.

He killed the light from his phone and got out of the sedan. The warm, muggy night air greeted Brad as he carefully shut his door without any residual noise. One final sweep of the rooms of the motel and its grounds showed no signs of surveillance of any sort, signaling that he could move about without being captured by cameras.

Adjusting his ACDC t-shirt over the top of his jeans and pulling the bill of his black ball cap further down on his head, Brad made for the steel staircase. He had grown used to blending in and not drawing attention to himself. Though he was barely twenty, Brad had completed numerous assignments without ever being detected or failing a mission.

His boots pinged off the steps as he ascended the staircase. He constantly scanned the parking lot and rooms as he neared the landing of the second floor. So far, all was as expected with no surprises that he could foresee.

Brad causally walked down the stretch of balcony past the rooms and shut blinds until arriving at his destination. One final glance at the closed doors around him and Brad advanced on Mr. Talbot's room.

A symphony of pleasurable noises was emitted through the door. Each groan and holler indicated the businessman was more than enjoying his weekly rendezvous.

With a soft but firm rap on the door, Brad listened as the couple ceased their primal grunts. A brief moment of silence lingered followed by lowered voices and shuffling feet.

"Yes? Who is it and what do you want?" a breathless, quickened voice asked.

"Yes, sir," Brad started as he got into character. "We've received reports from other guests of an odd smell coming from your room."

"An odd smell?"

"Yes, sir."

"I don't smell anything. They're mistaken."

Brad maintained decorum and said, "I understand, sir, but we'd like to check for ourselves and make sure there isn't a gas leak or other danger to our guests. For this inconvenience, we're going to comp your night's stay and offer you a voucher for a free future reservation."

The muttered voices persisted until he replied. "Fine, but make it quick."

As the door's deadbolt retracted and it pulled away from the jamb, Brad dipped his shoulder and rammed the door, forcing his way into the motel room. He quickly shut the door behind him, engaged the lock, and pulled his FNX-45 from the waistband of his blue jeans.

Mr. Talbot stumbled back from the door, dressed in nothing more than a white robe. His bulbous gut pressed against the loose knot keeping the flaps of the covering from coming undone. Beads of sweat raced down the sides of his clammy flesh as he raised his arms. The room smelled of cheap cleaner and generations of bad decisions.

"What the hell is this?" the portly man snarled.

A naked, older, blonde woman hidden under the ruffled sheets of the queen-sized bed ventured a scream, but Brad shushed the shivering hooker and controlled the scene.

"Keep quiet and do not make a single sound. Am I clear?"

She nodded her compliance as she whimpered through pursed lips.

"Please. I don't know who you are or what you want, but if it's money or other valuables that you're after, I can give you what I have in my wallet." Mr. Talbot turned and tipped his head at his trousers draped over the backrest of a brown, wooden chair behind him. "It's in my back pocket. Take what you want and leave."

"Shut up."

Brad kept the HK aimed at the fat man's skull as he looked over the room, then at the partially cracked door leading into the bathroom. The motel room's aged wallpaper barely clung to the walls. The furniture was about as old and worn as the walls were. So was the ancient, tube television.

High-heeled black boots stuck out from under the woman's garments that had been tossed in the middle of the floor. Her small, black purse rested on the top of the dresser next to the TV that had muted adult programming playing.

"Is there anyone else in here?" Brad asked.

Mr. Talbot shook his head and said, "No. It's just us."

The woman's frightened whimpers seeped from the white covers crammed against her mouth. She trembled in the bed as tears smeared the thick, black mascara around her eyes, darkening each socket.

"Listen. Please take what you want," Mr. Talbot said on the verge of crying. "I have a wife and three kids. I swear I won't report this to the authorities. You have my word."

Brad approached the quaking, plump man, grabbed him by the scruff of his robe, and shoved him toward the bed without acknowledging the plea. Then he checked the time on his wrist watch. It was 10:20 p.m. He needed to conclude his business and exit the room.

"There has to be some sort of arrangement we can make here." Mr. Talbot pushed up from the bed and sat down next to the weeping hooker as Brad dialed up the volume on the tv.

The mixture of grunts and moans would muffle the coming noise.

"I know we can–"

A single round fired from the HK45's suppressor in a whisper, silencing Mr. Talbot. The bullet punched the bald man's forehead. His head snapped back as blood and brain matter sprayed the white, dingy sheets. He collapsed back onto the mattress, pinning the woman's legs under his body.

Frightened, the hooker belted a scream that was instantly silenced by the TV's speakers. She kicked her legs and pressed into the headboard, but couldn't escape.

Brad leveled the HK with her head and squeezed the trigger without pause.

Another silenced report fired from the gun and punched her skull. Her head flopped back against the padded headboard; then she dumped over onto the mattress.

No witnesses were to be left alive, regardless of whether they were part of the assignment or not. That was the rule.

Having completed his task, Brad kept the volume on the TV high and then removed the cell phone from his back pocket. He angled the camera lens at their deadpan faces and snapped a picture for confirmation of the kills.

With the pictures recorded, Brad stowed the pistol in the waistband of his jeans, deposited the phone in his back pants pocket, and then advanced toward the door. Brad glanced through the shut blinds to confirm the balcony was clear; then he gripped the door handle with his gloved hand.

As the television's scratchy speakers continued to blare inside the room, Brad opened the door wide enough to slip through to the balcony. He shut the door behind him and strode toward the landing of the steel staircase. Then he descended to the bottom step and marched toward his car.

Wrestling the car keys from his front pants pocket, he opened the driver's side door and plopped down onto the seat. Brad then removed his gloves and chucked them onto the passenger side floorboard, and reached back and grabbed his cell phone.

He typed *Mission Complete* in the text message containing Frank Talbot's picture and hit send. Then Brad started the Corolla and exited the parking lot the way he came, vanishing into the night.

Chapter 2

Brad's morning started early the next day. It was 6:15 a.m. He had already been up and about for over an hour. He'd slept little during the night, but he was used to running on fumes, and could always drown himself in endless energy drinks or coffee.

Sun shone through the window of his tiny house, which was sparsely decorated. A single twin-sized bed, a dresser, couch, footlocker, and a kitchen table with two chairs were the extent of his furnishings. He sat at the small round table and stared off into the distance as he cleaned his HK45. For Brad, it was one of the ways to decompress after a job. The monotonous task of deconstructing the firearm, cleaning it thoroughly, and assembling it back together was therapeutic.

Over the years, he had grown proficient in handling the weapon. From a young age, Brad had been trained to use firearms and to know them inside out. Respect his tools of the trade and they'd treat him well. As time passed, each gun he used felt like an extension of him.

He secured the slide into place. Then Brad slapped the magazine into the mag well. He placed the weapon on the table top next to his cleaning kit.

The tools were organized in an orderly fashion on the soft, light-gray mat before him. He was taught that to be proficient at his craft one had to be methodical and precise in every aspect of his life.

Brad glanced past the weapon to the book to his right on the edge of the table. *Manhattan Heights* was one of his favorite reads. He had been an avid reader for as long as he could remember. Other than cleaning his gun, reading the adventures of his favorite heroic character helped relax Brad after a job. It pulled his mind out of a world with which he wasn't fully quadrated. Sure, he killed people, and he was among the best, but the *why* always found a way to niggle at him.

Two hard knocks sounded at his front door. He checked his watch. Right on time.

"Come in."

The door opened with a slight squeak. Additional sunlight flooded into the entryway as Mya Black entered his compact dwelling.

She was all business as usual but flashed a brief smile Brad's way as she stepped through the doorway. Her long, black hair was pulled tight into a ponytail and swung with each step she made. Not a hint of makeup coated her perfectly tanned skin, but Mya didn't require such trivial things. She had a natural beauty that made her far more pretty than any cover model could ever attempt to achieve.

"How'd it go last night?" she asked.

"No issues. Completed in less than ten minutes."

"Excellent. Not that I'm surprised. You're nothing if not punctual."

"I try to be."

Brad enjoyed their banter, regardless of the topic. Mya was one of the few people on the compound with whom he'd grown close. They had a kindred spirit that blossomed over the years since early childhood. Having relations, they knew, was forbidden and met with severe punishment as it was deemed a distraction from maintaining focus and discipline. Cobalt came first, second, and third, and there the list ended. Anything else would not be tolerated by the instructors, or their leader, Morgan Rojas.

"Have you slept?" Mya asked while studying Brad's tired face. "You don't look like you got even a wink of sleep."

"I drifted off here and there when I got back late last night, but nothing solid. I'm just glad it was a close assignment and not overseas, but either way, I'll manage. It's what we do, right?"

Mya nodded and then said, "Right. It is." She turned and trained her ear at the door. "Well, let's stop by the mess hall and grab you some coffee or an energy drink. You need to be awake and alert, more so than what you look like right now. They'll be passing out assignments shortly, and you don't want to catch another lecture or waste disposal duty, do you?"

Brad shrugged at the thought of collecting the compound's waste and then stood from his chair. "It's not the worst thing they could charge us with doing."

"If you say so." Mya backed toward the doorway as Brad carried the cleaning kit and mat to his footlocker. He deposited both into the hold, and then secured the HK45 in his assigned weapons lockbox. She continued. "Just remember that when you're grabbing those soggy trash bags and tossing them into that nasty dump cart. And don't forget, Asher's trash will be mixed in, so you would be handling his trash as well. He would love to see that."

Brad hesitated midstride, his brows furrowing in disgust. "You're right. I can't give him the satisfaction. But it won't come to that." He followed Mya outside and then shut the door behind him.

"That's what I like about you, Brad. You're confident and ballsy, borderline arrogant."

"Yes. That's all part of my charm."

Mya gave one last smirk as they got on the move. "That it is."

Chapter 3

A BUZZ OF ACTIVITY swarmed the grounds of the sprawling compound that was nestled in the valley of dense sylvan within the Blue Ridge Mountains. The expanse of the community had grown since Brad's arrival thirteen years ago. A steady flow of recruits funneled into Virginia's hidden training facility, which housed more than twenty kids of varying ages and walks of life. He couldn't remember how he'd arrived at such a place or any of his life previous to his arrival, but it had been his home ever since.

The property was dotted with a multitude of buildings across eighty acres of prime land. It was self-sustained by and for the cadets, instructors, and guards who lived on-site.

They had everything required to live and train in the remote depths of Virginia's backcountry— from barracks to an infirmary, an armory, training rooms used for lectures, offices occupied by instructors and other personnel, ancillary housing for higher-ranked operators, multiple helipads, and even an airfield.

The small airfield was used to take off and land from the far, east side of the compound. Only the craziest of pilots would dare risk the dirt runway that offered little room for error within the walls of trees. Luckily, they had three such skilled pilots who made piloting the nimble aircraft up and out of the short span of the runway look like child's play.

"I don't know about you, but I'm glad we are not stuck in those barracks anymore," Mya said as they passed a large sheet metal building. "I like my privacy, and in there you have none."

"No one was dumb enough to sneak a peek at you when you were changing. Well, not except for Jimmy, whose head you cracked for gawking at you."

"Yeah. He was a quick study," Mya replied. "He still won't look me in the eye to this day."

Brad, Mya, and a handful of senior operators working in the field were given private quarters away from the barracks that housed the children in training. It was a bonus reflecting how hard work paid off when they met goals set by their handlers.

The mess hall had a fraction of the bodies that would be stuffed into the building soon to retrieve breakfast.

Three of the instructors huddled around one of the tables sipping coffee and shoveling eggs and bacon into their mouths. All were former military, but that was about as far as their distinction went. No further information was given as it didn't matter. If they said jump, those under their command asked how high.

Out of the three burly bearded men, Brad had the best relationship with Ronan Sherman. Don and Shane weren't bad, but they certainly didn't go out of their way to coddle the kids in any sort of way.

Ronan tipped his head at Brad, who parroted the gesture.

"I think you need a Monster or a Red Bull," Mya said as she perused the cooler stocked with a variety of bottled water and energy drinks. "Coffee isn't going to cut it in a pinch, and you can't pound both. Not enough time."

"Give me the Monster. It will do for now." Brad said. "Downing both at once will give me the shakes and make it harder for me to concentrate during our briefing."

Mya opened the case, then removed one of the chilled 16-ounce cans and handed it to him. "Assault is still your favorite, right?"

"It is." Brad took it from Mya, popped the top, and took a sip.

"A bit on the nose, isn't it? Assault flavor, I mean."

"It is, but I like the taste."

Brad guzzled half the can in less than a minute.

"If that doesn't wake you up, I don't know what will." Mya picked out a Red Bull from the cooler and took a hearty gulp from the slender can.

Don and Shane stood from their seats then headed for the side exit. Ronan whistled their way and waved his arm at them as he trailed the two other instructors.

Brad checked the time. It was 7:15. This morning's briefing would start in exactly fifteen minutes. Not a minute later.

"Come on, hot shot. Let's go. We can finish our drinks on the way. I'd rather be early than late."

Chapter 4

THEY ARRIVED IN THE briefing room with five minutes to spare. It was sparsely dotted with what operators the organization had on-site, which, at the time, wasn't many. Most were out on assignments, leaving a mere few left behind for details. Besides Ronan and the other instructors not tied up with kids, there were a total of nine people present.

Mya and Brad funneled into the middle section of perfectly lined chairs and secured two seats behind Asher Rojas and Neil Stanton. The two men chatted in low voices as the pair sat in the light brown, folding chairs.

Two more operators rounded out the selection of young men and women to receive orders that day, Marci Davies and Blane Johnson. The duo looked like they could be twins, seeing how they mirrored each other. It was unclear if they were related since no one had memories outside of the organization. Cobalt was the only family they had ever known.

As Brad adjusted his backside on the cushionless chair bottom, he caught sight of Ronan staring his way. The elder instructor locked gazes with him as Asher Rojas turned in his seat and faced Brad.

"It's nice to see that the best damn operator in the world could grace us with his presence this morning. I was beginning to wonder if you'd show up." Asher checked the time on his watch and said, "You're normally here well before anyone else. Cutting it a bit close, huh? Did you have nightmares last night, Jones?"

Asher was cocky and arrogant. A smug smirk resided on his well-groomed, olive-toned face. Not a day went by that he didn't bust Brad's balls.

It had been that way since day one. Their supposed rivalry matured into a bitter contempt for each other. At least, that's how Asher saw it since he felt that his father showed favor to Brad instead of him, but Brad never saw it that way. To him, Asher had always been a sniveling little shitbird who siphoned power he never earned from his father, Morgan Rojas. Asher was the only kid on the compound with a biological parent present, and it didn't help that said parent was the leader of the entire organization; in many ways that made Asher invincible. It was a detail he never let anyone forget.

Instead of allowing Asher to dig under his skin, Brad let the snide comment slide off him. Now wasn't the time for bickering or heated discussions as Brad knew that he was being baited into a trap with their briefing about to commence.

"I'm good. I appreciate your concern, as always. It's nice to know that you care so much," Brad replied.

One thing Asher hated was not being able to get a rise out of Brad. It irked him to no end, and Brad's day continued to improve as he watched Asher squirm ever so slightly in his chair with irritation.

"Funny, Jones." Asher's lips pursed and his brow furrowed.

"How about you face forward and stop being a dick this morning," Mya said while keeping her voice dialed down. "Just because you're the boss man's son, doesn't mean you can't suffer consequences. We're all bound by the same rules. Don't forget that."

Asher cut his dagger-like stare at Mya, and then he opened his mouth to respond when Ronan cleared his throat.

All chatter ceased immediately. Asher faced forward, tabling their discussion for a later time.

Silence ensued as everyone provided their utmost attention to the head of Cobalt, Morgan Rojas, as he entered the room.

The instructors squared their shoulders and stood at the ready. Each man and woman waited as Morgan took his spot behind the podium at the front of the room.

Morgan was all business as usual as he set the files clutched in his hands on top of the podium. Despite being in his late fifties, the leader of Cobalt was in impeccable shape and good health. No one dared to challenge his command, knowing full well how lethal his hands were and how fluent he was with most types of weapons.

"This won't take long seeing as there aren't many of you here at the moment. We have several assignments on the docket," Morgan started in his suave, Latin American accent. "I've been mostly pleased by our recent missions stateside and abroad. We've completed each on time and with no residual fallout. All targets and objectives have been met with success and that means more work is coming in."

Brad gently tapped his boot on the floor as Morgan shuffled through the files before him.

"Now, I've got four different assignments here that need your best work. One will require a team of two while the remaining three will be single-man missions."

Ronan approached the podium as Morgan opened each file, glanced at the contents, and then closed the manila flap.

One by one, Ronan dispersed the assignments to the small group of men and women. Marci and Blane got the two-man mission, while Mya, Brad, and Neil got the remaining three. That left Asher as the odd man out.

As they each opened their respective files, Asher spoke up before Morgan could proceed.

"Um, where's my detail?"

"All assignments have been handed out. You'll be staying behind for now," Morgan answered.

"Why? I thought we had more work than we could handle." Asher shot back in a defensive tone. "At least, that's what was said during our last brief, unless that was a lie."

Morgan stared at his son but said nothing at first. His kid was the only one who dared to question his father. No one else muttered a single syllable. The air thrummed within the deafening silence.

"We'll discuss matters afterward. For now, you sit there, stay quiet, and listen."

Asher pressed his luck with his father, twisting the tension to another level that none of them had openly witnessed before.

"Jones just got back from a detail late last night and you're already handing him another one? I'm ready to go and can handle whatever it is you assigned to him."

Hammering his fist down hard on the top of the podium, Morgan leaned forward and stabbed his finger at his kin.

"You will sit there silently and stop arguing with me. I'm in no mood for it. Am I clear?" A short pause from Asher provoked Morgan to repeat his question, his voice dropping to a low timbre. "Am I clear?"

"Yes, sir."

The disdain in Asher's tone was apparent. The father and son had butted heads on more than one occasion, furthering the rift between them throughout the years.

After the heated exchange, Morgan regained his composure, relaxed his stiff stance, and asked, "Does anyone have any questions or concerns about their assignments?"

Not a single person spoke up. Brad had only started studying the file before Asher derailed their briefing, so he hadn't had the chance to gain a hold on the particulars of his job yet.

"Excellent. I expect the same outstanding work as always from each of you. Our margin of error recently has improved. That pleases me. Let's keep that up and not get sloppy. You've been trained for perfection and I expect as much."

And with that, Morgan tipped his head at the instructors, and then exited the room. He offered no additional glance at Asher, who whispered into Neil's ear.

"You heard the man," Shane said in a booming, commanding voice. "Get those asses up and legs moving. For those that have details, make sure you're prepped and ready for departure. As with Commander Rojas, we expect precision out in the field."

Each of the operators stood from their chairs and funneled out of the briefing room to the corridor. Brad and Mya were flanked by Asher and Neil while the instructors hung back discussing various matters.

"Jones. A word?" Asher asked in a stern bark.

Brad paid him no mind as he skimmed the file's contents and continued walking down the hallway next to Mya.

"Don't ignore me you piece of shit." Asher grabbed a handful of Brad's shirt and yanked, stopping him.

"What the hell?" Mya asked.

With one fluid motion, Brad spun on the heels of his boots and grabbed Asher by the arm. He shoved him forward into the wall as the files he carried fell to the floor. Ratcheting his forearm up behind his back, Brad applied the painful hold while pinning the side of his face to the wall. "Don't ever grab me like that again."

"Get your damn hands off of me, Jones!" Asher shot back as he tried to wiggle free of the hold. "I'm going to ruin you!"

Mya tugged on Brad's arm which locked Asher's in a bent position. "It's not worth it, Brad. Let it go."

"Yeah. You better listen to her, Jones!" Asher said as he fought to maneuver his arm out of the hold.

"Jones. Let him go. Now!" Ronan stood in the doorway of the briefing room, facing them.

Brad did as commanded and released Asher's arm as the instructor marched toward the group. Taking a step back, Brad gathered his file from the floor as Asher turned to face him.

Extending his bent arm, Asher advanced on Brad who held his ground. He got inches from his face and stared him down.

"Get going, Asher," Ronan said as he approached the feuding men. "It's done and over. Your father will be expecting you."

Jabbing his finger at Brad, Asher said, "You got that one for free, Jones. Next time, when your protector isn't around, your ass will be mine." Asher then stormed off down the hallway with Neil by his side.

Chapter 5

MYA EXCUSED HERSELF AS Ronan escorted Brad outside, far from the open ears of his fellow instructors. The pair crossed the expanse of the compound in the direction of Brad's unit located at the far end.

"Don't mind Asher. He doesn't like the fact that you're better at this than he is. It eats that boy alive."

"I don't think I'm better than anyone else here," Brad replied as he wedged the file under his arm. "We all have our talents and specialties. I can't help it if he has an ax to grind with me. I never asked Commander Rojas to show me any kind of favor. I don't require the attention as some do."

Nodding, Ronan said, "True, but Commander Rojas knows talent when he sees it. There isn't one area you aren't ranked highest. Hand-to-hand combat. Marksmanship. Surveillance. You're at the top of each category. As with all things, those that perform well get treated as such. It's only fair."

Brad didn't see himself as talented as Ronan made him out to be. Sure, he could handle his own in a fight and was able to use a variety of guns and knives with surgical precision, but that was only because Ronan had seared that training into his psyche from an early age. When you've eaten, drunk, and slept the life they had, it was bound to dig itself into your bones and reform you from the inside out.

"The only talent I possess is being able to take a beating and jump back up. Other than that, I'm just doing my job for the family."

Ronan patted Brad's shoulder; Brad stood a good six inches shorter than his mentor. "There's no doubt about that. I can't recall the last time I've seen someone take such a thrashing during sparring sessions and act as though it was nothing. That's not always a good thing, Brad. One has to know when to stay and fight, and when to live to strike another day. You can't do that if you're dead."

"I'll remember that. Although, I doubt the other instructors, or Commander Rojas, view that in the same way. We're taught to complete our assignments by whatever means necessary. Perfection. No room for error. Life and death are secondary to that."

Even with the stern teachings and tough upbringing within the Cobalt family, Ronan always found a soft spot for the kids in his charge. He was tough and yet showed compassion when his peers weren't around. Such feelings of well-being were never a blip on the organization's radar, as the world was cruel and dangerous. And so was the work they conducted.

As they neared Brad's unit, Ronan asked, "How have you been doing?"

"As in?"

He clarified. "You've seemed...distracted, as of late. On edge, even."

"I'm fine. Just focused is all," Brad answered with an indifferent shrug. "I've been a bit tired lately, but that's nothing new. A good night's sleep will fix that."

"And you're sure that's it?"

"I am. What else would there be?"

Brad had been feeling off in a way that he couldn't describe and he didn't want to talk about it. There was no room for feelings of remorse for those that they dispatched while on assignment, so it was a moot point.

Ronan stopped as did Brad, out of respect for his mentor. A quick scan of the surrounding area ensured no one was within earshot, and then Ronan said, "If you ever need to talk about anything that's bothering you, I'm here to listen. Okay?"

His words were sincere. They dripped with care, something that Brad was used to from Ronan, but that's about where it stopped. No one else cared about their mental state as long as they were still able to operate. They were assets, tools even, used how and where the organization saw fit. Completing jobs was all there was and nothing would change that.

Curious glances from passing instructors and their charges ended the conversation. Ronan cleared his throat as the two-way radio attached to his hip crackled a deep, raspy voice.

Sherman. Where are you at? I need you down at the gun range for a moment.

Ronan removed the radio from his belt and brought the mic to his mouth. "I'm on my way. Be there shortly." He fixed the clip mounted on the back of the device over the top of his black belt, and then said, "When you get back, let's have a better chat, all right?"

"Okay."

"Watch your six out there and remember your training. You'll be just fine."

"Always."

Chapter 6

BRAD CHECKED HIS SMALL black go bag as per his usual pre-deployment ritual. Each operator in the field carried a standard load of currency, alternate IDs, and passports. That didn't include whatever weapons they deemed necessary for the job they had been given.

In the event of being exposed to the authorities, they were to cut and run, then lay low until the heat subsided before returning to the compound. To date, Brad had never once had to resort to abandoning the only family he knew and had no plans of doing so if he could help it.

After meticulously checking each item in the bag, and adding his book, *Manhattan Heights,* to the contents already inside, Brad zipped it closed. He then double-checked the file again to ensure he had the proper attire and knew what weapons he needed.

It was another stateside op in their backyard. A residential neighborhood in Chesapeake, Virginia was Brad's destination. His target was Andrew Snider. No additional details about his target were supplied under the photo of the older, gray-haired man or the picture of his quaint, two-story home.

The mission parameters of the job were clear-cut and concise. Eliminate the target and retrieve a thumb drive from his office. Above all, no loose ends were to be left untied.

His phone buzzed a second later. Brad thumbed the power button, applied his thumb print to the screen, and checked the unread, securely sent message that contained the mark's name and address. Then he set the phone back on top of the table.

Given the scope of the job, and that the home was more than likely located in a suburb, Brad opted for his trusty HK45 with the suppressor. It was silent and efficient, two things the mission required. Before heading out, he'd stop by the armory and procure a few knives as a backup in addition to the pistol. It was good practice to be prepared for the unexpected, even if the mission seemed like a cakewalk.

Brad gave one final look through his go-bag as a knock at the door drew his attention to the entrance. Before he could reply, the door opened to Commander Rojas standing in the doorway.

"Sir. I was just on my way out. What can I do for you?"

Rojas entered the unit, shutting the door behind him. "I wanted to stop by and wish you well on your upcoming assignment."

"Thank you, sir. I won't let you down." Brad made sure to button his posture up a bit more and square his shoulders when speaking directly to the head of the organization. Rojas wasn't known to drop in on his people in such a way. Usually, his underlings would relay messages or dole out punishment.

"I also wanted to apologize for Asher and his outburst earlier. I must admit, he's like I was at that age. Passionate. Determined. Stubborn. Hard-headed."

Those weren't the words Brad would have used, but he dared not venture that sort of response. Asher was still Morgan's kin and blood always ran thicker than water.

"It's not a problem, Commander Rojas. There is no need for an apology."

"Please, Brad. Call me Morgan."

"Yes, Commander Rojas. I mean, Morgan."

It went against Brad's training to refer to him as anything other than Commander Rojas, or Sir. To everyone in the compound, as far as Brad knew, that was the standard and a line that should never be crossed.

Morgan shook his finger at him and smiled. "That's what I like about you, Brad. You're cool under pressure and remain focused. You know when to apply the right amount of force and when to back off. From the moment you arrived, I knew there was something special about you. I'm glad that you proved me right."

"I'm just doing my part. Nothing more. Nothing less."

"That you are, son." That word struck a chord with Brad. He had never been referred to in that manner by anyone except Ronan, who said it sparingly and away from others.

Such language blurred the lines of authority and made Brad wonder why Morgan had done such a thing. He dared not question his motivation verbally, but it did make him curious.

"Your assignment is stateside, correct?" Morgan asked.

"Yes, sir. Chesapeake."

"Perfect. I know that you're coming off the heels of another job, but you're my go-to operator right now. Out of all the young men and women here, you're a cut above the rest."

Brad bobbed his head. Even though he did not require praise, the recognition was nice to hear for a change.

"I'm glad that my performance has been acceptable."

"It's been more than acceptable, son," Morgan replied. "I hope that your peers and the younger cadets take note of how a true operator works in the field, including Asher. You're setting the bar high."

"Thank you. I'll do my best to not let you down."

Morgan clapped the side of Brad's arm while smiling. "That's what I like to hear." He then said, "After this job, I want to talk to you about a few things; there are some opportunities that I would like to have you be a part of."

"What sort of opportunities?" Brad's interest was piqued, causing him to wonder where Morgan was heading with the cryptic conversation.

"Don't worry about that right now," Morgan replied as he waved his hand in front of him. "We'll have time to talk in the coming days after you return."

"Sounds good, sir. I look forward to hearing what you have to say."

"That you will, my boy. I can promise you that." Morgan turned toward the door and then backed up. "Well, I'll let you finish getting ready. I have some matters of my own that need tending to. Do us proud out there."

"I will, sir."

Offering one last smile, Morgan opened the door and ducked outside to reports of gunfire that popped off in the distance from the gun range.

The door shut, muffling the cracks of gunshots that Brad had grown accustomed to hearing at all hours of the day. As he moved to the table and snatched up his pack, Brad couldn't help but dwell on what opportunity Morgan had for him.

But he would find out soon enough. For now, Brad had a mission to complete. He carried the pack out of his unit and made for the armory, ready to start his job and finish out his next assignment.

Chapter 7

THE DRIVE TO CHESAPEAKE took a little over four hours to make, placing Brad in the city after 2:00 p.m. Road construction and a stop at a gas station for fuel stretched his timetable, but not by much.

Brad was somewhat distracted as he cruised down U.S. Highway 17. His thoughts drifted from the conversations he'd had that morning with Ronan and more so, Morgan. Asher was another sore spot that grated on Brad's nerves, but he quickly erased the brat from his mind.

Morgan had planted a seed in Brad's head, one that he couldn't let go of. Given his upbeat demeanor, and approaching Brad himself, it ramped up the young assassin's imagination into overdrive.

What sort of opportunities would be presented? Brad was far too young and green to be offered an instructor position within the Cobalt organization. He still had a lot to learn and was unsure of his ability to teach others. The missions he had completed thus far were successful by all standards, but Brad was a stickler for honing his craft and becoming a better operator with each job he put under his belt.

He ultimately dismissed the instructor's notion as preposterous. No way would that happen at his age and level of experience. Besides, he was far more valuable in the field than tied up at the compound to train newbies. So, what then?

Nothing seemed to fit that popped into Brad's mind as he navigated his black Corolla along the outskirts of Chesapeake toward Lone Grove East where his target resided. He dismissed the nagging idea and realigned his wandering thoughts back to the job.

His mark, Andrew Snider, was all that mattered right then. Everything else was secondary. His task for the day was to complete the mission and return to home base.

As Brad steered the compact sedan along the snaking road, he studied the town and kept a keen eye open for police. He was mindful of traffic cameras and any highway patrollers within the community.

This was the first time he had been to Chesapeake. Most of the assignments he had been handed sent him all over the eastern seaboard and middle America. One group mission sent him and Mya to Spain the year before, but that was the extent of his international travels.

Brad retrieved the secured message on his device and confirmed the address one final time as he neared the entrance of Lone Grove East. 2516 North Hawkins Lane was where Andrew Snider lived. He placed the phone back in one of the open cup holders on the center console and drove down the two-lane road that ran perpendicular to the brick wall that encompassed the community.

Massive homes reached into the sky, far above the lip of the wall's top. Brad figured Mr. Snider was wealthy and had gotten tangled into some business that he shouldn't have, resulting in him being marked for deletion by Brad's organization.

Even though the operators weren't given specifics of why Brad couldn't help but wonder what each of the people they removed could have done to warrant being killed. It had to be for the betterment of the country or some other important reason. What else could it be?

Up ahead, the entrance to the upscale suburb came into view. A white Cadillac Escalade emerged from the blind corner of the wall and hooked a left onto the narrow road. Its body was spotless and reflected the sun with a shine as it rolled past Brad.

He kept his head trained straight ahead and flicked the blinker down. Brad nudged the brake and pulled into the entrance of the community that was dripping with a vibrant array of colorful flowers, trees, and bushes. As he piloted the Corolla past more castle-like homes and manicured lawns, Brad examined each house while making his way to the Snider's property.

Down the street from Brad's current position, he spotted another entrance at the far end. It provided an alternate route out of Lone Grove East in case his mission didn't go as planned. Having more than one exit was ideal, regardless of the location and situation.

Brad turned onto North Hawkins Lane and drove slowly while glancing out of each window. According to the layout, 2516 had to be on the right side of the street.

As he passed 2510, then 2512, Brad looked ahead for any vehicles parked in the driveways. A red, shiny Chevy Corvette caught his eye, but it wasn't on the Snider's property.

He slowed to a crawl on the street in front of the correct address. No cars were in the elevated drive. Both garage doors were closed and he couldn't get a visual inside the two-story home from the street. It was unclear whether or not Mr. Snider was home, but it didn't matter. He had to somehow check to see if he was there.

A patrol car appeared in Brad's rearview mirror. No lights flashed from the top of the vehicle as it causally drove by North Hawkins Lane. The unexpected arrival of the police tried to foil Brad's mission. It wouldn't stop him from completing his task but made him adjust his approach on the fly.

Brad drove down the remainder of the street and hooked a left on Saint John Lane. For now, he'd lay low until nightfall, then, under the cloak of night, Brad would return and execute his order with lethal precision.

Chapter 8

NIGHTTIME CAME AFTER 9:00 p.m. and with it, Brad's chance to move. He'd spent the remainder of the day resting in his car in different parking lots of businesses close to the residential community.

The delay was annoying, but a necessity to minimize his exposure to the Snider's neighbors and the squad cars that patrolled the high-end community. After his initial surveillance of the area, Brad hadn't gone back to the home until now.

An update on the mission's status was provided as Brad parked his Corolla a block away from the Snider's residence. The sedan's black body blended well with the growing darkness.

He secured his HK45 into the front waistband of his pants and stowed two separate knives in each of his boots. Black gloves were stuffed into his back pocket and the keys were removed from the ignition.

Brad exited the Corolla, made his way to the sidewalk, and hopped over the curb. His stride was relaxed instead of stiff and rigid. He refrained from twisting his head too much at the homes he passed. An overabundance of trees and bushes helped conceal him as he made his way down the curving concrete path.

Street lights were staggered at random spots along the road. Their bulbs cast a warm yellow hue at the thick, green grass that was edged and perfectly cut.

Dogs barked in the distance. Cars passed by heading in both directions but none braked as they drove past him.

Brad preferred to conduct jobs under the cloak of night whenever possible. It minimized risk and provided cover that one couldn't have during the day. He was confident in his ability to handle whatever situation he'd encounter, but he had his preferences.

As Brad followed the sidewalk toward the Snider's residence, he studied the home's lack of interior lighting. The front porch light was on and an SUV now resided on the left side of the driveway.

There was no activity outside of the home and from what he could see there was none inside either, which made gaining entry a bit easier.

He followed the sidewalk down to the street and crossed the road toward the home. Brad slipped by two sedans parked at the curb and headed for a row of dense bushes that separated the Snider's property from their neighbors.

His plan of entry was to go in through the back of the home. It would provide the best cover. From the intel he'd received in Andrew Snider's file, there was no mention of an alarm system.

Staying low, Brad worked his way around the outside of the home until he reached the expansive backyard. No dogs barked from inside, easing his mind from having to contend with an animal. Brad enjoyed the company of dogs and wanted to avoid having to kill one that threatened his job.

He maneuvered his way onto the stone patio and past the lawn furniture and a grill to the French doors. A wall of windows lined the back of the home wherein no blinds were installed.

Brad ducked and stalked the entrance while peering at the interior of the dwelling. His hand plucked the black gloves and a ski mask from his back pants pocket. He put each one on and then tested the doorknob.

It was locked, but Brad figured as much. It was nothing he couldn't bypass with the lock-picking kit that he had in his right front pocket.

The kit's leather pouch housed the tools needed to skirt the door lock. Plenty of practice had honed Brad's skills and reduced the amount of time needed to gain entry.

Over the next five minutes, Brad worked the doorknob's lock until it gave. He gathered his tools back into the leather pouch, deposited them into the pocket of his jeans, and gripped the knob.

Slowly twisting, Brad readied himself to bolt if an alarm blared. The knob stopped after a half rotation clockwise. He held a bated breath and carefully pushed the door inward.

No alarms sounded within the home. It was dead quiet, silent as a graveyard. For now, he was in the clear, but that didn't ease his mind. He would feel relieved when he was back in his car and driving away.

Brad slipped into the dining room and pushed the door shut behind him. It settled into the jamb with a low click. He then retrieved his HK45 and got on the move.

The home was huge and had vaulted ceilings. A rich, leathery scent tainted the cool air that offered a reprieve from the warm humidity outside.

Lights from the kitchen appliances and sconces on the wall illuminated the hallway ahead of him and the cooking area to his right. Brad kept to the shadows as much as possible and listened for footfalls or noises that signaled movement.

One of the mission objectives was to find the thumb drive. Brad figured it would be kept in an office desk drawer and would be as good a place as any to start. Most wealthy men like Mr. Snider had an office. It seemed to be a standard for business-minded folks. The real question was where it might be located.

As Brad swept the bottom floor in silence, a light flickered into existence down the long hallway. He stopped and aimed the HK45 at the glowing yellow light that shone from the partially open door.

Moving quickly, Brad scuttled along the wall and skirted by paintings and tables decorated in various décor that he didn't bother identifying. That wasn't why he was there.

The suppressor of the pistol aimed at the light. Brad advanced on the door and craned his neck, but he couldn't get a visual of who was inside.

A flash of movement passed by the opening and then across the room that Brad identified as an office, or a study, from the bookcases he spotted against the far wall. Mr. Snider had to be inside, or so he hoped.

His shoulder nudged the door and pushed it open. He stepped lightly and entered the room with the HK trained at the gray-haired man standing in front of a large cherry wood desk.

Brad pushed the door shut and hit the light switch in one fluid motion, thrusting the cavernous office into blackness.

Startled, the man shot upwards from his bent posture and flung his body around to the entrance. Only the outline of his features could be seen in the murky office.

A scant bit of light shone from the angled blinds covering the windows on the man's face, allowing Brad to confirm that he had found his target.

Mr. Snider muttered in shock as he struggled to speak. "Who? What?"

Brad advanced on the trembling man who leaned back on the desk. "Where is the thumb drive?"

"Thumb drive? What are you talking about?"

Standing less than a foot from his target, Brad smashed the pistol against the side of his skull. A faint yelp sounded as Snider collapsed to one knee. "Don't play games with me, Mr. Snider. I want the thumb drive you have, now."

Kneeling before Brad, he raised his arm and presented his palm in submission. "Okay. Just take it easy, all right?"

"Hurry up and get it." Brad grabbed a fistful of Snider's shirt and yanked him to his feet.

As Snider edged his way around the corner of his large desk, Brad stayed put and then checked the door. He asked, "Is there anyone else in the home with you?"

Snider rolled his high-back chair from the desk and sat down in the seat. "No. It's just me. My wife and daughter are out of town."

Brad glanced at the top of the desk and caught a glimpse of Snider in a picture with a woman and a kid. Half of the image was cast in shadows, partially concealing their smiling faces.

Part of him was relieved to hear that the woman and child weren't in the home. More people to contend with increased risk of mission failure; moreover, he had no interest in killing more people than necessary, especially a child. To Brad's horror, his gut twisted at the thought of hurting the little girl smiling out at him from the picture. He stood frozen, enraptured by their happy faces. It was as if he was a bystander watching himself but unable to make his muscles move. He was torn between finishing the mission and fleeing the scene to regroup and rein in his emotions. Sweat beaded across his brow and trickled down his back. What in the hell was happening?

The squeak of a drawer pulled him back to himself, his training kicking in again.

"Hey. No funny business back there. I can promise you that you're not quick enough, so don't even try it. Get the thumb drive and hurry up."

"I'm working on it," Snider replied. "It's in the bottom left drawer and there's no light, so I'm trying to find it blindly."

"Try harder. Work faster."

"Do you know what's on this drive? It contains data on some powerful men that could ruin their world."

"Not my problem. Hurry it up."

"Of course, it isn't. It's never anyone's problem. That is the problem."

"Less talking."

Another ten seconds passed before Snider dumped the small device on the desk pad. "There. That's what you're after. Please take it and go."

That's not how this goes, Brad thought with a tinge of unfamiliar dread. As he reached for the black thumb drive, the door to Snider's office opened.

Brad whipped around and aimed the pistol at the shadowy figure standing in the doorway.

"Andrew, are you..." she said, then froze. Pure panic washed over the woman as she lingered in the doorway. "What's going on?"

"Valerie. Sweetie. Don't move or say another word," Andrew replied in a strained, worried voice. "Everything's okay. Just stay calm."

"You lied," Brad said as he grabbed the thumb drive from the desk pad and shoved it into his pocket. "Damn it!"

"I know and I'm sorry," Snider replied, fear-stricken. "Please, don't hurt my family. I beg of you. You've got what you wanted. There's no need to go any further with this. We have no idea who you are."

"Unfortunately, Mr. Snider, that's not the way this works."

Brad pointed the gun at Valerie, hesitating, trying to think of another way. But he knew she would talk, risking his crew, his family. He knew in his gut that there wasn't another way. He glanced at the picture, the happy family moment memorialized on film. Seconds passed. The room froze as if the entire world was holding its breath, waiting to see what he would do next.

Then everything happened at once.

Valerie launched herself toward her husband, the sudden movement causing Brad to flinch. The HK fired a single round, the bullet spiraling through the air and finding a new home in Valerie's head, killing her upon impact. She stumbled back into the hallway and collapsed to the floor.

"Valerie!" Mr. Snider sprung from the chair in a fit of grief and rage. "You damn son of a bitch!"

Brad pivoted on his heels in one fluid motion and placed two rounds into Snider's torso as he bolted around the desk.

He crumpled to the floor and hit it with a heavy thump, face first.

Brad stood in the silence. It was too still, too quiet. No more whimpers or pleas, no panicked breaths or furtive movements. Only Brad and the thrumming of his own heart, beating an accusing rhythm– *Murderer... Murderer... Murderer...*

With the thumb drive secured in his pants pocket and the target down, Brad didn't know why he did what he did next, but he couldn't just leave the family photo staring out over the carnage. He rushed to the desk, and with shaking gloved hands he fumbled with the back of the picture frame. Finally, he freed the backing and removed the photo. Folding it in half, he slid it into his back pocket and headed toward the door. He stepped over the woman's dead body and rushed down the hallway.

By all accounts, his mission was complete.

As Brad neared the cavernous living room, a figure moved about on the stairs to his right. Instinctively, Brad leveled the barrel of the HK at the figure. It ducked back behind the wall's edge as he approached, whimpering and afraid.

Cloaked in shadows, a frightened young girl huddled on the steps and pressed into the wall. She was barefoot and had a nightgown on. Her arms cradled both bent legs. She glanced up at him through the murkiness, her messy hair flailing in every direction.

Brad closed his eyes, his traitorous heart punching a hole through his chest. This was the moment, he knew, that would define every consecutive moment for the rest of his life. Would he become someone who could kill a child? Or would he be a failed assassin, willing to put the only family he'd ever known at risk?

She cowered before him; her whimpers and cries sounded vastly different from those of adulterous men and their hookers.

The training that was drilled into him from an early age battled inside him.

Eliminate all witnesses.

The family's smiling faces burned a hole in his mind.

No loose ends.

No exceptions.

Brad did the unthinkable.

He lowered the pistol and stuffed it back into the front waistband of his jeans. If hesitating to kill the parents was him cracking, then this was his snapping point. Everything inside him broke loose, and he couldn't be in that house for another minute. He retreated from the hallway and across the dining room to the French doors.

The young girl vanished from the stairs as he threw open one side of the door and ran outside. He fled around the corner of the home and down to the sidewalk, then to the street.

His boots hammered the pavement like a race horse on the run. He leaped over the grass and the curb, after which he sprinted the length of the walkway toward his car.

None of the homes he flew by showed activity from the glances he gave them. For now, it seemed as though he was in the clear.

Brad followed the curved walkway to his car and skirted the back bumper. His gloved hand fished the keys of the Corolla out of his pocket as he advanced on the driver's door. He threw it open, ducked inside, and slammed the door shut behind him.

Firing up the car, Brad peeled away from the curb and down the street. He ripped the ski mask from his head and tried to control his panicked breathing, his body refusing to believe that it was getting enough oxygen. Black dots jumped around the edges of his vision. He had to pull himself together or this night was going to get a whole lot worse.

He removed his right glove with his teeth while navigating the streets of the upscale neighborhood.

After taking several deep breaths through his nose and releasing them slowly, he was able to force himself to focus on the task at hand. Switching the phone on and applying his thumbprint, Brad hesitated on penning the two words that he'd grown used to sending. It was a partial lie and one that he wasn't sure he'd get away with. If push came to shove, he'd find a way out of the hole into which he had now dug himself.

Exiting the community from the opposite way he entered, Brad typed *Mission Complete* in the text box. He then fired off the message as he merged onto the two-lane road. Brad dumped the phone into the passenger seat and punched the gas, leaving Lone Grove East behind him.

Chapter 9

THE FOLLOWING DAY WAS a mess of confusion shrouded in a sense of failure. It stole Brad's ability to think straight, but at least no one had questioned him about the mission– yet. Still, he had a massive weight tied to his shoulders that he couldn't shake and thus he needed the council of his instructor and mentor.

Brad made his way to Ronan's office early in the morning. It was before 7:00 a.m. His head pitched downward and he avoided eye contact with the few people he passed. Brad tried to act natural, but fracturing at the seams last night had thrown him off his axis, and Brad didn't know how to deal with it.

Visiting Ronan and divulging such a blunder was a risky move. He had no idea how his mentor would respond since he was an instructor, and loyalties ran deep. But Brad had to get what happened off his chest. He would accept the consequences, whatever punishment came down on him, if Ronan decided to pass it along.

He knocked on the closed door three times. There were no windows to Ronan's office so Brad had no clue if he was inside or not.

"Yes," a muffled voice replied from within.

Twisting the doorknob, Brad opened the door and poked his head inside. Ronan sat in his chair behind his gunmetal gray, steel desk. No one else was with him.

"Do you have a second to talk?" Brad asked.

"Of course. Come in and have a seat."

Brad entered the chilled room and shut the door behind him. His heart ran at a gallop. Nervousness twisted his stomach and his palms were clammy. His mouth was dry and tacky. He licked his lips and took a seat in front of the desk.

"How'd everything go yesterday?" Ronan asked. "I heard you were delayed a bit."

"Yes. There were a few bumps in the road but the job was completed."

"That's good to hear." Ronan paused for a beat; then he asked, "How are you doing since our talk? Any better?"

Brad said nothing.

The question made Brad want to writhe in his seat, but he remained still. His hesitation wasn't lost on Ronan, however, who knew Brad well enough to know when something was on his mind.

"What is it? You know I can read you like a book, right? Always have since you were a pup."

With his eyes downcast, Brad leaned forward in the seat and said, "I think I might have messed up last night."

"How so? From what I heard the mission was a success. The thumb drive was retrieved and all targets were neutralized. That sounds like it went off without a hitch. Case closed."

Brad looked up and met Ronan's gaze, wrestling with whether or not he should fully commit and unburden himself of the lie, but there was no going back now as Ronan knew something was up, and he'd press until he uncovered what it was.

"Well, not all of the targets were...handled."

Ronan inched forward on the edge of his seat, closer to his desk. "So, then, you didn't complete the mission as reported?"

"That's correct."

"What loose end was left untied?"

He gulped. "The daughter."

"Did she evade you somehow, or were you interrupted before you could finish?"

"Not exactly." Brad ran his fingers through his grungy hair that hadn't been washed in days and sat back in the chair. "I froze. No. I didn't just freeze, I panicked. I'm not sure why. I had her dead in my sight but couldn't pull the trigger. She was right there."

The image of the girl trembling and her voice quivering had haunted Brad since the encounter. He couldn't shake the sadness inside that went against the upbringing he had.

There was no room for emotion.

No sadness.

No remorse.

No fear.

A mindless killing machine was what they trained him, and the other operators, to be. Now, in the early days of his career, Brad felt like he had failed the family who had raised him.

Ronan remained calm and didn't unload on Brad. Not that he thought he would but he figured he'd at least lecture him on protocol and how he'd botched his op, even if by an insignificant portion.

"Okay. Let's work this out." Ronan scooted his chair back and stood. "The girl didn't see your face, did she?"

"No. I had my ski mask on."

"Good. That's good. So, she can't identify you, then?"

"Correct."

"Just so we're clear, both parents are dead?"

"Yes."

"All right. Here is what we're going to do," Ronan said while pacing his office. "We're going to keep this under wraps and between the two of us. No one else is going to know. Do not say a word to anyone."

"How is that going to work?" Brad asked. "Won't they know from news reports once the story breaks? We both know it will."

"Perhaps, but we can play it off that you didn't know she was in the home. Hidden somewhere out of sight and you were forced to leave before you could search the home. I don't know. We'll figure something out."

Brad asked, "So, you're not going to pass this up the chain then?"

"No. I'm not."

"Why? Won't you get in trouble if they find out you knew about it ahead of time and didn't say anything?"

"Because the organization doesn't take kindly to failure, much less lies, and I don't want anything to happen to you," Ronan answered. "I'm more forgiving than they are. And don't worry about me. I can take care of myself."

"Perhaps I should go to Morgan and explain what happened before they find out from the news or the folks who hired us. He might understand," Brad said, desperately searching for a favorable result. "Somehow, I seem to have gotten in well with him. He wants to speak with me about some new opportunity."

Ronan was quick to shut down the suggestion. "No. Under no circumstances do you do that. This stays between us. Stick to the plan and this will pass. I'll make sure of it."

"I can't believe I botched this so bad. I've never frozen like that. Even on my first solo op, I was flawless, precise. No hesitation. What's wrong with me? Why did I do that?"

"I'm not sure." Ronan made his way to Brad and sat on the lip of the desk in front of the confused young man. "I think, for now, you should stay out of the field until we can get to the bottom of whatever is bothering you. Again, I'll work it out. If anyone asks, you're not feeling well and I have removed you from active duty. Leave it at that. Your mind has to be clear and free of distractions. Right now, it's not. I should have spotted this sooner, and for that, I'm sorry."

"It's not your fault but mine. The blame rests on me alone."

"Don't beat yourself up." Ronan consoled Brad as best he could by patting his shoulder. "We'll get you straightened around and back in the game before too long. You probably just need some rest, is all. They've been using you a lot lately. That's what happens when you're the best."

Brad got up from the chair and made for the door, pausing before he exited. "And what if resting doesn't fix it? What if there's something else going on with me?"

"Then we'll cross that bridge when we come to it. And Brad..."

"Yes?"

"Off the record, I think you made the right call. There's no room for sloppiness in this business, but God help us if there is no longer a place for mercy."

Chapter 10

DAYS HAD PASSED SINCE Brad's admission of failure to Ronan. No swift punishment came from Morgan or the other instructors. The mission he'd willingly lied about hadn't been brought up again, much to Brad's surprise.

After spending the majority of his time in his housing unit "not feeling well," Morgan finally summoned Brad to his office on the evening of the third day. The leader cared not about any such illness as he had business to discuss with the up-and-coming assassin.

Brad headed to Morgan's plush office located in his mansion-like residence on the west side of the compound. It was decorated with lavish paintings and priceless artifacts Morgan had procured from around the globe. He enjoyed spending money and living large.

A hint of trepidation sprouted inside of Brad as he closed in on the double doors leading into Morgan's office. The meeting was expected considering how he'd wanted to speak with Brad about plans he had for him. Still, that knowledge didn't resolve the angst boiling in his gut.

He fought tirelessly to master his emotions and to present a confident front that wouldn't give away his deceit. Before walking in, Brad knocked on the door and waited for a reply.

"Enter," Morgan said from inside.

With a deep breath and a slow exhale, Brad entered the lion's den. He was not only greeted by Morgan, but by Asher, and a few other instructors as well, gathered around the huge conference table. Ronan was nowhere to be seen.

"Sir. You wanted to see me?"

"Yes. Come on in, Brad, and have a seat." Morgan gave a jovial smile, stood from his chair, and waved him over to the empty seat next to him.

Brad shut the door behind him and marched past two of the instructors to the plush black leather chair.

Asher eyed him the entire time. A resting scowl burned a hole through his head as he slouched in his chair and tapped his fingers against the top of the conference table.

"How are you feeling?" Morgan asked as he took his seat. "Ronan informed me that you were under the weather after returning from Chesapeake."

Sitting down and rolling his chair forward, Brad said, "I'm doing better." He didn't want to offer too much information. Men like these were keen on catching lies, and the more Brad talked the more he risked making a slip.

"I know I've been running you ragged, but with the amount of work we've received, it's been a necessary evil," Morgan offered. "All that matters is that you're back to form and ready."

Brad nodded as if he had no other recourse but to do so. "I am, sir."

"Good." Morgan then faced the instructors and Asher, who looked miserable and said, "For the past few months, I have been thinking of the future and what it means for the Cobalt family. What we do here is important work. This well-oiled machine is a marvel in and of itself, one that I'm proud of and hope that each of you is as well."

Asher smacked the table's top, interrupting his father's speech. "I'm going to stop you right there, Pop."

Disgruntled, Morgan said, "We discussed this already. I've made up my mind. You will sit down and shut up, or–"

"I will do no such thing," Asher shot back at his father, raising his voice. His malevolent glare flared with rage while locking horns with his father. "He lied to us and you're allowing it to slide? That's not how we operate or how you've handled such matters in the past. You know that since you set the rules."

Brad's throat moved. A lump formed. He swallowed and remained silent as Morgan glowered at his now-standing spawn who had hijacked his meeting.

"This has been resolved and explained by Ronan," Morgan said. "One cannot kill what they do not see, can they? Do you have that magical power to be able to do that? If so, then why haven't you?"

Asher guffawed and pointed at Brad. "Don't tell me that your golden boy over here couldn't locate a helpless girl in a home. Please. I'm not buying that, and neither is anyone else." He cut his hard gaze to Brad and continued his rambling. "Do you know what I think? He went soft. Choked, even. After all, for some, putting down an adult is easier than, say, killing a kid. What I think is that he knowingly let her go, and then he lied to us, his family. That cannot and will not stand." He turned back to his father, an imperious grin on his face. "Per your rules, of course."

Morgan scoffed at the notion of Brad willingly lying to them. "Are you so blinded by jealousy that you think your brother would betray his family? I'm disappointed in you, Asher, for being so small and simple-minded."

"He is not my brother!" Asher shot back. "Or perhaps you'd rather have your golden boy as your son since you seem to want to put him ahead of your actual kin. Groom *him* to take over."

Confused, Brad's brow furrowed. What did that mean? Did Morgan want him to take his place at the head of Cobalt?

A glance at Morgan confirmed the possibility as their eyes locked. Morgan said nothing to Brad but remained in the trenches of verbal warfare with his unruly brat of a son.

"Every operator here is your family. All are your brothers and sisters in arms. That's the way it's always been. Furthermore, this is not a kingdom. Just because you're my son, that does not make you my heir. I will appoint whomever I find capable to handle this position. But I'm done arguing with you right now about this, Asher." Morgan exhaled a heavy sigh; then he said, "What is it going to take for you to get past this so we can move on? Shall we take him outside and place a bullet in his head? Will that appease you?"

Asher considered the notion by tapping his finger on top of the empty chairs tucked under the lip of the conference table. "As much as that sounds tempting, and it does, I think, for now, a different example needs to be set. After all, rules are in place for a reason. It's what keeps this organization thriving."

"And what example would that be?" Morgan asked as he leaned forward and rested his forearms on the glossy conference table top.

Flashing a devilish smile, Asher said, "I'm glad you asked because I have the perfect thing in mind."

Chapter 11

BRAD WAS LOST, TRAPPED in a bitter conflict between father and son. The power grab was apparent and so was Asher's contempt for not only his dad but Brad too. His string of bad luck over the past few days was far from over and was teetering on turning deadly.

"What are you going on about, Asher?" Morgan asked, growing tiresome of the argument with his ingrate son. "You're on thin ice as it is, boy. I'd not forget that."

"No, Father. It is you who has been on thin ice for quite some time," Asher replied as he approached the closed double doors to Morgan's office. "You've gone soft and become gullible in your old age. It's time that we adhere to the principles you've set as the foundation for any op that we're on."

"And what's that?" Morgan asked.

"Complete the mission, fully. No loose ends."

Asher opened the door and then stepped out of the way.

A lone guard stood in the doorway with a young girl. But it wasn't one of their own who lived on the compound or a new arrival. No. It was Andrew Snider's kid. The daughter Brad had failed to kill.

Morgan shoved his chair back, and then stood in a huff. "What in the world is going on here, Asher? This is highly irregular. Why is she here?"

Brad shot upward as well, shocked at the sight of the girl.

"To make things right and for your golden boy to finish the mission that he failed to complete," Asher answered in an eerily calm tone as he bobbed his head at the guard, who escorted the blindfolded young girl into the meeting room. "I know that normally we would jump on this opportunity to bring another lost soul into the family, but she will make a perfect example which must be made."

Her lips quivered the same as they had that night Brad had killed her parents. In the light, he was able to fully see the girl's features that were marred by pain and fright. Her cheeks were flushed and her blonde hair was a complete mess. She looked to be around six or seven years of age, but that was the least of Brad's worries right then.

To Brad, he knew all too well what Asher had planned and why he had snatched the girl. This wasn't about making a point or setting a precedent for the organization. No. It was about torturing a young man who felt little physical pain and how to twist the knife into his gut.

"Lord, son. You have crossed the line here and have gone off the deep end," Morgan said while shaking his head in disappointment.

"Do what you want with me, but there is no reason to hurt the child," Brad said, pleading for the girl's life. "She doesn't need to be hurt and has suffered so much already. Please. Don't do this."

Asher took the trembling girl from the guard and placed her in front of him. The smug smile of satisfaction grew wider as he squeezed her shoulders.

"See, father. That's the weakness you've bred into your troops. Now we're pleading for lives to be spared that should no longer exist?"

"I will not tolerate this production that you're putting on any longer." Morgan glared at the instructors still seated at the table, then barked at each of them. "Why are you still sitting there silently? This sort of reckless behavior is not how we operate."

"Because, Dad, they are about as tired of you as I am," Asher answered. "Today marks the start of a new beginning."

The instructors nodded their agreement with the treacherous son, who had won the men over through his conniving to plant discord and doubt among the men with daily acts of small rebellions and traitorous words that went unchecked. It shocked not only Morgan, who couldn't speak at first but also Brad who parroted his gaped mouth and wide glare.

Right then all that concerned Brad was removing the child from harm's way. Something clicked inside of him, overriding his programming of being an elite assassin and lethal killer. He wasn't about to stand by and watch her life be taken.

"Asher. Why don't we settle this, just you and me? Leave the girl out of it and we can handle our disagreements among ourselves."

"Oh, we will, but not before you finish your job first, brother," Asher replied, facing the quaking child standing in front of Brad. "You're going to put a bullet into her skull. Right now."

"No, I am not," Brad said defiantly. "She will not be harmed."

"Pathetic. I knew you didn't have the stones for this." Asher bobbed his head at Shane, the instructor, who then stood and pulled a pistol from behind his back.

Morgan marched past Brad in a fit of rage toward his son and the girl. "I'm beyond finished with this and you, boy. This time, you have gone too far."

"I haven't even gotten started!" Asher pulled his Glock 19 from behind him and trained it on his father. "As I said, things are going to change today. It will be a new dawn for Cobalt, but I'm afraid that you won't be around to see it."

The barrel of Asher's Glock lined up with Morgan's wrinkled forehead. He forced his father backward, past Brad who stood in silence while trying to formulate a way out of the perilous situation.

"I will have your head for this!" Morgan said, piqued by the betrayal. "The only example to be made is going to be of you."

Asher forced his father back into his chair and kept his pistol aimed at his head. "Let's get this over with, shall we?" He glanced at Brad, and then tipped his head at the blindfolded girl. "If you will, brother. I can promise you that a quick death is far more humane than what could happen to her if you don't put her down, now."

Caught in a no-win situation, Brad devised a half-cocked plan that more than likely would get him killed alongside the girl, but desperation and guilt compelled his actions.

"Okay. Fine. You win, Asher. I'll do it."

Whimpers from the frightened girl built. Her entire body shook as Brad advanced on her. She looked around aimlessly, unable to see the man who had ruined her life, and now, was tasked with killing her for no other reason than a grudge between feuding assassins.

"Now, take the gun and finish the child," Asher ordered.

The guard standing near the girl pulled his holstered Sig Sauer P320 and presented the grip to Brad.

He took the weapon and stood before the child, towering over her like the Grim Reaper, which was how he now saw himself.

Staring at the helpless girl, Brad felt a huge weight of remorse pull him down further into his pit of despair. It tore into his soul as easily as the bullets had into her parents. He'd become a monster, but he never realized until it was far too late.

"Today, brother," Asher said, growing impatient. "Pull the trigger. Free yourself."

Brad's finger pressed on the trigger a hair tighter; then he glanced at the guard standing not more than a few feet from them from the corner of his eye.

His posture was relaxed. He looked away from Brad to Asher who belted a heavy sigh.

"Do it already or I'll–"

A scuffle broke out behind Brad. Grunts and shuffling feet presented a chance for him to act. A single report sounded as he switched targets from the little girl to the guard.

Fire spat from the muzzle of the P320 at close range. The .45 ACP bullet punched the guard's skull and exited the back of his head.

In one fell swoop, Brad lowered and scooped up the child, then ran for the closed double doors as the guard crumpled dead to the floor.

A swarm of activity flourished at Brad's back as Asher barked orders at the instructors. Before the deviant son could get another shot off at Brad, he passed through the door and bolted down the hallway.

Chapter 12

LUGGING THE FLAILING, SCREAMING girl under his arm, while taking on fire was no small feat. Her body jerked in every possible way, testing his hold on her as they ran out of Morgan's home.

"Stop wiggling so much, kid. I'm trying to save you," Brad said to the girl who thrashed her legs and swung her arms wildly.

The instructors gave pursuit out into the sprawling grounds of the compound. There was no way that Brad was going to make it across the stretch of land to his unit.

He closed his arm around the girl's waist to keep her from slipping and falling. It was cumbersome at best to carry her, return fire, and dodge incoming ordnance with any sort of efficiency.

His P320 sent round after round at the trailing men who matched his sprint across the compound.

Headlights flashed ahead, ripping across the grounds and barreling toward them. Eluding the speeding vehicle was going to be impossible while also keeping two steps in front of Morgan's backstabbing goons.

Making it out alive seemed less and less likely, and the end of the road was near. But Brad wasn't going to stop. They'd have to gun him down first.

A bullet zipped past the duo. It caught the meaty outside of Brad's left triceps. It burned hot, but he maintained his breakneck sprint and bore the pain as a truck approached them.

Muzzle fire flashed from the driver's side of the pickup. The bullets flew past Brad as he ducked and trained what dwindling supply of ammo the P320 had left at the cab.

But something odd happened that Brad didn't expect. The truck stopped and cut hard to the right. Inside the cab, behind the wheel, was Ronan.

"Get in!" he said while firing at the instructors and guards rushing toward them.

Brad didn't argue as he trusted Ronan with his life.

His mentor scattered the trailing men as Brad deposited the girl into the backseat of the truck. He climbed in after her and slammed the door shut.

The truck launched forward as its tires bit into the ground. Its back end swung wide as Ronan hammered the gas and sent the pickup into a violent lurch that thrust Brad into the backrest.

"Keep your head down, boy!"

Ammunition pinged off the truck's body. Cracks of gunfire caused the girl to squeal under the barrage of incoming fire.

Brad shielded her body with his, protecting her however he could. From his vantage point, all he could see out of the window was the darkening night sky and the tree limbs under which they passed.

The uneven terrain of the road jostled them about as the truck gained speed. It hopped over high spots and bottomed out in the ruts, punishing their bodies in the backseat.

"Are you two okay back there?" Ronan asked, his voice stressed.

"We're alive if that's what you mean," Brad answered while staying below the window's edge. "I got nicked in the arm, but nothing fatal."

"And the girl?"

"Fine enough."

She didn't say a word but grunted and screeched instead. Brad assumed the traumatic experience had done a bit of damage to her.

"Hold on!" Ronan said.

A loud crash sounded. The truck jolted as if they'd collided with something.

Gunshots lessened as the seconds ticked by. Brad sat up slowly and peered out of the back window at the compound from which they now fled.

"They'll be mobilizing shortly and coming after us," Ronan said while piloting the truck through the forested area along the dirt road that snaked in and out of the trees.

"Yeah. Asher killed Morgan right there in front of us."

Ronan sighed while working the steering wheel from side to side. "That little bastard. I knew he was a piece of trash, but never thought he'd stoop so low as to gun down Morgan. I had plans of getting you out of here after overhearing some of the instructors speak of mutiny, which wouldn't have boded well for you."

"It's a safe bet that Asher wants me dead, but not before making me suffer first."

Headlights sliced through the dense woods behind them. There were several pairs of lights exiting the compound after them.

"Okay. This is what we're going to do," Ronan said, calming his strained tone. "You're going to take the girl and disappear somewhere far away. Asher brought her into the organization and didn't plan on her living. That's a loose end on his part that will have to be tied off, along with you, and now me."

"What about you?" Brad asked, not fully understanding the plan laid out by Ronan. "We can go together. There's no reason to split up."

"That's not how this is going to work, son." Ronan killed the lights and slammed the brakes. Then he shifted into park and jumped out of the cab. "Get up front, now."

"Stay down in the seat, okay?" Brad said to the girl as he climbed over the backrest and dropped into the driver's seat.

Ronan appeared with a rifle clutched in his hands at the open door. "Keep the lights off for as long as you can. The woods are dense and should supply enough cover for you to blend in. You'll hit the highway about a mile up."

The door slammed shut, sealing Brad and the girl inside the cab.

"You don't have to do this. Come with us."

"No. I'm going to buy you as much time as I can. It's the least I can do for you." Ronan shouldered the rifle and clapped the body of the pickup. "Now go."

Much to his dislike, Brad obeyed. He shifted the truck into drive and hit the gas, sending the pickup jumping forward.

As he followed the overgrown path through the dense woods of the Appalachian Mountains, Brad peered at the side view mirror and watched as Ronan sprinted up the familiar road they'd taken to enter the compound, firing his weapon.

The reports made him flinch; he was worried that Ronan would fall and give his life for him, and that this would be the last time Brad would ever see his mentor and friend.

Chapter 13

BRAD AND THE GIRL had escaped Asher's reach, but they were far from out of harm's way. Brad knew their tactics and how resourceful Cobalt was. To fully vanish from the face of the earth, and be safe, their old identities would have to be erased for them to survive and move on.

Brad clutched the steering wheel tighter than he realized while guiding the pickup down the desolate night roads into the backwoods of North Carolina. Anger brimmed under the surface as he pictured Ronan being killed or tortured for his disloyalty. The worst part was that Brad couldn't save his friend.

It made him sick to his stomach. Acid boiled in his gut and threatened to charge his mouth, but Brad held it off. So much had gone wrong because of him. Regret was a powerful beast, one that sunk its fangs deep.

But there wasn't time for self-loathing and pity, not while he had the girl with him. She wasn't built for a life on the run, and she didn't deserve as much. The dire mess she had gotten trapped in wasn't her fault. Brad owned it and vowed to make it right however he could.

As the miles ticked by on the dark winding roads that led them to nowhere, in particular, Brad wrestled with what to do with the kid. He was an assassin, conditioned and trained to stay off the grid and move in the shadows, strike when the enemy least expected it, and vanish without a trace. It was his best weapon, aside from his formidable fighting and weapons skills.

Brad peered over the top of the seat's backrest. The girl was motionless in the black depths. Only a hint of her silhouette was visible. As far as he could tell, she hadn't removed the blindfold and left it in place. The stress of the ordeal had worn her down to the point of passing out from the horrifying experience.

As Brad faced forward, he spotted a sign marking the next closest town coming up. He missed the name but caught that it was ten miles up the road. His truck was running low on gas and he'd have to stop soon or risk being stranded with the girl.

They entered the outskirts of Woolhope, North Carolina in the dead of night. Not a single soul stirred within the community as he followed the narrow road into the downtown area. All of the businesses were buttoned up and closed, making it seem abandoned.

Street lamps illuminated the intersections that were absent from other vehicles at that ungodly hour. No Sheriff or police were spotted as the pickup crept through the isolated community.

Up ahead, along the town's main street, Brad spied a gas station's illuminated pylon sign. It was the only station he'd seen in hours. Given the time of night and lack of people out, now was as good a time as any to try and get some fuel. He had no money on him, but that was a problem he'd find a way to overcome by whatever means he could.

Brad maintained a slow, steady speed and minded all traffic signals and laws. Even though he didn't see any local law enforcement in the area, that didn't mean some lonely deputy pulling the graveyard shift wasn't in his squad car somewhere, waiting for someone to break the law.

The intersection's light flashed yellow, then red. Brad stopped at the thick white line painted on the recently laid asphalt, anxious for the signal to turn green.

His finger tapped the top of the wheel as he surveyed the streets for approaching headlights. He then checked the rearview mirror for any trailing vehicles appearing at his back over the hill. Even though he felt confident in losing their tail, Brad was vigilant in watching their six.

Down the street to his right, Brad caught sight of what looked to be a church. The building was lit up with darkness around it.

A plan formed, one that sent him driving through the green hue of the traffic signal toward the church. He wasn't sure if anyone was even inside, but given his lack of options, Brad had to check and see. The girl's life depended on him being able to find someplace safe for her to go, and a church, for now, seemed as good as any place to leave her.

As Brad pulled up along the curb, he studied the main entrance within the elaborate architecture of the religious sanctum. Flood lights brightened the intricate details of the structure which stood out among the darkened buildings around it.

There were no windows on the front that allowed him to see inside. Brad couldn't just leave the girl in the middle of the night and drive off.

He killed the engine and shut off the headlights. After wrestling with what to do next, and scouting the area, Brad decided to get out and see if anyone was there. He checked on the girl in the backseat, who remained still, and then he exited the truck.

While walking up the stretch of sidewalk toward the building, he couldn't help but scan the empty parking lot to the right for vehicles and then to the businesses at his left. It felt awkward approaching the church in the middle of the night like some sort of heathen or vandal, but he had no choice.

Brad climbed the short stack of concrete steps to the landing, and then approached the door. Being so close to the church made him uneasy because of his line of work. As he raised his arm to knock at the door, it cracked open.

A black-clad figure stood in the shadows of the entryway. Brad dropped his arm and stood at ease so he wouldn't startle the person before him.

An older gentleman opened the door wider. The low light behind him gave Brad a glimpse at his features as he came into focus. He had a mustache and a bald head. If he had to guess, the man looked as though he could've been in his late fifties or early sixties. The man gave a warm, inviting smile that eased Brad's apprehension from what he was about to unload on him.

"Yes, son? What can I do for you?" the man asked politely. "Are you in need of prayer? Anyone showing up to a church in the middle of the night in that loud monster of yours must be in dire straits of the Lord's counsel."

Tongue-tied, Brad gulped and then cleared his throat before responding. "Um, no sir. It's a bit more complicated than that, I'm afraid."

"It always seems to be, son, but I have found that whatever is troubling you, there is a way out of it." The man spoke with kindness and without irritation, given the late hour. He appeared tired from the bags under his eyes, but his smile was bright. "Please, come in, and let's discuss whatever it is that is bothering you. I make it a point to keep the doors to the church open at all hours for those souls who need it. You never know when you'll require the Lord's guidance."

Brad glanced back at the truck, then at the priest. "I know this is going to come off as strange, but this is a matter of life and death."

"Oh?" He raised his brow and then asked Brad, "Are you in some sort of trouble, son?"

Ignoring the man's question, Brad held up a finger and retreated to the truck. He moved quickly, transitioning from a stroll to a sprint. Brad opened the back driver's side door and carefully removed the girl from the seat. Cradled in his arms, he lugged her back to the church where the priest met him at the base of the steps.

"What I need from you right now is to listen and not ask a bunch of questions."

Confusion wrinkled his forehead at the odd request, but the priest obliged.

"This girl right here is in mortal danger and needs protecting. She has no family and is by all accounts, alone." Brad didn't give the priest a chance to back away or answer before he deposited the motionless child into the man's arms. "I know how weird this must seem, but this truly is a matter of life and death."

"What sort of trouble are the two of you in?" the priest asked while glancing down at her. "I think it best if we contact the Sheriff's office. They'll be able to help."

Brad emphatically shook his head, dismissing the notion. "Please don't do that. Not right now, at least." He calmed his nerves, took in a deep breath, and then said, "Listen. She is in danger whether you believe me or not. Bad men will be looking for her, and they will go to great lengths to find her. That can't happen. For now, please give it a few days. When you do contact the authorities, make sure this stays under the radar. No press or anything like that. Her life depends on it."

Befuddled by the odd request, the priest struggled for the right words to say while holding the child in his arms as Brad walked away. He looked at the blindfolded girl and then back up at the young man who had dropped her off in his arms then retreated to the truck.

"What do I tell the girl when she wakes up? I imagine she'll be scared and wondering what is happening."

As Brad slammed the back driver's side door shut and then opened his, he said, "Tell her she's safe now, and that I'm sorry for everything that's happened to her and her family."

"But, who are you? I never got your name. What is her name?" the priest asked as Brad climbed into the cab of the truck.

"Just do as I said if you want her to stay alive," Brad said as he slammed the door shut.

Brad started the truck, flipped on the headlights, and then shifted into drive. His boot mashed the gas pedal, sending him skidding away from the curb and up the street. He gave one final look into the rearview mirror at the church that grew smaller before turning onto one of the side streets and disappearing, for good.

For now, Brad hoped the Snider's daughter would be far removed from Asher's reach.

Only time would tell if he had done enough to give the child a chance at a normal life. But one thing he knew for certain as he pulled the picture of the girl and her family from his pocket– he wasn't going to leave her safety in the careless hands of fate. He couldn't be an active participant in her everyday life, and he knew he was beyond any redemption for what he had done, but he could protect her like a condemned guardian angel from Hell, otherworldly and invisible, ever-waiting to destroy anyone who made the terminal mistake of coming after her.

Chapter 14

Sledge piloted his gray 2005 Chevy Silverado truck up I-95. Traffic was especially heavy that Wednesday. It made it cumbersome for Sledge to get back to his room at the Motel 6 he stayed at on the outskirts of Jacksonville, FL. in an expedited manner.

Blood ran from the knife wound on his right side. The warmth collected at the waistband of his pants and underwear. It wasn't a fatal laceration, but one that did require attention to ensure it healed properly and didn't get infected.

The mirrors revealed no law enforcement in tow. Sledge was keen to maintain as low a profile as possible when out to keep off the authority's radar.

Since escaping Cobalt over a decade ago, Sledge assumed the name of his favorite character from the book series, *Manhattan Heights*. His former persona, Brad Jones, was all but dead to the world.

He thumbed the blinker and merged onto the off-ramp. Sledge followed the three cars ahead of him along the winding road to the intersection, and then he hooked a right and drove to the entrance of the motel.

Whenever possible, Sledge stuck to such establishments that dealt in cash and didn't care to ask many questions. He avoided using credit cards and always came off as forgettable, but likable. Folks seemed to remember jerks they'd encountered, but cordial, polite individuals skated by without further thought.

Sledge entered the motel from the back entrance and parked his truck near his bottom-floor room. As with most of the motor inns he'd frequented over the years, the clientele mostly stayed the same, especially during the day. His haggard and rough appearance more than matched that of the patrons in the lodge, and he wouldn't attract any unwanted attention.

Pulling the keys from the ignition, Sledge got out of the cab and made his way to the room he'd rented three days prior. His arm clutched his side as he walked normally, cognizant of the surrounding vehicles and any people going about their business.

He unlocked his door and ducked inside, then, out of habit, locked the door and wedged the guest chair under the handle for an added security measure. It wouldn't stop someone determined to get in, but it would slow them down. The blinds were drawn and the curtains closed, leaving no opening for someone outside to peek into his room through the window.

Tossing the truck and motel room keys onto the small table, Sledge moved to the back of his lodging where the sink was located. He switched on the dimly lit bulb that buzzed from the surge of electricity. His first aid kit was washed out in a light yellow hue that shone from the incandescent bulb.

The sink had a grungy brown stain in the basin. Surface cracks splayed like ghostly fingers within the marble. Both the hot and cold knobs of the faucet looked as if they belonged to another time.

Sledge pulled his shirt over his head, tossed it onto the counter, and then began inspecting the damage to his side. Just as he thought, the cut wasn't too deep, but it stung like it was trying to make up for its lack of depth. A bit of cleaning and liquid stitches would suffice in closing the gash.

As Sledge grabbed a washcloth from the bathroom and ran the coarse fabric under the tepid tap, he stared into the mirror. A haggard, tired man reflected in the glass. His torso had healed cuts along his muscular chest and six-pack abs. Some of the lacerations healed better than others, but a hard life lived was evident from the damage that was visible on his body.

Soaked with warm water, Sledge applied a thin layer of soap to the washcloth and then cleaned the area around the skin. His pain tolerance was high; he barely flinched from the contact of the rag pressing to the gash.

It soaked up the blood on the skin and from the wound. He folded the rag over and made another sweep over the damp skin before depositing the bloody rag in the basin.

After retrieving a clean-ish towel, Sledge patted it dry and then pulled out his liquid stitches. He pinched the skin together and applied a bead of glue across the ripped flesh. It was a sloppy job but it didn't have to be perfect.

Next, Sledge plucked a bandage from the kit and stuck the white pad over the gash. It was a hair small to completely cover the area, but the stickiness of the bandage didn't interfere with the glue.

Hospitals were a no-go as they liked to ask questions, especially when it came to such injuries as knife wounds or gunshots. The only time Sledge would consider going was if he'd suffer a wound outside of his scope of being able to treat it.

Exhaling, Sledge threw the towel at the counter and leaned on the edge of the wall near the jamb of the bathroom. Exhaustion set in fast even though it was barely 2:00 p.m.

For the past three days, Sledge had been tracking down a known drug dealer who enjoyed employing minors to spread his product across Atlanta and down into the northern tip of Florida. The low-life piece of scum was a minnow in a much larger sea of sharks for whom he worked. Still, Sledge managed to remove the criminal from the streets, although his methods of doing so could be considered ethically ambiguous, and would likely result in him being labeled as a vigilante if anyone were paying attention. But he didn't care what anyone thought of his approach to the deviant men. Those who employed his services of exacting justice were grateful for the lengths to which he went, and didn't bat an eye when it was served.

Sledge made his way to the king-sized bed; then he stuffed the 1911 pistol he carried under the pillow. It wasn't his HK45 that he preferred in the past, but Sledge found the 1911 as reliable and robust as the HK.

He collapsed onto the rigid mattress that sprang and popped from his bulk hitting it. A half-empty bottle of vodka was near the clock on the nightstand, ready for him to pound his troubles away and find some rest if he so desired, but Sledge let the spirit be and stared at the ceiling instead.

The clatter from the air conditioning unit filled the dead void of silence in the room. He'd grown used to the annoying noise that had become a constant in most of the inns in which he stayed. At least it pumped out cool air and gave him a reprieve from the humidity.

Within minutes of lying down, Sledge found comfort on the firm mattress. As the seconds ticked by and his brain drifted off into a sea of nothingness, Sledge released another heavy sigh and then passed out, dead to the world.

Chapter 15

A CAR BLARING ITS horn interrupted his deep slumber at 4:30 a.m. Sledge sprung from the mattress with the 1911 aimed at the door. The thick haze of sleep smeared the view of his bewildered gaze. His heart pounded against his chest from the sudden disturbance.

Much to Sledge's relief, no one was inside his room. The door and chair were as he left them the previous day. Muttered voices sounded outside of his room then trailed off as lights flashed at the window.

Sledge lowered the gun and sat on the edge of the bed. Yawn after yawn made his eyes water and mouth gape open. He'd had no plans of sleeping as long as he had, but his body was running on fumes and had finally crashed.

Once he gathered his bearings, Sledge stood and trudged to the bathroom. Before leaving the motel and driving back to Atlanta, he settled on taking a shower to fully wake him. Being alert was one of the keys to knowing one's surroundings.

He stripped off his boots, socks, pants, and then underwear in the doorway of the bathroom as the lights flickered on. The assault of the white bulbs overhead made him squint and divert his gaze to the floor.

The chill of the tile from the air conditioning unit pumping out cold air probed his bare feet as he made for the shower. He rotated the handle slightly up, switching on the flow of sputtering water that spat from the showerhead above.

Sledge didn't wait for it to warm up but instead, he climbed into the cold grip of chilled water that shocked his system awake. A shiver flooded his body at first, but he held fast under the cold waterfall that splashed his face and body.

In less than ten minutes, Sledge had washed with the ivory soap and tiny, standard, generic shampoo and conditioner bottle provided, dried off and got dressed in the same clothes save the bloody shirt he had discarded the prior day.

Within his go bag on the floor at the base of the bed, Sledge dug out a fresh shirt that clung to his toned, muscular, slightly-wet frame. Putting the shirt over his head and pulling it down aggravated the laceration on his side, but it wasn't anything that completely hindered his movements.

Inside his pack near the top of the opening, Sledge spied one of the books in the *Manhattan Heights* series. He had read each of the ten novels numerous times and knew them by heart. If quizzed, Sledge did not doubt that he could answer any questions asked. Being an avid reader to fill what little free time he found continued to be one of the few pleasures Sledge had in his life.

After brushing his teeth and collecting his belongings together on the bed, Sledge cleaned the counter and basin of any blood; then he deposited the ruined towels and shirt in the trash.

It was standard operating protocol for Sledge to clean up and remove such evidence. Even though he was no longer an operator, the baseline teachings he'd received during his youth and teenage years proved invaluable as an adult. To date, it worked flawlessly.

Sledge peered out to the parking lot from the corner of the window as he removed the guest chair from under the silver handle. Old habits were hard for Sledge to shake.

Night laid claim to the area, but dawn would be coming soon. He snagged the truck keys from the table and left the room key where it lay; then he carried the thin trash bag and his pack out of the room to the Silverado. After tossing his pack into the cab, Sledge dumped the trash from the room into the provided dumpster in the parking lot and then returned to his truck.

He scaled the side of the Chevy and settled into the firm driver's seat that had splits forming in the leather. The truck had loads of miles but ran well. It wasn't a head turner, which was perfect since Sledge preferred the subtle look of an ordinary vehicle that blended in with most automobiles on the road.

The engine cranked and the truck roared to life. Sledge placed the 1911 in the magnetic holster mounted at the base of the steering column. It was easily accessible and concealed, perfect for surprise encounters that required its use at a moment's notice.

Sledge switched on the headlights, drove out through the back entrance of the motel, and retraced his route back to I-95, which wasn't but a mile or two up the road. Traffic was sparse that Thursday morning and moved much faster as he made his way to I-75.

While cruising along the interstate, Sledge's phone pinged, indicating that a message had dropped into his encrypted messaging account. For him, it was one of the more secure civilian apps that provided a level of encryption that couldn't be hacked by any novice. Only hackers, crime syndicates, and government organizations would have the experience and means of being able to break through if they so desired, so Sledge remained mindful of such things and tried to keep his language vague whenever speaking with clients.

He applied his thumb print to the screen of the phone and pulled up the received message. A single word was delivered.

Update?

Sledge preferred to meet in person and provide the clients he served with a briefing on the job after receiving his final payment, instead of messaging. To him, it was a better business practice to do it that way, and it kept individuals from trying to scam him.

A short response was penned as he steered the truck past an eighteen-wheeler.

Job completed.

Most of Sledge's clients were down-on-their-luck folks or those who were in despair for various reasons. Everything from drugs, rape, prostitution, and gang violence afflicted those desperate souls in some form or fashion. He handled nearly any case presented and based his fee of service on what the individual could afford. Several times, he did the jobs for free, or just got paid by whatever means the person or family could afford. Those rare clients he took on that had the bankroll to pay out filled those gaps of lost income and more than gave him enough money to live off of.

Sledge put the phone, face up, on his lap as another message dropped into the encrypted app.

That is good news. We thank you for your service and for your help in our family finding some peace for our son. As agreed upon, the final payment of five thousand US dollars has been sent to the account you provided. Thank you again, Mr. Sledge, for everything.

It warmed Sledge's heart to hear how grateful they were. Money wasn't the point and his goal wasn't to be rich, but folks seemed more than willing to pay for his services to fix whatever problem they had. Sledge had made it his mission to help those who couldn't find justice within the legal system. So far, he had done just that.

Chapter 16

HE ARRIVED IN ATLANTA after 10:15 a.m. Most of the rush hour traffic had thinned out, making his commute through the city easier than if he'd gotten there earlier, but traffic in Atlanta was almost always terrible.

His stomach rumbled its displeasure at its lack of food. Sledge couldn't remember the last time he'd eaten anything more than processed foods from gas stations. Protein bars, nuts, and energy drinks were his primary food source, along with whatever else he grabbed while on the move. It worked in a pinch but wasn't sustainable for long periods.

West End Diner was his favorite spot in Atlanta to eat when he had the time to do so. They had some of the best southern cooking and coffee in the south and more than satisfied his grumpy gut.

Sledge pulled into the diner's driveway at 10:45. The morning crowd had mostly dispersed, leaving the parking lot with a sparse amount of vehicles and patrons. He didn't care much for crowds and stayed away from mobs of folks as much as he could, so the sight of the mostly-empty diner improved his mood.

The restaurant had a traditional 1950s retro vibe to it as if a scene from the past was plucked therefrom and dropped into modern times. Sledge loved the aesthetic about as much as he did the amazing food.

As Sledge entered the diner, he felt a sense of calm drape over him. The West End Diner had been one of the few eateries Sledge had frequented over the years. Though he tended to drop in at night, his rumbling stomach wouldn't allow him to put off eating any longer.

Sandra gave Sledge a warm smile and waved at him from behind the long winding counter. The waitress had been employed at the West End Diner for as long as Sledge could remember. She was a delight to visit with each time he dropped in, and her thick southern accent more than complimented her inviting personality.

"Well. If it isn't Mr. Sledge dropping in for a day visit," Sandra said. "I thought I'd never see you in here unless it was dark outside."

"Ha-ha. I do come out during the day and haven't burst into flames, so I guess I'm not a vampire as you mentioned," Sledge replied.

"Well, honey, I had my doubts. But I'm glad to see that you're not."

Their brief banter session ended with each of them chuckling as Sandra retrieved two plates of heaping food from the galley and delivered them to two older gentlemen at the counter.

"Grab a seat, sweetie. I'll be with you shortly," Sandra said as she grabbed a pot of coffee and refilled the men's white coffee mugs.

Sledge tipped his head and found his way to the far corner of the diner. The table he liked to sit at was unoccupied at the moment. It was the best seat in the house as it put his back to the wall, allowing him to see the entire restaurant.

Music from the 1950s played from the speakers at a reduced volume. Elvis Presley belted his throaty tune of Hound Dog as Sledge collected two packets of Sweet'N Low from the holder and pulled two napkins from the dispenser.

Sandra strode up to the table with a fresh pot of steaming coffee and a white mug that she put in front of him. Her grin widened on her ageless, dark-skinned face that, to Sledge, didn't make her look a day over forty.

"How is my favorite customer doing this Thursday morning?"

"Pretty good," Sledge replied as he watched the coffee pour into his mug. "How are you doing? Did that book you wanted come in yet?"

"Oh. I'm living the dream every day. And no, I'm *still* waiting for that darn book to arrive," Sandra jokingly said as she topped off the mug. "It's taking them forever to get it in." She paused for a beat. "If my knight in shining armor would come through those doors and sweep me off my feet that would be great. If I were a young woman, you'd be in trouble, sir. But, I imagine your girlfriend wouldn't care for that."

Sledge tore off the top of the sweetener and dumped the sugar substitute into the coffee. "Now, Sandra. You know that I only have eyes for you."

"Oh, child. You shouldn't get started on me this early, pretty boy." Sandra's smile widened further, if that was possible, as she fanned her face with the plastic diner menu. "You keep sweet-talking me like that, and you're going to be in for it."

"Promises. Promises."

Sledge was a good-looking man by all accounts. His rugged look, square chin, and muscular build more than enticed the opposite sex to flirt with him. But Sledge didn't see what others did. All that he saw was a broken man trying to do right in a world full of wrong.

"Are we getting the usual today, sweetie, or are you going to be adventurous and try something different?" Sandra asked while presenting the menu to him.

No thought had to be given to the matter. Sledge enjoyed the diner special that consisted of two eggs over easy, three slices of not-too-crispy bacon, a sausage link, two pieces of toast, and three warm buttermilk pancakes drowned in maple syrup and real butter.

"I think we'll go with the diner special. I can't stray from my favorite. It's too good."

Sandra didn't scribble anything down and said, "That it is. I'll be back shortly with your order, handsome."

As Sandra hauled the menu and coffee mug back to the counter, Sledge examined the folks who were in the diner at that time. Generally, he would have his nose stuck in a book, but he decided against it this go-round and instead, sat there slouched in the red bench seat.

He sipped on the scalding coffee while taking care not to burn his mouth. All seemed calm and right as he set the mug down and licked his lips.

A heated discussion two tables up from Sledge broke out between a man and a woman. The man's voice rose to an angered shout that he struggled to keep under wraps. He faced Sledge with a portion of his identity concealed by the woman's head, at whom he barked.

From what he could see of the irritated man, Sledge surmised that he was more than likely abusive from the way the woman's body flinched with each scolding he put on her. His wiry facial hair and unkempt appearance lent credence to Sledge's assumption of the man. He didn't look like a pimp but more like a jilted partner who received some bad news.

The other people in the diner minded their business and went about their meals, ignoring the man's clucking tongue that reprimanded the woman for some reason Sledge couldn't fully make out.

She tried to stand and exit the booth they were in, but the man grabbed her by the forearm and forced the quaking woman back into the seat.

For Sledge, the aggressive move was far enough, and he aimed to stop it before it went any further.

Chapter 17

THE WOMAN PLOPPED BACK down in the seat. Her muffled cries loomed large as the man kept hold and wagged his index finger at her. He caught sight of Sledge staring his way and shifted his focus from her to him.

Sledge continued sipping on his coffee as the snarling man got up from the booth and made his way to him. He'd saved Sledge the expense of having to get up himself and approach them.

"Do we have a problem, pal?" The man asked, reeking of stale cigarette smoke and liquor, among the more potent body odors that came off of him in waves. "I couldn't help noticing that you were staring at me. I don't like that."

Swallowing the coffee in his cup, Sledge shifted his glare up at the man. "No problem here, pal except for the fact that I don't care for the way you're treating that lady. Only pieces of trash do that."

"Is that so?" He pressed his dirty rough hands flat to the table top near the edge. There were nicks on his skin and his knuckles were bruised, indicating that he was a brawler and didn't mind throwing punches.

"It is. A man who does such a thing is weak in my opinion. Probably has a small dick to match his small ego."

"Are you serious right now? I could slit your throat and bleed you out on this table and not think twice about it." The man's threats were idle at best and caused little for Sledge to be concerned about.

Sledge matched his intense gaze and said, "How about you do this? Leave the diner, without the woman, and perhaps I'll only break a few of your fingers and not your entire hand that you used to grab her with."

The man snickered at the response but didn't heed the warning. His pride and arrogance wouldn't allow it, especially in front of an audience that could hear them speaking.

Lowering down and getting closer to Sledge's face, his left hand shifted behind his back as he jabbed his right index finger at him. "I'm going to–"

In one fluid motion, Sledge snatched the man's finger and broke it, then slammed the side of his skull down on the table top.

The jarring noise of his head bouncing off the surface sent heads twisting toward Sledge's table. He leaned toward the man's face while smiling at the old men parked at the counter.

"Now, unless you want the remaining fingers broken, I suggest you exit forthwith. I'm feeling generous and you're testing my good will. If you so much as look at that woman again or contact her in any way, that'll be the last thing you'll ever do. I can promise that."

He grunted a response and whimpered from his broken digit.

Sledge said, "Nod your head if you understand."

He bobbed his head while trying not to cry.

"Good. Now, get out of my sight and let these good folks in here finish their meals in peace," Sledge said as he eased his grip from the man's skull. "Go be a waste of space somewhere else."

Sandra stood in the open space between the counters holding Sledges plates of food as the man stood straight. Clutching his bent finger and holding his hand to his chest, he stomped toward the entrance of the diner and stormed out the door.

A portion of Sledge's coffee spilled onto the white table top. He dabbed the mess with the napkins as Sandra delivered his meal of hot breakfast food.

"Are you okay, sweetie?"

"Right as rain. There was a misunderstanding on his part that needed clearing up."

"That's one way of putting it." Sandra slid the plates onto the table across from Sledge as he finished wiping up the coffee. "Let me get a rag to clean that up for you."

"Don't trouble yourself. It's taken care of." Sledge placed the damp napkins at the edge of the table near the wall and then pulled his plates of food toward him as if nothing had happened. "This looks and smells wonderful. Give my compliments to the cook, would you?"

"Sure thing, sweetie." Sandra glanced at the woman who was now facing both of them from her seat. "Are you all right?"

She nodded but gave no verbal response.

Sledge dug into his bountiful plate of southern goodness which made his stomach growl even more. Clutching the fork and knife, he got to work on cutting the eggs and mixing the runny yoke with the whites.

"If you need anything else, honey, don't hesitate to ask, okay?" Sandra said.

"Yes, ma'am," Sledge replied with a warm smile.

As Sandra walked off, and as Sledge took another bite of food, the timid woman approached his table and stood patiently with both hands clutched at her waist. She hesitated to speak at first but finally did as Sledge met her shiny eyes.

"I don't want to be a bother, but I wanted to say thank you for what you did." She spoke softly and had a young face that put her age around the early to mid-twenties.

Her cheekbones were visible and the garb she wore hung loosely from her rail-thin frame. She glanced at his plate of food twice while trying to hide the fact that she was hungry.

"It's not a problem. I made the point of him leaving you alone clear. He got the message."

"Well, thank you again. If this wasn't my wake-up call to make better decisions, I don't know what is." She gave a forced smile, glanced at Sledge's plate of breakfast food one last time, and said, "I'll let you finish your meal in peace. Have a nice day, sir."

As she turned to walk away, Sledge spoke up. "Would you like to join me?"

She paused and shot him a glance over her shoulder. "I don't want to intrude. I feel as though I've already ruined your meal."

Sledge waved his hand at her as he swallowed the bit of food in his mouth. "Nonsense. You haven't ruined anything." He then pointed at the seat across from him and said, "Come on. Have a seat and join me."

A smile replaced the downtrodden expression on the young woman's face. She was more than eager to sit with him as she slid her legs under the lip of the table and scooted to the center of the bench seat.

"Sandra, can we have a menu over here, please?" Sledge asked the waitress stationed behind the curved counter.

"You got it, doll."

The woman removed the purse from her shoulder and put it toward the edge of the table and wall.

"Here you go, sweetie," Sandra said as she placed the plastic menu down in front of the angular woman. "I'll give you a second to look it over and be right back to take your order."

"I think I'll have whatever it is he's eating," she replied while bobbing her forehead at Sledge's food. "It looks good."

Sandra picked up the menu and said, "Wonderful choice. That's his favorite as well. I'll get this order put in. It shouldn't take long."

"Thank you, ma'am."

"You're welcome, sweetie." Sandra then asked, "Would you like some coffee or water?"

"Water, please."

"Coming up."

Before Sandra walked away, Sledge said to her, "Make sure you put this on my bill."

"You got it."

Slightly embarrassed by the gesture, the woman lowered her head in shame. "Thank you for that. I'll pay you back. I promise. I don't like having debts over my head."

"You're welcome and don't worry about it," Sledge replied. "I'm happy to do it. Just do me a favor and pass on the good deed to someone else who needs it."

She smiled brightly as more tears formed. "I sure will."

"Perfect."

"I'm Cathy Renner by the way."

"It's nice to meet you, Cathy. I'm Blake Sledge."

Chapter 18

CATHY GOBBLED DOWN THE plate of food in record time and Sledge paid the check. They went their separate ways afterward as the lunch crowd filed into the diner.

Sledge's schedule was now open since he'd completed his latest job in Jacksonville, but luck being as it was, he knew it wouldn't stay that way for too long. Problems were abundant in the world. A day barely went by when his phone didn't ping a new opportunity to apply his skills. Word of mouth spread about his services of help and hope to those who needed it, increasing his workload as the years ticked by.

With nothing pressing at the moment, Sledge jumped at the chance to run some errands that he had been forced to put off for the last few weeks. One of them was dropping in on the computer repair shop Sledge used to fix equipment.

He wasn't the biggest tech guy in the world, but he managed well enough. His operation was small and about as streamlined as he could make it. Being an army of one was preferred for security reasons, but at times, Sledge wished he had another set of hands to do research and communicate with potential clients while he focused more on completing jobs.

Mac's Computer and Electronic Repair was Sledge's second home and rivaled that of the West End Diner. Few spots within Atlanta garnered such frequent visits from Sledge, but he had to eat and have his equipment running at optimum performance. There was no better place in the city than Mac's for the latter.

Sledge ducked out of traffic and rolled to a stop in the empty slot at the curb in front of the repair shop. His truck grumbled an unsatisfied rasp as he shifted into park and killed the engine while peering at the building.

Bars covered the windows and the glass door. "Mac's Computer and Electronic Repair" was written in a graffiti-style font on the right window in large, bold, colorful lettering.

A smaller matching cling was stuck to the front of the door as well as a sign that displayed it was open to the public. The shop wasn't located in the best part of town, but issues regarding robberies were few and far between for the business.

The shop never had a ton of foot traffic inside when Sledge dropped in, but they always stayed steadily busy fixing computers and other electronic equipment. The owner, Mac, was hardly ever there. He left the day-to-day operation to his one employee, Trixie, who was smart as a whip for a nineteen-year-old girl who had a mouth that got her in trouble more times than Sledge could count.

As he exited the truck and made his way around the hood toward the curb, two surly men dressed in tracksuits emerged from the entrance. The meathead on the left stuffed a wad of cash into his right pants pocket as they strode down the walkway, away from the shop.

Sledge studied the men for a moment as he approached the barred door, then he entered the shop. A bell rang, indicating his presence.

The repair shop was cluttered with myriad computer towers and various electronic components lining both walls on either side. The items weren't arranged in a methodically organized manner but in more of a messy configuration that made it hard to shop and discern what was what.

Rock music pumped from the boombox perched on a shelf nestled in the back left corner above a towering stack of leaning cardboard boxes. It wasn't anything Sledge listened to, as the high-pitched squeal of the singer grated on his nerves. He preferred older rock to the new-age junk that kids and young adults considered music.

At the far end of the shop, near the register, Trixie's normal spot was vacant. She wasn't in sight, nor was Mac, but that wasn't unusual.

The swinging gray metal door leading into the stockroom swung open. A young woman with purple and black hair emerged, staring at her phone and chewing gum. Her fingernails were painted black and she wore a scant bit of makeup to accent her flawlessly light skin.

"Yes. How can I help you?" Trixie asked in a lifeless voice without looking up as her fingers struck the face of her phone.

"Maybe switch that garbage off on the radio to another station that plays real music for starters," Sledge replied with a smirk.

Trixie lowered her phone and placed the device on the counter near the register, and glanced up at him. "I would, sir, but our radio doesn't pick up senior stations. I do apologize. For that, you'll need to return to your assisted living home."

Sledge enjoyed their back-and-forth banter. She was witty and extremely intelligent. "Hey, now, that's below the belt. You do realize that I'm in my early thirties, right?"

"Oh, that's right. I forgot," Trixie said with a wry grin. "It's hard to remember that when you act like you're a billion years old."

"Not a billion. Maybe a million."

"That's still old as dirt, Sledge."

"Perhaps."

Trixie sat on the black stool behind the glass counter as Sledge approached the register. Her leg was raised, the heel of her boot resting on the edge of the stool as she held onto her leg.

"What are you out doing today, besides giving me a hard time?"

"Oh, just taking care of business since I'm back in town."

"Vacation?"

"I wish. No time for that. Too busy."

"You have to make time or you'll crash and burn. Look at me. When I'm here, it's basically like being on vacation."

Sledge snickered at the comment. "Yeah, that's the impression I get. This place isn't exactly a resort."

"Hey, you can lead one man's trash to another man's treasure, but you can't make it drink," Trixie quipped while waving one arm toward the disheveled array of randomly stacked computer parts, with wires splayed in every direction on the shelves like a Price is Right model.

Sledge couldn't help but laugh. "Fair enough."

"It's all in the mind of the beholder, Sledge. Don't forget that." Trixie tapped the end of her finger to her temple, then she asked, "Anyway, are you picking up today or dropping off?"

"Picking up. Is my laptop ready?"

"You mean that clunker you're limping along by making me slap more Band-Aids on it?"

"It's only four years old," Sledge countered. "I wouldn't consider that to be a clunker."

"In terms of electronics, and especially computers, that's ancient." Trixie lowered her leg and hopped off the stool. "And to answer your question, I got it running, and faster mind you."

"Perfect. I didn't doubt that you would be able to. You're one of the best in the city when it comes to fixing gadgets." Sledge rested his elbows on the countertop but didn't fully put his weight on the smudged glass. "How are you doing? Staying out of trouble, I hope."

"Oh, I'm doing fine, but trouble seems to find me whether I want it to or not," Trixie replied while sifting through the mess of equipment on a four-shelf, black rack. "You know as well as I do that I'm a good girl, but I always seem to get caught up in precarious situations. It's not my fault."

Right, Sledge thought, knowing better than to believe in that bald-faced lie. She was cunning and had side businesses that involved computer schemes that he'd heard her speak of while on the phone.

"Were those two Neanderthals who left a minute ago in the tracksuits part of that trouble that happens to track you down?"

"Those two goons were here looking for Mac is all," Trixie replied as she removed a laptop from the second shelf from the bottom. "I try not to involve myself in whatever business dealings he has going on. I show up, do my stint in paradise, and then head home to my crappy loft apartment."

Since coming to Mac's, Sledge had taken a shine to Trixie. They had a good rapport and formed a comfortable and predictable bond. He had few friends by choice and preferred to stay alone, but Trixie was an exception he made.

"Okay. I'm just making sure you're not being harassed is all. Certain men don't mind roughing up and intimidating women."

Trixie carried the laptop to the counter and placed it in front of him. "Yes. I know how you are, Sledge. You make it a point to let me know that each time you come in here. I'm surprised you're not a father, because you've mastered caring a bit too much quite well."

Even though she spoke as if it annoyed her, Sledge knew by her smile that Trixie appreciated his thoughtful nature.

"I have to protect my investments. If you're not here, who else is going to fix my equipment? Certainly not Mac, he's not nearly as skilled as you are."

"No need to suck up to me. I've already fixed the problem," Trixie shot back while lifting the lid. "I'd save those compliments for another time, but that's just me."

Her finger pressed the silver power button but the unit refused to fire up. She stood on her tippy toes and studied the screen, trying to figure out why it wasn't booting.

"Maybe the battery is dead?" Sledge said as she flipped the unit around toward her. "Do you still have the charger I brought in?"

"Yeah. It's around here. I'll have to track it down. I may have forgotten it on the shelf."

While Trixie moved away from the counter and scoured the mess of cords, cables, and equipment piled on the shelf, Sledge's phone pinged from his back pants pocket.

He removed the phone and checked his encrypted app which showed a new message had been delivered. Sledge opened it and skimmed the three sentences as she arrived back at the counter holding something black and long in her hands.

"Okay. I think I got the right power cord and brick."

Trixie plugged the tip of the cable into the side slot and powered on the unit. In less than three minutes she had the laptop operational and was clacking her nails against the keys.

Sledge penned a quick response to the request for his assistance with an issue that wasn't listed within the lines of panicked verbiage.

"Is that your girlfriend or work?" Trixie asked as she stared at the screen.

"Work," Sledge answered as another message dropped in, listing nothing more than an address.

"We need to find you a woman, someone to loosen you up. You always seem so uptight."

Sledge responded to the message with, *Be there in half an hour*, then stuffed the phone back into his back pocket.

"I'm not so sure that a woman would care for my hectic schedule. My work can be demanding at times."

"Is brooding a profession?" Trixie asked as she spun the laptop toward him. "Just wondering."

"Maybe."

Trixie ran through what she'd done and how she'd upgraded the system's memory and removed a bunch of clutter from the hard drive.

To Sledge, the laptop seemed to perform better than it had previously. Its response time was quicker and the lag time after each mouse click was immediate.

"For now, this should keep you running, but I'd suggest you start considering upgrading," Trixie said. "This wasn't a high-end unit to begin with, so there is only so much that can be done. It wouldn't be worth doing too many more upgrades at that point; you could buy a new one with the latest bells and whistles. If you want, when you're ready, I could build you a sweet-ass rig without all of the ad junk and programs they stuff in here. That crap does nothing other than take up space and suck power from the processor. I'd do you right by it."

"I'll keep that in mind for when I'm ready," Sledge replied. "Seeing how you work on these, I have no doubt you'd put together an amazing system."

"Oh, for sure. I don't do too many custom jobs for just anybody," Trixie said while flashing him a smile and winking as she placed the laptop and cord in the case he had left with her. "It's my way of giving back to the elderly community."

"You just had to go there, didn't you?"

"I never miss a chance to bust your balls," Trixie said as she handed him the case.

She rang up the transaction and Sledge paid her in cash, all one-hundred-dollar bills. Shutting the till Trixie gave Sledge his receipt for the work performed and he stuffed it into the unzipped pocket of the laptop case.

"Thanks again for getting it fixed up," Sledge said as he backed down the length of the open walkway toward the entrance. "Do me a favor and try to stay out of trouble, will ya?"

Trixie took a seat on the stool and shrugged while smirking. "I'll do my best but make no promises."

"Fair enough, I guess."

"You stay out of trouble as well. Don't let work get you down too much."

Sledge knew that wasn't going to be the case. Each referral he received was never a pleasant one. But he was okay with that. Life was hard and unfair most of the time. So when people were shoved to the ground, and had their faces rubbed in the dirt, he was the one who picked them up and made things right.

As he opened the door and stood in the doorway, Sledge said, "I'll do my best, but make no promises."

Chapter 19

HIS TIME SPENT AT Mac's put Sledge slightly behind schedule, extending about ten minutes past the thirty-minute timeframe he quoted to the client. Traffic didn't help either as it slowed Sledge's progress in reaching Tuxedo Park.

For some, the prospect of doing business with an individual in such an expensive neighborhood would send dollar signs sprouting in their heads, delighting in how much they could charge for services rendered. Sledge, however, kept to his mission of helping people first and making money second, regardless of their social stature.

Upon entering the outskirts of the lavish subdivision, Sledge raked his attentive gaze over the lush manicured lawns and mansions that dotted the expansive property. Expensive luxury sedans and SUVs occupied the driveways within the upscale neighborhood.

The Silverado paled in comparison to the vehicles he passed. They made his ride look more like a piece of junk, unfit to cross into their neck of the woods.

Tuxedo Park was the wealthiest and most well-known subdivision in Buckhead and had been for ages due to it being the home of the Governor's Mansion. Sledge cared not for political figures, regardless of their affiliation, as he saw both sides of the aisle as cronies and thieves of the American people.

Sledge viewed the address again while following the curve of the street that passed a castle-like home with a pond right next to it. His destination was up on the left, secured behind a steel fence and a wall of shrubbery that lined the inside perimeter with its thick leafy limbs.

He slowed and pulled into the mouth of the drive, then stopped at the closed gate. Sledge rolled down his window and looked at the intercom box mounted on a gooseneck black pole. Installed on top of the wide boxy unit was a camera directed at the window.

As Sledge reached out of the window and aimed his finger at the white button at the front of the intercom station, the gates jerked and then swung inward, allowing him to pass.

No voice came from the intercom, so Sledge assumed the client saw him on the camera and buzzed him in. He pulled forward and drove through the gate at a modest speed of ten miles per hour. Once Sledge got clear of the gate's edge, both sides closed and settled into place.

The tarred driveway wound through well-kept landscaping that lined the sides of the private drive. A bountiful blend of flowers and plants sprang from the earth in a colorful, vibrant array.

Up ahead was the Claymore Estate, in the middle of a large swath of green lush land that separated the homes on either side of the stone mansion by several acres. Sledge soaked in the scenery and searched for a security detail out of habit, knowing the odds that people with such wealth would have protection on-site.

Much to his surprise, Sledge couldn't spot any uniformed men or suits patrolling the grounds as he neared the circle drive. He could see nothing but landscapers tending to the perfectly-shaped bushes and lawn.

Sledge followed the curving concrete drive to the front of the home. A massive fountain, with stone dolphins frozen in mid-air as water shot from the center tower, was centered in the middle of the driveway.

Rolling to a stop, Sledge shifted into park and killed the engine. After removing his keys from the ignition, he climbed out of the cab and slammed the door shut.

He moved around the hood and crossed the wide drive toward the brick steps, which had marble lions perched on pedestals on either side of the landing. Nothing screamed that the Claymores had more money than they knew what to do with than the abundance of pointless display pieces they had.

The hand-carved Mahogany door ahead cracked open as Sledge approached the entrance. A gentleman in his early fifties appeared in the doorway, distraught and clutching an old-fashioned, rock glass half filled with brown liquor. His silver hair was slicked back and his skin had a nice bronze tint to it. He was clean-shaven and wore a white Polo shirt, pressed khaki slacks, and brown dress shoes.

After taking another hearty drink from the tumbler, he lowered the glass from his lips and extended his hand to Sledge. "Thank you so much for coming to meet with us on such short notice, Mr. Sledge."

Mr. Claymore's grip was firm but not overly tight. His hand was smooth as silk, indicating to Sledge that the man didn't perform hard labor. Muscles flexed in his defined biceps, squeezing against the bands of the polo's sleeves that hugged his arms.

"It's not a problem, sir. You caught me at the right time it seems."

"Please, call me Brian. Sir is too formal."

"Sure. No problem."

Brian downed the rest of his drink and tilted his head at the interior of the home. "Come inside and we can get started."

Sledge entered the cavernous mansion and stepped clear of the doorway as Brian closed the door. It hit the jamb with a deep thud that echoed through the spacious residence.

"We'll go back to my office and get started with why we reached out to you," Brian said as he moved swiftly down the long, wide corridor that had paintings and art pieces on display. "My wife is waiting for us there."

Their shoes clicked off the marble floor. Both men moved with purpose as Sledge had to keep pace with the hastened jaunt of the distressed man.

After arriving at a set of closed floor-to-ceiling double wood doors, Brian pushed his way into the room where a younger, blonde woman stood in the middle of the spacious study.

She bit at the tips of her nails and stared at the floor before glancing up at them. Her flawless face was riddled with fright and sadness. The woman looked to be in her early to mid-forties, but she could have been much younger than that.

"This is Mr. Sledge, sweetie," Brian said to whom Sledge assumed was his wife.

Sledge extended his arm to the woman as she scuttled toward him. "It's nice to meet you, ma'am."

"Please. Call me, Mandy." She shook his hand and sniffled, fighting to keep back a flood of tears that formed in each of her swollen, bloodshot eyes. "We do apologize for bothering you and requesting such a quick meeting, but we're at our wits' end and we're not sure what to do next."

"It's no worry at all." Sledge released her hand, which was just as smooth as her husband's.

She backed up and offered him a seat in one of the leather guest chairs at a round table.

They each sat down in the chairs and got to the crux of why he had been asked to come. Placed on top of the table was a manila file.

"So, tell me, why is it that I'm here today?" Sledge asked while taking his seat.

Brian put his rock glass on the table top and cleared his throat. Although he was more composed than his wife, Sledge could still see the hurt in the man's face as he fought to keep his emotions from overtaking him.

"I know your time is valuable, Mr. Sledge, so I'll cut to the chase." He glanced at his wife who wiped the wetness from under each of her eyes, and then he said, "Our daughter, Kim, was kidnapped six days ago after school. She never made it home. So far, the police have no leads, and there has been no contact made with the kidnappers."

"Not even a ransom request?" Sledge asked.

"No," Mandy answered. "It's like she fell off the face of the earth. Her friends know nothing. We're pretty close with a number of them and they all say they saw her at school this past Friday, but they haven't seen or heard from Kim since then."

"How old is your daughter?" Sledge asked.

"Seventeen," Mandy replied.

"So, high school then. Does she drive to school, ride with a friend, or take public transportation like a school bus?"

Brian answered without hesitation. "She drives her car. A red convertible Mercedes-Benz E-Class."

"Okay." Sledge soaked in the details while going through the list of pertinent questions he had in his head. "Have the authorities tried tracking the vehicle? Those sorts of luxury sedans generally have vehicle locators on them."

Mandy said, "That was one of the first things they did, even after we told them we tried to track the car as well. Neither of us had luck in doing so. Like Kim, it's as if the car's GPS or whatever system it has to locate it has been disabled."

Sledge sighed. "I have to ask, so please don't take offense, but is there any chance she could have run away? Sometimes young people can get wild ideas. Did she ever rebel? Did she fight with you guys a lot or buck the rules?"

Mandy's response was immediate, "No, nothing like that. I understand why you have to ask, but I assure you, Mr. Sledge, she is a model student and daughter. She has her whole life ahead of her, and she's excited about that life. She would never run away. She wanted- *wants*, to be a veterinarian. She always has, and she's already taking courses for it." Desperate tears fell down the broken mother's face.

Before Sledge could venture another question, Brian sat forward on the chair and then put both arms flat on the table. "Listen, Mr. Sledge. We're desperate here and know that time is of great importance. The longer Kim is missing the odds of us ever finding her will go down. We know this. The police have assured us repeatedly that they are on the case and working tirelessly to uncover any leads."

"I do understand your cause for concern and I'm sorry that your family is having to go through such a tough time," Sledge said, "but the questions I'm asking are important and help me get a sense of the trail of events that led up to her going missing."

Mandy reached for the file on the table and then scooted it toward Sledge. "This has everything we know about the case. Nothing has been left out. We've been more than cooperative with the authorities about our daughter."

Sledge picked up the file and glanced through the police report. An image of Kim was paper-clipped to the folder. She had long, straight brown hair. A dimple resided in the middle of her chin as well as in her cheeks when she smiled. She was pretty and, similar to her mother, had flawless skin free of birthmarks or freckles that he could see in the picture.

"We know you're not a detective or a private investigator. Your name came up from a friend of ours who heard the sort of work you do and he provided your contact info to us," Brian said.

"And what sort of work did you hear about?" Sledge asked, peeking over the top of the folder.

"The kind of work we could use right now," Mandy answered as if his methods and tactics were acceptable. "Our daughter's life hangs in the balance and we just want her home by any means necessary. You come highly recommended, Mr. Sledge."

Brian patted his palm on the table. "We understand discretion and have been informed of how you operate. No one knows about us reaching out to you. Not even the police. This is a contained matter and will remain that way unless you feel otherwise."

"As far as money goes," Mandy said, "that will not be an issue. You have a blank check written. Whatever the figure you arrive at, it will be acceptable. We are dead serious about finding our daughter and want to incentivize you enough to ensure that you go the distance to find her."

After listening to the desperate parents plead their case Sledge closed the folder and placed it on the table before him. He hated hearing of the young girl missing and had a few ideas spawn inside his head as to what might have happened. His primary guess was human trafficking.

With her age and appearance, Kim would be a prime target for such deviants to snatch up the young female for the black market. American women were a hot commodity among foreign elites who paid top dollar for them. He hadn't personally worked a case that involved human trafficking, but Sledge knew of the industry and wanted nothing more than to see it burn to the ground.

His finger tapped the file, and then Sledge said, "Okay. I'll take the case and do what I can to find your daughter."

A grateful head tilt came from the father as well as a flood of tears from the mother.

"Thank you so much, Mr. Sledge," Mandy said.

"Yes. Thank you. You have no idea what this means to us."

"You're welcome." Sledge made it a point to clarify one important aspect of his work to manage his client's expectations. "I do need to make one thing clear before we get started."

"And what's that?" Brian asked while holding his wife's hand in his.

"I don't make promises. That's never good business. But what I can say, and guarantee, is that I will do everything within my power to find your daughter. Of that, you can rest assured."

The parents exchanged looks, and then said, "Agreed."

"Perfect. Let's get to work, then."

Chapter 20

FOR THE NEXT HOUR, Sledge rummaged through Kim's bedroom and clarified any pending questions he had that weren't immediately addressed in the file he was given. Notes were scribbled inside the folder, and then Sledge exited the home for his pickup.

As he made his way across the driveway, Sledge's phone dinged with a message from the secured encrypted software he used. All communications were to be sent from the software. No phone contact was to be made from either party. That was his rule and non-negotiable.

The first installment for his services was confirmed by Mandy Claymore through the message. Twenty thousand dollars had been deposited into his account, to which the parents agreed and Sledge accepted. The remaining balance was open-ended, but he had no desire to take advantage of the wealthy family.

Sledge climbed into the driver's seat and placed the file under the wide armrest. Next, he started the pickup and drove around the fountain and then down the private road toward the gate.

After exiting the estate, Sledge decided to head back to his home and start researching the case further. He wanted to study the material given to him in-depth, and doing so required a bit of time. He was good at tracking people down and uncovering messes, but it always happened after he had done his homework.

As he navigated the Atlanta traffic back to his home, Sledge chewed on the details of Kim's disappearance. From what her father had said, the family had no enemies to speak of. They were rich, and most times that was more than enough incentive for unscrupulous thugs to target them.

Mandy didn't work and was a stay-at-home mom.

Brian was an investment broker at Infinity Global Investment Group. The firm handled large accounts and Brian was one of their biggest brokers who managed the group's elite clients. To Sledge, that threw up red flags. Perhaps Brian had crossed the wrong people or made some bad deals. Only time would tell if that was the case.

Sledge piloted the Silverado down the street in the warehouse district of the city that was far from being revitalized. Most of the buildings in the area were in bad shape and falling apart. No businesses occupied the shambly structures and traffic was zero in the area. It was the perfect place for Sledge to call home while also being off the radar.

The building was listed under a shell company he had established. It was the perfect cover and one that, so far, had not drawn attention. To anyone looking at the paperwork on the property, it read as legit and straightforward, leaving no gray areas for anyone to want to investigate further.

Pulling down the alleyway, Sledge drove exactly one hundred feet to a closed roll-up door. He then thumbed the button on the garage door opener and steered the truck inside as the door retracted into the building.

As soon as the tailgate cleared the entrance, Sledge lowered the door and killed the engine. He removed the keys from the ignition, gathered the file, and both his go-bag and laptop, then departed the cab.

His home was an open workspace that covered more than five thousand square feet of, to him, prime real estate. A portion of the spacious warehouse had been sectioned off for living quarters while the remainder housed surveillance equipment, weapons, tools, and his muscle car that he tinkered with between jobs.

Sledge secured his go-bag in the fireproof safe set within the floor of his bedroom and then he headed to his office to dive into Kim's disappearance.

The laptop Trixie fixed was cast to the floor as he rounded the shatterproof glass top of his workstation. Sledge dropped into the seat of his leather chair, and swung toward the two curved, thirty-two-inch black monitors.

He opened the file and ran his finger down the middle of the folder. One by one, Sledge removed each piece of information and spread them out in front of him.

For the rest of the afternoon and part of the evening, Sledge sifted through the reports and notes taken with a fine-tooth comb. From what he read, the police had been thorough in taking the Claymores' statements with no missing details. All they had discovered thus far, which wasn't much from what he had been told by the family, was listed within the documents.

The detective assigned to the case was Shawn Wentworth. From what the Claymores said, he had been attentive to their questions and was eager to solve the case as well.

Even though the file mentioned Kim didn't have a boyfriend as far as the family knew, Sledge wondered if that was the case. He had to cross off as many possibilities as he could to steer his focus in the right direction, and quickly since he was racing the clock to find her, the clock had a significant head start.

Sledge scanned her social media accounts for clues but found nothing useful. Kim was active and posted daily, but never mentioned a guy she might have liked or was seeing. He dug through countless random videos and posts that offered little value.

One constant that Sledge did notice, however, was a girl that Kim tagged regularly in pictures of them together. Amanda Watson. The pair looked close from the way they interacted in the videos he watched and posts they made.

Amanda's notes in Kim's file were limited to a brief statement to the police, which had nothing to offer about her friend. From what Amanda told the authorities, when school ended on Friday Kim left Grady High School in her Mercedes alone and the teen spoke of no plans afterward to her.

In Sledge's experience, teenage girls always knew more than what they said in questioning, always. Especially those as close as Amanda and Kim appeared to be. Sledge marked Amanda's name on a scratch sheet of paper, then circled it. She was a prime person to check with and to see if any details had been left out of her statement.

The more Sledge dug into the details and lack of leads, he couldn't help but veer toward human trafficking. Kim could have been targeted on her public social media accounts and then tracked for weeks to learn her patterns. Revealing so much of one's life on the internet was a game of Russian roulette. Each harmless post and check-in provided opportunities for those within the business of trafficking young women to target their next victims with ease.

For Sledge, he had no digital footprint to be traced. He minimized his exposure and kept off of the web as much as possible. With no family or friends to speak of, that made living like a ghost easier and kept him off of Cobalt's radar.

Rubbing his eyes, Sledge stood from his chair with Kim's photo pinched between his fingers. The hour had grown late by the lack of natural light that funneled in from the windows around the warehouse.

Sledge checked his wristwatch. It was after 9:00 p.m. Tomorrow, he'd start his hunt for Kim, and hopefully, find her before it was too late.

Chapter 21

GRADY HIGH SCHOOL WAS a buzz of activity as students funneled out of the building that Friday afternoon and fanned out to their vehicles and buses. Kids from all walks of life mingled as they chatted and laughed.

Sledge waited in his Silverado truck that was parked at the curb near the school. From his vantage point, he had a clear visual of the front of the parking lot and the building. He studied each of the kids that went about their business, trying to find Amanda Shaw.

Her image had been committed to Sledge's memory, which was as keen as an elephant's. It had improved tremendously since he left Cobalt, though he couldn't remember anything before he arrived at the group's facility in Virginia during his youth.

Amanda had fiery red hair and freckles on her face. Her height and body type matched that of Kim's, tall and sleek. Sledge put her at around 5'9" and her weight at about one hundred and thirty pounds.

As cars exited the school and buses funneled out through their private drive, Sledge struggled to find Amanda's white Range Rover in the meld of shuffling vehicles. The last thing he wanted to do was pay a visit to her home, not unless it was a last resort. He wanted to catch her out in public and to do that, he had to tail her for an opening to speak with her about Kim.

Cars of all makes, models, and conditions drove off in either direction of the busy street. Among the long line of vehicles was a white Range Rover that came into view.

Sledge squinted through the windshield of his truck at the driver. The side windows of the luxury SUV were tinted so dark he couldn't see through them. The girl behind the wheel had long, flowing, red hair and appeared to be alone. No one was in the front passenger seat or the back as far as Sledge could tell.

She hung a left and cruised down the road, staying under the posted speed limit of twenty-five miles per hour for the school zone. Sledge pulled out from the curb and followed the teen as she continued down the road.

Amanda didn't head home right away but piloted the Rover along the street where she eventually stopped at a gas station for fuel. The parking lot of the Sunoco station was semi-busy with minimal folks at the pumps. Sledge pulled into the lot and parked his truck near Amanda.

Before getting out, Sledge located the cameras on the property. Two were mounted under the awning and positioned in a way that shouldn't capture his face if he played it right. His time to move and speak with her was now.

Sledge got out of the truck and made his way toward the hood of the Range Rover. His stride was casual. He didn't want to startle her or look out of place. That wasn't his goal.

Amanda's back leaned against the glimmering body of the Range Rover as she glanced at her phone. The end of the fuel nozzle was buried into the SUV as gas poured into its tank.

"Miss Shaw?"

She flinched. Her relaxed posture stiffened as she stood straight from the Rover. A naked fear swarmed her face as she backed away, nudging the black rubber hose attached to the pump.

"I'm not going to hurt you, Amanda," Sledge said calmly.

"Who are you and what do you want?" She couldn't help but look Sledge up and down as if to measure what his intentions were, approaching her as he had.

"The Claymores have employed my services to help track down their daughter, Kim."

"Do you have a badge that I can see?" Amanda asked.

"No. I do not. I'm not with the Atlanta Police Department. You can say that I'm sort of like a private investigator, an independent."

Her tense body relaxed some but not by much. "Okay. Again, what do you want? I've already told the police, and that detective, Shawn Wentworth, everything I know. There should be a document or whatever showing what I said."

"I've seen that, but I was hoping to maybe pick your brain a bit more about Kim and the days leading up to her disappearance," Sledge replied.

"My intentions here are to find your friend as quickly as possible. Her folks are distraught about what's happened to their daughter."

The handle clicked, signaling that the gas tank had reached its fuel capacity. Amanda viewed the face of the pump and then removed the nozzle from the opening of the Range Rover without responding to Sledge's request.

"It won't take long. I promise. You may have some information that could help me in tracking down your best friend," Sledge said. "Kim is your best friend, right? You do want her back home and to be able to see her again, correct?"

"Of course I do," Amanda shot back as tears formed while she screwed the cap in place on the gas tank. "She's been my best friend since we were little kids. Kim is like a sister to me."

"Then help me find her. Five minutes is all that I'm asking. We can talk somewhere public; you can pick where. After that, you're free to leave and I will not bother you anymore. I promise."

Amanda glanced to her left, past the steel column of the awning, then back to Sledge. "All right. We can talk across the street at that burger joint."

"That will work for me."

Chapter 22

AMANDA WAS UNEASY IN her chair. Her weight constantly shifted and her fingers twiddled with a nervous tick. She was guarded. Sledge couldn't tell if it was because she knew more than she had let on, or if she was worried about her friend. Either way, he'd know soon enough.

"Okay. What is it that you want to know?"

"How was Kim acting the days before she went missing?" Sledge asked, studying every twitch and move Amanda made. "Was she acting differently? Did her mood change any, like growing quiet or angry?"

"Nope. Kim seemed fine. I mean, we had some tests going on at school that week that she was stressing about." Amanda's shoe tapped the floor under the table. Although subtle, Sledge picked up on the nervous tick. "She prided herself on making good grades. Her parents expected as much from her, nothing but the best. Anything less than that was frowned upon whether they said it out loud or not."

Sledge nodded, logging her response in his head. "Did she stress out every time there was a test?"

"Most times, yes. Kim's parents have high expectations for her future. It's hard to achieve such things with a crap GPA."

"Okay." Sledge paused for a beat before continuing, thinking about her statement.

Kim was stressed the days prior because of an upcoming test. Despite them alluding otherwise, her parents expected perfection from their daughter, increasing her anxiety. Teens under such weight to perform to maintain grades were known to dabble in certain drugs to aid them in staying awake and studying.

Amanda checked the time on her white watch and looked toward the front of the restaurant. Her tells of unease were growing more intense as their conversation progressed.

"Do you know if Kim ever dabbled in drugs of any kind?"

The mere mention of drugs caused Amanda to twitch quite a bit more, even though she tried to keep from doing so. "Not that I'm aware of."

"So then, she never used Adderall, Molly, or anything related?" Sledge explained his reason for the questioning. "I ask only because it seems that under such pressure, as described by you, and how Kim was expected to perform at high levels, she might require a stimulant to help her along. Or maybe during those times you two were having so much fun in those videos she posted on her social media; that was a way for her to unwind, and maybe you too. I don't know."

She dipped her chin and lowered her head in shame. It appeared that the weight of her knowing more than she had led on was eating Amanda alive on the inside.

"Were you two taking any of those drugs or anything else? Remember, I'm not the police," Sledge said, gently forcing the issue.

Amanda ran her wrist under her nose and sniffled. After a momentary pause, she nodded her admission.

"Which ones did you two take?"

"Kim was taking Adderall and Molly. Maybe some other stuff. I don't know." Amanda lowered her arm and sniffled again. "I did Molly and coke a few times."

"I'm guessing no one else knows this, right?" Sledge asked. "I noticed in the report you said no when the police mentioned drugs."

"A few of our other friends knew we had taken some Molly and even Xanax here and there, but most everyone did at parties," Amanda replied, maintaining her decorum. "It wasn't that big a deal."

"So, Kim's parents don't know about the drugs, then?"

"Lord, no." Amanda's face twisted as if she'd whiffed a horrible odor. "They would have killed her if they knew about it. Same with my parents, they overreact about the smallest things."

It's not a small thing, but okay, Sledge thought.

"Killed her?" he asked.

Amanda gave him an irritated look that only teenage girls can achieve, "You know what I meant."

"Who was your supplier?"

Another hard pause came from Amanda. She rubbed the back of her neck, seemingly afraid to mutter the name.

"It's okay. You can tell me," Sledge said. "Whoever sold it to you won't know it was you who told me. I promise."

Finally, Amanda said, "His name is Drake Connor. Kim met him online and we all started hanging out a few months ago. They were just friends. Nothing more."

The name Drake Connor didn't ring a bell. He hadn't been listed in the report as a person who had contact with Kim.

"So, they didn't have a romantic relationship of any kind?"

"Not that I'm aware of," Amanda answered. "He acted like he did but she shut him down. You know, like touching her shoulder and trying to kiss her. It was creepy to me but she brushed it off. I think Kim, and well, I, went along with it because he supplied the you-know-what to us. Looking back, it was really stupid and I'm regretting it now. But we didn't think anything of it, just living in the moment. You know?"

"Well, we all make mistakes. It's what we do afterward that defines who we are," Sledge replied, understanding her remorse.

Amanda shrugged. "I guess."

"Why didn't you mention this to the authorities?" Before she could conjure that look again, he hastily added, "I understand the obvious of being in trouble, but your best friend is now missing. This Drake fellow could have had a hand in Kim's disappearance."

With no small amount of reluctance, Amanda said, "Because he threatened to have me and my family killed if I ever mentioned his name. I don't know if Drake did the same with Kim or not. That's why I said nothing about Drake at first but eventually called Detective Wentworth after they didn't find Kim right away. I thought they would, you know? I thought she'd show back up and we'd be laughing about all of this by now." Amanda leaned forward with her elbows on the table, cradling her head in her hands.

Sledge was shocked at this revelation, though he remained calm on the outside. Interesting that Detective Wentworth knew, but it wasn't mentioned in the reports.

Her phone buzzed from below the table. She lifted it and looked at the screen with bloodshot eyes that glistened.

"I know that was tough to say and I appreciate you taking the time to speak with me." Sledge gave a warm smile as he felt bad for the girl.

She typed away on her phone and then said, "I need to get going."

Before she could stand and leave, Sledge asked one last question. "Do you have any idea where I might find this Drake Connor?"

"He's a bad person, mister. Not someone you want to get tangled up with." Amanda's phone buzzed again, furthering her mounting frustration as she stood. "Believe me, I regret daily ever speaking to him."

Sledge stood as well. "I can handle myself. Trust me. All I need is a place or an address to start from."

Amanda sighed, and then said, "Try the Blue Oyster Club on Harwell Road. Drake tried to get Kim and me to go there one night with him but we said no. That's about as good a place to start as any, I guess."

"Thank you, Amanda. What you've told me is helpful."

As Amanda walked by Sledge, she stopped, and turned around. "I do hope you find her. My life hasn't been the same since she disappeared. I want my best friend back."

"I'm going to do whatever I can to find her. You can count on that."

Chapter 23

SLEDGE SAT IN HIS truck and searched the internet for a Drake Connor. The results were many and spanned across the country. He wanted a face to go with the name, and to get a sense of what he was like, other than the piece of trash Amanda made him out to be, which, doubtless, would prove correct.

The fact that Connor had met Kim online furthered his suspicion of human trafficking, as drugs were a good way to lessen a woman's defenses and make it easier to manipulate her as well. Again, Sledge had no proof of such things, but his gut told him so.

After searching through social media and not finding Drake Connor as a friend of Amanda or Kim, he sifted through dozens of men by that name in a general search. Finally, Sledge stumbled upon a Drake Connor who lived in Atlanta. The young man pictured looked to be in his early twenties, handsome, and well-groomed.

By all accounts, he was the personification of vibrant youth. His photo told Sledge that he was confident, likely to the point of arrogant, and probably a smooth talker. He had to be to get in with the type of teen girls he had.

Since Sledge had a possible lead to go on, he pulled out of the fast-food chain's parking lot and made his way to the Blue Oyster Club, which he staked out until night came. He was used to sitting idle for long periods and patiently waiting for his mark to present itself. An experienced hunter knew how not to rush the hunt, as patience paid off in the end.

Neon lights from the gentlemen's club beamed their bold colors above the upscale joint. It was like a moth being drawn to a flame, or sailors being lured into a siren's seductive call. Both were appropriate analogies for the strip club.

An assortment of luxury vehicles and everyday rides started filling the parking lot at around 10:00 p.m. Men in suits exited their luxury sedans and sports cars while those dressed more casually merged with the throng of businessmen funneling into the building.

Drake wasn't among the masses clamoring to get inside, at least, not that Sledge could tell. There would be no nabbing him outside, it seemed. To get a possible bead on the young man, he'd have to venture inside the club and look around.

Sledge got out of his truck and crossed the street toward the entrance of the club's parking lot. Additional vehicles arrived and drove by him, heading for the blacked-out double doors of the establishment.

He kept his 1911 tucked in the waistband of his jeans and draped the bottom of his shirt and jacket over the weapon to conceal it. Sledge wasn't as nicely dressed as most of the men entering the club, but figured he wouldn't stand out too much given the overall clientele.

Manning the door to the club was a thick, no-neck bouncer. Muscles protruded from every part of his torso. His chest was thick and broad. His arms were about as big as Sledge's thighs. He looked like a bodybuilder or a football player, perhaps a linebacker. It didn't matter in the end. Sledge was experienced in hand-to-hand combat. Training always prevailed over brute strength, and very likely the man didn't have the type of training Sledge did.

One by one, men shuffled into the club. Sledge merged with the crowd, passing the bouncer without receiving so much as a single glance from the big man.

Inside, men paid their cover charge to gain entry. A big-breasted blonde behind a bulletproof window took their money and buzzed them past the door.

She flashed each of them a wink and a playful smile while enticing the men with her visible assets. Most ate it up and tried to flirt before being moved on. They were probably the type who thought the strippers loved them when they stuffed wads of cash into their G-strings.

"How are you doing tonight, doll face?" the blonde asked Sledge while smiling at him.

The music blasting from the closing door muffled her voice, making it hard to hear her.

"Good. And you?" Sledge asked as he pulled a twenty-dollar bill from his pocket and slid it under the opening to her.

"Better now that you're here, sweetie." She snatched the money with her long, red-painted fingernails and deposited it into a lockbox stuffed with cash. "I hope you'll look for me a bit later. Maybe we can have fun."

"Maybe."

She winked and then buzzed the door. It opened to the din of music and the DJ shouting into a microphone.

Sledge made his way inside the dark club lit only by the bright lights from the stage and the much dimmer light at the bar areas. Cigarette smoke choked the air and made it cumbersome to breathe. That was one vice Sledge had never been tempted by.

Scores of scantily dressed women dotted the club. Several were on stage, shaking and gyrating their half-naked bodies to the hip-hop music, as guys whooped and hollered while trying to stuff money into their panties. Other women mingled among the guests, trying to sell what Sledge figured to be a personal lap dance.

He paid the females no mind and roved through the debauchery before him. Sledge was glad Kim and Amanda hadn't taken Drake up on his offer of them coming here. It was certainly no place for young girls to be.

The gloom and smoke hindered Sledge's ability to spot his target within the seedy club. Flashing lights showed snippets of the seated men and those standing near the stage.

None of them fit the image Sledge had of Drake in his head; he was much younger and likely more fit than the men he was seeing. He didn't expect him to be wearing a suit, but to be more casually dressed considering how he supposedly targeted young teenage girls.

Women strutting by Sledge winked and ran their fingers up his arm to his neck or up his back. He failed to fall into their traps and continued about his business.

Most of the tables throughout the club were occupied. Not a single seat close to the stage was available, or anywhere else for that matter.

Sledge headed for the curved bar to get a drink and to ask around to see if anyone had seen Drake. Blending in was key to not raising suspicion.

A tan brunette stationed behind the bar served up drinks to the waitresses who waited for her to fill their orders. Bottles of beer and tumblers filled with various colors of liquor sloshed about as the barkeep stacked the beverages onto the round trays and sent the waitresses off to deliver them.

As Sledge rested his elbows on the bar top, the tan brunette asked in a shout, "What can I get started for you, handsome?"

"Bud Light."

"Sure thing, doll." The barkeep moved quickly, grabbing his bottle from the cooler, popping the top, and then sliding it down to him in under a minute. "Are we starting a tab tonight?"

Sledge fished out a fifty from his pants pocket and handed it to her. "No, but maybe you can help me out."

She snatched the money from his hand and then said, "If you're looking for that sort of party, you need to ask one of the girls out on the floor. I'm off limits."

He took a drink of the ice-cold beer, and then said, "That's not what I'm after."

"Then why are you here? If you're not looking for ass and tits, then you're in the wrong place, friend. That's all we have to offer."

"I'm looking for a guy. Maybe you've seen him around."

"Again. Ass and tits. The gay club is farther up the road if you're into that sort of thing."

While taking another drink of beer, Sledge pulled out his phone and showed her the picture of Drake. "Have you seen this man in here before?"

"Your business is not my business. I'm paid to deliver drinks, not trouble." Her hands continuously moved from one task to the next. A barrage of orders was shouted from the waitresses at the far end of the bar looking for drinks to deliver to the wild men.

Sledge slapped another fifty-dollar bill on the counter.

The barkeep sighed and indulged Sledge by glimpsing at the photo on his phone, then said, "Yeah. I've seen him around. He's a regular."

"Is he perhaps here tonight?" Sledge deposited his phone back into his pants pocket while sipping on the beer.

"Why do you want to know?"

"I just need to ask him a few questions. Nothing major."

It was a lie since Sledge had a feeling it would be a bit more than a civil conversation.

She cut her gaze to the right but never turned her head. "He's in the corner of the club. The one surrounded by multiple girls and the three bald dudes guarding them."

Sledge nursed his beer, turned from the bar, and followed her line of sight to the meatheads standing at attention and the little pissant, Drake, indulging in the club's topless dancers.

"I appreciate it."

"You didn't hear that from me, okay?" The barkeep gathered a handful of beer bottles from the cooler beneath the bar and placed them on the counter.

"Hear what?" Sledge winked and downed another gulp of the light beer; then he put the half-empty bottle on the counter.

He moved away from the bar and licked his lips, ready for whatever came next.

Chapter 24

MUSIC PUMPED FROM THE speakers. Women danced to the rhythmic beat as hordes of men shouted with glee at their glistening wet flesh. None of the strippers pulled Sledge's narrowed stare from his target as he maneuvered his way toward the corner of the club.

As he drew closer, Sledge evaluated the surly men guarding Drake. Each wore a deadpan glare that swept over the club. Their arms were tucked against their chests and their hands were clasped together at their waists. They were imposing sentries that steered drunken men away from their set perimeter, but Sledge wasn't so easily deterred.

Two dancers stood from Drake's lap while another sat beside him, running her fingers through his hair. They each took him by the hand and pulled him from the wrap-around, purple, leather couch that was cast in a rainbow of flashing bright colors.

The four of them departed the corner and passed between the wall of guards to a nearby opening that had a neon light that read "Private Suites" in a vibrant, red glow.

One by one, the sentries followed the women and Drake into the darkness, vanishing into the corridor.

Sledge moved around a table full of howling men who had two dancers shaking their assets for them. His neck craned and he peered into the opening of the hallway while making his cautious approach.

The 1911 remained hidden in his waistband. For now, it was to be used as a backup in case he needed its muscle. Despite how much he wanted to kill the garbage human, Sledge required answers and the deviant puke was going to give them to him, whether he wanted to or not.

Upon entering the cold, shadowy corridor, the music lessened. Recessed lighting built into the ceiling above cast a light purple hue that shone at the floor about every five feet.

Closed doors lined the walls. Each had a number mounted to their painted, black fronts. A glut of sultry noises loomed from each room as Sledge followed the curving corridor to the three men who appeared around the bend.

They stood like statues, motionless and facing forward. Sledge watched each of them while making his approach.

One of the guards nearest to Sledge spotted him and held up his hand. From what Sledge saw, Drake's room was the last at the end of the hallway. There were no private rooms past his and no exits.

"Turn around and leave," the big man shouted at Sledge as he faced him, blocking his path with his wide frame. "This room is taken."

Sledge jabbed his thumb over his shoulder while ignoring the throaty bark of the sentry and said, "I think there's been a mistake here. See, I don't give a shit."

He kicked the guard in his balls, causing him to double over. Then Sledge palmed the back of his thick, bald head and rammed his knee into the man's face.

The crack of bone sounded in the tight corridor. The sentry's upper body shot upward from the impact. His legs wobbled from the devastating blows and he swayed. Sledge drove him back into the other two men who reached for their guns wedged in the waistband of their trousers.

Before they could manage to get their guns freed, the yelping big man hindered the other guard's movements as he collapsed to the floor. They moved sluggishly and didn't appear to be professionals. That much was certain.

Both men abandoned their weapons and relied on brawling and brute strength to handle Sledge. Their hands balled into tightly packed fists as they surged toward him. The man closest to Sledge launched an arcing right cross at him that he managed to easily deflect.

He grabbed the man's arm and placed him into an overarm pressure lock; then Sledge kicked the other guard in his gut, ripping the air from his lungs and sending him tumbling backward into the wall.

Without letting go of the man's limb, Sledge bent his arm toward him, and then he grabbed his own wrist with his free hand. He thrust his elbow upward, striking the guard square in the chin.

The pop made from the blow rattled the big man and sent his head snapping backward. Sledge drilled him in the gut with two hard punches, then landed a blistering right cross that cranked his head to the side.

Sledge hammered the other guard's skull with a kick to the face, removing him from the equation. With all three of the guards down and out of commission, Sledge set his sights on the closed door.

The bass from loud music blared in Drake's room and vibrated the door. Sledge was certain that he hadn't been given away to the lowlife drug dealer or the other patrons of the club who hadn't emerged into the corridor, giving him the advantage to pursue his course of action and get some answers.

Chapter 25

SLEDGE TWISTED THE DOORKNOB and barged into the private suite where Drake was receiving a lap dance from one of the strippers while the other two danced for him, completely naked. As the blonde woman straddled his waist and leaned back into him, Drake ran his hands up her front toward her breasts when he locked eyes with Sledge.

The enjoyment of the moment vanished. Panic swelled on Drake's face as he glanced down toward the floor, no doubt spotting his men out of commission in the hallway.

He scrambled to get up while tossing the naked woman on his lap onto the seat. The two women dancing with each other paused and glanced at the door.

Terror filled both of their faces as well as the woman who had resided on Drake's lap. With the music pumping loud inside the private suite, it silenced the strippers' screams as they fled for the door, hurrying to escape while they could.

Sledge maneuvered around the women and closed in on Drake as he stretched across the red leather couch to a platform that had drugs and a pistol sitting on its top. Before he could take hold of the weapon, Sledge kicked him in the side and knocked the wind out of him.

Clutching his ribs and writhing from the flat of his back, Drake mouthed something but Sledge couldn't make out what was being said from the annoying din of music engulfing the space. After removing the thug's gun from the table, Sledge located the controls for the speakers on the wall and switched the music off.

The thumping rap music ceased and silence took hold within the suite, allowing Sledge to hear Drake's groans. Dismantling his weapon, Sledge dropped the pieces to the floor and approached Drake as he tried to stand and make for the entrance.

Two steps were all Drake could get before Sledge cranked the man's chin with a sharp right jab. It dazed Drake and sent him stumbling to the floor.

"How about we don't try that again, okay?" Sledge asked while he examined the cocaine cut into nice, neat lines on the glass top of the table. "That's rather rude to do when someone is trying to speak to you."

Drake palmed the side of his reddening face. His lip was busted and his hair was now a mess. He flipped over to his backside and clutched his ribs while glancing at Sledge with a malevolent glare. "Who the hell are you and what do you want?"

"The who doesn't matter; it's what I want that you should be concerned about." Sledge strolled toward him, relaxed in his movements.

"Do you have any idea of who I am and the connections I have?" Drake asked grimacing from the blows Sledge had landed on him. "I'm the last person in this club you want to mess with, pal. Attacking me and my men was the worst mistake of your life."

That's highly unlikely, Sledge thought.

The puny man's idle threats were the same as every other thug Sledge had encountered. None held any weight nor shook Sledge's resolve.

As Drake scooted on his butt toward the doorway, he stabbed his finger at Sledge who stalked him. Before he could mutter more drivel, Sledge snatched his finger, bent it sideways, and then got Drake to his feet.

Both of his eyelids pinched shut. Drake gnashed his teeth and growled as Sledge applied pressure to the digit and tweaked the man's wrist at an unnatural angle.

"How about we stop running our mouths and focus here," Sledge said, maintaining a firm hold on the appendage. "I want to know why you were targeting Kim Claymore."

"Who?" Drake asked with a whimper. "I don't know anyone by that name."

Annoyed, Sledge smashed Drake's nose with his free hand. A meaty thump sounded from the contact as Drake's head snapped back.

"What did I say? Don't jerk me around. Answer the questions, or so help me, I'm going to make you wish you were dead."

Blood leaked from both of Drake's nostrils down to his upper lip. Sledge kept watching at the doorway while conducting his interrogation.

"Okay, man. Christ!" Drake said in a shout as Sledge jacked his arm in the air as if to throttle him more. "That's the rich kid from Tuxedo Park, right?"

"Yes, you piece of trash. The one you gave the Adderall and Molly to," Sledge replied. "What hand did you have in her disappearance? Spill it and perhaps I won't beat you into a pulp."

"I don't know what you're talking about, man," Drake answered with a twisted, pained frown. "The only thing I did was sell drugs to her. That's all. What are you, some kind of private investigator?"

"Not exactly."

Sledge peered at his watch, knowing that he had spent far too much time in the suite with Drake since pummeling his men in the hallway. If he had more men inside the club, they'd be coming soon after the strippers fled the scene in terror.

Before Sledge could utter another word, Drake slashed at Sledge's waist with a switchblade knife. The tip sliced through the fabric of Sledge's shirt and missed flesh as he sucked in his gut and hopped back.

Drake jumped at the chance to run and bolted for the doorway while carrying the knife. The scared man rushed out of the suite and hooked a left as he leaped over the legs of his men on the floor.

Giving pursuit, Sledge stormed the entrance to the private suite and darted out into the corridor. He raced after his target as Drake ran the length of the curved hallway in a dead sprint toward the pulsating music of the club.

The frightened drug dealer continually glimpsed over his shoulder at the entrance to the hallway as Sledge emerged from the darkness after him. Drake stumbled into men crowding the club as women performed on stage, trying to escape while he could.

Two men approached Drake who jabbed his finger at Sledge marching onward toward them; he was undeterred by the size of the goons locking onto him.

As Drake threaded his trembling body by the henchmen and rushed for the entrance of the packed club, Sledge engaged the two men who now carried pistols. He disarmed one with ease by knocking the barrel toward the floor and then prying the weapon from the man's hand, but not before it discharged a harsh bark that trumped the music.

People in the vicinity scattered like roaches, clearing the area. The women on stage stopped their routine and retreated to the back of the stage as fast as they could.

Amid the chaos, Sledge caught one final glimpse of Drake who merged with the throng of people shoving their way out of the double doors of the entrance to the club. Then he vanished.

Sledge kicked the gun away and rammed his elbow into the goon's skull as his partner looked for a clean shot but failed to find one. The blow rattled the thick man and weakened his legs, but he didn't go down immediately and blocked Sledge's path.

His partner closed the distance between him and Sledge in seconds. He thwacked Sledge with a glancing blow across his chin that rattled his cage. Stars burst as he stumbled back, slightly dazed by the brute's heavy hand.

He charged Sledge with his arm cocked and then launched another arcing right cross that Sledge expertly deflected. Taking hold of the man's wrist and using his forward momentum against him, Sledge flipped him end over end onto a table.

Glassware was sent from the tabletop onto the floor as the man's flailing body skidded across the top and onto the ground. Sledge scooped up one of the turned-over chairs and smashed the steel legs into the other man's side, knocking him hard onto the floor.

Discarding the chair, Sledge rushed to the entrance to try and catch up with Drake before he got away. He pushed the tinted glass doors open and ran out to the parking lot where he was confronted by the meaty bouncer.

As people cleared the club in panic, Sledge caught a glimpse of Drake climbing into the driver's side of a black BMW parked in a reserved spot toward the front of the lot.

The meaty bouncer tried to grab Sledge with his large hand. His fingers swiped at his shirt but he couldn't find purchase on the clothing.

Sledge skirted by the bouncer and shoved him as he focused on the BMW.

Brake lights flashed red; then white lights emerged as the BMW tore out of its parking spot in reverse. Tires squealed as the front end whipped around, facing the street.

The bouncer stayed on the offensive and tried to restrain Sledge but failed to contain him. A single strike to the man's throat sent both of his hands clawing at his neck as he collapsed back into the building's wall.

Sledge rushed the BMW as the vehicle raced toward the street, dodging what few people remained in the lot. The car narrowly avoided running over the bystanders who jumped clear of the sedan as it careened out into the road.

Horns blared from other drivers that Drake nearly clipped with the front end of his ride. The BMW's rear tires spun wildly as its back half rotated a full ninety degrees in the middle of traffic.

Shooting down the sloped drive to the road at full tilt, Sledge made for his truck as the BMW righted its course and took off down the street. He climbed into the driver's seat, fired up the engine, and punched the gas, sending the pickup in a forward jerk after his mark.

Chapter 26

TAILING THE LUXURY SEDAN, Sledge kept within striking distance as he piloted the Silverado past the slower-moving vehicles. His headlights shone at the trunk of the BMW as it swerved erratically into oncoming traffic.

Cars ahead of Sledge slammed their brakes and jerked into his path to avoid colliding with the BMW. He pumped the brake and worked the steering in one fluid motion as he skimmed by the honking vehicles.

Despite Drake's attempts to ditch his tail, Sledge wasn't easily deterred. Every sharp turn that caused chaos on the streets, and sent cars into Sledge's path, couldn't keep him from Drake before the weasel could slip away.

Sledge punched the gas and surged ahead of a yellow hatchback that blocked the street. The truck's engine revved a throaty roar as it shot by the car toward the Beamer.

Drake hung a nail-biting right turn at the street ahead. The sedan cut in front of an approaching van that came to a sudden skidding stop. It steered out of the van's way and clipped cars parked at the curb, damaging its front end.

The reckless driving of the drug dealer was now endangering civilians. Sledge had to end this while he could before someone got hurt or the police showed up. Neither would work in his favor.

Gaining on the nimble sedan, Sledge pushed the truck up the straight-away at max speed. The needle moved upward in the speedometer as the headlights shone at the BMW's tinted back window. His front bumper stalked the Beamer's trunk, closing to less than four feet before making contact.

As Sledge sought a pit maneuver to stall the sedan, Drake cut to the left and made for an alley at dangerous speeds. Instead of making a tight turn into the narrow opening of the buildings, he made a wide arc that sent the hood of the sedan crashing into the corner of the building.

The BMW jolted from the collision. Metal crunched as smoke leaked out from under the crumpled hood. The driver-side door of the Beamer flung open as Sledge stopped directly behind the sedan.

Drake climbed out past the exposed airbag that had been deployed and collapsed onto the pavement. The headlights of the Silverado revealed a gash above Drake's forehead.

Placing the truck into park, Sledge jumped out of the cab and advanced on the drug dealer who crawled along the concrete, then tried to stand and run.

"And where the hell do you think you're going?" Sledge asked as he landed a boot into the mid-part of Drake's spine. "I wasn't finished talking."

The drug dealer collapsed onto the ground, prone on his stomach. Sledge flipped him over to his back and straddled the man's waist. Bunching his fingers into the front of Drake's silk shirt, Sledge jerked him upward from the concrete.

"Running was a dumb move. It seems you're not too smart. All I wanted was answers to a few questions and now you've royally pissed me off."

Part of that statement was a lie. Sledge wanted the deplorable man to suffer for preying on the girls and threatening to harm them.

Spitting to the pavement from his bloody mouth, Drake stared up at Sledge with a dazed look.

Police sirens sounded in the distance. Soon, they'd be on-site and Sledge didn't want to be in the vicinity when the authorities arrived.

He dragged Drake's meager frame across the pavement back to his pickup. Sledge then scooped him off the ground and shoved the drug dealer into the back seat of the cab. He gave little resistance to being handled as he flopped onto the seat, disoriented and hurt from the crash.

Sledge climbed into the cab through the open driver's door, slammed it shut, and then drove off as the din of sirens converged on the street behind him.

Chapter 27

DRAKE GLANCED ABOUT THE empty plot of land with a bewildered gaze from outside of the pickup. Blood seeped from the wound on his forehead, trickled down to his chin, and dripped onto the ground. He tried to stand and use the truck's bed to help him get up, but wobbling legs made that difficult to achieve.

Lights from Atlanta gleamed like stars from all around them. There wasn't a building within earshot of the sector of the city to which Sledge had driven them.

"Now that we have some alone time, how about you stop wasting mine and tell me what you know about Kim Claymore." Sledge stood before Drake with his hands on his hips. A disgusted scowl formed on his face as he glared at the man who had a hand in Kim's disappearance. "Come clean with what you know and perhaps I won't break every bone in your body."

"I didn't do anything to her," Drake said, pleading his case with his hands raised in submission.

"I know learning is hard. It looks like you need a refresher course." Sledge hammered his nose with a jab, furthering the damage already done.

Drake howled and cupped his nose with his hand. His dress shoes stomped the earth in frustration.

Sledge continued, "Don't lie to me. If you want to feel real pain, then keep it up. I'm not stupid, so don't act like you're going to weasel yourself out of this. Again, I know you had contact with Kim and her friends. You sold them drugs and threatened to hurt them if they said a word about it. That, in and of itself, begs for me to beat the living shit out of you."

"I only threatened them to make sure they wouldn't squeal to the authorities. I didn't mean it."

Sledge raised his eyebrows.

Drake lowered his hand and said, "Look, I can't tell you. They'll kill me if I do."

"And what do you think I'll do if you don't?" Sledge removed the 1911 from his waistband and aligned the muzzle with Drake's forehead. "Come clean or it's lights out. I doubt anyone would lose sleep over a piece of trash preying on young women. I know I won't."

"Shit. Fine, man." Drake's strained voice boomed loudly in the night sky.

"Better." Sledge lowered the 1911 to his side and then said, "Tell me why you targeted the girl. I know you met Kim online and conned her into meeting you. I'm skeptical it was only to just sell her drugs, and since there has not been a ransom attempt, it's safe to say that this isn't about getting money from the parents."

"I don't know why she was targeted," Drake answered as he wiped away the blood running from his nose. "All I was told was her name and that I needed to gain her trust. The drugs were secondary to that and helped me get in deeper with her. She's a nobody as far as I'm concerned. I don't decide who is targeted. I'm just the one who plays the part and kicks them up the river."

"So, you're part of a human trafficking ring in Atlanta then? I'm guessing that's what has happened here, right? You gained her trust, pumped her full of narcotics, then passed her off to be auctioned to the highest bidder?"

With eyes downcast, Drake bobbed his head but didn't mutter a verbal reply.

"Who do you work for? I want the names of everyone involved and, more importantly, who you ditched Kim with."

"I don't know their names."

Sledge glared at Drake as he aimed the gun at his shoe and popped off a single round near the man's foot. The bullet punched the dirt and made Drake flinch and jump.

"We're doing well here. Let's not ruin it with more lies. Okay?"

Frustrated and scared, Drake belted a throaty hoarse response that rose in volume. "I'm not lying! I receive instructions on a burner phone. That's it. I'm nothing more than a middleman, pal. I'm nobody."

"You certainly weren't acting like a nobody at the club," Sledge replied. "I don't know too many nobodies that have bodyguards. Plus, if I recall correctly, and I do, you did threaten me by saying that you have powerful people in your corner."

"Listen. All I did was deliver the girl as requested. I don't ask questions and do as I'm told. You live longer and make a hell of a lot more money that way if you keep your head down and go with the flow."

Sledge lunged forward and wrapped his fingers around Drake's sweaty neck. His hand closed like a vise grip, squeezing with all of his might and choking him.

Drake struggled to breathe. Gurgling noises sounded from his gaped mouth as his legs kicked.

"It must make you feel like a big man doing what you do, huh?" Sledge asked in a demented growl. "It's pieces of shit like you that make me sick to my stomach. You're a waste of space that serves no productive function in society. Maybe I should go ahead and put a bullet between your eyes. Do the world a favor and rid it of one less leech feeding on it."

Gurgling sounds emitted from Drake's mouth. His body squirmed against the bed of the truck as he tried to breathe.

But Sledge couldn't end Drake, regardless of how much he wanted to. He still needed answers and wasn't quite finished with him yet. Plus, he wasn't a cold-blooded killer. Not anymore.

After calming down, Sledge released his taut grip from the humbled man's neck. He then took a step back as Drake gasped for air and coughed.

"Where's your burner phone?"

Drake cleared his throat, spat to the ground, and then stood upright. "In my car."

"The Beamer you crashed?"

"Yes." Drake's voice was scratchy and hoarse, making him sound more like a chain smoker who had a throat disease.

Christ.

"Why is it there and not on you?" Sledge asked, annoyed.

"Because I was off the clock at the club and, well, my car is normally a safe place."

Sledge sighed and massaged the bridge of his nose with his index finger and thumb. There was no doubt that the authorities had arrived on the scene to secure the crash site.

A tow truck would have impounded the sedan and taken it to the Atlanta Police Department. To get to the burner phone, Sledge would have to get inside the perimeter of the city's impound lot. The one caveat was whether the police had discovered the phone, which Sledge hoped they hadn't yet.

"Where in the car is the burner phone?" Sledge asked as he patted Drake's pants pockets down.

"Glove box," Drake replied without hesitation. "What are you doing?"

Inside his front right pocket, Sledge felt another phone wedged deep down. He pulled it out and wagged it at Drake.

"This. Do you have a password to get into it?"

"No," Drake said.

Sledge confirmed as much and got into the phone without having to enter any sort of authentication. "Good."

"Are you going to kill me now?"

Cramming Drake's phone into his back pants pocket, Sledge said, "I should, but no. Consider this your lucky day. You won the lottery."

"Thank you."

"Don't thank me." Sledge clarified. "You're going to get out of Atlanta and disappear. Fall off the grid. I don't care where you go but wherever that is, you better keep that nose of yours clean and make sure I never hear your name or see your face again. As of now, you're no longer in the human trafficking business. Am I clear?"

Drake gulped and took the threat seriously. "Yes."

In his extensive work history, Sledge realized that the full range of responses to threats boiled down to two base reactions– complete denial that the threat existed, or pure, God-given, self-preserving fear. Sledge saw the latter in Drake. "Good. Because, if I do hear of you again that will be the worst day of your life. I can promise you that."

Chapter 28

AFTER DISCARDING DRAKE AT a random curb, Sledge left the shaken young man in his rearview and then made his way to the city's Police Property Unit. Given the nature of the accident and the likelihood of the Beamer being linked back to the disturbance at the club and subsequent car chase, Sledge didn't think it would be towed to one of the local wrecker yards. Not yet, anyway.

The burner phone was the next puzzle piece to tracking down Kim and bringing those involved to justice. He just had to get to the device before the police could find it.

While driving the dark city streets lit by lamp posts, business signs, and bright building lights, Sledge thumbed through Drake's private phone for additional clues. It was a quick search and one that didn't bring any new details to life.

Sledge discarded the phone to the hold within the armrest and mulled over everything Drake had told him. As much as he hated being right, Sledge's gut feeling about what happened to Kim was spot on. Now that he knew it involved human trafficking the real questions were, who were the mysterious players that had contacted Drake, and where were they keeping Kim?

A week was a long time for her to be moved to any place on the planet. The black market worked twenty-four hours a day, every day. Sledge had his work cut out for him, but he never backed down from a job. Although he tried to not make promises, one that he always did make was that he'd give his all and do what he could for the clients who procured his services.

Upon his approach to the city's property unit, Sledge slowed and parked at the curb a block down from the fenced perimeter of the lot. He cut the engine and got out of the truck, and then Sledge moved to the sidewalk and scuttled to the corner of the private yard while hunched.

The street had zero activity. No cars drove by and foot traffic was null. This gave him time to sneak into the yard and hunt for the sedan while using the cloak of night to conceal his presence.

Sledge grabbed hold of the diamond-shaped links and prepared to climb when he noticed that the bottom corner where the fence met the metal pole appeared bent and loose. His boot nudged the fence, confirming that the bottom part was indeed not fully attached.

Removing his hands from the fence, Sledge stooped and pulled up the corner. The space provided was not huge but it looked to be big enough for him to thread his frame through it.

He lifted the fence higher, thereby widening the gap as far as it would go. Then he stooped and passed through the opening to the other side.

After securing the bent part back into place, Sledge advanced out into the yard, looking for the sedan. He kept to the shadows and close to the cars and trucks that resided on the lot. The darkness in the area, although a blessing, was also a curse since he struggled to get any sort of visual of the black luxury car.

His search went on for the next fifteen minutes until he finally crossed the wreckage. Drake's BMW was in dire straits. The front end of the car was a crumpled mess, but the rest of the vehicle appeared to be in relatively good condition.

Sledge snuck down the passenger side of the vehicle and tugged on the handle of the door. It opened without restriction, granting him access to the sedan.

The interior light came to life, illuminating the car in a yellow hue. Sledge quickly flipped the interior lights off and pulled out his phone to use the screen's light. He worked fast and searched the vehicle for the burner phone, starting with the glove compartment.

It was mostly empty except for a stack of papers crammed into the hold. He dug through the contents and discovered a black flip phone nestled under the papers toward the back. That had to be Drake's burner phone. Bingo.

He plucked the device from the hold and closed the compartment door; then he reached for the side of the passenger door. As he did, headlights shone into the yard from the main entrance gate, followed by the grumble of what Sledge thought to be an engine. He quietly pushed the door shut and held his position until he could gauge who it was and what was happening.

The burner phone went into his back pants pocket as Sledge slunk toward the trunk of the BMW. He rose slightly and craned his neck to scan the area.

At the locked gate of the lot, two men were standing in front of a wrecker. They had no vehicle loaded on the flatbed truck. One paced the length of the entrance while the other man spoke on a phone and leaned on the fence.

They hung around another five minutes before retreating to the wrecker's cab and driving off. Sledge made his way back to the part of the fence he entered through, crawled out to the sidewalk, and then stood up. Having retrieved the burner phone, his next move was to track down the men who contacted Drake, and for that, he would need some help.

Chapter 29

SLEDGE SPENT THE MAJORITY of the night into the early morning hours trying to track down the owner of the incoming numbers received by the burner phone. It proved useless in the end since the numbers appeared to be tied to other burner phones online without any names attached to them.

He had slept more than a few hours before the sun rose and beamed into the warehouse through the large windows. His desk wasn't nearly as comfortable as his bed, but Sledge had crashed just the same on the glass top next to his keyboard.

Standing from his chair and stretching, Sledge shook the sleepiness away and conducted his daily routine. After a cold shower that shocked him awake, and getting dressed in under ten minutes, he moved on to the kitchen for a cup of strong coffee.

As he waited for the machine to dispense the cup of extra dark roast, premium, blended java, Sledge decided to reach out to a contact he had in the Atlanta Police Department.

Officer Rick Jenkins had helped Sledge out on previous cases with cell phone tracking and looking up vehicle plates, as well as other items. The two men crossed paths years prior when Sledge saved the young officer's life one night while Rick was on patrol. Since then, the pair fed one another leads but kept their business dealings under the radar.

Sledge put his phone on speaker and set it down on the counter next to the coffee machine as Rick's number rang. His finger tapped the smooth surface of the granite as the call connected and a gruff voice answered from the other end.

"*It's a little early, ain't it?*" Rick asked, sounding as if he had been awakened from a deep sleep.

"The sun's up. It's not that early."

A thin line of black coffee sputtered into the large white mug Sledge had stationed on the platform.

"*If you say so.*" Rick cleared his throat and grumbled. "*I had a long night and didn't get much sleep.*"

"Take a cold shower. That will wake you up."

"*Maybe if you're a psycho, sure.*"

"Have you tried it?"

"*No.*"

"Then don't knock it until you have," Sledge replied as the last bit of coffee dropped into the wide-mouth mug.

"*As much as I love our banter, what is it that you're after so early that couldn't wait until later?*"

"Information."

"*Why else would you have called except for that?*"

Sledge sipped on the black coffee and made his way to the round table in the kitchen where Drake's burner and personal phones waited. "For starters, I enjoy listening to you bitch and moan. That's my favorite way to start my day."

"*It's better than coffee if you ask me.*"

"Anyway, I've got a few phone numbers I need traced. I think they're prepaid jobs, so it's doubtful you'll get names. But locations would be a good place to start."

Rick was now up and moving around. Sledge could hear the officer rummaging about his apartment.

"*What sort of mess have you taken on now?*"

"I'm helping a family out is all. Nothing big."

"*Yeah. Right,*" Rick replied with a snicker into the receiver. "*It's never nothing when you're involved. I've never met a single person who hunts for problems like you do. It's either bad luck or bad judgment.*"

"Maybe both."

A momentary pause filled the phone before Rick said, "*Sure. What are the numbers?*"

Sledge read off the three separate numbers from the burner phone to Rick.

"*Okay. I got them logged.*"

"When do you think you can get back to me?"

"Time-sensitive?"

"Yes." Sledge flipped the lid shut on the phone and put it on the table.

Another brief pause came from Rick and then he said, *"Give me a few hours to shower and look presentable. I'm on rotation for the early shift today. Yay me. I drew the short straw it seems."*

"Is a few hours going to be enough to look presentable?" Sledge asked. "You may want to tack on an extra hour or two."

"Go to hell, Sledge."

"Been there. I don't recommend it."

"Anyways. Is there anything else before I let you go? Some of us need to get to work."

"Yeah. One last thing. It'll be brief."

"Goody. Shoot."

"What do you know about Detective Shawn Wentworth?"

"Not much. He's been on the force for about six months now, I think. What little I've heard about him seems good, though. Why?"

Sledge couldn't shake what Amanda had told him about telling Wentworth about Drake, who had then omitted the dealer's name from the police report. It was a nagging itch in the back of his mind that he couldn't scratch, regardless of how much he tried.

"Just curious is all. I've heard his name floating around."

"Right." What sounded like water running boomed from the phone's speaker. *"I'll be in touch later this morning. Call or message?"*

"Message."

"You and your protocols. I'm surprised you called this time."

"It's important and I couldn't wait for you to check your messages."

"Sure. Talk soon."

The call ended with a click. Sledge lowered the phone from his ear and stared blankly at the wall, wondering if Wentworth was a good cop, or if he was involved in Kim's abduction. To find out the answer, Sledge would have to pull on that string to see what he could find.

Chapter 30

THE MORNING WORE ON as Sledge waited for Rick to call him back with whatever details he dug up on the phone numbers. Each passing second felt like an eternity when Kim's life hung in the balance, but Sledge had learned that patience and vigilance were keys to success. One had to be methodical in the approach and not let emotions dictate actions. That was easier said than done, though.

Sledge contacted the Claymores through the encrypted app with a vague update that he tried to spin as positive. By all accounts, it was more than what he had at the beginning of taking on the job of tracking down Kim.

They were grateful and asked for specifics, but Sledge didn't divulge details yet. He wanted to wait until he had a bit more to go on before doing so and not provide false information that could muddy the water.

During times of crisis, people's emotions steered their actions. Logical reasoning was hampered and typically thrown out of the window. They hired Sledge to complete a job and had to trust that he would do exactly that.

After the update to the Claymores, Sledge plotted out his day and what his next moves would be. He was big on contingencies. If plan A fell through, he'd have two other backups to fall back on. That's how he operated and completed all of the assignments with a high success rate.

At the moment, a lot rested on Rick's shoulders and what he could find out from the numbers. If that proved to be a dead end, Sledge had contacts throughout the city and on the streets that he could tap for information.

Druggies, petty crooks and other scum rounded out his assortment of informants. All had been busted by Sledge for one reason or another. He spared the gutter trash from an early grave or a ticket to the big house in exchange for being his eyes and ears on the streets. Like Drake, if they made a wrong move, it was communicated to each person he let go that it would end poorly for them. None dared to test his limits, knowing how dangerous he was.

His phone buzzed from the white folding table Sledge stood at as he reassembled his 1911 pistol. Rick's name and cell phone number popped up on the screen.

Slapping the fully stocked magazine into the grip's well, Sledge put the gun down and grabbed the phone. The message was short and to the point. No fluff. All that was listed were the numbers Sledge had given Rick with their current locations. Two of the numbers were not stationary, but they were in the city at least. The third phone number, however, had an address typed out next to it. That would be Sledge's starting point.

He typed *Thanks* in the outgoing message bar and then hit send.

Rick replied immediately. *You owe me. Don't forget that.*

I never do.

Chapter 31

IN THE TRAILING MINUTES of receiving the update from Rick, Sledge had climbed into his pickup and exited the warehouse. He headed down the alley to the street and hooked a right without stopping.

Sledge navigated the bustling city of Atlanta in a rush while also trying to be mindful of not drawing attention from the authorities. He brought Drake's burner phone with him in case a call was received so he wouldn't miss it.

The phone rattled in the cup holder of the armrest as Sledge closed in on the address Rick provided. This was a dynamic situation and could change on a dime if the user of the phone got back on the move. Once on-site, the real fun would begin with finding the phone, and its handler.

Under the gun, Sledge felt the pressure as he cleared the changing yellow light of the intersection ahead. He made a tight right turn onto Grand Blvd. and continued up the road. The location of the device was pinged at a local coffee shop, Java Palace.

Cruising up the road, Sledge whipped the Silverado across the street and parked in one of the empty spaces at the curb down from the coffee shop. He shifted into park and killed the engine while staring at the entrance of the targeted business.

Fifteen minutes had passed since Sledge received the details from Rick via encrypted message. It was going to be challenging to find the phone in the shop without raising suspicion.

An idea formed as Sledge removed the keys from the ignition, grabbed Drake's burner, and got out of the truck. Crossing in front of the pickup, he stepped onto the curb and made his way down the sidewalk toward the entrance of the coffee shop.

Sledge kept his phone stowed in the back pocket of his jeans and clutched the burner in his hand. Upon approach, he flipped the lid open and thumbed the down arrow of received calls until he reached the correct number that corresponded to the address where he was currently located.

Two women emerged from the building, laughing and chatting with paper coffee cups clutched in their hands. He skirted past them and grabbed the edge of the door before it closed; then he slipped inside.

It was after 10:30 a.m. but the Java Palace was humming along with shallow lines of people waiting at the counter to place their orders. A strong scent of roasting coffee permeated the air. Names were called out for the drinks ready and waiting to be picked up.

The tables in the shop were mostly occupied by those typing away on laptops, reading books, or just taking in the buzz of activity within the business or outside of the large window facing the walkway and street. It was a mixture of businessmen dressed in suits and casually attired men and women seated at the small round tables going about their daily lives.

Sledge studied each of the patrons with a calculating glance as he made his way to the back of the line of folks waiting to put in their orders. Each person seated was a suspect, but who was it? Even worse, had he missed his chance?

Still clutching the burner phone, Sledge dialed the number, set the call to mute to clear the background noise, and then brought the phone to his ear. As the device connected, Sledge viewed the crowd of folks seated and standing to see who answered their phones at that moment.

Three monotone rings sounded from the device before it clicked and the call connected. A brief pause loomed from the speaker, but background noise could be heard.

A man seated in the corner of the shop reading a newspaper brought his flip phone to his ear as he set the paper down on the table. An agitated voice spoke in a whisper that had a slight southern drawl. *"Why are you calling me? This isn't how it works or how we operate. We call you. Not the other way around."*

Sledge advanced in the line while observing the man and his body language. His attire was that of other men in the coffee shop.

From what Sledge could see, the man was dressed plainly in a red ball cap and a black t-shirt. He was well-groomed and looked to be in his late forties, with a white complexion without any sort of tan to indicate he spent time outdoors.

"Hello?" He asked into the receiver again, but Sledge didn't answer.

After a few seconds, the call disconnected and he stood. The newspaper was left on the table as he thumbed the keypad of the phone while heading toward the entrance of the shop. Sledge had found his mark.

Lowering and flipping the phone shut, Sledge deposited the burner into his front pants pocket and stalked the man out of the shop. He had experience in tailing his targets without being detected and was good at blending into his environment.

Keeping a good bit of distance between them, Sledge followed the man down the sidewalk. He pulled his phone out from his back pocket and held it in his hand. If his target turned around, Sledge could make it seem as though he was viewing his phone instead of following him.

He trailed the man for three blocks through Atlanta's downtown. Not once did he turn in suspicion. He made additional phone calls from the burner that lasted less than a minute each as they ultimately arrived at a parking garage off Luckie Street.

Sledge hung back about fifteen feet as the man in the black ball cap stepped between a couple holding hands, forcing the man and woman to release their hands and move out of his way. Annoyed, the man paused and shouted a slew of colorful words at Sledge's mark, which fell on deaf ears.

The couple went about their business as the woman calmed him. Sledge walked by the couple and tracked the man to the entrance of the parking garage.

A car horn honked up the street. The man in the black ball cap stopped, as did Sledge. He shuffled to the wall and hid behind a portion of concrete that protruded out as the man peered over his shoulder. After sweeping the sidewalk, he faced forward and got back on the move.

Waiting an additional few seconds, Sledge poked his head around the bend and followed his mark up the parking garage's walkway and then across the lower level. The majority of slots were taken by cars with only a few being open. Tires squealed from vehicles entering and exiting the garage. Engines sounded louder within the stacked decks of concrete, reducing one's ability to hear anything other than the roar and echoes of cars as they piloted in and out of the garage.

Sledge gained on the man, cutting the distance between them to less than twenty feet. His hand retrieved the 1911 pistol from the waistband of his pants. He held it down at his side and walked faster as his mark pulled keys from his front right pocket and then ducked down to the driver's side of a light blue sedan.

Hunching, Sledge watched him from over the hood of a red, two-door coupe parked next to his vehicle. The man gave no glance his way as he unlocked the driver's door and lowered down into the seat. Sledge rushed around the trunk of the red coupe and down to the passenger door of the light blue sedan.

In one fluid movement, he yanked the passenger-side door open and dropped into the seat of his mark's ride. Startled, the man removed his hold from the key wedged into the ignition and reached for his waist.

"I wouldn't do that if I were you," Sledge said while training the barrel of the 1911 at the man's side.

The man froze and then raised his arms in submission. "You're the one who called earlier from Drake's burner?"

"Bingo." With his free hand, Sledge felt around the man's waist while keeping the pistol locked on him. "I had to flush you out and you took the bait."

"Who are you?"

"A concerned citizen."

He sized Sledge up and then asked, "Concerned about what?"

"A missing person with whom you are now linked." Sledge pulled an HK45 from the man's waistband. The weapon was similar to the one Sledge used during his days with Cobalt.

"What missing person?"

Sledge tossed the HK45 to the top of the dash and then said, "Come now. Let's not play dumb. I have Drake's burner phone which means I've made contact with him. That's how I tracked you down. It was smart using those prepaid phones but they can still be traced and aren't foolproof."

"Is he dead?"

"He's in the wind. I think you'll have to find someone else to lure your victims in. Drake's off the table."

"He'll be dealt with. I can assure you of that." The threat of Drake meeting his end wasn't lost on Sledge but that wasn't his concern.

"Who do you work for?" Sledge asked. "And where is the girl?"

He said nothing.

"Let's not do this. It will not work in your favor."

"My employer is not someone who takes threats lightly. Their reach is vast and they have the means to end your life with a simple snap of their fingers." He snapped his fingers to drive the point home. "You are way over your head and want nothing to do with this. I promise. My advice to you is to leave now and disappear because the alternative is far worse."

Sledge didn't scare easily. His mind had been conditioned to stare evil and danger in the face and not blink. The man before him was the least scary person Sledge had ever encountered, and his weightless warning fell flat and failed to hit the mark.

"I appreciate the concern but I'll take my chances. Now, tell me where the girl has been taken."

The man said nothing and stared at him with a deadpan expression.

Sledge sighed, and then said, "Okay. I guess we're going to do this the hard way."

Chapter 32

THE MAN SMIRKED AT the comment. He didn't appear to be afraid of Sledge. His relaxed body didn't tremble under the threat of pain or death, which piqued Sledge's interest.

Most people that Sledge encountered under similar circumstances shuddered at the hint of what he'd do to them. Generally, they displayed their fright and crumbled under the weight of anxiety, then spilled their guts; but not this guy. He had a calmness about him that made Sledge ponder why he was so cool while being held at gunpoint.

Sledge cracked the man's temple with the bottom of the 1911 as an incentive to tell him what he wanted to know or suffer the consequences. The impact rocked the man slightly, but he absorbed the blow and then shook it off. Still, he remained steadfast.

A line of blood leaked from the tiny gash made by the weapon. It trickled down his cheek, then to his chin.

"Kim Claymore. Where was she taken after Drake handed her off to you? Tell me now or I'll empty this magazine into your side."

"Then you'll never find her," the man replied. "You see, my employer, and that of Drake, is far more dangerous than you. Their network is vast and they are entrenched deeply in multiple avenues of business. You're one man on a crusade facing an army of ruthless men who will not hesitate to burn your world to the ground."

"Again, I'd be more concerned about your well-being than mine. I've dealt with far greater enemies than the likes of you and whatever organization is funding your human trafficking ring in the city." Sledge nudged the 1911 into the man's ribs and said, "Now, enough stalling. You're going to take me to wherever it is that you're keeping Kim. While we're driving there, you can fill me in on who your employer is. Are we clear?"

The man glared at Sledge then tipped his head but ventured no verbal reply.

Sledge said, "Good. Start the car and let's go."

As the man moved his hands toward the steering wheel and started the engine, Sledge removed the gun from his side. He tucked the weapon under his other arm to conceal the gun while keeping it trained at him. He retrieved the HK45 off the dash and stowed it in his waistband. "Let's start with your name."

The car shifted into reverse and they backed out of the parking space. The driver refrained from speaking further and offering up anything else on his own. He'd gone silent and gave an occasional glance to Sledge from the corner of his eye while piloting the sedan toward the exit of the garage.

"We'll circle back to that. Tell me who has employed your services to kidnap helpless teenage girls?" Sledge asked, wanting to know more about the dangerous organization funding the human smuggling ring. "I'm curious who they are."

There were many bad syndicates in the world, in fact, too many to count. Sledge had most of them on his radar and had dealings with several from past jobs that dealt in various illicit activities like drugs and weapons distribution.

The man said nothing and remained tight-lipped as they coasted toward the narrow drive leading to Luckie Street. As Sledge glanced at him waiting for a response, a beige SUV materialized to their right and cut in front of them without braking.

Instead of stopping, the driver punched the gas and sent the sedan crashing into the side of the SUV as it skirted the curb. Metal crunched from the impact. Both airbags deployed from the steering wheel and the dash in front of Sledge.

A hint of smoke tainted the air from the explosives used to deploy the airbags. The bag punched Sledge in the face, disorientating him long enough to allow the driver to make his move.

He opened the driver's side door and climbed out as Sledge did the same with the passenger door. With witnesses around, and him still needing the man alive to find Kim, Sledge held his fire. He would have to run him down on foot instead of placing a bullet in him.

As the man sprinted down the exit toward Luckie Street, Sledge rushed around the trunk of the sedan and peered into the cab of the SUV.

The driver and passenger of the SUV appeared okay as he ran past their car after his target. Both the man and the woman rubbed the back of their necks and glanced out of the windshield at Sledge as he sprinted toward the street.

With his gun still out, Sledge put the weapon in the front waistband of his pants and focused on running down the mark. Discharging his piece in public would do way more harm than good.

His boots hammered the concrete like a racehorse. He cut in front of a car pulling into the garage to the walkway where the man in the black ball cap gained a sizeable head start on him.

Sledge was well-conditioned and able to hack at the lead. The distance between the men reduced with each wide stride they made, getting him closer to the mark.

His mark cut through some bushes and leaped out into the street, narrowly missing getting hit by an approaching van. The vehicle's horn blared at the man who skirted its hood without stopping, and at Sledge who mimicked his path into the road.

They merged on the sidewalk and continued their chase down the walkway past pedestrians who jumped out of their way as they zipped by. There was little chance of Sledge allowing his one good lead to escape. Without him, he'd be back to square one, which meant finding Kim would be less likely.

The man glanced over his shoulder to Sledge. A pained expression of exhaustion twisted his face as he tried to go faster but was unable to.

In a desperate attempt to lose the tail, the man ducked inside a building as an older, gray-haired woman emerged onto the sidewalk. He shoved her out of the way and bolted inside the closing glass door. She didn't go down but stumbled back into the wall.

"Are you okay, ma'am?" Sledge asked while slowing enough to cut into the building.

She stood straight and jabbed her finger at the door, then she rambled off a string of colorful words with a scowl. Sledge took that as a yes and rushed inside the building after him.

Thundering footfalls clomped down the narrow hallway. The man had attained a larger lead as he cut around a blind corner and stomped his way up the stairs.

Sledge matched his stride and pushed harder, vowing that the man wouldn't lose him. Too much was riding on his case.

Staircase after staircase was traversed to the roof. Despite black ball cap's best efforts to ditch the troublesome tail, Sledge refused to yield and maintained his pursuit.

The man was first to emerge out of the building onto the roof. He slammed the door behind him as Sledge scuttled up the steps after him. His feet shuffled in a blur of speed as he advanced toward the closed door.

Sledge exploded out onto the roof and hunted for his man, who was now hidden. His chest heaved and his nostrils flared from the strenuous chase that brought them to the top of the building. As he moved away from the closing door, footsteps sounded at Sledge's back.

He detected the man's movements and spun around with both of his arms raised. Each hand was balled into a tightly packed fist as black ball cap lunged at Sledge with the knife he held. The tip stabbed at his chest, but Sledge hopped back and smacked his forearm down with his fist.

Frustration and pain contorted the man's face as he shook off the blow. He raised the knife as both men moved in a circle, each waiting for the other to make their move.

"You don't want to do this, pal," Sledge said. "Tell me where the girl is and maybe you'll make it out of this alive."

"I'd be more concerned about you than me."

The man stabbed at Sledge's gut but he side-stepped the attack, then punched him in the skull. He was quick, but Sledge was faster and more experienced in hand-to-hand combat.

Shaking the sting from his head, the man lunged forward once more with the knife raised and ready to strike. Sledge caught his arm in midair and stopped the man's forward momentum, then he punched him twice in the stomach and threw him onto the ground, end over end.

A harsh gruff sounded from black ball cap's mouth as he landed on his back. He wheezed and clutched his gut while slowly getting to his feet. His wallet had fallen from his side pocket, but he hadn't noticed.

Sledge advanced toward him, not giving the man time to recover. His speed was impressive. He moved faster than the man could react after the devastating hits rattled him.

Propped up on shaky legs, the man backed away and stabbed at him with the knife. His arm swung the blade from side to side in a sweeping motion that kept him at arm's length.

As he neared the edge of the building, Sledge slowed his advancement and backed off. The man glanced at the lip and back to Sledge; then he stepped up onto the ledge.

"Whoa there, let's not do anything stupid," Sledge said as he slowly crept toward him. "It's not worth going out like that. I can promise you, pal. Why don't you come down from there and we'll talk this out?"

He wobbled while facing Sledge. A purposeful look of steadfastness came over the man as he leaned back. "You don't get it. I'm already dead. And so are you."

Sledge moved fast to snatch any portion of the man's body, but he wasn't quick enough. As he reached the edge of the building, Sledge heard the man's body slam into the concrete with a sickening thump.

The knife was still locked in his fist as he lay on his back. Blood pooled under his head from the impact busting his skull open.

People in the area took notice of the horror. A blood-curdling scream snapped Sledge out of his trance as he pushed away from the building's edge and out of view from the street below. He retreated to the doorway and scooped up the man's wallet while on the move. Priority one was vacating the area before the police arrived.

His one viable lead to finding Kim was gone, and now Sledge was back to square one with no idea of where to go next. He had the man's wallet, at least, and prayed that he'd find something useful inside it.

Chapter 33

TRENT GESNER. THAT WAS the dead man's name that opted to end his life rather than tell Sledge what he knew. It was a surprise move that Sledge didn't see coming until it was too late for him to do anything about it.

Sledge made it back to his truck by way of alleys and side streets. Sirens sounded in the direction of the building where Gesner had jumped to his death. He walked causally up the sidewalk from the opposite direction with his head tilted down at an angle and moved past the bed toward the driver's side.

A police cruiser flew by on the street and took the intersection ahead at full tilt. Tires squealed from the cruiser as Sledge climbed into the cab.

He dumped Gesner's wallet on the passenger seat and started the truck. Sledge then shifted into drive and pulled away from the curb normally to not draw any wandering gazes his way.

Merging into the street behind a line of cars heading south, Sledge dissected Gesner's final words before he took his life. Who was he so afraid of that he'd rather jump than go against his employer? There wasn't a bit of hesitation in Gesner while on the ledge. He acted as if leaping from the building was a better way to go out than daring to face the people for whom he worked. That sort of power and influence to control people was hard to accomplish, but not impossible.

Sledge tapped the top of the steering wheel as he drove through the city toward his next stop. Shawn Wentworth was a person of interest involved in the case, and Sledge wanted to see if his gut was right about him possibly having a hand in Kim's kidnapping.

It was after 1:00 p.m. when Sledge arrived at Shawn's home. He parked across the street on the curb and studied his residence. The detective's home was a single-story, gray, brick house that was void of character. No landscaping spruced up the property's rather dull appearance.

The lawn looked as if it hadn't been cut in weeks, with weeds sprouting up taller than the blades of grass. All of the windows were covered with drawn blinds that kept him from being able to see inside the home from his truck.

A black, Toyota 4Runner sat in the driveway, indicating that the detective should be at home. From what Sledge found during his research, Wentworth was recently divorced and had two young kids who lived with their mother in Atlanta. Even though Rick had nothing bad to say about the detective, Sledge wasn't so sure, but soon he'd find out if he was on the level or part of the criminal ongoings taking place within the city.

After a car drove past Sledge's truck, he got out and made his way toward the detective's home. He moved up the driveway and past the 4Runner to the concrete walkway that led to the porch. This wasn't a stealth mission, but more of a social call that didn't require covert tactics. He wanted to hear what the detective had to say first before he jumped to conclusions.

Sledge trotted up the three steps and advanced toward the door. He knocked twice then checked one of the nearby windows. Seconds passed before the door unlocked and opened.

A man stood in the doorway staring at him. He was dressed in brown slacks, brown dress shoes, and a white, button-up shirt with black vertical stripes. His tie was thrown over his right shoulder. He dabbed a napkin to his thin lips while he looked Sledge over. "Yes? Can I help you?"

"Hi, there." Sledge flashed a warm, inviting smile. One he had perfected with practice. "I was hoping to catch you and wanted to see if you had a moment to speak about a case that you're working on."

Wentworth peered at the street and surrounding area while staying inside the home. "Which case and who are you?"

"I'm working with the Claymores on their missing daughter's case. I came across your name as the detective assigned from the department."

"Um...I didn't know the Claymores hired a private investigator," Wentworth said. "That's news to me."

"I'm not a private investigator so to speak. They recently procured my services."

"And what services are those?"

"The kinds that handle sensitive matters such as theirs," Sledge answered. "May I come in? I won't be too long. I promise."

Wentworth hesitated for a minute; then he backed away from the doorway while opening it wider. "Sure."

Sledge walked into the home that was sparsely decorated. It looked like that of a divorced man who did not care about furnishing a bachelor pad.

A single couch, a coffee table with a cooked TV dinner on its top, and a TV mounted to the far wall rounded out the living room. The walls were devoid of pictures. Not a hint of his life was on display.

The door shut behind Sledge as Wentworth moved around him. Through his dress shirt, the detective's muscle tone was visible. "So, what can I do for you Mr...."

"Sledge will be fine." He surveyed the home and peered down the hallway before turning to face him. "I wanted to see how things were coming on your end. Perhaps we could swap notes since we're both after the same thing– finding Kim."

"Well, Mr. Sledge," Wentworth said as he stood between the couch and coffee table, "I do appreciate the offer and your reaching out, but that's not the way I, or the department for that matter, conduct an investigation."

Sledge wasn't easily deterred and countered with, "I understand. Rules and protocols get in the way of progress at times. We're after the same thing here. It's been over a week since her disappearance and the family is anxious. They're scared beyond all belief, and rightfully so. Their daughter has been snatched up by unscrupulous fiends."

"So, you think she's been kidnapped?"

"What other possible reason could there be?"

Wentworth said, "Perhaps she ran away. That wouldn't be uncommon considering her age. That does happen."

"True, but the impression I got from the family didn't hint at a runaway."

Sledge examined Wentworth's mannerisms, which were free of any tells that alluded to foul play. The detective maintained eye contact at all times and didn't divert his gaze. He was relaxed and not on edge.

"I'm not saying that's the case. We're leaving all possibilities on the table while we dig further into the investigation."

"You've spoken to Kim's best friend, Amanda, right?" Sledge asked, knowing full well that he had.

Wentworth tipped his head. "We have. She has provided us with leads that we're currently looking into."

"Yes. I've spoken with Amanda as well. Sweet girl who misses her friend and wants her back." Sledge blocked the TV with his hands cupped behind him while facing Detective Wentworth. "It's a real shame what happened to them. Messy business, drugs are. They ruin so many lives."

Tossing the crumpled napkin in his hand onto the coffee table, Wentworth asked, "What are you getting at? I feel you dancing here so please, do us both a favor and spit out whatever it is that's on your mind."

Here was a man who didn't like beating around the bush. Sledge appreciated the candor and directness.

"Why was Drake's name stricken from your report? Out of all of the files I looked through given to me by the Claymores, he's not mentioned once. Why?"

Confusion washed over Wentworth. His brow furrowed and his nose crinkled. "I have no idea what you're talking about. Mr. Connor is a person of interest. That hasn't changed."

"So, you didn't remove him from the file?"

"No. Mr. Connor was brought in for questioning but we had to release him for lack of evidence," Wentworth said. "We are keeping an eye on him, though."

"Then how would his name get stricken from the report?" Sledge was refusing to let the issue go. "That sounds highly suspect if you ask me."

His assumption wasn't lost on Wentworth. Accusing an officer of being dirty was treacherous grounds, but one that Sledge ventured on regardless.

"You come into my home and accuse me of being a dirty cop?" Wentworth squinted and pursed his lips. His body teemed with anger as he stabbed his index finger at Sledge. "I don't know who the hell you think you are, but I don't take kindly to people showing up on my doorstep and then insulting me. I'm not dirty. I never have been and never will be. I hate dirty cops and if someone has doctored my report, then I will look into it and see who did."

The two men stood toe-to-toe, staring each other down. The tension increased as neither man said a word.

Sledge could see the fire in his eyes, but it wasn't from having a lie being unearthed. No. It was the look of a man who had conviction and his principles called into question.

"My apologies, but I had to be sure you weren't on the take."

"I'm not."

"Do you have any guesses as to who could have changed your report?"

Wentworth took a step back from Sledge and said, "Not off the top of my head. I haven't been with the department for too long, and haven't spent much time with the other officers. I'm not there to socialize. I will be looking into that case file for sure, though."

"It could be a simple mix-up," Sledge said as he didn't know for certain if a corrupt badge had infiltrated the department. "I have a nose for these sorts of things and it was telling me that something wasn't adding up."

"The Claymores can rest assured that I'm not crooked and that I want their daughter back home. I'm not going to rest until that happens."

Wentworth's passion impressed Sledge. The detective didn't strike him now as being a dirty cop. He had more than convinced Sledge of his commitment to locating Kim, which the family desperately needed.

Still, the inconsistency warranted further investigation, to sniff out a mole in the force covering for the group operating in Atlanta that was snatching kids.

"I do apologize for showing up on your doorstep and insulting you with such accusations," Sledge said. "I had to be sure you weren't involved in this mess."

"Well, I'm not." Wentworth removed his tie from over his shoulder and straightened it against his chest. "Few things in life get my feathers ruffled, but having my character called into question is one that will set me off fast."

"I understand." Sledge glanced at the door, feeling as though he had worn out his stay. Before leaving, he had one question left to ask. "Have you ever heard the name Trent Gesner?"

"I have, but only in passing at the department," Wentworth replied.

"What do you know about him?"

"He's a scumbag linked to some deep pockets," Wentworth replied.

"How so?"

Wentworth explained. "Gesner has been brought in several times over the past two years for different crimes, but nothing sticks. Weapons charges, drugs, and racketeering. Each case launched against him hits a dead end. He always has the same lawyer who shows up too; the lawyer word-vomits a bunch of fancy legal jargon, and poof, he's out." Wentworth snapped his fingers for added effect. "Just like that. I haven't seen it personally, but other detectives in the unit have painted a rather vivid picture of his character."

"Has he been tied to any crews in the city or does he have any known associates?"

"Marko Vega. He's just as big a fish that we haven't been able to land yet." Wentworth approached Sledge and asked, "Why are you asking about Gesner? Do you think he has some involvement in Kim Claymore's disappearance?"

Sledge raised his brow as he headed for the door. "Are we sharing notes now, detective?"

"Sounds like we are."

"Gesner may be involved, but I'm still working out the finer details."

He didn't want to mention much more considering that soon Wentworth would undoubtedly learn of Gesner's death, and Sledge didn't want to be tied to him if he could help it.

As Sledge gripped the doorknob and turned to leave, Wentworth said, "If you do find that Gesner or Vega is tied to Kim's case, please let me know. They are big players. You'll need the backup to bring them in."

Sledge opened the door and stepped outside onto the porch. "I'll think about it. I doubt he'll be much to contend with."

"I wouldn't underestimate Gesner or his associates."

With a smirk, Sledge said, "I won't. Have a good day, detective."

Chapter 34

ANOTHER POSSIBLE LEAD HAD come to light after Sledge's visit with Detective Wentworth. A name was better than nothing and gave him a direction on whom to target next. From the sound of it, Marko Vega was the man who'd bust the Claymore case wide open and guide Sledge to the larger organization funding their cell in Atlanta.

With each person he'd encountered since agreeing to work for the Claymores, Sledge moved up the criminal ladder toward an unknown enemy. Soon, he figured he'd uncover much more than anyone had and shine a light on the seedy underbelly that ran under the city's nose.

Before Sledge dove deeper into Marko Vega, he decided to stop at Mac's Computer Repair and check on Trixie since he was in the area. She was a good kid and smart as a whip. The thugs who left the shop the prior day weighed on his mind. He didn't care for the two goons doing whatever business it was with her instead of Mac.

It was getting later in the day when Sledge arrived at the repair shop. The time was 3:40 p.m. and soon, Trixie would be shutting things down for the day. But, much to Sledge's surprise, the shop was already closed, or so the sign facing the street indicated.

His truck idled at the curb. He peered at the closed sign hanging on the door from the inside. The shop didn't close for business until 4:30. They still had over forty minutes.

The lights were off in the building and Sledge didn't spot any movement near the front. A feeling tickled his gut that something bad was going down, but he didn't know what it might be or if the day's events just had him on edge.

Sledge killed the engine and got out of his truck. In a quickened stride, he slipped around the hood of the Silverado to the sidewalk. He marched to the entrance while scanning for Trixie inside the murky store.

As he squinted and peered through the glass door, Sledge spotted no movement inside. Neither Trixie nor Mac were stationed behind the counter at the back; he did, however, locate her black backpack near the register on the counter, which furthered his gut feeling that she was in danger.

He gripped the silver door handle and tugged, but the door refused to open. It was locked. Sledge tugged harder on the door, and then pounded the glass with his fist.

The stock room door swung open. A man appeared in the doorway, but it wasn't the same man from the previous day. He was taller and big, but Sledge couldn't make out much more than that from the shadows concealing his face. It wasn't Mac. Mac was much shorter and rounder than this guy.

Refusing to leave, Sledge persisted in hammering the door. He wanted in the shop and he wasn't going to let up until he got inside.

The mysterious man moved around the sales counter and advanced to the entrance of the shop. A scowl twisted the man's appearance. He had tattoos along both of his muscular arms and one on top of his head. Several piercings dangled from his nose, lip, and ears.

He stared Sledge down at the entrance and pointed at the sign without speaking, indicating that the shop was closed. Sledge continued jerking on the silver handle and knocking on the door despite the obvious attempt of the tatted man shooing him away.

Growing somewhat agitated, the tatted man retracted the deadbolt on the door and then pushed it open. As soon as the bell dinged above the entrance, and before he could launch a warning, Sledge pulled the glass door from the man's hold and forced his way inside.

Sledge rushed him and smashed the side of his head with a sharp right cross. Then he went low to the midsection and worked on the ribs with quick jabs.

"What did you do with the girl?"

The tatted man favored his side and squinted at him as he steadied his footing and shook his head. Again, no words were spoken as he snarled and clenched his hands into fists and raised his arms to shield his face.

He threw jab after jab at Sledge which was expertly dodged. The strikes were fast but sloppy. His footwork was abysmal and he didn't follow through with each punch lobbed.

As the tatted man's arm blew past his head, Sledge ducked and moved to his blind spot, delivering rapid punches to the kidneys; then he kicked the back of a knee. The man's leg buckled and he dropped to the floor while panting and wheezing.

Without giving the tatted man a second to stand and regain his focus, Sledge smashed his fist into the side of his skull. The tatted man collapsed to the dingy tile floor as the stockroom door squeaked open.

Sledge pulled the 1911 from his waistband and trained it at the shadowy figure now standing in the doorway. A different individual stood in the murkiness. His hand dove toward the top of his pants for what Sledge gathered to be his gun.

"Nope. Keep those hands up."

He complied and raised both arms in the air.

"Is the girl back there in the stockroom?"

He nodded.

"Trixie?"

"Yeah." Her voice was a bit weak, but she answered his call.

"Are you okay?"

"Mostly."

Sledge wagged the gun at the gentleman in the doorway to come toward him.

With fingers pointed at the ceiling, the equally tatted and muscular man maneuvered around the sales counter and out into the open plot of the store where Sledge and the man's partner were.

Trixie ambled from the stockroom. Even though Sledge couldn't see her face clearly, the way she moved indicated that the two men had roughed her up some.

"Did you touch her?" Sledge asked the man standing before him.

"That bitch owes..."

Sledge smashed the 1911 on the man's skull and said, "Not what I asked."

The thug righted his hunched stance and then spat on the floor. He glowered at Sledge while licking at the corner of his mouth.

"I don't know why you're here or what you want, but if you ever, I mean EVER, come around here again or bother her, I will end you. And believe me, it will be the worst day of your life." Sledge kicked his partner, who was still writhing on the floor, in his side. "Take your dipshit buddy here and leave, before I change my mind about allowing you two to live."

The two men lumbered toward the door while glaring at him, then at Trixie who advanced around the counter. They pushed out of the store and out onto the walkway until they were no longer in sight.

"I'm surprised to see you here today," Trixie said as she rubbed her right arm.

"I was in the neighborhood and thought I'd drop in and harass my favorite tech." Sledge stowed the 1911 back in his front waistband and then turned, squaring up with Trixie. "What was that all about? More business dealings with Mac?"

Trixie probed her busted lip, which started to swell, with her fingertip, "No. They weren't here for Mac."

"You?"

Eyes downcast, she bobbed her head.

"Why?"

"It's a long story involving bad people," Trixie answered as she leveled her gaze on him. "You shouldn't have gotten involved. Seeing how you wrecked that one dude and sent them scrambling out of here with their tails between their legs, you seem like you can handle yourself pretty well, though."

Sledge waved his hand at her while viewing the bruise on her left cheek. "Don't worry about me. I can take care of myself."

"That's evident."

He looked her over from top to bottom. "What did you do to get mixed up with thugs like that? The truth, please."

She sighed. "Yes, dad." Trixie then gave a condensed recap of what happened. "I was hired to do tech work for a company and well, things didn't go as planned and they wanted their money back."

"That's a pretty thin reason for such men to pound on a woman," Sledge replied, not believing the story. "The truth, please."

Trixie rolled her eyes, turned, and walked toward the register where her bag was located. "Fine. I was hired to hack a database and alter records, but instead, I planted a virus in the people's system who contracted me, and that crashed their network, then I turned them over to the authorities."

"What?" Sledge was stunned by the admission. It took him a minute to comprehend that Trixie was far more than just a computer geek. "So, let me get this straight. You're a hacker?"

"Yeah. I have been for a while." She plucked her backpack from the counter and placed one of the straps over her shoulder. "A girl has to eat and pay bills. Mac is cool and all, but what he pays isn't enough for me to live on. This is the first job I've done that backfired on me. It wouldn't have been a problem but these guys were assholes and treated me like shit from the get-go. I taught them a lesson while getting half of my pay."

Sledge glanced at the entrance to the shop, then said, "Sure, but at what cost? They've already been here to rough you up. It could've turned deadly if I hadn't intervened."

"True, but if I lay low for a bit and allow things to cool off, maybe it will be fine. They're not local; just their goons are."

"Do you honestly believe that?" Sledge asked, unconvinced and knowing better. "If they found you here, then they can find you at your home. It's not that difficult."

Trixie shrugged. "I guess so. What choice do I have? This is my mess and I'm responsible for cleaning it up. This isn't the first time I've been threatened."

That didn't make Sledge feel any better about the situation. Bad men who were wronged and stolen from tended to hold grudges. He knew they'd be back, and with reinforcements, to collect their money and her life. He couldn't allow that to happen.

"This isn't your problem to mess with," Trixie said as she headed for the entrance. "I'll figure out how to handle them. I usually do."

Sledge trailed her, not liking the idea of her being in danger. "Why don't you come back to my place? There's plenty of room and it's secure. You'll be safe. I promise."

"No offense, but you're a bit older than what I generally like," Trixie quipped as she peered at the walkway in front of the shop.

"It's not like that," Sledge shot back. "I can assure you my intentions are nothing but noble."

Trixie opened the door, ringing the store's bell above the entrance. "I know. I'm just giving you crap. It's what I do. But seriously, you've done enough. I can't ask you to involve yourself anymore."

"You don't have to. I'm volunteering to do so." Sledge held the edge of the door for her as the two of them exited the store.

She allowed him to pass; then she locked the door behind them. "Well, I do appreciate it. I'm not one to ever ask for help. It's easy to do that when you don't have people you can count on in your life."

"You do have a friend in me," Sledge said. "Besides, I need my computer tech in one piece. Finding another one that's as good as you would be a pain."

"That it would," Trixie said as they made for his truck. "And don't you forget it."

Chapter 35

Upon entering the warehouse, Trixie was more than flabbergasted. Her chin dropped and her eyes bulged. She leaned forward on the seat and peered out of the windshield as the truck stopped inside the industrial building.

"This is your home?"

Sledge cranked the gear shifter on the column into park, and then said, "Yep."

"All of it?"

"Yes. You seem surprised."

Trixie unbuckled her seat belt while blindly reaching for the passenger side door handle. "I am. This isn't what I pictured your home would look like. It's a warehouse, right?"

"It is a warehouse that I converted. I like my space. What were you expecting?"

"To be honest, a tiny one-bedroom apartment," Trixie answered. "Not a massive warehouse like this. I can't say that I've ever met anyone who has done this before."

"I guess that's fair. Now you have." Sledge switched the engine off, removed the keys, and then opened his door. "Come on. Let me show you around."

They got out of the truck while the rollup door's wheels clacked into the tracks behind them as it closed with a hollow thud. She draped her pack over her shoulder and looked the cavernous building over from right to left.

"And all of this is yours? You don't have a roommate or girlfriend living here with you?"

"Nope. It's just me. It's rather solitary."

"I can tell." Trixie glanced at him and asked, "You're sure I'm not imposing? I don't want to be a thorn in your side."

"That's the last thing you are." He was at her side and swept his hand across the expansive interior of the warehouse. "As you can see, I've got more than enough space for both of us. There's an extra bedroom in the back you can use, and a full kitchen with a stocked fridge and pantry. Internet access. TV. Whatever you want."

Trixie brought her hand up to her nose; then she looked away from Sledge.

He noticed and asked, "What's wrong?"

She didn't answer, not at first.

"It's just nice having someone who cares enough to help me out like this and who isn't after anything in return. Usually, when a guy would offer such hospitality, there was a hidden price tag attached that came up later. But you don't seem like that kind of guy."

Sledge spoke softly, "That's not the way it is here. The only thing I want is for you to be safe and to feel welcomed. That's my main priority and only concern."

"I do feel welcomed. There's no doubt about that." Trixie smiled and dabbed the wetness away from under her eyes onto her forearm. "Just so you know I probably won't be here for too long."

"There's no need to rush out," Sledge replied as they traveled across the building toward the living quarters.

Trixie said, "Well, I don't have any extra clothes here with me and I do have my job at Mac's that I can't miss out on. I'm not exactly rich and live paycheck to paycheck. If I don't show up, he'll not only dock my pay but he might fire me for not showing up and for bringing trouble to his shop. I wouldn't blame him if he did. From what I've seen, he has enough problems of his own and doesn't need any more added to his plate from me."

"I'll stop by your place and pick up your clothes and personal items the next time I head out," Sledge said as he accompanied her through the kitchen, toward the hallway leading toward the bedrooms, bathrooms, and his office. "It'll be safer that way. Whoever you got mixed up with will probably be staking out your place, waiting for you to show."

"Won't that put you in danger?"

"No more than you. I can handle anything those goons throw my way. Don't worry."

"Okay. If you say so."

Sledge thought about Trixie's job at Mac's and what that income meant to her. She wasn't averse to putting in hard work and paying her way. Even though working at the repair shop seemed like a pain to do, she did what was necessary and showed up to complete her shifts. Given the circumstances, Sledge figured Mac would understand Trixie taking some time off. If he didn't, Sledge would persuade him otherwise.

"As far as Mac goes, I think he won't have an issue with you steering clear of the shop for a bit. With what happened there today, you should stay low for his safety and yours."

"That's all well and good, but what if he doesn't like that I'm not showing up?" Trixie asked as they stopped at a closed door. "He doesn't hand out vacation days. Also, don't forget about that little thing called money. I have bills and debts that need to be paid."

"Mac will understand. When you call him, don't tell him where you are and that you'll reach out soon," Sledge replied. "As far as money goes, we'll work that out, so don't worry about it. I got you, okay?"

Trixie nodded and stared at Sledge. Then she said, "You know, I can honestly say that you're one of the few genuinely nice people I've crossed in my life. I have a pretty good B.S. radar that goes wild when men try to 'help me,' but with you, it never goes off. I might sound like a broken record, and I don't mean to be all sappy, which I'm usually not, but thanks for being a good guy. It means the world to me."

"You're welcome, but there's no need to thank me." Sledge smiled at Trixie as he reached for the doorknob. "Anyway, this is your bedroom here." He turned the knob, walked inside, and then turned on the lights.

The bedroom wasn't overly big, but it wasn't small either. It had a crisp white paint job on the walls that made it feel larger and less cramped. A twin-sized bed, dresser, writing desk with a chair, and TV mounted to the wall rounded out the furniture.

As Trixie moved about the room and dumped her pack on the edge of the bed, she took it all in. "You know, for a bachelor, you're pretty clean. I'm impressed yet again."

"I'm glad you approve." Sledge directed her attention to the two doors in the bedroom. "The bathroom is to your right. It has a shower if you want to get cleaned up. Towels are in there as well." He tilted his head at the other door near the entrance of the room. "That's the closet. Once I bring you some clothes, you can hang them up or put them away in the dresser, whatever you like. This is your space."

With her hands placed on her hips, Trixie looked it over and then looked at Sledge. "Sounds good. I might rinse off and relax a bit. Truth be known, I haven't been sleeping well in a while and am a bit tired."

"Do as you please. If you get hungry, fix whatever you like in the kitchen."

"Thanks. I will."

"Do you need anything else?" Sledge asked as he moved into the doorway.

Trixie thought about it for a second, then said, "Not that I can think of. What are you doing the rest of the day?"

"Work. And I figured I'd run by your place to gather up your clothes and anything else you want. I'll go ahead and do that first so you have your stuff here. Don't worry. You're completely safe."

"That would be great. I'd like fresh clothes to change into instead of getting back into the clothes I'm already wearing," Trixie replied as she dug her laptop out of her pack and placed it on the desk. "I might get a bite of food in the meantime and when you get back take a shower."

"That will work. I won't be long."

Trixie scribbled her address down on a notepad with a pen next to the paper. She tore it off and handed it to Sledge. "This is my address. There's a suitcase in the closet you can stuff my clothes in and a brown tote you can shove my hygiene products into if you don't mind."

Sledge took the paper. "Not at all. I want you to be comfortable here."

She then fished out a set of keys from her left front pants pocket and gave them to him. "Here's my apartment key. The lock can be a bit tricky. It sticks at times."

"Nothing I can't handle. Be back shortly."

As Sledge started to close the door, Trixie said, "Thanks again, Sledge, for being a good dude. It's nice to know good men exist in the world."

Sledge smiled then said, "You're welcome."

Chapter 36

TRIXIE'S FINAL WORDS SPOKEN to Sledge before he left to retrieve her belongings bounced around inside his head. If she only knew the truth about the kind of man he used to be, would she still consider him a good person?

So many wrongs had been committed in his younger days. Mistakes were made and lives were ruined for his employer without him knowing if he was on the side of good or evil. He had been brainwashed and soaked with lies. Sledge hated being taken advantage of, but he couldn't change the past.

His mission now was to redeem his soul and cleanse the stink of evil that clung to him, once and for all. He was no longer a killer aimed at targets about which he knew nothing, but rather a man set on a long path of redemption in an attempt to atone for his sins. Perhaps one day, it would be enough.

Sledge parked out front of Trixie's apartment building and sat in the truck as he surveyed the immediate vicinity. The area was in the lower-income district of Atlanta which had its fair share of robberies and violence. Most of the buildings were in dire need of repair, inside and out.

Weeds grew from the sidewalks and trash littered the area. Homeless individuals camped out in plain view on the walkways and in the alleys. Drug deals went down at street corners in broad daylight, which Sledge was easily able to view from his idling truck.

The cars parked at the curbs had no visible occupants in them. From what he could ascertain, a final sweep of the street indicated that whomever Trixie screwed over was not staking out her apartment.

Satisfied that the coast was clear, he got out of the cab. He pocketed the keys, marched to the flight of steps, and then climbed to the entrance.

A musty odor punched him as he opened the door and advanced inside the entryway. The unpleasant stench made his nose crinkle so he avoided the staircase and opted for the bank of elevators.

His goal was to get in and out as fast as possible with no issues. He'd get her belongings and bounce before trouble had a chance to stop him.

After pressing the button located on the wall between the two elevators, Sledge took a step back and waited for whichever carriage arrived first. He checked the time on his watch and noted that it was 5:30 p.m. Once Sledge finished at Trixie's place and got back, he had to dive back into Kim's case and track down Marko Vega's hotspots within the city.

The carriage to his right pinged as it settled into place. A second later, the door retracted and revealed an elderly woman with a brown and white Pomeranian clutched in her arm. The dog growled at Sledge and snapped at him as she shushed the squeaking canine.

"Stop that barking, Beatrice."

She petted the dog's head and flashed Sledge a smile that showed her stained, yellow teeth. Her white hair was capped by a red, Gatsby, Linen, Cloche hat that sat crooked on her head. Her bent, wrinkled finger pushed on the bridge of her glasses as she slid them further up on her large nose.

Sledge put his boot at the base of the door and draped his arm across it to keep it from shutting as she ambled toward him. With a warm greeting, he said, "Ma'am."

Her legs didn't move too fast as she shuffled by him. The cheap perfume the elderly woman wore couldn't mask the mothball scent and body odor coming from her meager, tiny frame.

"Thank you, dear. Such a gentleman."

Growling under its breath, the Pomeranian glared at Sledge as the pair made for the entrance of the building. The woman spoke to the animal as if it understood everything she muttered to it and might reply.

Sledge stepped into the carriage and thumbed the fourth-floor button. The door skipped shut and jerked upward with a whine. Gears above him worked and clinked as the overhead light flickered and buzzed. It wasn't the worst elevator Sledge had ever been in, but it was pretty close.

It dinged a soft tune marking its arrival. The door opened to a dimly lit hallway that was more foreboding than anything else. Sledge stepped out of the carriage and hooked a left down the hallway, then another right that took him in the direction of Trixie's loft.

His ears were attuned to the slightest sounds looming from the spaces he passed as well as the corridor. He spied no movement ahead or behind him. No footfalls matched his own as he strode up to her residence.

He dug the keys out of his pocket and stared at them while trying to decide which one worked on the door. He noticed a bit of light shining near the jamb. The door was cracked open.

Stuffing the keys back into his pocket, he pulled the 1911 from his waistband and took a position against the wall to the side of the entryway. Another glance in either direction of the hall confirmed no movement.

Sledge extended his arm toward the door and pushed it open; then he carefully peered into her place with his gun trained ahead. As the hinges creaked and the door swung until it stopped against the interior wall, Sledge raked his narrow gaze over her tossed apartment.

What few pieces of furniture she had were tipped over and sliced open. Broken dishes and glassware were scattered across the wood floor and countertops.

The fridge hung open as did all of the cabinets in the kitchen. He guessed that the men pursuing Trixie had already visited her and left a while ago.

Upon entering the loft, Sledge shut the door and did a sweep that resulted in him finding nothing more than destruction and damage to her property. The people she'd screwed over were pissed and not about to let it go. Even if they recovered the money she stole from them, an example had to be made, and that generally resulted in death. Sledge couldn't, and wouldn't, allow that to happen.

He got to work and gathered her clothes from the closet and quickly stuffed them into her suitcase. He filled it in record time as he crammed what he could into it, knowing that she'd never return.

Next, Sledge stuffed the tote full of bathroom products; then hauled it and the suitcase to the front door. He had spent a little over fifteen minutes in the loft and it was now time to leave.

A knock sounded from outside. Two short raps at the door snapped Sledge's attention to the entrance. Instinctively, he pulled the 1911 back out and aimed the barrel at the edge of the door.

His heartbeat was steady. Not a hint of anxiousness lurked in his grasp of the gun grip or his breathing. Years of intense combative training had molded his body and refined his emotions to a razor's edge.

Another knock sounded, followed by a woman's voice speaking softly from the other side of the door. "Trixie. Are you in there, girl?"

Sledge lowered the pistol and peered through the peephole, noting a short, black-haired woman standing at the door. No one else was in view behind her, but that didn't mean a trap hadn't been set using the woman as bait.

She knocked again, refusing to leave. "Come on, girl. Open up and let me know that you're okay. Those two dudes left already. I'm worried about you."

Twisting the doorknob and keeping the piece out of sight, Sledge cracked the door open and wedged his boot at the base to thwart any sort of potential attack.

"Trixie isn't here."

"Oh." The young Latina woman's brow arched as she peered at Sledge. "I thought she was. I heard someone rummaging about in here and figured it was Trixie."

"No. I stopped by to pick up a few of her things," Sledge replied while glancing in either direction of the corridor.

"Is she okay? Are you her dad?" the woman asked. "I've not seen you around before and didn't think she had family visiting or even any relatives close by. At least, not from the way she spoke."

"She is fine and no, I'm not her father. I'm a friend helping her out. That's all." Sledge secured the 1911 in his pants behind him as he skirted around the edge of the door and stepped out into the hallway while shutting the door behind him.

The woman craned her neck to peek inside, but couldn't see around his body. He didn't want her to see the mess as it would only increase the questions she asked.

"Did you happen to see the two men who came by here earlier?" Sledge asked while blocking the entrance to the loft.

She folded her arms across her chest and tipped her head. "Not a very good look, just as they went in and shut the door. They were bald and had tattoos but that's all I could see."

Bald. Tattoos. It sounded like the same two meatheads from Mac's.

"Do you remember around what time they came here?"

Her finger tapped against her chin while she glanced at the floor. "I want to say it was like 3:00 or a bit before then. I'm not sure. I didn't see when they left, though."

Sledge asked, "Have they been by here before today?"

"Not that I'm aware of. If they have, then I missed them. Trixie has never said one word about those guys. They are not the sort of people she'd associate with. They looked sketchy if you know what I mean."

"I do." Sledge then said, "Just know she is safe. Nothing bad will happen to her. I can promise you that."

"I hope so because she's a good person and my friend. I've always worried about her," the woman replied. "Please tell Trixie that Camella wanted to know how she is, will you?"

"I will."

"Thank you."

The door behind the woman opened. A young boy stopped at the doorway. He looked to be around six years old and had a head full of bushy, black hair.

She spoke in Spanish, which translated to *get back inside.* The boy obeyed and slammed the door shut.

"I must be going. Please give Trixie my best and I hope to speak to her soon."

"I will."

Camella opened her apartment door and vanished inside while speaking Spanish at a raised volume. The deadbolt engaged with a loud click as the woman's voice was reduced to a muttered bark.

Sledge ducked back inside Trixie's pad, gathered her suitcase and tote; then he exited the loft toward the bank of elevators. Taking the carriage down to the first floor, Sledge made for his truck, dumped the luggage onto the back seat, then climbed into the cab and took off, speeding down the street. He headed back to the warehouse without additional stops, wondering what sort of mess Trixie had gotten herself wrapped up in.

Chapter 37

FOR THE REMAINDER OF the evening, and into the early morning hours, Sledge shifted gears to Kim's case now that Trixie was settled in his place and made herself at home. She had kept to the spare room and only made brief appearances when hungry or thirsty, which suited Sledge fine since he wanted her to feel comfortable.

Marko Vega was a person of major interest and one who would hopefully be the key to finding the missing girl. Detective Wentworth painted the man as a slippery fish who always managed to wiggle out of jams using outside sources. He was the next bad actor who Sledge believed would connect the localized criminal network to a much larger player that bankrolled their operation.

Hours ticked by like minutes as Sledge poured through research on who Marko Vega was, and the sort of business dealings in which he was involved. His web search provided little to go on as not much was listed about the notorious felon. With bits and pieces scattered throughout the internet, there weren't too many dots to connect.

Frustrated, Sledge pinched the bridge of his nose, sighed, and then leaned back in his desk chair. His eyes were strained from staring at the computer screens for hours on end. He ran on fumes and his body was tired, but how could Sledge rest when a girl's life hinged on him being able to find her before it was too late?

Needing to clear his head and gain some clarity, Sledge forced his body out of the chair where he was camped, grabbed his favorite book, *Manhattan Heights*, and strolled into the hallway. His boots shuffled along the floor to the kitchen where he deposited the book on the table, and then made a cup of coffee and waited as it brewed.

He checked the time and groused at it being after 3:00 a.m. His efforts were commendable but that meant little if he wasn't able to advance the case forward. Each second that went by meant his chances for success in rescuing Kim were diminished. That couldn't happen.

The coffee finished brewing with a hiss. After pouring a cup of the dark roast, Sledge carried the hot mug to the table and took a seat in one of the chairs. As he sipped on the scorching brew, Sledge cracked the book open and stared at a photo wedged into the crease.

It was a picture of a smiling, happy family, a husband, a wife, and a little girl. They were huddled close together with the small girl wedged between the man and the woman. The child was the focus of Sledge's interest. He had spent countless hours reliving the moment when he got the photo, and who the girl was. So much regret and heartache were tied to the image that it broke his heart. Few things in the world destroyed a man like Sledge, but knowing the pain he'd caused that family some twelve years prior haunted him daily.

He plucked the picture from the book and brought it closer. As Sledge focused on the little girl, he thought of Trixie and how he'd ruined her life that fateful night long ago. Not only did Sledge kill her mother and father, but he put her in the crosshairs of Cobalt who wanted to tie up any loose ends.

After dropping her off at that church in North Carolina, Sledge remained in Trixie's life from a distance, watching over her and ensuring that she'd always be safe from Cobalt so that she could grow up to have a normal life. His efforts proved inadequate in the end, as she was bounced from foster home to foster home until striking out on her own at the age of seventeen, forever hindered by what he had done to her.

Movement from the hallway snapped Sledge from his trance of guilt. He blinked away the wetness forming in each eye and stuffed the picture into the crease of the book with which he had grown up. Slamming it closed, he half expected Trixie to emerge and catch him at his most vulnerable, but she never did materialize from the blackness of the hallway.

Sledge stood from the chair and grabbed his book. The trip down memory lane put a damper on his mood and stifled his ability to think clearly; he was inundated with guilt that added to the fatigue plaguing him. But rest wasn't what Sledge wanted because that was when the nightmares came to haunt him.

Arriving at his office, he spotted his desk chair twisting from side to side. Sledge opened the door further and discovered Trixie planted at his desk, clacking away at the keyboard.

"What are you doing?" He asked while entering the office. "I thought you were sleeping."

Trixie rolled back from the desk's edge and spun in the chair toward him. "I'm a night owl. That and I don't sleep much. I got a few winks earlier in the evening, but with everything going on, I haven't been able to shut off my mind. It runs constantly and makes it hard to relax."

"I can understand that. I suffer from the same thing." Sledge put the book on his bookshelf and then faced her. "There's fresh coffee in there if you want it. I don't sleep much, either."

"Thanks. I could smell it. When I was heading toward the kitchen, I noticed your office light was on. With you being so old, I figured you'd be in bed well before 10:00 p.m. nightly." She cracked a wry grin at the comment.

Sledge couldn't help but smile. It helped mask the pang of guilt as he looked at her. "Believe me; my body would probably appreciate the proper amount of rest. If it wasn't for coffee and energy drinks, I wouldn't function at all."

"Same. I pound energy drinks when I'm seated at my rig. It focuses my mind and keeps me on task without straying." Trixie twisted in the chair and tilted her head at the screens. "Speaking of rigs, this is a nice setup you have here. It's a far better unit than that piece of crap you brought in recently. I'm surprised you have a system like this. And here I thought your tech skills were abysmal."

After taking a long sip and swallowing the coffee, Sledge said, "I do all right for a one-man operation. I'm not overly tech savvy, but I can hold my own when it's needed."

"Or when you need an extra set of hands," Trixie replied. "I guess that's why you dumped your junk off with me to tinker with it."

That wasn't the reason Sledge visited Mac's repair shop regularly. Each piece of equipment he brought to Trixie to fix was a way for him to be close to her without revealing his true intentions of keeping an eye on her. With her being in his home, more would be revealed, so he had to think on his feet until he dared to be upfront with her about who he was and how they were connected.

"Two hands are better than one," Sledge said as he stepped forward. "You're good at what you do. Why wouldn't I take advantage of that fact? If recent events are any sort of indicator, it seems as though your tech skills far exceed upgrading aging laptops and ancient drives."

"I am a woman of many talents." Trixie pointed at the screen and then asked, "What are you working on here? Maybe I can give you a hand. It would be a way for me to pay you back for your kindness and for saving my bacon, which I'm grateful for even if I don't act like it."

Sledge thought about it for a moment. Her skills were impressive, and having her close would allow him to watch her better. That unknown factor of whom she screwed over still grated on his nerves and made him consider if she had inadvertently gotten caught up with Cobalt. He had no proof, but it begged to be considered.

"Okay. You can help me out this one time. After that, we're even."

"Deal." Trixie pressed her fingertip to the search bar of the internet page and asked, "So who is this Marko Vega, and why are you searching for him?"

Chapter 38

OVER THE NEXT FEW hours, the duo hung out in his office huddled around his computer. Trixie helmed the rig and typed furiously as Sledge towered behind her, leaning on the back of the chair.

"I always wondered what it would be like hunting someone down," Trixie said as her fingers moved from key to key across the keyboard. "At least, I'm assuming you are a private investigator since you've never actually told me whatever it is that you do. You could be a bounty hunter. You've got the menacing look for the part."

"What I do is a mixture of several things," Sledge answered as he yawned. "People hire me for a myriad of reasons, one of which is tracking individuals who are lost, hiding–"

"Or kidnapped? I'm guessing that's where you were going."

"Yes. That too."

"Does this Marko Vega have something to do with a kidnapping case?"

"He's a person of interest for a case I'm working on. That's all I can say."

"Well, that's no fun." Trixie pounded the keys on the keyboard as she stayed glued to the monitors. "Whoever this guy is, he doesn't have much of a digital footprint. Most of the searches I've conducted and databases I've tapped aren't coming up with much on him. I know where to look and the results are limited at best. His name could be an alias, which is what's throwing off the results. That's a possibility. Or..."

"Or what?"

"Someone is scrubbing the web of his name and purposefully keeping him hidden," Trixie said. "It would take some doing, but it's not impossible."

She had gotten more information on Vega, if even by a fraction, than what Sledge had been able to gather during his session in the seat. It was better than nothing and got him closer to tracking down the man.

"Did you happen to get a location of known hangouts?" Sledge asked as he stretched his arms and yawned again. "The detective I got his name from didn't provide any more than Vega's name."

"I haven't yet, but I'm working through some searches here and we can see where it goes." Trixie stopped for a moment and stretched her neck, then popped her fingers.

"Why don't you get up and take a break? You've been going after it for hours now and have done well. More than I asked for. We're even if that's why you're still plugging away at it."

Trixie spun in the chair and slid her right leg under her left. "Oh, I'm good. This is what I enjoy. I don't care to watch TV or read. My enjoyment comes from hacking away at the keys. It helps me decompress and relax. I know that might sound weird, but it's true."

He understood and had his ways of relaxing. To each their own. "I get it and appreciate your willingness to help."

"Of course." Trixie studied his face a second, then said, "Why don't you go lie down and rest? I can handle this from here. I can tell you're tired since you keep yawning every five minutes."

"I'm good," Sledge replied as he glanced at his watch. "It's after 5:00 a.m. and I've got business to handle today. I'll rest later."

"Knocking heads can wait for a bit," Trixie shot back with her lips pursed while she stared up at him. "You'll be more alert and able to think clearly after resting. Now, you insisted that I listen to you and come here where it was safe. I did, so listen to me now. Go lie down and rest for a few hours. When you get up, I should have everything compiled on what I've dug up on Vega. Then you can go about whatever it is that you need to do today."

Sledge was reluctant to give in even though he knew she was right. His brain would work better and keep him sharp after a bit of rest. Squaring off with Vega would test his gumption and skills, requiring both to be sharpened to a fine point.

"Fine. I'll go crash for a bit. It won't be too long. Just long enough to shake this tiredness."

"Whatever works, do it." Trixie got up and made for the door while passing by Sledge. "I'm going to grab my pack and set up my laptop. I've got software and channels I can use that should help our case."

"Our case?" He asked, as she paused for a beat in the hallway.

"Yes. You're not getting rid of me that easy."

As she vanished down the dark corridor, Sledge snatched the Manhattan Heights book from the shelf. He then removed the photo of Trixie and her family stuffed in the binding of the pages, knowing that he'd have to find a safer place to put the picture that would be far from her reach.

Chapter 39

His phone buzzed its annoying alarm, snapping Sledge from his slumber. With a sigh and a face thick with sleep, he rolled to the left and mashed his finger against the screen.

Sweet silence was his once more, but he wouldn't bask in the comfort of his bed. Work had to be done and he had to get up and move. A girl's life hung in the balance. Her kidnappers didn't care if he was rested or not.

Sledge got off the mattress, stretched his arms, and repped off twenty jumping jacks to get his heart pumping. Next, he transitioned to the floor and pounded out fifty push-ups and sit-ups that got his blood moving.

After a quick shower and tending to the knife wound on his stomach, Sledge dressed in clean threads and headed out of his bedroom toward the office. It was after 10:00 a.m. by the time he completed everything.

Much to his surprise, Trixie wasn't in the office. Both of Sledge's monitors were dark and her laptop and pack were missing. He hadn't bothered checking her room before coming to the office. With how determined she was in digging up material on Vega, Sledge figured she'd still be grinding away. That wasn't the case.

As he turned to head to her room, she called out to him from the kitchen. "It's about time you got up, sleepy head. I was wondering if you were alive or dead."

Sledge advanced up the hallway to the kitchen where Trixie stood at the counter near the refrigerator. "Funny. I felt like I was dead."

"Do dead people snore?" Trixie asked as she moved the carton of eggs, package of bacon, bread, cheese, and a stick of butter toward the stove. "I ask because you were snoring loudly. It was so quiet in here that I heard it and wondered what it was. At first, I guessed a freight train or a plane flying overhead. Nope. Just you, sawing logs."

He didn't know if he snored or not. Being alone made that impossible to know, much less care about. "That's news to me. I hope it wasn't too much of a bother."

"Not at all. I'm just giving you a hard time, Sledge. You don't snore too badly." Trixie bent down and pulled out the storage compartment under the stove while she continued speaking. "Now, one of the foster families I stayed with did the same thing. That man snored so loud it was impossible to escape. He toyed with death many a night for that, among other reasons that I won't bore you with."

His throat moved at the ominous comment and he advanced the conversation past her stint with the foster family. "What are you doing over there?"

"I'm going to make some breakfast if I can find the right size pan." Trixie hunted one down and put it on top of the front right burner near the food. "Awesome. I've been craving a fried egg sandwich for most of the morning, but I figured I'd wait until you got up before making it so I didn't have to do it twice. One and done. And before you say no, you want one. Trust me."

Sledge didn't argue and made for the table where her laptop was. The screen faced her and there was an open can of Monster next to it.

"Did you find out anything else about Vega?"

"I did, after some trenching." Trixie dabbed her finger blindly at the laptop and said, "Take a look at the screen. You want cheese, right?"

"Sure." Sled sat down on the chair and spun the laptop around as Trixie worked on cooking the food.

Several images populated the screen of a well-groomed, darker-skinned man. Sledge placed his heritage somewhere in the Middle East. He had a neatly trimmed, black beard and a cunning smirk. His right ear was pierced. A dragon tattoo was etched onto the side of his neck and slithered up toward his jaw.

Until that moment, Sledge had no face to go with the name. Now, he did.

"Where did you find these images? I couldn't put together much on him when I looked."

As Trixie cracked an egg on the side of the pan and dropped the contents to the heated bottom, she said, "Two words. Dark Web. The place to go for bad guys. And a few other resources I back-channeled into as well."

A knot formed in Sledge's gut from hearing how she'd gathered the intel. From the way Trixie spoke, it sounded like she'd hacked into government agencies to see what they had on Vega.

Before Sledge could open his mouth to voice his concern, Trixie cut him off.

"And to answer the question that's on the tip of your tongue, they won't be able to track the IP address. I went through multiple servers spread across several countries, so we're in the clear.

"Also, I used a Tor browser to access the Dark Web. It's anonymous and the web page requests are routed through a series of proxy servers operated by thousands of folks around the globe, so we're good there. This isn't my first rodeo. I know what I'm doing. Don't worry."

That was easier said than done since Sledge worked in the shadows and tried to stay under the radar as much as possible. A lot rode on that fact since he didn't know all the players to which Cobalt was tied. It made a huge difference for not only him but Trixie as well.

"Okay. Just checking. And it's my job to worry when you're talking about hacking networks. You never know who is watching. That, and there is always someone better out there than you. Don't get too cocky."

"I'm the right amount of cocky, thank you."

"I can see that."

Sledge trained his focus back to each of the photos that contained Marko Vega with an assortment of people. Trent Gesner was one of the individuals Sledge spotted but that was about it. All of them had a shady vibe about them that he couldn't shake.

The sizzle of the eggs frying in the pan played in the background as Sledge scrutinized each image in further detail. His stomach rumbled from the rich smell of eggs frying in butter.

Trixie whistled and danced at the stove subtly while tossing bread into the pan. One wouldn't be able to tell that her life was threatened recently and that her world was now a tangled mess. It spoke volumes, though, seeing how being here with him made her feel secure enough to not let it bother her. Not that it did much if anything when he suggested she stay with him until things cooled off, whenever that might be.

He asked, "Did you happen to dig up an address for this clown during your surfing session? The pictures are great but I need locations as well."

"Yes and no." Trixie opened the bacon, sniffed inside the package, then reeled in disgust. "Lord. We're going without bacon. It's pretty rank." She dumped the package into the trash and then went back to the pan as the eggs popped and crackled.

"What does that mean?"

She clarified. "He doesn't have a home address listed anywhere that I could find, which means someone is blocking it again or his residence isn't listed under the name you have. One thing I did find is that in one of those photos that your man is in, the building in the background is a meat packing plant here in Atlanta. Davidson Meats. Part of the name is visible and I was able to piece together the rest by doing a simple search."

Sledge looked back through the pictures and found the last half of Davidson and the first three letters of meat in the background behind Vega. Although slightly blurred, it was visible once he found it. "That's some good work." He was taken aback by the efficient work Trixie had done. "This is way more than I expected you to dig up."

"Don't underestimate me." Trixie removed the pan from the heat and dumped a sandwich onto a plate near the stove; then she put the pan back on the burner. "I might be young but I've got loads of experience. It's easy to do when you don't have much of a social life and spend all of your free time tinkering."

"Well, I'm seriously impressed by what you've done here. This should help with the case I'm working on."

"That would be great if it does." Trixie finished making another egg sandwich and brought two plates to the table after switching off the burner and removing the frying pan. "Breakfast is served." She put one plate down in front of Sledge, who had pushed her laptop to the side.

He sniffed at the wonderful aroma coming off of the sandwich. The bread had a golden buttery outside. Melted cheese draped over the edge of the fried egg white that was speckled with pepper. For such a simple meal, it looked amazing to Sledge who was accustomed to scavenging for food in his kitchen most days.

"This is great. And it smells good. You didn't have to do this, Trixie."

"It tastes even better. Life changing." She stood and tore strips from the paper towel holder and handed one to Sledge. "I had to learn to cook for myself at an early age so I perfected a few dishes. I thought I would share one of those with you seeing as you don't seem to care a lot about sleeping and eating."

As they ate and conversed, Sledge thought about the exceptional work Trixie had done on Marko Vega. She proved to be capable behind the keyboard and worked her magic to uncover data that to a novice would seem impossible. Her skillset was remarkable and she was driven, and fearless even when faced with those who wanted to harm her.

He asked, "How's your cheek and lip feeling? There's a nice bruise forming."

Trixie patted the paper towel to her mouth as she finished chewing and swallowing the rest of her meal. "It's better. Still tender and sore to the touch, but fine overall. I don't lose sleep over such things. It was caused by me so I can't complain too much. When you play dangerous games, you assume the risk for any blowback."

Sledge polished off the remainder of his meal, wiped his hands clean on the paper towel, and then tossed it on top of the plate that was still streaked with egg yolk the bread hadn't soaked up. "I'm glad it's not bothering you much. That could have gone the other way fast."

"Perhaps, but it didn't. I'm glad you dropped in when you did." Trixie dug her fingers into her back pants pocket and removed her phone. "I should call Mac and let him know what's going on. I didn't yesterday. He should know so he can make whatever arrangements he needs to."

"Before you call him, I want to run something by you."

Trixie glanced up from her phone with her finger hovering above the screen. "What's that?"

"Why don't you come to work for me?"

"Doing what? Cooking you egg sandwiches."

"No, but that wouldn't be frowned upon." Sledge then said, "You can help me out on cases. Research and stuff. I'm juggling everything and I manage, but having someone as proficient as you are would relieve me of that so I can focus more on what needs to be handled."

She held onto the phone and mulled over the proposition without responding. The wheels turned and her head bobbed as she thought about it.

He added. "You'll also be paid. We can work out the details on that later, but I can promise you that it will be worth your while. Seeing how dangerous it is for you out there right now, you've got nothing to lose."

After a moment of silence, Trixie said, "Let me think it over. I appreciate the offer and understand what you're saying, but I'd still like to think about it before I answer, if that's okay with you?"

"Sure. Of course. This isn't a time-sensitive offer but a standing one." Sledge leaned back in his chair with one hand on the table and the other on his lap. "Go ahead and call Mac and fill him in. As you said, he should at least know what's going on with you at the moment. I would advise not telling him where you are. If those guys come back, he can have deniability, which protects him and us."

"True." Trixie started to tap away on her phone; then paused to look at Sledge once more. "You're serious about this right? Me coming to work for you and all?"

"I am. We'll get your bills handled and get you set up somewhere other than your room." Sledge clarified one point. "My one stipulation is that you keep this quiet. No one knows that you work for me. What we do here stays private and isn't shared with anyone. This is a biggie for me and is not negotiable."

As much as Sledge wanted Trixie close to better protect her, he also had to cover his behind. His work made enemies at times and maintaining discretion was crucial.

Trixie said, "I'll take that under consideration and I do understand. That Vega dude you're tracking seems like a real scumbag. Trust me, I don't like seeking out problems, but I also don't run from them either."

"I know you don't. Make your call to Mac and let him know what's happened." Sledge stood and took their plates to the kitchen sink; then he deposited both into the bottom. "I'm going to get ready to head out shortly to check on that meat packing place. Do you have the address handy?"

"I do, boss man," Trixie said with a smirk. "I'll get it to you before you leave.

"Sounds good."

Sledge found it amusing and comforting to hear her consider his proposition. All he wanted for Trixie was a normal life, free of dangers from their past that she seemed to have blocked out. Maybe one day she'd be able to have such a future where he could not.

Chapter 40

Sledge couldn't help but wonder what sort of mess he might walk into at the meat packing facility. There could be a drug deal going down or an arms shipment arriving for distribution across the greater Atlanta area. Maybe. All were plausible.

In the end, it could just be a normal business operating with no underlying illegal deals transpiring, so Sledge had to consider that. Not everyone at the plant could be on Vega's payroll; most were likely just going about their daily work with no idea of what was happening beneath the surface.

His main hope and his concern for the day's mission were that he'd come across the group's human trafficking ring and find Kim, or at least find a concrete clue to indicate if she was even still in the city. Sledge worried that she might have already been sold to some Saudi Prince to add to his harem or some other deviant that got their jollies from having their way with underage girls. It was a race to find her before it was too late. So far, he wasn't so sure he'd be able to deliver Kim Claymore to her parents, and that killed him.

With additional magazines laid out on the workbench where he kept his weapons, Sledge's hands moved as if they had a mind of their own. Repetition made doing most tasks easier. The two magazines he had fully loaded were ready to go.

One by one, Sledge stowed the magazines on his person. He then added a double-edged, combat knife to the sheath at the small of his back and a four-inch gambler's dagger to the sheath secured around his lower leg near his boot. This rounded out his arsenal with the 1911 that was ready to go with a round chambered.

Footfalls played off the concrete floor as he secured the pistol into the front waistband of his pants. He turned away from the table as Trixie approached.

"Here is the address of the Davidson Meat Processing plant." Trixie handed him a torn piece of paper as Sledge adjusted the bottom of his coat over the top of the jeans he wore. "It looks to be on the other side of town."

Sledge took the paper, copied the address to memory, and then stuffed it into his front pocket. "Thanks. Did you get ahold of Mac?"

"I did. It was a short conversation. He didn't want details even when I tried to tell him," Trixie replied. "For now, he told me to take whatever time I need and that I'm welcomed back whenever. I think he's saying that because he's not going to be able to find anyone else who will work for his crap pay and the crummy environment."

"Probably not."

"Do you always pack heavy when going out on jobs?" Trixie asked, calling out the additional magazines he had on him. "That's a lot of ammo."

"It's better to have it and not need it than to need it and not have it," Sledge replied. "These aren't the sort of folks I'd trust to have a simple conversation. I don't plan to go in guns blazing, but I'm not going to lie down and take a bullet to the head."

"Man. And here I thought I was the only one diving deep in shark-infested waters. Seems like we're more alike than we thought."

"It seems we are." Sledge started across the warehouse toward his truck with Trixie following next to him. "But that is nothing for you to worry about. This building is buttoned up tight and has surveillance. No one knows that I'm here, so you'll be safe. I promise you that. I cover my tracks well."

Trixie nodded at the weapons cages. "Will I be able to get a company firearm?"

"Do you know how to handle a gun? Have you ever shot one before?"

"No, but I'm a quick learner. Besides, it could sweeten the pot on making my decision to come on board as your tech girl. Tech support. Information handler. Whatever you want to call me in the chair."

As Sledge dug his keys out from the left coat pocket, he asked, "Does that mean you've made up your mind?"

"Maybe. I'm considering it. It's right up my alley," Trixie answered. "I could do it with my eyes closed and without breaking a sweat. From what

I can tell, you've got a pretty tight operation here. I could make it better, but that's me."

"That's good to hear and I don't doubt it." Sledge moved around the hood of the Silverado to the driver's side. "There's always steady work coming in, so it's never a dull moment."

"Seems like it." Trixie looked over the truck, and then asked, "Why do you drive this thing when you have that sweet-assed muscle car parked in the back like it's done something wrong? This truck is so plain and that car is, well, awesome."

"It's a work in progress," Sledge answered as he got into the truck. "It runs and operates just fine, but still needs some adjustments. Plus, what's going to draw more attention to the streets? This tin can or that black beauty?"

"The muscle car for sure," Trixie answered. "No contest there. Not unless you like plain old trucks that someone's grandfather would drive."

"Exactly." Sledge started the pickup, rolled down his window and then he slammed the door shut. "It's about blending in and not being flashy on most days, especially when I'm going out on jobs. That car is memorable. It's a classic. This truck is not. See the difference?"

"I do, but the muscle car would be more fun to drive." Trixie raised her hands and then said, "That's me, though. If you throw in me being able to drive it as part of your perks package then that should seal the deal."

The smile Trixie gave Sledge indicated that she wasn't serious about that being a condition of her coming on board. It wouldn't hurt but no one drove his car except for him.

"Nice try but I don't think so. You're pulling out all of the stops, aren't you?"

She shrugged. "Hey. You can't blame a girl for trying to get what she can. You approached me with this. Not the other way around. I can't help that I'm a badass."

Sledge snickered at the comment as he pressed the button on the garage door opener. "You're too modest. Thanks for not letting this go to your head."

"It's your fault." Trixie tapped the hood with her hand, then said, "Be careful out there, and don't get shot up. Not until we've had a chance to go over the healthcare plan and perks package. I'm not going to let that muscle car go so easily."

"I can see that." Sledge shifted into reverse as the rollup door ceased its upward movement in the tracks. "Be back in a bit."

The truck backed out of the mammoth opening into the alleyway. He punched the opener and closed the door as Trixie disappeared into the depths of the building.

Instead of going his usual route, Sledge drove down the narrow corridor in the opposite direction to the next street over. It was the quickest path to take that would land him at the plant sooner than going the other way. Every second and minute counted and he had to make the most of each.

Traffic bustled along without much of an issue. No wrecks or road construction stalled the snaking lines of cars running on the freeways and side streets.

Sledge peered out of the windshield at the cars ahead of him, determined to find Marko Vega and get what he could out of him about Kim. Pounding him to dust or using other tactics weren't off the table and were always deployed when a subject was holding their tongue instead of giving him what he wanted.

One thing Sledge hoped to learn from the smug-looking man was who was funding their operation. They had major backers who were able to scrub Vega from most internet searches and get him out of jail without as much as a slap on the wrist. The latter was more important seeing as Sledge's digital footprint was near nonexistent as well, but the other was problematic. Whoever bankrolled Vega and his crew had power, connections, and most of all, boatloads of money to pay off public officials.

Exiting the freeway and taking the winding off-ramp to the street below, Sledge cruised through the changing yellow light and hooked around the corner. Another mile up the road landed him at the edge of a fenced wall of diamond-shaped steel that stretched down the road and reached what he guessed to be eight feet into the air. As Sledge slowed and coasted alongside the fence, he located the name on the side of the white building that took up most of the property. Davidson Meat Processing.

Sledge steered the Silverado to the curb and stopped. His keen gaze surveyed the plant as he put the truck into park and switched off the engine. Before moving in for a closer look, Sledge did a bit of recon from the safety of his truck.

There were no surveillance cameras in sight on the tops of the steel fence posts that he could identify. The buildings nestled on either side of the plant looked vacant at the moment as evidenced by the growing weeds sprouting up from the concrete and the lack of vehicles parked around the structures.

A lush landscape of green grass, flowers, and trees blanketed what bit of land wasn't consumed by the enormous plant. It had the appearance of a regular business, but Sledge had his doubts about that.

Not a hint of activity buzzed anywhere close to the property's fenced perimeter or within the grounds; having men patrolling with firearms wouldn't work to sell the lie.

The streets had little to no traffic and the Davidson plant was the only business that remained open. It was almost like it was off limits to the public, but without signs indicating as much to keep from being overtly obvious.

To Sledge, it was the perfect cover for Vega to conduct his illegal operations under the guise of a legitimate business going about its daily grind. If Vega was smart, and it appeared he was cunning, all sorts of illicit activity would be happening under everyone's noses, one of which Sledge assumed would be the group's human trafficking ring.

His gut told him that he'd find something out inside. What that was remained to be seen. To find out, he'd have to venture onto the property, and that's exactly what Sledge planned to do.

Chapter 41

As SLEDGE PREPARED TO pull away from the curb and stow the Silverado in an inconspicuous spot before advancing on the perimeter, the grumble of a big rig approached from the west. It's throaty engine whined and sent Sledge crouching in the driver's seat.

He peered out of the side window and watched as a white delivery truck rolled past him. Davidson Meats was plastered on the side of the rig. It slowed as it neared the gated entrance, and then pulled into the drive. The gate jerked and retracted, granting the truck access.

Sledge sat straight in the seat and drove off down the road as the wide-body rig continued toward the plant. It hooked a right at the mouth of the parking lot, which had vehicles parked in front of the building.

The Silverado was tucked behind a building down from the plant's fenced perimeter. It wasn't too far away, but enough to keep it out of view so it wasn't setting on the road for an extended period.

Pocketing the keys, he worked around the shuttered business toward the far end. A quick look past the blind corner confirmed that the coast was clear, allowing Sledge to advance on the fence.

No signs were visible indicating that the fence was electrified. Several No Trespassing signs were plastered along the run, but that meant little in keeping Sledge out.

He roved the grounds and the building for folks outside before making his move. With the area clear, Sledge backed up about six feet and charged full steam ahead. He launched into the air and slammed onto the fence.

His fingers gripped the steel and the tip of his boots wedged their tips into the openings. In one fluid motion, Sledge climbed up and over in less than ten seconds. He dropped to the ground and then scuttled to the nearest hulking tree; then he moved on.

Sledge made his way across the expanse of the property using the vegetation as a shield. Two decades' worth of covert operations proved pivotal in gaining access to the plant. He preferred to work under the cloak of night, but Kim didn't have the luxury of him sitting on leads that could result in her possible rescue.

The delivery truck he'd spotted earlier was backed in at one of the plant's docks. It was one of four other trucks similar in color and size that were already stationed at other docks. From his point of view, Sledge couldn't see what was going on behind the rig. He scampered across the lot to the far side of the trucks; he saw no movement around them. Staying low, he skirted by the hoods and stalked down the driver's side to the elevated concrete platform ahead.

A hint of cigarette smoke tainted the air as he drew closer. He spied no men on the platform but the stale stench indicated that they were in the immediate area.

For now, Sledge kept the 1911 tucked away. The weapon was his fail-safe and could be pulled at the drop of a dime. He was a quick draw and could go from unarmed to on target and firing within a second or less if the need arose.

Hunched at the dock wall near the back of the delivery truck, Sledge stood and scanned the platform. Sounds of motion confirmed that the dock had activity, but not close to him.

He craned his neck and glanced around the edge of the rig. The truck that had recently docked had two men standing near its enclosed, cuboid-shaped cargo area on the dock. One was dressed in plain clothes, jeans, and a t-shirt. The other was outfitted in a dark gray jumpsuit with Davidson Meats embroidered on the back and a matching, gray ball cap that was turned backward.

Both men conversed while smoking. They stood relaxed as clanging emitted from the hold of the rig. The exposed grip of a pistol poked above the plainly-clothed man's jeans, confirming Sledge's gut feeling that nefarious activities were transpiring on the grounds.

As much as he wanted to yank the 1911 out and go to work on removing the men, discretion would be a key factor here. Jumping the literal gun was foolhardy and wouldn't get Sledge any closer to solving this unfolding, and escalating, mystery.

Wheels clacked inside the truck. Both of the men standing on the dock cleared the path of the rig. Another plainly-dressed, bald man emerged seconds later with a pallet jack trailing him. It hauled a large, wooden crate across the platform to the gaping mouth of the retracted rollup door.

The bald man batted the dangling plastic flaps covering the entrance with his arm while wheeling the crate into the plant. He vanished from sight, leaving the other two men alone on the dock.

Sledge formulated a plan to gain entry to the building without being seen. This mission, as did most, required stealth and finesse. There were times a sledgehammer approach was needed, and this wasn't one of them.

He hunkered down in place and waited for the two chattering men to separate before making his move. The plant worker shifted toward the rear of the truck and worked on closing the door while the armed man took one last drag from his cigarette and flicked it to the ground before passing through the swaying, plastic flaps.

The plant's bay door wheeled down afterward, sealing off the building from the outside. Sledge glanced at the jumpsuit that finished securing the delivery truck and advanced across the dock toward him.

He pulled a phone from his pocket and viewed the screen while puffing on his half-smoked cigarette wedged between his bearded lips. His gaze never peered up from the device as he headed to the entrance at the far side of the platform.

While distracted by the device's screen, the man presented his back to Sledge and made for the entrance. It was go-time.

Sledge leaped onto the dock's edge and stalked the man. His footfalls were silent. He moved quickly, cutting the distance to mere inches without so much of a twitch or pause from his prey, allowing him to strike with flawless precision.

As the worker reached out for the silver door handle, Sledge made his move. He slipped one forearm under the man's chin and locked his fingers over his other arm. His other hand pressed against the back of the man's skull and shifted his ball cap askew; then Sledge squeezed.

His chokehold was set before the man could respond with a shout. He thrashed his body in terror, unable to view who had gotten the drop on him in his blind spot.

The phone clutched in his hand crashed to the dock's platform with a clatter. The cigarette followed, bouncing off Sledge's forearm to the ground.

Its tip burned his flesh, but that didn't loosen his hold. Sledge kicked the phone to the mound of discarded cardboard and pallets tossed into a corner.

He held firm and dragged the flailing man's body to the pile of waste. The restricted blood flow to his brain from the chokehold killed the man's fight. Before long, he had gone completely limp in Sledge's arms. He was unconscious and little more than dead weight.

Sledge hauled his limp body around the perimeter of the trash in the corner. The stacked pallets and bent cardboard provided cover to allow him to remove the jumpsuit from the plant worker and assume his identity.

In no time flat, Sledge had the uniform stripped from the man's body. He quickly maneuvered the garb up his stomach and fed both arms through the holes. Sledge then zipped up the front and put the cap on his head in the same way the man wore it.

One part of the ensemble that was an outlier was the man's badge. The two men looked nothing alike. Hair color, facial hair, and bone structure. All were vastly different.

The saving grace was the fact that the image imprinted on the laminated plastic was tiny and blurred unless viewed up close. From afar, it would play the part. If he was approached, then all bets would be off.

Chapter 42

PART ONE OF SLEDGE'S plan had gone off without a hitch. No one emerged onto the dock as he stepped out from the stack of pallets toward the entrance. Now, it was on to part two.

He approached the door and paused. There wasn't an access panel, telling Sledge he should be free to enter the building without restriction.

The door opened with ease. A blast of cool air punched him from the interior of the plant as he marched inside. His hand guided the door into the jamb so that it couldn't slam shut and draw attention his way.

Sounds galore engulfed the plant. The meld of machinery churning away made it hard to hear. The section of the plant he had entered appeared to be a staging area for inbound and outbound shipments as well as storage for boxes and other supplies.

Towering orange, steel uprights ran perpendicular to the bay doors. Their scale was immense, reaching to the ceiling and stretching as far as Sledge could see. Each had its four-tier shelves packed with crates, flattened meat boxes, and shrink-wrapped pallets that hid their contents.

Both men who delivered the wooden crate were gone. The area, for now, was clear of workers or armed men patrolling the storage section of the plant. It stood to reason that perhaps such measures weren't needed. After all, when thugs felt untouchable, it lured them into a false sense of invulnerability and caused them to become lax with security.

He adjusted the ball cap and pulled the bill down to block his face. With his head tilted slightly forward, he got on the move to see what he could find.

Vega was his main target. Any others were obstacles in his way in getting to Kim. It was unclear whether or not the Middle Eastern man was at the plant right then, but Sledge planned to scour every inch of the building to find out.

As he skulked down the corridor flanked by the mammoth steel racks, Sledge glanced at the pallets stored at ground level and up top. He paused and scrutinized the square-shaped containers. No markings of any kind were branded or painted onto the wood surface.

It was hard not to assume that the crates didn't house weapons or drugs. Seeing the armed delivery driver confirmed they were hauling something of value that Vega didn't want to be compromised.

Sledge wanted to pop the tops of the crates within reach, but that wasn't why he was there. Drugs and weapons were a distraction to his objective. Kim was the prize.

Instead, Sledge removed his phone and snapped as many pictures as he could while he continued to the end of the racks. No flash emitted from the device. Picture after picture was taken blindly as he trained the lens on the pallets he passed.

The two delivery men emerged from a different section of the plant ahead of Sledge. A cloud of cold air exploded out from the plastic hanging flaps as they conversed and funneled up the middle aisle toward the front of the warehouse.

He kept low and hid behind the containers on the floor while shifting to the edge. The men spoke at length and ventured further away, leaving Sledge's sight as they disappeared around one of the uprights.

That crate was important, but Sledge didn't know why. Not yet, at least. He scuttled past the upright's beam and made for the cold storage opening where the men had exited. The area was free of movement, allowing him to dip inside and investigate what they had dropped off.

Sledge parted the plastic and slipped inside the cooler. The temperature dropped instantly as the chilled gust of air brushed over his exposed skin. Between the jumpsuit and the clothes he had on underneath, it was more comfortable than cold.

More orange steel racks populated the cavernous cooler. Similar crates and pallets were stacked neatly on the shelves, but there was a slight difference in what resided in the space.

At the opposite end from where Sledge was were five men. Three were outfitted in black coats. They carried automatic rifles and acted like sentries, guarding the other two similarly dressed men who had their backs turned to him.

Sledge crouched and made for cover before being spotted. A towering stack of cardboard strapped to pallets hid him from view. He skirted outside of them to the far edge and waited for visual confirmation on whether or not he had found Vega.

Chapter 43

THE TWO MEN STOOD shoulder-to-shoulder while facing what Sledge guessed to be the crate that was just delivered. They leaned forward and chatted as the guards around them surveyed the area.

Come on. Give me a good look at your faces, Sledge thought as he patiently waited for the two mysterious men to turn.

From the back, the man on the right looked like Vega. He had the same haircut but that was a far cry from definitive proof.

Sledge had to get closer. There was no other option. Being idle for too long increased the risk of exposure and a deadly encounter with additional armed men that he assumed were roaming the plant.

As he plotted out the safest path toward the group, the two men turned and shook hands, confirming that the man on the right was indeed Vega. Bingo.

A coy smirk slid across Vega's face. He held something square in his hand, but Sledge couldn't make it out. It had to be a brick of cocaine or a similar drug, ready for distribution.

His partner's identity, the man over whom Vega fawned, was hidden by one of the guards. The way Vega smiled and bobbed his head in a subservient way to the man indicated he was of considerable authority to Vega, but who was he? That was the principal question.

Both men left the area by way of another entrance ahead of them. All three guards followed on their heels, leaving whatever product was delivered unattended.

Sledge made his move away from the cover of stacked boxes and down the open lane to the far aisle where the crate in question was.

One of the delivery men from earlier pushed through the plastic flaps into the cooler as Sledge crossed by the opening. He spotted Sledge immediately but didn't go for his weapon tucked in the waistband of his pants.

"What the hell are you doing back here?" He asked in a hoarse rasp. "This area is off limits."

In a blink, Sledge fell into character and faced the armed man. His head remained tilted forward to hide his face as if he was too scared to even look at him.

"I'm sorry, sir. I must have gotten turned around. This plant is pretty big."

The delivery man paused and then asked, "Are you new here? I don't recall seeing you before."

"Yes, sir, I am. Just started," Sledge replied in a submissive voice while keeping his head angled downward. "I do apologize if I'm in a restricted area. I'll vacate immediately."

Two steps forward were all Sledge could manage before being confronted by the gruff gunman. He snatched Sledge by the bicep and squeezed, then he asked, "What's your name?"

His head cocked to the right as he tried to view the badge that was turned askew, hiding the identity of the worker from whom Sledge had stolen the jumpsuit. He reached for the laminated plastic to flip it over when Sledge attacked.

He wrenched his arm from the delivery man's hand; then he rammed the heel of his palm up into his nose. The blow was quick and connected with such force that it snapped the man's head back and sent him stumbling onto the heels of his combat boots.

Sledge followed up with a jab to his throat, severing the gunman's ability to call for backup. Blood streamed from both of his nostrils down to his upper lip. He made a raspy, garbled hack and fumbled for the pistol wedged in the waistband of his pants while Sledge grabbed his wrist and landed a head-butt to his already bleeding nose.

A crack sounded upon impact. The guard's unsteady legs buckled. He collapsed onto the concrete, hitting it with a thump, and unconscious to the world.

The body had to be moved and concealed as Sledge didn't want to alert the plant to his presence. He grabbed the gunman's wrists and dragged him across the ground to an open section between two pallets of goods stationed under one of the uprights. His body was crammed into the tight opening well enough that he wouldn't be seen from the side, but he would be visible if viewed head-on. Time was running short. He had to move fast.

Sledge adjusted the jumpsuit and scurried to the far aisle, then down to the open crate that was left exposed by Vega. Upon his approach, the contents of what was stored in the container came into view, confirming Sledge's suspicion.

Rows of white square packages took up half the space of the crate while a mixture of rifles and handguns filled the remaining half. Drugs and weapons aided Vega's criminal efforts on top of the human trafficking.

But that wasn't Sledge's mission at the moment, he reminded himself. He had to leave the crate and track Vega down to get answers to questions that hinged on life and death.

He snuck out of the cooler and sought out Vega and his mysterious guest. Wearing the company jumpsuit allowed Sledge to blend in with the workers going about their business as if major arms and drug deals weren't being conducted right under their noses.

Maybe they knew about it and didn't care, or perhaps the men and women employed by the bogus business had been forced to comply. A large majority that Sledge saw working appeared to be foreign. It didn't matter one way or another. This operation was done for as soon as he got his hands on Vega.

Sledge spotted more of the men dressed in black coats ahead being funneled around a blind corner. His pace quickened and he tipped his head forward a hair more as he approached the junction.

A forklift drove up on Sledge's six o'clock. Its steel frame clanked and rattled as its rubber tires gripped the slick concrete surface. The load the lift truck hauled was a shrink-wrapped pallet of Davidson Meat boxes. Sledge wondered if perhaps the white containers had drugs stuffed inside as a way for Vega to move his product throughout the city, and possibly, the country.

Its horn sounded as it rumbled by Sledge, who cut down the aisle the men in black coats had taken and then hooked a left without slowing. The smell of propane tainted the air as the rickety lift truck went about its business.

At the end of the aisle were the three gunmen who stood outside an office. They meandered about with their rifles hanging from their shoulders.

It didn't seem as though they had much concern about anyone crashing their party.

The blinds of the office were tilted at an angle but not fully closed. From where Sledge stood, he counted three people inside speaking and dealing. Vega was one, but the other two were unknowns.

Sledge stopped at an elevated metal desk. Its top wasn't flat but rather, slanted. Papers fastened to clipboards populated the cold surface. He made it appear as though he was checking the invoices and production numbers printed on the sheets while he snuck infrequent glances toward the meeting that was taking place.

Vega opened the blinds and spoke to his criminal backers while waving his hand at the plant as if indicating something in his conversation. This gave Sledge a clear view of the gentleman who accompanied Vega, but not the third member whose long, black hair he glimpsed. It wasn't a man, from what Sledge could tell, but rather a woman.

As Sledge examined the man's face, a light bulb sprang on in his head. He had seen him before. His features had aged since their last encounter some twelve years prior, but Sledge never forgot a face, especially the face of someone who worked for his former employer, Cobalt, that appeared to be closer to finding him now than ever before.

Chapter 44

His body froze in place. He couldn't move, paralyzed by the sight of Shane, one of the instructors from Cobalt's criminal network who had betrayed their leader, Morgan Rojas, and sided with his son, Asher.

They were the backers of Vega's and Trent's Atlanta empire. It all made sense now and connected dots that, simply put, sent Sledge into a tailspin of worry. Kim's case had brought him back into the fold of a massive crime syndicate that blew everything out of the water, and not only complicated his investigation but also threatened to expose Sledge and Trixie if he was discovered.

"You there!" A heavily accented Spanish male voice sounded from behind Sledge as he put the clipboard down on the slanted top of the desk and backed away.

As Sledge turned around, he was confronted by one of the plant's workers outfitted in a matching jumpsuit but with a durag covering the top of his skull.

Rattled by the revelation of Cobalt being in his backyard, Sledge's brain malfunctioned, causing him to lose his train of thought and render him unable to respond coherently.

The man's gaze shifted down from Sledge's face to his badge. His eyes widened as he looked up, realizing Sledge wasn't the same person as the one pictured. He opened his mouth and shouted at the top of his lungs while backing away.

All three of the gunmen protecting the meeting between Vega, Shane, and the mysterious black-haired female, locked onto Sledge. They abandoned their posts near the entrance of the office and charged at him while removing the slings attached to their rifles.

Sledge unzipped the front of the jumpsuit and dug out the 1911 pistol while retreating. Vega's pompous grin morphed into a snarl as he exploded out of the office with Shane trailing him, the woman hidden behind the muscular physique of the instructor.

The foot soldiers rushed Sledge with their rifles shouldered. Vega boomed a commanding order over the ensuing bedlam of activity, that he wanted the intruder alive.

On the run, Sledge fired at the gunmen chasing after him. He nailed the man to his left in the right thigh, taking him out of commission. The other two ducked and scattered for cover wherever they could, then gave pursuit once more.

In a dead sprint, his mind flushed with angst, Sledge tore ass around the blind corner while glancing over his shoulder. The reports of gunfire sent workers in the area scrambling out of his path and the line of fire. They viewed him as the bad guy, which was ironic considering what sort of business was happening inside the plant.

Vega's foot soldiers bounded around the corner of the wall toting their already-shouldered rifles. Controlled bursts of gunfire popped off from the weapons, sending rounds zipping by him. Their shots targeted Sledge's arms and legs. The goal was to disable him long enough to be questioned. He knew the score and what that would entail, especially with Cobalt on-site.

Sledge ducked inside one of the freezers that had its door cracked open and slammed it shut. Two Hispanic women huddled together in the corner, dressed in full-body freezer suits and beanies. They glanced at Sledge; then hey diverted their gazes as he looked away from them.

He backed away from the large door with the 1911 trained on the entrance. His shoulder nudged a slab of butchered meat that dangled from hooks. Five rows of carved, processed animal flesh hung from the chains that connected to the ceiling above.

Each piece of meat Sledge bumped into sent the carcass into a pendulum swing. It distorted his view and made it harder to find a way out other than the way he'd come in.

The door swung outward and three of Vega's men stormed into the deep freezer. Sledge caught snippets of the armed thugs as the swaying beef disrupted his view. They fanned out, each taking a section of rows and advancing down the narrow lanes between the slabs of raw processed meat.

Sledge retreated toward the back of the freezer. The clinking chains and the whirling fans mounted to the walls and ceilings disrupted any noise that wasn't able to rise above the din of chilled air blasting into the hold.

Instead of discharging his pistol and revealing his position, Sledge opted for the gambler's dagger he had stored on his lower leg. He plucked the dagger from its sheath, ducked, and then shifted to the left.

Wielding both weapons in either hand, Sledge stalked the gunman tracking directly behind him. The team of killers refrained from speaking and moved steadily up their respective rows. They shoved the slabs of beef out of their way with the rifles while sweeping left to right.

Voices crackled over their radios, booming loudly inside the freezer. The jumbled mess of chatter disrupted the men long enough to allow Sledge to strike.

He shot upward from his crouched stance and jammed the tip of the blade deep into the man's neck. The tempered steel sliced through his carotid artery. Blood poured from the gash as Sledge pulled the knife free.

The gunman palmed his neck and stumbled back into one of the hanging chunks of beef. He then flopped to the grated floor below, hitting it with a heavy thump.

In one fluid motion, Sledge trained his attention on the second guard two rows across from him. The man shoved the carcass out from in front of him while trying to get a lock on Sledge.

As he made his approach and leveled the barrel of his rifle at Sledge's chest, Sledge threw the dagger. It twisted in the air, end over end. A blur of black steel gleamed in the overhead lighting that illuminated the deadly weapon.

It punched the gunman squarely in the chest and sent him tumbling back a few steps while his weapon angled toward the grates. Sledge wasn't sure if it was a kill shot, but it did enough to remove him from the board.

Heavy footsteps thundered behind Sledge, shaking the grates underneath him. Before he could turn and fight, the buttstock of the third gunman's rifle cracked Sledge's skull. It didn't make full contact, but instead was a glancing strike that caught a portion of his head, knocking the ball cap off and ringing his bell.

Sledge remained alert and coherent, though dazed, as the gunman sought a clean shot at his legs or arms. His feet moved and he ducked and weaved as the rifle barked from close range.

Fire flashed from the muzzle.

A single bullet speared the frozen air and nicked Sledge's outer left thigh and caught a scant bit of meat. It burned, but the swarm of adrenaline pumping through his veins dulled the pain.

The empty casing pinged off the grate as Sledge brought the 1911 to bear and fired. His adversary was formidable and knocked the barrel away with the rifle's buttstock, then launched forward with a knee thrust at his midsection.

Sledge absorbed the blow and bent over, but he rallied quickly and lunged at him. His shoulder dipped and he plowed into the gunman's chest, driving him back through the copious amounts of frozen beef that hung from the hooks.

With his back exposed, Sledge received shot after shot from the man's elbow stabbing his spine. Each strike felt like a hammer smashing his bones to pieces, but he didn't falter.

Both men fought, trying to outmaneuver the other. Sledge got a clear shot of the man's feet. His pistol aimed at the tip of his boot and he fired.

The bullet punched through the top of the boot. The man belted a painful roar as it connected with tissue and bone. His balance waned as he removed pressure from his injured foot while still trying to hold his position.

Sledge shot up and landed an uppercut under the wounded man's chin. His head flung back as he crumbled to the grate.

In his periphery, Sledge spotted guard number two writhing on the grates. The knife he hurled at the man was no longer protruding from his chest. It must have popped free when he hit the ground as the coat kept it from digging too far into the meat.

As men thundered toward the freezer from outside, Sledge lumbered out of the hanging slabs of beef to a walkway near the wall. He rushed down the length of the room and pushed his way out through a door.

It dumped him into a different section of the plant that looked vaguely similar to the warehouse from where he entered. He turned and slammed the door shut with a loud thud.

A set of wide bristle brooms leaned against the orange steel rack next to the entrance. They wouldn't work in securing the door and stalling the approaching mob of hired guns. To have a chance to escape and regroup, Sledge had to book it and make for the dock.

He took off in a wide stride then cut left, then right up one of the aisles. His feet moved a mile a minute as he focused ahead on the bay doors that were visible through the open parts of the storage racks.

The hairs on the back of his neck stood on end as the gunmen pursued him up the aisle. The multitude of footfalls increased from one pair to more than he could count.

Sledge rounded the steel leg of the rack and then hooked past more sealed crates set to ship out. Weapons fire discharged at his back. The bullets punched the closed bay doors and the wall ahead of him. He exploded out of the exit he first came through and emerged onto the dock.

At the moment it was clear of any immediate threats. No one was in the area, neither worker nor hired gun. Sledge grabbed one of the pallets and dragged it to the door, then wedged it under the handle to buy him some time.

As he backed toward the edge of the dock, the door quaked from inside. The pallet held in place under the barrage of beating fists and shoulders ramming it. Sledge then jumped from the dock and charged across the parking lot to the field in a mad dash, knowing full well that he had only seconds before the gunmen would open the other dock doors and continue their pursuit. The stakes of his mission had completely gone off the rails, leaving him unsure of what to do next beyond running for his life.

Chapter 45

COBALT WAS CLOSER TO Sledge than it had been in the last decade. Not only had he possibly exposed himself to the sheer force of the criminal juggernaut, he now put Trixie in danger as well if they discovered her, too.

His mind reeled with a tangled, tattered mess of mixed emotions as he raced back to his hideout in his truck. He wasn't so much scared for his life as he was for Trixie's. Sledge had vowed to keep her safe from Cobalt, and now, his missing person case had thrust them both into a precarious situation.

He pushed the Silverado hard through intersection after intersection, ignoring the changing lights. Tires squealed and horns honked as he straightened out the steering wheel.

What if they're following me? Sledge thought as he checked the rearview mirror, then both side mirrors. Other than cars and trucks that he pissed off while speeding around them, no vehicles gave him pause that Cobalt was on his heels.

The beating of his heart inside his chest was amplified tenfold. His normal spike of adrenaline during a mission wouldn't steal his nerve but surprises such as these didn't happen every day, especially when one wasn't looking for or anticipating their worst fear.

Sledge knew Vega had a big backer, but Cobalt was never considered. The clandestine organization was keen on working in the shadows, but he would have never thought they were involved in a crime ring this far from the compound. Is this something new that Asher implemented since taking the helm, or had Sledge unwittingly been a part of an organization capable of sex trafficking? Asher was as ruthless as they came, willing to make an example of Sledge by making him kill a little girl, but that was

Asher's action, not that of Morgan Rojas, who was explicitly against it. Sure, he knew Cobalt wasn't sending its assets out to spread world peace, but he always wanted to believe that the marks he was assigned to dispatch were Cobalt's way of taking out the trash.

His heart lurched at the possibility that his trusted mentor, Ronan, would willingly partake in such atrocities as human trafficking. During his time as an operator, Sledge was never informed of their other ventures, which he now understood included drugs, weapons, and the trafficking of women. How wide was Cobalt's reach? How deep did their trenches dig into the underworld? Sledge's head spun. Everything he thought he knew came crashing in on him. And worse than any other thought– how was he going to protect Trixie now?

Fuck! You stupid idiot!

He punished the steering wheel with his fist, angered by the ramifications of what he had now set in motion. Being careful and operating under an alias proved viable, but would it still stick and protect them?

The unanswered questions were many and came in waves that didn't let up. Sledge hadn't been thrown like this for a long time but knew now that because of him, Trixie could pay the ultimate price. *Because of him. Always because of him.*

Brakes locked the tires as Sledge torqued the wheel. The truck's rear swung wide in the road as he aimed for the drive leading down the alleyway. His boot transitioned to the gas pedal and pinned it to the floor.

Its engine revved as the pickup flew down the corridor at full tilt. As Sledge neared the side entrance to the warehouse, he thumbed the garage door and slipped inside, narrowly grazing the rubber bottom with the roof of the truck.

Once clear, Sledge closed the door, stopped the truck, slammed the shifter into park, and shut off the pickup. He sat there for a moment in the cab listening to the ticks of the hot engine beginning to cool off, attempting to wrangle in his scattered brain that was firing off scenario after scenario.

One big problem, among many that Sledge feared, was that his inconspicuous ride was now burned. He could no longer trust that it could be used without Cobalt being able to track it within Atlanta.

Part of Sledge had regrets for taking the case. He couldn't see the future to know what would be coming, and that was a big problem for both him and Trixie.

He removed the keys and got out of the truck. The hollow thud of the driver's door slamming into the body of the pickup echoed inside the warehouse. His boots clomped across the floor. A wild, unhinged gaze twisted his face in a mask of rage and uncertainty.

As he entered the living quarters of the warehouse, Trixie confronted him from the hallway leading to their bedrooms. He paced about, trying to come up with what to say to Trixie and what to do next.

"I take it from your angry demeanor that the meat packing plant was another dead end?" Trixie asked as she allowed him to vent his frustration. It took a second for his visible injuries to register as she met his gaze. "Oh, man. You're hurt. What happened? Did you find Vega?"

Sledge stared at her blankly at first. The words to respond escaped him. All he could see in Trixie was the child whose life he had ruined and changed forever. Another misstep on his part placed them both in the crosshairs of a much larger and more dangerous enemy than Vega could ever hope to be.

"I did, but we have a problem."

Trixie advanced toward Sledge as he averted his gaze to the floor. Dried blood matted the side of his skull where the buttstock of the rifle had cracked him. She examined the abrasion on his head and looked him over for other injuries.

"If by a problem you mean you taking a slight beating, then, yes, we do have a problem." She gripped his sweaty chin and turned his head to the right to inspect the extent of the damage. "But it doesn't appear too bad that we can't patch it up. Let me get the first aid kit and we can–"

He snatched both of her wrists. With eyes wide, Sledge peered deep into hers as guilt twisted his stomach into knots. "Just stop for a second, okay? I'm fine."

"You're not fine." Trixie jerked her arms from his taut hold. "Far from it. You come barreling in here like a madman then say you're fine? That doesn't work for me. What has gotten you so on edge? You're rattled, something I never thought I'd see, but here we are."

"I think I messed up, maybe. I don't know."

"How did you mess up?" Trixie's concern grew as she flanked him. "Will you please tell me what is up with you? I'm starting to think you've got a split personality or that hit to the head crossed wires because the smooth-talking Sledge I know has checked out and some crazy mad man, who is being all manic and spitting nonsense at me, is here now instead."

Sledge wanted to come clean and tell Trixie the truth, but how could he? If he revealed the lie it would further complicate matters that didn't need to be muddied any further right then. That wasn't priority one. Her safety was all that mattered to Sledge. His vow to protect her trumped everything else, and he had to make sure he stuck to that by any means necessary.

"We need to get out of the city at once."

"Out of the city? Why? You're starting to scare me."

"You're going to have to trust me on this," Sledge replied without further detail. "It's for your protection."

"Protection from what? Stop being so cryptic and tell me what has you so beside yourself, will you?"

He snapped at her without thinking before he opened his stupid mouth. "Trixie, just do as I say, all right? I'm trying to make sure you're safe."

"Well, now you're just pissing me off." She didn't care for his raised tone and sharp tongue. The frown and furrowed brow that formed indicated as much. Her nostrils flared as she folded her arms and huffed at him.

"First off, don't ever raise your voice at me like that again. I'm not a child and don't appreciate being spoken to as such." With her arms still locked against her chest, she continued, "Secondly, I'm not going anywhere until you tell me what it is that's put you so on edge. I deserve to know as much seeing as you wanted to bring me in on your operation here. If the heat is dialed up because of Vega, then say so and allow me to make the decision that is best for me. You're not my dad or protector. I'm a grown woman."

A grown woman? Sledge didn't see Trixie as anything other than the child he simultaneously ruined and saved. He couldn't get past it, regardless of how much he tried. Guilt had a way of doing that. But she was also right in the fact that he had brought her on board. For their partnership to work and function properly, they had to be upfront with each other. But Sledge couldn't completely unveil every detail to her. Not yet.

He caved, and then said, "You're right. Here's what's going on."

Chapter 46

Trixie listened as Sledge gave her the rundown of what had happened at the meat packing plant, minus Cobalt's involvement. He stuck to the topic of Kim's case. The blast of information did little to shake her resolve as she bobbed her head and soaked it in.

"So, you don't know for sure that Vega, and his employers, know who you are and where you live, then?"

"I don't," Sledge replied. "That's the problem here. I don't know the sort of connections Vega's partners have. We know he's connected since his backers are constantly bailing him out of jail and covering his tracks. It takes deep pockets to do such a thing, and it's hard to say what they will and won't be able to figure out with their extensive resources."

After a minute of silence, Trixie said, "Well. I'm not worried about them and you shouldn't be either. Nothing is saying that they even know who you are and where you live. I should know since I did a bit of digging on you and can't find much on the web, so you've done a pretty good job on that front."

Sledge's throat moved. "Oh, you have?"

"I have because I was curious about you, but that's beside the point right now." Trixie approached him and said, "We have to see this case through. I can't tuck tail and run knowing that we could have helped in rescuing Kim and didn't because of a little heat. Is there risk involved? Yes, there is but that's to be expected when evil people are involved. For once, I'd like to use my skills to help save people instead of screwing stupid businessmen out of cash who think they're smarter than me. I might be young, but I've done plenty of stupid things to last me a lifetime. Perhaps now I can use these fingers for good and bring that girl home."

Listening to Trixie made Sledge gleam with hope. Maybe he hadn't ruined her as badly as he'd thought. She had made mistakes and gotten involved with the wrong crowd, but she was willing to spit in the face of looming danger and hold the course to save the missing girl. It was enough to make him reconsider staying put and finishing the assignment. The Claymores counted on him to succeed, and although he didn't verbally promise to bring their daughter home, Sledge vowed to himself that he would give his all in trying to make it happen.

"You're right."

"I'm what?"

"I said you're right," Sledge said again, knowing full well she heard him correctly the first time. "We need to finish this case and find Kim. I let the unknown of what could happen to you get the better of me and it messed with my head. I know you're a grown woman and all, but I can't help but be a bit protective."

"That's because you're a good man. You may not think it, but it shows in your actions." Trixie flashed a warm smile, and then asked, "What's our next move, now that we got that settled? I doubt heading back to the Davidson Meat Plant would be worthwhile since they know it's on our radar now."

Sledge agreed with a head tilt. "Yeah. Vega isn't dumb." He then thought of Drake's phone and the two extra numbers listed in the incoming and outgoing call logs. "If I give you a few phone numbers, can you look them up and see what you can find out? Locations, names, etc. The whole gambit?"

"Sure. Are we talking prepaid numbers? Because those will be anonymous and shouldn't have names attached to them, though, if active, I might be able to at least get a location on the device. Also, if they're tied to Vega, it's certain that he's deactivated them and got new phones and numbers by now. These guys don't come across as amateurs."

"As far as I know, yes, they are prepaid and you're more than likely right, but we need to be sure about the numbers," Sledge replied. "The phone is in my office. The numbers will be in the call log. See what you can find out about each of the numbers."

"I'm on it." Before Trixie walked away, she said, "We should tend to that cut on the side of your head. It might need stitches."

"I'll take care of it. You focus on digging up what you can on those numbers."

"You're the boss."

Trixie retreated to the office as Sledge removed his phone and punched in Wentworth's number while walking down the hallway toward his room.

The phone connected and rang three times before he answered.

"Detective Wentworth."

"It's Sledge. You got a minute to talk?"

"A few. How did you get this number?"

"I just did." Sledge passed through his bedroom to the bathroom. After turning on the lights, the mirror above the sink reflected his haggard face from the incursion at the plant. "I've got news you're going to want to hear and act on."

"Oh, yeah? Like what?"

"Vega, and a shit ton of weapons and drugs." Sledge grabbed a rag from the cabinet, dampened it under running water, and then cleaned the wound on his head. "Consider this a Christmas present from me to you."

"So, you're Saint Nick, now?"

Sledge removed the phone from his ear, put it on speaker, and placed it on the edge of the white pedestal sink while he dabbed at the abrasion. "Sure, though, I'm neither fat nor jolly."

"Where are the guns and drugs located?"

"Davidson Meat Packing in town," Sledge answered as he gently wiped at the dried blood matted to his hair and skin. "You'll want to move quickly before he has a chance to remove any evidence from the premises. Limited time offer, I'm afraid."

"You've put eyes on the drugs and weapons?"

"I have. I even got into a bit of a skirmish with his men as well." Sledge squinted and got closer to the mirror while inspecting the damage to his skull. "That's why this is a time-sensitive matter. If you move now, it'll increase your chances of nabbing the goods before they can all be moved. It's your call, though."

Wentworth sighed into the phone. *"You're being straight with me here, right, Sledge? If I gather the cavalry and we barge in and find nothing, it's going to make my life a living hell and make the department look like incompetent fools. Neither of those is conducive to a long, viable, police career."*

"I've seen the drugs and guns myself. I'm shooting you straight, Wentworth. They were delivered by Davidson Meat trucks in wooden crates," Sledge answered as he pressed both hands on the top of the sink. "My guess is that they're using the plant as a front to move their product in and out. It could be one of many locations across the city and state that's doing so for all I know. Again, that's why I'm telling you to move your ass if you want to have the best chance of nabbing them red-handed."

"Have you found anything else out about Kim Claymore since we're sharing? The guns and drugs are great and will help against bringing down Vega if they're there, but Kim is my main priority at the moment."

"Not yet, but I'm still working on it," Sledge replied. "Do you have anything new you want to share?"

"Nothing concrete. I've got feelers out to my contacts on the streets. So far, no one has said a word. I think they're more scared of Vega and his partners than anything else."

Sledge parted the damp hair around the wound and then inspected it. "Maybe you need to squeeze them? A bit of pressure can yield results. That's been my experience anyway."

"Thanks. I'll keep that under advisement, but do me a favor and don't tell me how to do my job and I won't do the same to you," Wentworth shot back. *"The only reason I haven't ordered you to stay out of the investigation is that we're under the gun and need to find her. That's all I care about right now."*

The wound didn't appear too bad and the bleeding had stopped. Sledge let it be, popped a couple of aspirin for the headache, and said, "I don't think that would go down as you think it would, Detective. But that's beside the point. Our goals are aligned. Get to the plant and check it out before that piece of garbage can remove the evidence. If you find out anything new, hit me up. I'll do the same."

"Watch yourself, Sledge. As I told you before, Vega is a heavy hitter and not to be taken lightly. You may hit hard, but he can knock you down for good."

"Thanks for the warning. Talk soon."

Sledge ended the call and left the bathroom with his phone in hand. The bloody rag remained wadded up on the edge of the sink as he exited his bedroom and made a beeline for the office.

Trixie sat in his chair with her laptop stationed to her right. Her fingers moved at a blistering speed as she switched from her rig to his keyboard.

"Tell me you've got me something new on Vega?"

"Those numbers listed in the phone are toast. Deactivated so that's a dead end." Trixie jumped from one computer to the other, pounding the keys. "Did you handle that wound on the side of your head yet, or are we going to ignore it?"

"It's not that bad. I cleaned it up and popped a few aspirins. We're good."

"I'm not so sure that constitutes good, but okay." She spun around in the chair and slid the phone back to him. "What do we do now that the phone is a no-go?"

Sledge thought on it for a moment then realized he had a contact he could tap. It was a long shot on if he'd help him or not, but Sledge was at the end of his rope, and desperate times called for desperate measures.

"I've got a contact I can reach out to and see what he knows. He supplies me with surveillance gear and other goodies while also keeping an ear to the ground."

"It's better than what we currently have."

"That it is. Keep scraping the web. If you find anything out, let me know."

"Of course. If you need me to run any names or location intel, hit me up. I'll be right here working my magic." Trixie cracked her fingers.

Before leaving the office, he said, "Also, if any of the perimeter alarms are tripped, I want you out of this building ASAP. There's an emergency exit at–"

"I know where it's at. I've made myself familiar with the building," Trixie replied. "Your security system is legit as well. State of the art. I'm not surprised seeing what all you do."

He was glad she made herself at home and felt safe there. That meant the world to him. "Good. Keep those eyes and ears open. I'll be in touch soon."

"Sure thing."

Chapter 47

HIS 1970 CHEVROLET CHEVELLE SS roared down Atlanta's city streets. The bulky but nimble muscle car ran smooth and solid, despite needing a bit more work on the engine. A slight clatter sounded from under the hood, but it didn't detract from the vehicle's performance; it responded to the slightest pressure on the gas pedal and a turn of the wheel with his pinky.

Oscar's Pawn Shop was coming up, past the intersection, and down the road about half a mile. It had been several months since Sledge had spoken to him. Their last encounter was a result of him needing additional ammo and gear for a job that Oscar happily provided. Money was king and Oscar was more than willing to relieve Sledge of his.

Instead of parking out front on the curb, Sledge opted for the alley. He stowed the Chevelle behind a dumpster and walked the remaining way toward the sidewalk to his doorstep.

Similar to Mac's place, Oscar's shop was fortified with steel bars mounted behind the windows and on the door. One big difference was that Oscar had tons of surveillance within the building. He didn't shy away from keeping a loaded .357 Magnum revolver and Mossberg 590 12-gauge shotgun under the sales counter for those criminals stupid enough to attempt robbing him.

The store had two guests inside speaking with Oscar at the counter. Both the woman and the man looked sketchy in their tattered dirty rags. They twitched as if on drugs that had them paranoid. The woman jerked her chin over her shoulder at Sledge and stared at him with large wild eyes while her partner peddled their box of electronic components that peeked above its top. Sledge figured the contents stuffed in the box were hot and that the duo was trying to unload them for cash as was the case in other pawn shops the world over.

Oscar peered at the items causing the sides of the box to bulge outward with a deadpan stare. Both of his large hands rested on the counter. To most, he was an intimidating man and commanded respect just from his sheer size. He stood a staggering six-foot-six and was all muscle. His head was shaved and his goatee was neatly trimmed to a thin line that outlined his mouth and chin. Looking at the big bull, one would think he played football in his past life, and they'd be right. High school and then college ball at LSU. Eventually, he fell in with the wrong crowd which led him into a seedy underworld of crime and mayhem that wrecked his football career and damaged his future.

He glanced away from the couple and spotted Sledge milling about the various pawned items on display. A slight head bob between the two men served as an informal greeting.

"Hey. Right here," the tweaker said as he snapped his fingers in front of Oscar's face. "Do we have a deal? These are some quality products that you'll be able to move. No problem."

"Come on, babe. Let's take our stuff and go," the woman said while grabbing her partner's shoulder. "He doesn't want what we have and he isn't going to change his mind. We can't help that he isn't smart enough to see a good thing when it's right in front of him."

Her partner wrenched his shoulder from her hand and shouted in her face. "Will you shut up and let me handle this? I don't remember asking you for a damn thing."

Sledge grinned at the bickering addicts and stayed out of the conversation. There was no need to intervene. Oscar had it under control even if it didn't appear that way.

"I think it's time you two take your box of stolen car radios you've lifted out of my store. Now," Oscar finally said in a deep commanding voice.

"Stolen!" the crazed man screamed back at Oscar, vexed by the insult. "How dare you insult us like that? I can't believe what this monkey said to me."

The slanderous remark boiled Sledge's blood. He glared at the man who was sinking further into anger and clenching his fists.

Oscar, on the other hand, remained calm, even after being insulted by the pasty, scrawny, white male who was not even in the same realm as him.

"First of all, the serial numbers have been scratched off the few radios I can see on the top. I imagine the rest are similar," Oscar said as he squared his shoulders at the two belligerent patrons. "No reputable business will want that junk in their shop, including me. Secondly, if you speak to me like that again, I'll knock all of your teeth out of your skull and you'll be on a soft foods diet for the foreseeable future." He jabbed his thick finger at the entrance. "Now take your box of junk and get out of my store while you can still do so on your own."

The woman took the request to heart and backed away from the counter, but her partner wasn't as easily swayed. He held his ground, shoved the box to the side, and lifted the front of his shirt while also going for the register to his left.

Sledge moved to intervene but Oscar beat him to it. The big man snatched the raggedy man's wrist before it could reach the register. He then pulled the .357 Magnum from under the counter and wedged the barrel of the revolver to the man's forehead as he clutched a tiny .38 Special that paled in comparison.

Whimpers sounded from the woman who retreated from the man held under threat of having his brains removed from his skull. She glanced at Sledge and then back at the two men at the counter.

"Put the gun on the counter, slowly. Do it now," Oscar said while keeping the .357 in place.

"Sure, sure. Just take it easy, okay?"

Sledge held back and watched as the rail-thin man put the revolver on the counter in front of Oscar.

Oscar vehemently said, "Now, take your shit and leave. The gun stays. Consider it payment for me having to have tolerated your presence for this long. If I ever see either of you in my store again, you won't be walking out of here. Am I understood?"

The duo nodded but didn't venture a verbal response.

"Grab the box and come on Jeffry." The woman hoofed it across the store past Sledge to the entrance.

Her partner clutched the box and retreated after her as Oscar thumbed the hammer forward on the .357 and placed the weapon on the counter near his newly acquired .38 Special.

They couldn't get out of the store fast enough, shoving the door open and scrambling out onto the walkway.

"Another satisfied customer I see," Sledge said while tipping his head at the front of the shop. "Your customer service skills are improving. I'm impressed. I thought for sure you would have cracked his head for making that comment."

"I wanted to, but that's rather bad for business when you're punching folks in the head." Oscar stowed the .357 and .38 Special under the counter and smirked. "You were a lot of help. Did you enjoy the show?"

"It's quality entertainment. Some of the best work I've seen out of you."

"Doubtful, but okay."

The men shook hands and chuckled at the incident. They had forged a good rapport throughout the years; it had started rocky but eventually smoothed out.

"What's up Sledge man? I thought I heard that beast of a car you have rolling by."

"I figured I'd grace you with my presence since it's been a few months. You're my favorite gun runner and enforcer turned legit businessman in town."

"Funny. How many others do you know?"

Sledge tapped his finger on the counter. "Aside from you, I know none."

Oscar flashed his million-dollar smile and then shook his head. "Come on, Sledge. Stop jerking me around. What are you doing here?"

"Business. You got a few minutes to speak?"

"Well, it's business hours. Is this a conversation that needs to be kept under wraps and done in private?"

"Probably best if it is. I wouldn't have dropped in on you like this right now if it wasn't important. You know that."

"Whatever. You've done this several times," Oscar shot back while moving toward the open slot within the counter. "And it's always for a good reason. New case?"

Sledge couldn't disprove the statement. Most times, he had to move quickly or lose out on whatever lead he was after. "Yeah. A missing girl that's been gone now for over a week."

"That's a tough one," Oscar replied, cringing at the news. "Abduction or run away?"

"Abduction and human trafficking."

"No shit? You for real?"

"Yes. I wouldn't be yanking your chain on this, big dog."

As the deadbolt clicked on the door, the life ran out of Oscar. He had a ten-year-old daughter whom he got once a month from his former girlfriend. She was the apple of his eye and the center of his world.

"That human trafficking bullshit is about as bad as you can get. I've heard horror stories that would ice the blood in your veins." Oscar advanced on Sledge who faced him. "But what does that have to do with me? I know nothing about that world. You should know that already, though."

"I do, but I'm not asking about that," Sledge replied.

Oscar twiddled his fingers at him. "Come on. Stop beating around the bush and tell me what you're after so I can open my shop back up. I'll have you know that you're the only person I do this for. Don't make me regret it."

"The missing girl is tied to Marko Vega and his crew. I need to know everything you know about him, and I need some gear."

"Shit, brother." Oscar dipped his chin and pinched the bridge of his nose. "You sure know how to step in the shit, don't you? He's next-level bad news."

"It comes with the territory." Sledge then asked, "Can you help me out? That girl's life depends on it."

"You're a real bastard for coming here and dumping this into my lap. You know that, right?"

"I do, but I'll make it worth your while. I always do and I keep my word."

Oscar moved around him to the opening within the counter; then he motioned for Sledge to follow. "Are you coming, or are you going to stand there wasting time?"

Chapter 48

THEY LEFT THE SALES floor and ventured into the darkened back room of the shop, but that wasn't their final destination. A hidden door within the wall concealed by a tower of leaning boxes and a storage rack awaited the duo.

"You're positive the missing girl is tied to Vega?" Oscar asked as he slid the four-foot-tall storage shelf away from the door.

"Oh, I'm positive. There's no doubt about it." Sledge hung back as Oscar opened the door and stepped inside.

Lights in the ceiling above flickered on. The low buzz of electricity coursing through the halogen tubes filled the large room.

A variety of weapons lined both sides of the walls. Everything from pistols and shotguns to rifles was seated in their mounts, ready to be plucked. In the center of the room was a stainless-steel table with ammo and boxes of tactical gear stored under the long run that went from front to back.

The door closed and locked. Now, their business could be conducted.

"Did you have anything to do with his partner, Trent?" Oscar asked. His arms folded across his broad chest and he leaned on the edge of the lower cabinets that had gunmetal steel grates covering the fronts. "I heard the old boy had taken a nosedive from the roof of a building to the concrete. Splat. Messy stuff."

"I can neither confirm nor deny the fact that he opted to jump instead of talking. Their runner, Drake Connor, was somewhat useful, but not by much."

"Okay, Sledge." Oscar lowered his arms and braced the heel of his hand on the lip of the cabinet. "You're playing with fire here, bud. Those boys are connected, and bankrolled by some powerful people who don't mess around. I don't know who exactly, but word has it that they're big-time, international and shit. Someone who will mess up your world without thought."

"Yeah. So I'm finding out." Sledge then asked, "What do you know about Vega and his operations? Any clue as to where he might be housing the girl? I hit up one of his places recently, a meat packaging plant. I found guns and drugs. That was it. Granted, I didn't have time to fully check the place out."

Oscar thought about it and then pushed up off the cabinet. "I don't know off the top of my head. It's beneficial to one's health not to poke around the bear's cave. You tend to get mauled when you do."

"Again, I don't have the luxury of letting this go. The family that hired me to find their daughter is counting on me to succeed. I don't want to let them down, or the girl."

"You know as well as I do that the odds of her still being in Atlanta are slim to none." Oscar was the realist between them. His outlook, although bleak at times, aligned with what the facts presented to him. "If Vega did indeed snatch her up, she's probably been bought and moved on. I hate to say it, but you're chasing your tail on this one."

Sledge shrugged. "Either way, I have to be sure. Her family deserves as much and that slimeball and the people he works for need to be taken out."

"And you're the man for the job, huh? The lone gunslinger coming into town to clean it up?" Oscar's condescending remarks weren't without warrant, seeing as that's how Sledge viewed his mission of atonement for the people he slaughtered at the behest of Cobalt. "Don't get me wrong, brother. I think it's amazing what you do for folks, helping them as you do while putting your life on the line. It's commendable but also batshit crazy. Each case you get seems to get more dangerous."

"If I didn't know any better, I'd think you cared for my well-being."

"You're a good customer who pays and doesn't give me shit, most times." Oscar extended his arms out to encompass his selection of death-dealing weapons and gear. "Since you're determined to find an early grave, I might as well help keep you alive for as long as I can."

Sledge glanced over the array of guns, knives, and tactical gear Oscar had displayed and stored under the tables between them. "Don't worry, brother. I'm not going to bleed you dry. I still have a good bit back at the warehouse."

"What are you after? Body armor? Rifles? Knives?"

"A ballistic tactical vest, mainly. One that has storage and stopping power. Considering who I'm going up against, it might not be a bad idea to have the proper attire on hand."

Oscar smirked and ducked below the table. "I got something I think will work for you." He fiddled below while Sledge spied the assortment of pistols and rifles behind him.

"How's Trina doing?" Sledge asked while he waited. "It's been a while since I've seen her last."

"She's growing like a weed every day. I swear, each time she comes to stay with me, she's aged like two years. It's crazy."

"That doesn't surprise me."

"Here we go." Oscar stood and placed a black armored vest on the tabletop. "This is going to be the best vest I have on hand."

Sledge turned toward the table and said, "Now we're talking."

"This is the Sentry Plate Carrier Package from AR500 Armor." Oscar went through his normal sales pitch like he always did, even with Sledge. "It comes with a level III body armor, a MOLLE chest-mounted pistol holder that's universal, so that 1911 you cherish will fit right in." He gave a wry grin and continued. "It also has a double M4/AR-15 magazine pouch and a double pistol magazine pouch. The vest is made from 600D nylon to keep it light, but it's also rugged. You've got your adjustable padded shoulder straps, a drag handle, hydration tube/radio guides, and quick-release side buckles. This is the definition of the kitchen sink."

"Does it wash and fold clothes and fetch beer from the fridge?"

"It damn well could on future models."

"That's a huge selling point. May I?"

Oscar pushed the vest across the table to him. "Be my guest."

"Thanks." Sledge gripped it by the shoulder straps and let the vest hang from his hands. "I know it's a lot to ask considering it involves Vega, but would you mind tapping any contacts you have for where I might look? If it's going to be too dangerous for you to do that, then don't. I don't want to put a crosshair on your back, or your family."

"There are risks in everything we do and the decisions we make," Oscar replied as Sledge tried on the vest. "I can't promise what I'll dig up and how viable it will be, but I'll hit up a few contacts of mine and see what they might know."

"That's all I ask, brother." Sledge snapped the buckles in place and tested out the vest's comfort and how well he could move while wearing it. "I'm still looking, too, but two heads are better than one. Well, three if you count the detective on the case."

"As I said, no promises on what I find, but I will at least look into it." Oscar pointed at the vest. "It's nice, right? Comfortable and doesn't hinder your movement."

Sledge unbuckled the straps and then pulled the vest over his head. "It's nice, just what I was after. Hell, I would have taken it on the sales pitch alone. I think you're in the wrong line of work."

"Tell me about it but here we are." Oscar tipped his head toward the vest. "What else do you need for your vigilante mission?"

"Ammo."

"The usual, I take it?"

"Yep."

Oscar gathered three fifty-round boxes of .45 ammo and two cases of 5.56 NATO munitions for the AR-15 rifle he had back at his place. Each was placed on the table next to the vest.

"Anything else while you're here?"

"A tank if you have it?"

"I'm fresh out but I do have some on order."

Sledge looked over the stock of firearms one final time before answering. "No. I think this is good. The vest was my main concern and one can never have too much ammo on hand."

"That is something we can agree on."

"How much for the lot?" Sledge reached into his front pants pocket and removed a folded clump of bills.

"Say two thousand and I'll throw in a few magazines as well."

"Sounds fair." Sledge counted out three thousand and tossed the money onto the table.

"That's too much. I said two."

"Yes. Two for the gear and ammo, and one thousand for your time and trouble about Vega and the girl." Sledge held his hand up, stopping Oscar from refusing the extra money as he knew he would. "I know how you are, but this time is different. The risk is higher so you should be compensated for it. If you decide it's too much exposure, keep the grand and do whatever you want with it, or put it on my tab. I don't care. It's yours to do with as you please. Maybe buy that daughter of yours something nice. You're a good dad and man, Oscar."

Oscar palmed the crumpled bills and then stuffed them into the back pocket of his jeans. "Thanks, Sledge, but no need to suck up with compliments. You're already throwing money at me."

"I get told I do that a lot," Sledge smirked at Oscar who grabbed the cases of ammo.

"Because I'm such a great guy, I'll even give you a hand taking this out to your car."

"Don't expect a tip."

Sledge followed Oscar out of the weapons hold to the stockroom carrying the vest and the boxes of .45 ammo. "I know what you're up to but I'm not looking to part with my baby out there. It's not going to happen."

"Come on now. I only want to help you out, bud." Oscar portrayed a person who had been offended by the remark as they crossed the cluttered stockroom and passed through the exit to the alley. "My intentions are noble."

"Yeah, right. So says the cat that wants to help out the injured canary." The heavy exit door slammed hard into the jamb with a loud thud. "Hey, I think you have a feather sticking out the side of your mouth."

Oscar ignored Sledge's reply as he soaked in the shiny black body of the Chevelle. "That right there is a thing of beauty. You've done an amazing job in taking care of her. Sure beats driving that truck you have."

"So I'm told." Sledge moved ahead of Oscar, who was infatuated with the muscle car, and placed the ammo and vest on the ground. Then he pulled the keys from his front pocket and unlocked the trunk. "You can put that ammo back here."

"This is something for you to keep in mind, but if you ever feel the need to sell her, hit me up first." Oscar put the boxes in the corner of the trunk and stepped to the side as Sledge stowed the remainder of the gear in the hold. "That's all I ask. Give your boy first dibs since we're pretty much family and all."

"I'll keep that in mind." Sledge closed the trunk lid and turned toward Oscar who snapped out of his trance. "Seriously though, thanks for everything. Let me know what you find out on Vega as quickly as possible."

"I got you, brother. Like you, I try not to make promises, but I'll kick over a few rocks and see what comes scurrying out."

"That's all I'm asking."

The two men shook hands and parted ways. Oscar backed down the alley and made for the side entrance to the building as Sledge opened the driver's side door to the Chevelle. His phone vibrated from his back pants pocket. He removed the device before getting into the car.

Trixie's number flashed on the screen. He answered.

"Hey. Did you find something out?" No response came from Trixie, but Sledge could hear her breathing into the receiver, so he thought it was her. "Is something wrong? Hello?"

A calm male voice replied instead of hers. *"If you don't want to find bits and pieces of your friend scattered across Atlanta, listen close and do exactly as I say. Am I understood?"*

Sledge's throat tightened. His mind raced as he tried to figure out who was on Trixie's phone and more importantly, what they did with her.

"Yes. I understand."

Chapter 49

THE PHONE CLICKED OFF, ending the call with the well-spoken man and thrusting Sledge into a panic-induced race to save Trixie. He dropped down into the bucket-style racing seat and then slammed the heavy car door shut. In less than five seconds, Sledge had the Chevelle started and was flying down the alley to the street.

He merged onto the street without tapping the brake. The muscle car's tires gripped the asphalt as he cut the wheel hard right. He stomped the clutch down and slammed through the gears as he gunned it to the approaching intersection.

His instructions were simple. Bring twenty thousand dollars in cash to the supplied address in one hour. Do not contact the authorities or arrive one second late, or she would die.

Sledge peered at his watch while darting in and out of traffic. It was 2:15 p.m. He had fifty-five minutes remaining.

As he headed back to his warehouse, Sledge focused more on the man's voice and who he was rather than worrying about the funds. He had money stashed in his safe, more than enough to handle the request and save Trixie's life.

What grated on his nerves, more than not knowing how they got to her, was who exactly the men were. Sledge tossed out Vega and Cobalt since that wasn't their M.O. A ransom request was out of character for both. If they knew who Sledge was, the conversation would have gone down differently.

No. This was someone else who had ties to him or her. The only logical explanation Sledge could see was that it had to do with the people Trixie had screwed over on her last job. She made enemies that would not stop until they got what they were after and punished her for such betrayal.

After collecting the required amount of cash from his safe and stuffing the loot into a duffle bag, Sledge was back on the road to rendezvous with the men who held Trixie. He had seven minutes to spare as he pulled into the construction site of a new office building that was underway.

Its metal skeleton was visible in spots where the concrete walls hadn't been put into place. No workers were on the grounds as Sledge cruised through the yard.

Stacks of dense, red, steel beams dotted the rough landscape. Mounds of dirt and large machinery flanked him on either side. He drove around the back end of a bulldozer and headed for the site office located near the main construction area.

The single-wide trailer had two cars parked out front, a brown Ford Bronco and a nicer, black Lexus sedan. No armed men were in sight as Sledge rolled to a stop at the end of the trailer next to the Lexus.

He turned the engine off, removed the keys, grabbed the duffle bag from the passenger seat, and then got out of the car. The meld of sounds from the city played as background noise as he closed the car door and made his way toward the stack of concrete steps placed at the foot of the entrance.

Sledge hoped Trixie was okay and not harmed. Whoever had taken her didn't know about the problems they now found themselves facing. Soon, they would.

The door swung open. One of the bald, tattooed men that Sledge crossed in Mac's shop the day he rescued Trixie stood waiting for him. He clutched what looked to be a Glock 17 in his right hand while his left palm pressed on the inside of the door to keep it open. The jugheads didn't get the message he'd communicated before. Too bad for them as this time, he wasn't going to be as forgiving.

"Hold it right there," the bald, tattooed man said as he glowered at Sledge. "Is that the money you were told to bring?"

"It is. Twenty-k in cash." He craned his neck to try and peer into the trailer. "Where's the girl at?"

"Around." The tattooed man stepped out of the doorway and allowed his partner, whom Sledge had kicked the crap out of at Mac's shop, to emerge from the trailer and scuttle down the steps.

He closed in on Sledge and ripped the bag from his hand. The same glare contorted his features as he patted him down from top to bottom.

His 1911 was removed, as was the combat knife he had sheathed at the small of his back. Sledge made no moves against the disgruntled man who stripped him clean of his tools and then escorted him up the steps and into the trailer.

Inside, a man dressed in a navy blue pinstripe suit sat on the edge of a desk. His hair was perfectly sculpted and he was clean-shaven. He adjusted the thin, black-framed glasses on the bridge of his nose and then stood.

A devilish smile formed as he stared at Sledge while maintaining his distance from him. He cleared his throat and spoke while tapping the face of his Rolex watch.

"Cutting it a bit close, but we're pleased to see that you made it with time to spare."

It was the same man who had threatened to chop Trixie up and pepper the metroplex with her body parts.

Sledge glanced about the cluttered, stinky mess of the trailer for Trixie, but he didn't spot her. The building had a stench about it that smelled of body order and fast food.

Filing cabinets lined each side of the wall. A square folding table near the doorway housed stations of two-way radios that were scuffed and worn. A water cooler caked in dust was dry as a bone and had no cups lodged in its holder.

The desk behind the suited man had papers scattered across its top in disarray. Whoever the site manager was, he did a piss-poor job of being organized and tidy.

A closed door in the back right corner caught Sledge's attention. That had to be where they were keeping Trixie.

"She's safe, for now," the suit said while tipping his head at the closed door. "I must say, though, that she's gotten herself into a bit of a mess. Kids these days don't understand the consequences of their actions. That's partly why we have so many bad eggs in the world."

"If it's all the same to you, I'd like to get this over with," Sledge replied, not wanting to hear the man drone on. "You've got your money. I want the girl."

"Straight to the point. No fluff. That's how business is done." The suit directed his gaze to the thug holding the duffle bag. "Are we good?"

He skimmed the top layer of the cash stuffed into the duffle and then gave a thumbs up. "Looks like it's all here."

"I imagine it is," the suit replied as he leveled his sights back on Sledge. "Our friend wouldn't be dumb enough to show up thinking he could screw us over. Not after promising what would happen to her if he tried anything other than what we told him to do. That wouldn't work out too well for Trixie's future."

The bald thug marched across the trailer and disappeared into the back room. Multiple voices spoke at once, indicating that the men had more than just Trixie in there. Two were female and the other sounded like a small child.

One was Trixie as Sledge picked up on her barking at her captors. The other woman's strained, frightened voice seemed familiar, but Sledge couldn't place where he had heard it as it melded with the din of shouting.

"Who else is with Trixie?" Sledge asked.

"Bait," the suit answered as he smoothed out the front of his jacket. "We had to draw Trixie out of her hole. My boys here circled back to her neighbor who lives in her building across from Trixie. It doesn't pay to stick your nose into other peoples' business."

Sledge remembered her now; she was the young woman with the small child. Camella was her name. Sweet and sincere, and now paying an awful price for caring about her friend who had gotten tangled up with the wrong crowd.

Trixie was escorted out of the room by the bald thug. A nasty bruise formed on the side of her face, signaling that they had put their hands on her again. She jerked at her arm but couldn't escape the bald man's taut grip.

"Are you okay?" Sledge asked Trixie while maintaining decorum, even though he wanted to attack and kill the three men in the most savage of ways.

As soon as she put her eyes on Sledge, Trixie lowered her head in shame and simply nodded. Her embarrassment and shame clung to her like a second layer of skin that she wore openly.

"See. There she is, mostly unharmed," the suit said with a smile. "She's a bit of a handful, that one, and well, her friend and kid as well. Loud and mouthy."

Sledge wasn't about to abandon the mom and boy into the hands of such men. That wasn't going to happen. "I want the woman and child as well. You no longer need them since they've served their purpose."

"I'm afraid that isn't how this is going to go. You paid for this little pain in the ass alone, not the woman and boy." The suit playfully flickered Trixie's purple hair.

She wrenched her head away from his hand which was withdrawn. "Don't touch me."

"Feisty."

"I didn't know you had them as well," Sledge replied.

"Oops. Did I not mention that? Like your gun and knives, the boy and woman are tools to be used. When they are no longer needed, they are disposed of."

That wasn't going to happen. Sledge couldn't and wouldn't allow it, so he tried to reason his way out of the situation instead of resorting to violence.

"I don't know who you are or who you work for, but I'd rather things not get messy here. Let's come to an amicable conclusion where everyone walks out of here alive and no one has to be put in an early grave."

Sledge's warning hit on the men whom he pounded on the day prior, but their handler in the suit wasn't moved as he stayed the course and held his ground, unwilling to compromise.

"You were right about our friend," the suit said to his men who flanked Trixie and Sledge. "He's either stupid or doesn't value breathing." He approached Sledge without fear or hesitation and got within inches of him. His arrogance would be his downfall and bite him in the ass. "You know, on second thought, I think I'm going to bury you and the bitch with the woman and boy, but not before you watch as they are hacked into tiny pieces."

The sudden shift of the man's demeanor wasn't surprising to Sledge. Criminals, regardless of how well-dressed they were and spoke, were still conniving trash who couldn't be trusted. He'd planned for the deception, knowing that his sort of ilk didn't care for loose ends.

Sledge gave Trixie a quick look; then he trained his heated and focused stare back at the suit before him. "I want you to know that what's about to happen is on your shoulders. You should have cut your losses and forgotten about the girl because now, none of the three of you are going to leave this trailer alive."

A second passed before the suit guffawed and threw his head back in laughter. Trixie bunched both hands into fists, ready and waiting for Sledge to make his move.

"I'm done dealing with this Neanderthal," the suit said as he backed from Sledge and turned toward the desk. "Take them outside and dispose of the bodies while I check in. I want this wrapped up and finished quickly, but quietly."

As the tattooed man grabbed for his wrist, Sledge made his move. He stepped forward then drove his elbow back into the man's face. It connected with a meaty thump that sent him stumbling backward.

The man's arms sprang up in defense as he clamped his eyelids shut and gnashed his teeth. A guttural growl surfaced as blood ran from his nose.

Trixie stomped the bald man's foot that was holding her hostage; then she rammed him in the chest with her shoulder as he aimed his Glock at Sledge. She drove her legs and swatted at his face with her fists, putting her life on the line to keep him from firing.

Sledge kept the pressure on and made short work of the tattooed man who was unable to match his speed or block the volley of targeted strikes to his jaw and stomach. Each blow hit with a devastating force that crippled his attempts at launching a counterstrike and ended with Sledge prying the man's gun from his hands and putting two in his chest.

The reports boomed inside the trailer as the suit ran for the entrance. Sledge whipped around and swiped his legs out from under him, planting the frantic businessman face-first onto the laminated tile floor.

A yelp sounded from Trixie as the bald man cracked her in the skull with his Glock. She crashed into the wall and then dropped to the floor. He trained his weapon at her and lined up a kill shot as Sledge fired off a salvo at him.

Three rounds exploded from the barrel of the gun, one right after the other. Brass popped out the side of the weapon and pinged off the floor. Each bullet found a home in the bald man's torso, killing him upon impact.

A slight ringing flourished in Sledge's ears from the weapon discharging. It didn't stop him from hearing the suit scrambling to his feet and making for the closed door of the trailer.

Sledge placed a bullet into the back of the man's knee before he could flee. His leg gave and sent him hard to the floor. He belted a scream of agony while clutching his bloody leg.

Trixie shook off the blow and tried to stand. She used the wood panel of the wall to pull her torso up as Sledge towered over the groaning suit. She gathered her legs under her and steadied her balance.

"Christ!" the suit said as he writhed in the dirt collected on the tile at the entrance. "Ah! My knee!"

"I told you what was going to happen," Sledge said as he viewed his handy work done to the businessman's leg.

No witty rebuttal came from the suit. Only groans and moans of pure agony leaked from the injured man's mouth.

A phone rang but it wasn't Sledge's. The ring tone was different from his. He glanced about the trailer and spotted the suit's phone on the floor. An unknown caller displayed on the screen as it rattled against the tile and blared out its rhythmic beat.

With the gun aimed at the suit, Sledge retrieved the device and answered the call.

"Is it finished?" a robotic voice asked. "Have the girl and the man been dealt with?"

Whoever was on the other end of the phone used a voice modulator to change their voice to that of a robot.

"Not exactly, but your man dressed in the navy-blue pinstripe suit isn't faring too well. It's doubtful that he's going to make it. He got a nasty injury. Fatal even."

"You're him, the one who is messing with my affairs and protecting the girl."

"That's correct. I warned your men to forget about the girl and move on. They didn't heed my warning and now they're dead. Your wonder boy here in the suit is next on the chopping block. Their deaths are on you for sending them into the mouth of hell."

"Sledge, are we clear?" Trixie asked in a shout from the other room.

She spoke in a raised voice that was easily heard by him and no doubt by the person on the other end of the phone.

Sledge didn't answer Trixie as the robotic manipulated voice responded to him.

"Sledge? I've heard of you before."

"Good for you. If you have, then you know I'm not to be trifled with."

He said nothing.

"I'm going to be blunt. Cut your losses and end this campaign. The girl is off the table and no longer any concern of yours. I don't know who you are and frankly I don't care. This is one vendetta that you will not see to the end."

He said nothing but the subtle background noise that Sledge heard from the phone indicated the person was still active, and hopefully, taking his proposition to heart.

"I'll take your silence as you agreeing to my terms. I'll leave the cash here with your now-dead meatheads as a gesture of good faith that your score with Trixie is settled. If you do try to come for her again down the road, I will burn your entire world to cinder and make you regret ever starting this war in the first place. Make no mistake about that."

"The man in the suit."

"What about him?"

"I no longer require his services. Do with him as you please."

The line went dead. Silence filled the receiver before a steady beeping noise boomed from the speaker.

Sledge mashed the red button to end the call on his end; then he dumped the phone onto the floor. With a malevolent glare trained at the suit that was dragging his leg behind him toward the door, he said, "Looks like you've been cut loose by your employer. It seems you're on your own."

"Then you better go ahead and kill me now, because I'm nothing but a dead man walking."

"Well, you're not walking." Sledge aimed the gun at his chest, ready to fire. "Not anymore."

He placed two bullets into the suit's chest. His body jolted from the punch of the impact, ending the businessman's miserable existence in the trailer.

Footfalls clomped hard on the floor and rushed out of the far room. Trixie emerged a second later, panting and wide-eyed. After seeing that Sledge was okay, she breathed a sigh of relief. "Thank God. Are we clear now?"

"We're good." Sledge stowed the Glock in the waistband of his pants. He then retrieved his 1911 pistol and combat knife. He placed the bag of money on the suit's chest, as promised. Trixie, Camella, and her son ventured out of the room. "Come on. We need to get out of here before someone shows up."

Chapter 50

THEY MOVED OUT OF the site office in a single file line down the concrete steps to the dirt. The door to the trailer slammed shut with a heavy clap, sealing the dead bodies within.

Camella kept her child close. The boy walked at her side and clung to her hip like an alien growth. Tears rushed down the face of the frightened child as he whimpered into his mom's forearm.

"You're not going to have to worry about those bad men coming after any of you again," Sledge said as they rounded the hood of the Lexus to his Chevelle.

"How can you be sure that they won't send more men after her, or us?" Camella asked from behind Trixie.

Sledge made for the trunk of the Chevelle and popped the lid. "Because I got the point across of what would happen if they did." He tossed his extra weapons and magazines inside the trunk with the rest of his gear. "Trust me. They won't bother any of you again."

Trixie comforted both Camella and her son as they walked around the front of the muscle car to the passenger side. Her guilt for causing the monumental mess was evident by her sagging shoulders and lowered head. She whispered to Camella and opened the door as Sledge closed the trunk lid.

The mom and son ducked into the back seat as Trixie sat up front. Sledge opened the driver's door and settled behind the wheel. With keys in hand, he started the beastly car and pulled away from the site office.

As they quickly left the grounds of the construction site and pulled out onto the street, Sledge asked, "Where am I taking you two?"

"No police please," Camella replied. "My friend's house will be fine for now. I don't want to go back to my apartment or deal with the authorities."

Sledge bobbed his head, acknowledging the request. Seeing how quick Camella was to strike down going to the police when no one offered that up as an option made him think that either she or her son were in the country illegally, or they were just scared and needed time to decompress. Either way, it didn't matter to Sledge. He wasn't with border patrol and wanted to avoid putting more undue stress on both of them. The ordeal they'd just gone through was bad enough.

Camella guided Sledge through Atlanta to the suburbs where they landed in the driveway of a quaint home northeast of the city. It was a relatively short drive and one that didn't eat up too much of their day.

Trixie got out of the passenger seat and pulled the backrest forward. Both mom and son scooted out of the vehicle. Camella offered a final thank you to Sledge before bending Trixie's ear. The boy said nothing and clung to his mother, still shaken by the men who kidnapped them.

While the women spoke outside of the car, Sledge remained behind the wheel and peered at the houses lining the street. Each had a quaint feel to it that made him nostalgic for reasons he couldn't explain. Maybe it just reminded him of the way his childhood hero and namesake, Blake Sledge, grew up in his favorite book, *Manhattan Heights*.

To this day, Sledge couldn't recall his youth before Cobalt. He never knew if he had such a home or lived in a place as nice and peaceful as this neighborhood. Any time he tried to remember anything before Cobalt it was as if his brain was sifted through mud. He could see faint outlines of people, but everything was always shrouded in shadows. He didn't even know his real name.

"Blake," Trixie said, snapping him out of his thoughts.

"Yeah. What?"

Camella ducked and extended her hand at him. "Thank you again for everything."

Sledge shook her hand and smiled. "No need to thank me. I'm glad you and your son are safe. That's all that matters to me."

He caught a glimpse of the boy who stared his way. Sledge waved at the child who retreated to the other side of his mom, too timid to parrot the gesture.

A woman walked out to the covered front patio of the home and waited. Her arms folded as she stood rigid and worried.

Trixie and Camella hugged one final time before the mom and son peeled away and made for the home. The trio embraced one another and then disappeared through the doorway.

Sledge shifted into reverse as Trixie got back into the car. "How is she holding up?"

She shut the car door and then fastened her seat belt. "About as well as can be expected. Camella is a tough woman. She's been through a lot. Leaving her deadbeat boyfriend in Mexico, and making the trip to the United States with her son, alone and broke, would test anyone's character. That woman is the definition of badass."

"I would have to agree with you on that." Sledge backed out of the driveway and headed down the street.

On the way back to his warehouse, the pair sat in silence for the better part of the drive. Trixie peered out of the lowered window as the wind whipped the strands of her hair around. The guilt she carried was like a weighted pack strapped to her shoulders. It crushed not only her body but her spirit as well.

"I'm sorry for being such trouble. I wouldn't blame you for kicking me to the curb," she said with her head bowed in shame. "You have enough going on with that missing girl and those thugs who abducted her. All I'm doing is making your life harder."

Sledge waved off the ludicrous statement. "Nonsense. You're not doing any such thing. We've all made mistakes. Some big. Some small. But no one in the history of ever has gone through their life being squeaky clean." *And you have no idea how hard I've made your life,* Sledge thought.

"Yeah, but still, I could have gotten you, Camella, or her son, Danny, killed." Trixie refused to let up on the self-loathing that dragged her further into the depths of despair. "Maybe I'm better off being alone. People don't last too long around me. They either leave or end up dead."

He hated seeing Trixie so beaten down and feeling guilty about something that was entirely his fault, not hers. He was trying so hard to put the pieces of rubble that were her life back together for her. Perhaps it was too little, too late, but he wasn't about to stop trying.

"Let me be frank about one thing, okay?"

She looked up at him. "What?"

"You're a good person and deserve happiness. It's waiting for you. This is a rough patch that will blow over eventually." He glanced at the street ahead and then back to her. "Mistakes are to be learned from. As long as you're doing that, then you're heading in the right direction.

"Furthermore, you are not messing up my life. It's been nice having someone around. It doesn't make that warehouse feel so empty. And your work on digging up information on Vega has been pivotal in getting us closer to finding Kim. I quite literally couldn't have done that without you."

Trixie sniffled then dabbed her wrist under her nose. "You give a decent pep talk. It wasn't as hard and rigid as I thought it would be. Not bad for a hard-nosed detective badass."

"I thought it sounded pretty good."

"It did and it made me feel better. Thank you."

Sledge smiled. "As of now, you no longer have to work for such people as those scumbags back there since you're hanging with me."

"I'm grateful for you taking a chance on me. I'd much rather use my skills to help people than destroy them. I promise I'll bust my ass every day to pay off my debt and the risk you took with bringing your money to buy my freedom." Trixie paused a beat and then continued. "Truth be told, I didn't have the funds anyway. It was tied up to pay off another group of men to whom I was in debt."

"Again, it's over and done. Everyone is okay."

"Yeah. They are."

"Just so I'm aware, are there any other surprise guests that you owe that we should be expecting in the future?"

"No. This was my only outstanding balance, so to speak."

Sledge was relieved to hear that. It still niggled at him that Trixie was running these jobs right under his watchful eye. However, he couldn't have kept eyes on her every second of the day, so she had plenty of time to get herself into trouble without his knowledge. "Good. There is one other thing we need to work on soon, though."

"What's that?"

"You need to learn how to use a gun and a bit of self-defense. Not a bad thing for a woman to know in this day and age."

Trixie hiked her shoulders. "You're right. My recent blunders are a testament to that."

"Don't worry. Once we get past this case, we'll set aside some time and train."

"Does that include you letting me drive this car by chance?"

"Don't push your luck."

"I'm only asking is all," Trixie replied with a wry grin.

"I'm sure you are."

They rolled into the warehouse after 5:30 p.m. As Sledge got out of the driver's seat and moved to the trunk, his phone dinged a message. It was from Rick.

I got a bead on Vega through an informant of ours on the street, but you'll have to move quickly if you want to nab him. His detail will be light. Here is his home address. Sledge said the address in his head and continued reading. *Best to move in at night to keep a low profile. I doubt you'll have an issue moving in the shadows. Other than that, I've got nothing else. Good luck.*

Sledge typed *Thanks* and hit send.

"What's up?" Trixie asked from the passenger side of the trunk. "Did you get an update on Kim?"

"No, but I did on Vega." Sledge put the phone in his back pants pocket and popped the trunk lid. "We've got an address now of his home."

"Where'd you get it from?"

"A contact of mine who's helped me out on this case and others," Sledge replied, keeping Rick anonymous. "It seems as though Vega's security detail isn't too heavy at the homestead."

Trixie shifted her attention to the trunk at the ammo, vest, and duffle bag while Sledge rummaged through the contents. "When are you moving in?"

"Tonight. After dark when it's easier to skirt any guards Vega may have on the property and remain hidden."

"Good call."

"I'm glad you approve." Sledge hauled out the vest and duffle bag first.

"I do; just be careful. They know someone is on to them and will be more alert I imagine."

Sledge knew that was not only possible but certain. His actions over the past few days had ruffled the feathers of the criminal underworld and disrupted its paradoxical harmony. When one poked a bear, they had to be ready to face the beast head-on.

"I'll be better equipped this time. Don't worry about me. I can feel the noose tightening around Vega's neck. His days are going to be numbered if I have anything to say about it."

"That's what I like to hear because I like my new job and would hate to have to find another one so quickly."

Her foreboding and yet light-hearted comment made them both chuckle. Sledge wasn't opposed to dark humor when directed at his mortality.

"At least I know you care." He handed Trixie the vest and duffle bag. "Take these back to the weapons hold while I grab the ammo."

She took both items from him and walked off as he lifted the boxes of .45 ammo out of the trunk. Sledge had been granted another shot at Vega and he wasn't about to squander it.

Chapter 51

NIGHT CAME. A MOONLESS black sky dotted with few stars shrouded the city in darkness. It was the perfect time to go to work and conduct his hunt.

Sledge hit the road after 10:00 p.m. in the Chevelle. Traffic at that hour was scattered and thinned out. It made reaching Vega's secluded home nestled in the foothills outside of the city easier to reach without having to deal with the hustle and bustle of daytime activity.

This outing was different. He planned accordingly, not taking chances on the amount of security Vega had. The debacle at the meat packaging plant hammered home what sort of men he was dealing with, and the fact that Cobalt was back in the fold.

The ballistic vest he got from Oscar fit snugly, but it wasn't too tight. Its nylon material wrapped his side and chest like a warm hug. The steel plate in the center acted as a defense for chest shots if he did find himself knee-deep in a gunfight this go-round.

That wasn't the plan, however. This was a covert, under-the-radar type of campaign. Slip in, get what he needed, and get out without igniting an all-out gunfight where he was the outnumbered interloper.

There was a time and place for such ruthless carnage, but now he had to be like a scalpel, sharp and precise to exact Kim's whereabouts and status from the sadist who stole her.

In the back of Sledge's head, Oscar's input on Kim made him wonder if she was still alive or in the city. He knew the score and the odds of him finding her. Each day that ticked by reduced his odds, almost like winning the lottery's monster jackpot on a single ticket.

But Sledge played behind the eight ball most days and did his best work under the gun. If a rough life filled with blood and bullets had taught him anything, it was that grit and determination made men and forged character when shit went down. He had more than enough to go around and would see it through to the bitter end.

Few lamp posts lined the sides of the winding road that snaked toward Vega's home. Large swaths of blackness cloaked the Chevelle's body as it grumbled along at a slow but steady clip.

The area had no other homes that Sledge could see. No lights punctuated the ether to either side of him, thereby cloaking the remote location of Vega's dwelling.

A home came into view to his left. Like a beacon in the night, light shone from several windows of the massive mansion that resided in the middle of the sprawling grounds encompassing it.

It dwarfed the Claymore residence from what Sledge could see from the road. Even at night, its sheer size was something to behold. The old saying that crime didn't pay seemed inaccurate, as Vega's estate vigorously contradicted that notion.

Sledge pulled off the main road and tucked the Chevelle into a tight spot hidden among the trees and bushes. The car wouldn't be found unless someone knew exactly where to look; that didn't appear to be an issue given the lack of traffic on the narrow road.

The headlights cut out and the engine stopped its throaty grumble. Sledge moved with purpose and exited the vehicle; then he headed for the street.

His attire for the night's incursion was an all-black ensemble. Not a hint of color was noticeable on him. Each piece that covered his body blended with the blackness around him, making it difficult for enemies to see him coming. He had to be a scalpel instead of a hammer, utilizing precision over brute force.

He scuttled across the road to the grass; then he scaled the fence, covered with long, leafy vines, with ease. Up and over the top railing, Sledge landed and pitched forward into a roll then got to his feet. He removed the suppressed 1911 from the holster attached to his thigh and swept the open grassy plot of land as he made for the corner of the house.

The weapons at his disposal were minimal but in the right hands, lethal. He had the 1911 as his primary weapon. Two additional magazines resided in the bulletproof vest's pouches as backups. The combat knife was tucked in its sheath at the small of his back as well as another gambler's blade that was clasped to his ankle near the top of his black combat boots. He hated losing the knives and tried to keep spares for ones he had grown fond of.

No guards patrolled outside as he closed in on the home. Dogs were always a concern as well with such men as they liked to keep animals on the property as an added defensive measure and early warning system. One bark would stir Vega and any men he had inside or out that Sledge hadn't come across yet. That would hinder his chances for mission success.

His footsteps were muffled on the thick carpet of perfectly trimmed grass. Sledge moved along the back wall of the home while peering at the large windows. Blinds were angled enough to allow what bit of interior light there was out, but kept him from being able to see inside.

There were no flood lights mounted to the edge of the roofline with which he had to contend. It appeared he was in the clear and good to proceed as planned to breach the house.

Thus far, the mission had gone off without a hitch. Rick's intel on Vega's mansion was accurate. Sledge was relieved at the lack of outside patrols. He by no means dropped his guard but stayed alert, knowing that things were rarely as they seem.

As he reached the patio, Sledge detected flashes of light emitting from inside the dark first floor of the mansion. He trained his ear and listened to the subtle muffled noise that sounded from within.

Is that a TV? Sledge thought as he heard what appeared to be voices speaking.

He shifted down to the French doors of the home while checking his six and the backyard. There was still no hint of guards in the area. Inside, Sledge couldn't see any movement in the low light.

His stomach tingled with a nervous jitter. Something felt off now, but he couldn't pinpoint exactly what it was. Perhaps it was him being overly cautious. The dumpster fire that was the meat packing plant made him leery, but that wasn't a bad thing.

On delicate jobs such as these, it behooved one to be attuned to their surroundings at all times. Sledge, though, didn't have the luxury of contemplating entry or retreat. Not this time. With his back against the wall and no other leads to pursue, he decided to breach and move in while he had Vega so close. The reward was worth the risk.

Sledge picked the lock and moved in. His suppressed 1911 roved the interior, which was lit by only a few lamps that struggled to illuminate the monstrous footprint of the mansion. He pushed the door into the jamb and carefully advanced as the local news broadcasted from the massive TV hanging on the opposite wall.

These sorts of clandestine missions were nothing new to Sledge. He worked well at night and preferred such a cloak-and-dagger op when the opportunity presented itself. Shadows were an assassin's friend. Even though he had moved on from that life, the skills he acquired had become invaluable when he had to move under the radar and not be seen until the last second.

One variable Sledge didn't know was whether Vega had a wife or children. They wouldn't be touched or harmed, but not knowing what to expect grated on his nerves. He was there for the criminal and nothing else. It was a means to get to Kim and bring the young woman home.

As the TV blared the nightly news, Sledge wondered where Vega had scampered off to. The mansion was huge and he wanted to minimize his time inside, but he had to find Atlanta's crime lord. Getting in and getting out was the plan. The longer he stayed the risk of detection increased.

Sledge conducted a speedy sweep of the living room and kitchen while moving to the hallway. It was dark and had no lights illuminating the corridor in either direction. The flood of memories was hard to resist from previous missions that ended badly as he prowled the ritzy home.

A muffled clatter sounded from the floor above. It was almost like heavy footsteps running, but Sledge wasn't sure if he heard it correctly over the din of the TV.

He moved in to investigate and hit the landing of the wide-mouthed staircase that twisted upward along the wall to the second floor. Step by step, he climbed the stairs toward the top. No squeak came from the planks of wood from his bulk pressing down on them. He shifted on the move and checked the first floor, then back to the landing of the second. Both were clear.

As Sledge reached midway up the staircase, a flicker of light shone from the hallway below in the corner of his eye, and then it vanished. It was gone in a blink. There was no doubt in his mind now that things were about to get interesting.

Chapter 52

He paused on the steps and waited for a beat. The suppressed 1911 was aimed at the lower level as he hunted for the source of light that came and went before he could lock onto it.

His instincts kicked into overdrive. Sledge calmed his breathing and watched the shadows below for figures skulking in the blackness. The odds of the home being a setup for him built with each second he remained in the house. It was too strong to deny now. The biggest unknown was if Vega was inside or not.

Instead of moving down the steps to investigate, Sledge decided to head to the second floor and wait to see what happened next. From an elevated position, he had the advantage against a strike team if Vega had intended to send one in.

Each step made up the stairs offered little residual noise. He moved swiftly but silently to the landing, and then ducked behind the railing. A quick sweep of the hallway around him revealed no movements or sounds.

As he scanned the first floor, a black-clad figure moved up the corridor. Then another. Then another. A three-man... No, wait... A four-man team moved in a single file line.

They weren't professionals. Sledge could tell that from the way they moved. Their formation wasn't tight and their pacing was rushed instead of cautious and calculating. Maybe they were confident in their skills against a man they didn't perceive as that great of a threat, or they were plain stupid. Either way, Sledge would know soon enough.

Two of the men split off from the back of the pack and headed up the stairs while the other two pushed on up the corridor. Divide and conquer was their plan. It was a foolish misstep that benefited Sledge. Fewer men to take on at the same time were easier to handle quietly. Scalpel. Not hammer.

Sledge drifted back into the shadows of the hallway and moved to one of the first rooms he crossed. The door was unlocked. He slowly twisted the doorknob and pushed it open as the steps warned that the two-man team was nearing the landing.

As he ducked inside the bedroom and closed the door, Sledge banked on the men splitting up again to cover more ground. It was another mistake on their part. They were underestimating him.

He waited in the blackness of the room. Sledge caught shapes of what he thought to be a bed and a dresser. There were other objects inside but he couldn't make them out and focused on the approaching men coming down the hallway.

The door hung open about an inch, just enough to tempt one of the gunmen to take a closer look. They knew he was in the home. The only question was where.

Sledge scooted down the wall near the doorway. His 1911 aimed at the gap. He waited for one of the men to enter before discharging the weapon.

The booming clamor from the TV downstairs continued. Although not as loud where Sledge was, he still caught snippets of the broadcast echoing throughout the massive mansion.

With a steady finger on the trigger, he waited for one of the gunmen to present him with a target. Minutes passed before he heard their footfalls sounding in the hallway outside of the room. They were close and heading his way.

He mastered his breathing and stared at the gap without blinking. As soon as Sledge had them in his sights, he'd snuff them out, and move on.

One of the men approached the room he was in. They didn't come barreling inside like a bull, but they stopped and waited. The door squeaked open and swung into the room. A single, shadowy figure passed through the doorway with what looked to be a pistol double-gripped between his hands.

As he shifted his feet and swept the room, Sledge fired a single shot at close range. The suppressed 1911 kicked in his hands. Muzzle fire was nonexistent within the murk as the muffled report sent a bullet into the gunman's skull. His arms dropped down to his waist before the shadowy figure could muster return fire.

Sledge lurched forward and cradled the man under his arms before he hit the floor. His limp body was bigger than what Sledge could see within the gloom. Catching dead weight without making any noise was tough to do, especially when the target was large and heavy.

Muscling the dead weight, Sledge dragged the killer away from the doorway along the carpet to the corner of the room. He gently placed the body on the floor and faced the entrance.

His partner hadn't shown, indicating that Sledge was still in the clear. He advanced on the doorway and then peered out into the hallway.

The other gunman stalked the corridor down from the room Sledge was in. He kept to the center of the hall and swept his rifle from right to left. No backward glance was given over his shoulder as he veered to the next room on the left side of the corridor and moved in.

A look at the landing showed no additional men coming up the stairs. The second team was still below from what he could tell.

Sledge padded out of the room and stalked the man ahead of him. His pistol locked onto the back of the gunman's head as he listened at the door; then he nudged it open with the barrel of his shouldered rifle. He was unaware of Sledge's presence behind him as he carefully peeked inside the doorway.

Another muffled report spat from the suppressed 1911 at less than six feet. The bullet hit home in the base of the man's skull, killing him upon impact. This time, Sledge was unable to catch the body before it folded over and dumped to the floor with a dense thump.

Sledge stepped around the gunman's body and into the dark room. A muffled voice whispered from the dead man's head as Sledge grabbed his arms and towed him further inside the room. He then released his hold and felt for a wire and earpiece.

His fingers happened upon the thick coiled wire on the floor near the body. Sledge picked it up, put the earpiece in his ear, and listened.

Bottom floor is clear. He must be upstairs, the raspy male voice said. *Team two. What's your status? Any luck?*

Pinching the wire between two gloved fingers, Sledge dropped it to the floor and marched to the doorway. From the incoming transmission, he knew no one else was upstairs with him, but with both men dead and unable to respond, they'd be on their way.

As Sledge stepped out into the hallway, a beam of bright white light blasted his face from the landing of the stairs. He stopped dead in his tracks and raised his hand from the sudden burst of brilliance that temporarily blinded him.

"Contact!" a thundering voice said at the top of his lungs.

Sledge retreated into the room as the gunman at the stairs opened fire and advanced toward him. A salvo of rounds rattled off from his shouldered rifle. The bullets punched the drywall and the surface of the door as it slammed shut.

Wood splintered from the onslaught. The constant buzz of hot lead hammering into the room cumulated into a dizzy whirlwind of chaotic bombardment. It seemed as though the ragtag team Vega had sent into the home after him, wasn't as prepared and ready to face him as Vega had hoped.

Ducking, Sledge held his return fire and waited for his shot. He got clear of the door and huddled in the shadows across the room. His suppressed 1911 was trained at the entrance. Patience was paramount now. Don't jump the gun and fire blindly. Wait for the target to present itself, and then drop him. Clean and smooth.

The door busted inward and flew against the wall. A hulking figure stood in the doorway and swept from one side to the next. Sledge fired three rounds in quick succession. Each found their mark dead center in the man's chest, knocking him back out into the hallway, but he didn't go down.

His aim was true and on point. There was no questioning the placement. That should have been a kill shot unless he wore a vest. The two men he'd dusted earlier weren't body shots. Sledge adjusted on the fly and charged the door while the gunman gathered his bearings and brought the rifle to bear.

As he fired, the gunman hunched and retreated to the staircase while wildly spraying the corridor with the hope of tagging Sledge. His aim was off and he hit everything under the moon except for Sledge.

Sledge unloaded three more rounds at the fleeing man. Two went wide while the third caught the back of his leg. He cried out and fell to the floor, landing on his stomach with a heavy thump. His weapon stayed locked in his grip. He flopped over to his back, trying to raise the rifle and get a bead on Sledge as he converged on him.

Light from the stairs materialized and grew brighter as the fourth member of the strike team clomped toward the landing. His footfalls increased in speed as his partner groaned and aimed the barrel of the rifle in Sledge's direction.

A perfectly placed round was fired from Sledge's pistol into the side of the man's skull. Its silenced puff removed the third gunman as his rifle and head fell to the floor.

While on the move, Sledge hopped over the dead body and fired at the beam of light emerging from the stairs. He squeezed the trigger constantly, unloading at the gunman who halted his advancement, ducked, and fired while retreating down the steps.

Muzzle fire flashed from the rifle as a swarm of ordnance zipped by Sledge. One round sliced his left arm while two punched his bulletproof vest. It stopped Sledge cold and knocked him off balance. He dropped to one knee as the final gunman retreated down the stairs.

It didn't feel like the bullets made it through the vest. Sledge ran his fingers over the outside and felt dents in the plate but none breached. The chest armor had done its job.

Sledge stood and forged ahead. The gunman had a few steps left to make before hitting the first-floor landing. His chin wrenched over his shoulder as the gun-mounted light bounced at the marble floor. Before he could stop, turn, and fire, Sledge moved down the stairs while unloading the remainder of his magazine.

The weapon clicked empty as the .45 ammo puffed from the suppressed 1911 in a steady stream of fire. Most found their mark on the gunman's body; he absorbed the hellfire and fell backward down the remaining steps and crashed to the floor. His rifle clattered off the marble tile as he writhed from the flat of his back.

Sledge ejected the spent magazine and pulled a fresh one from the pocket on the front of his vest, then he slapped it into the pistol's well. After releasing the slide, Sledge trained the weapon at the moaning man as he hit the remaining steps to the tile.

Light from the rifle shone at the wall across from them. A trail of blood leaked from the corner of the man's bearded mouth. As the gunman reached under his back for what Sledge guessed to be a secondary gun or knife, he stomped on the man's arm and pinned it to the floor.

The bullet that clipped Sledge's arm stung, but the pain did little to steer his attention from the snarling man under his boot. He lined up the 1911 with the man's skull and interrogated him.

"Where's Vega? Where is he holding the girl?"

No response came other than grunts and moans of agony.

With a bit more pressure applied to the gunman's wounded arm, Sledge repeated his question in a stern and guttural tone, as if a man possessed. "Answer my question or I can promise you that a world of pain is heading your way."

"Eat shit," the man said, cringing and gnashing his teeth. "I'm not telling you anything."

Sledge removed his boot from the man's limb; then he bent down and grabbed him by the scruff of his shirt. Pulling him up to his feet, Sledge said, "Oh. You're going to tell me what I want to know, even if I have to beat it out of you."

The two men stood toe-to-toe in the cavernous corridor of the mansion, each refusing to budge from their position. He leveled his narrowed gaze and furrowed brow with Sledge, calling his bluff.

Shoving the 1911 in the man's face, Sledge angrily said, "Tell me where Vega has taken the girl, now!"

The gunman shifted his sights to the right of Sledge, then back to him. Was there a fifth contact Sledge didn't know about creeping up on his six? His instincts and intuition kicked in, telling him that something wasn't right.

As Sledge listened and cocked his head to the left, the gunman made a move against him. He pulled a pistol from behind him. Sledge caught the move out of his peripheral vision as footfalls sounded at his back. They weren't alone.

Suppressed gunfire popped off at the men. Sledge spun around while holding the injured gunman by his shirt, placing him between himself and the shooter.

A volley of bullets impacted the back of the man's vest. Sledge used him as a shield while battling the thug who took the brunt of the ceaseless gunfire. There were stray shots. Each bullet punched his vest while a lone round hit home in the back of the man's skull.

His head dangled forward and his body went limp in Sledge's grasp. Both of his legs buckled as the gunman fell to the floor while Sledge fired at the fifth contact that appeared out of thin air.

The new target dodged the return gunfire that Sledge struggled to accurately land while trying to handle the dead weight of the gunman, interfering with his ability to defend and engage. The mark moved quickly and wasn't as clumsy as the four men before him.

Before Sledge could land a kill shot, the HK clicked empty. He dropped the gun and used both hands to pick up the dead gunman to shield his body from the volley of shots coming from the fifth contact. Bullets pelted the body as it jerked in his arms from the impact until Sledge heard the sound he was waiting for—the assassin's gun clicked as the slide locked in place.

Sledge instantly dropped the body and ran toward the assassin as he reached for the sheathed combat knife at the small of his back. His opponent had already drawn his curved Karambit Tactical knife and lunged at him.

The knife twirled around his finger as he slashed upward with the tip grazing the nylon material of Sledge's vest. He knocked the man's arm away with his palm while backing and hunting for an opening to strike.

His adversary was relentless and matched his fighting style to near perfection. Every counter Sledge tried to launch was blocked by the well-versed killer who refused to let up and kept the pressure on him.

He moved with such speed that Sledge had to adjust his approach before the man could get in close. His footing wasn't as quick as the other guy's, but his strength and reflexes saved Sledge from several blows that sliced at his midsection and across both arms. The knife bit his flesh but glanced off before going too deep.

Sweat probed the slashes. Salt made them burn. Blood ran from the wounds, but Sledge ignored each injury and slashed and stabbed at whatever part of the man's body he could. He landed a right cross on the edge of his attacker's chin that sent him hard to the tile. But he recovered in a blink and swept Sledge's legs out from under him.

His back took the brunt of the impact. As he scrambled off the floor, he was overtaken by the masked killer who mounted him and sliced down with the Karambit at his throat.

Sledge blocked his arm. The razor-sharp edge of the curved blade was less than half a foot from slicing his throat open. His hand, clutching the combat knife, was tacked to the tile by the killer's knee that bore down on his forearm.

He had been out-maneuvered by the mysterious arrival that was by far a cut above the other men Vega had under his charge. The expert fighting skills portrayed by this fifth fighter had gotten Sledge off his feet and now threatened to spill his blood onto the floor.

The pair locked glares in the gloom of the mansion as the war for victory hinged on whoever wanted it more. More downward pressure was applied, bringing the Karambit closer to Sledge's throat.

Pushing upward against the black-clad figure who had mounted Sledge, he gained a bit of breathing room. He thrust his hip skyward and torqued his body at an angle that rocked the killer's balance. Sledge tipped to the right and removed the other guy's leg off of his arm, freeing the combat knife. He rolled the fighter onto his back and presented the combat knife to his throat as the tip of the Karambit pressed to Sledge's stomach.

Each man had the other in a compromised position. Given their tactical proficiency and fighting ability, either could deal a death blow and bleed the other out with a single slash.

Sledge dipped his chin and peered at the knife near his stomach; then he met the killer's focused glare once more. His eyes were fierce and cut right through Sledge as neither man dared to make the first move.

He parted his lips to ask a question to the fighter trapped under him when a loud bang echoed through the home behind Sledge. As he peered over his shoulder at the multitude of lights at the far end of the corridor, the Karambit slashed at his gut.

The tip sliced through Sledge's shirt and caught flesh. It raked the skin, cutting him from left to right. A knee to the spine and a hip thrust threw Sledge over his target and to the floor. He went end over end once and got to his feet as additional forces surged up the corridor.

Outgunned and outmanned, Sledge sheathed the blade and retreated into the living room as the expert killer he fought got off the floor. He crashed through the French doors to the outside and hoofed it down the property as lights waved like wands behind him.

Cracks of gunshots popped off as he surged toward the wall of steel fencing. He flinched and kept pushing as incoming fire zinged past him.

Sledge scaled the fence to the other side; then he dashed across the road to the dense vegetation where his car was hidden. His keys were plucked from his front pants pocket as he rushed down the driver's side of the Chevelle and got inside the car. He fired it up and backed out onto the road.

A twist of the wheel sent the front end whipping about. Sledge pumped the brake, slammed the clutch, shifted into gear, and then hit the gas. The muscle car jerked forward and raced down the dark deserted road as he wondered who the assassin in black was and, more importantly, how they knew he'd be coming.

Chapter 53

TRIXIE TENDED TO SLEDGE back at the warehouse after he arrived. He made it home without being followed by Vega's men or the new player in town. His wounds weren't too severe, but they had to be dressed, nonetheless.

"I had a bad feeling about this. Did you at least find out anything new before things went sideways?"

"All I know now is that someone tipped Vega off that I'd be coming." Sledge unbuckled the bulletproof vest and pulled it over his head. He threw it to the floor in frustration. Next, he removed his shirt and sat down in one of the seats at the kitchen table. "It was a complete shit-show. They had a four-man team show up at the house. And one other assassin that was separate from the four-man team. They knew I was going to be there. As far I as know, Vega was nowhere on the grounds. This was all for me and not a chance encounter."

She inspected the gash on his stomach and the damage done to his arms. "It seems to me as though you're being played by someone who's working with Vega. How else would he know that you would be there unless you were lured in on purpose?"

"Grab the first aid kit, would you?" Sledge asked as he explored each cut received from the Karambit and the graze from the bullet.

"Yeah." Trixie walked off to retrieve the kit while Sledge slouched in the chair.

The fight with the masked assassin piqued Sledge's interest. He mirrored a lot of the same moves as Sledge, countering and striking as he would. It was like fighting against himself, which made Sledge wonder who it was under the mask and tactical gear.

"Do you have any idea who would have sold you out to Vega?" Trixie asked. "It has to be someone who knows you're working on the kidnapping. Maybe that detective guy you've spoken to is the mole. There are corrupt cops. I wouldn't put it past any of them to be on Vega's payroll."

"It's not him," Sledge replied in a mostly calm and reasonable voice. "Detective Wentworth wouldn't have known I was heading to Vega's mansion tonight. I never mentioned it to him. The only person who knew about it was..."

That's when the epiphany hit him. His eyes bulged in shock. He shot up straight in the chair as the betrayal sank in. The one person who knew Sledge would be heading to the mansion was Rick.

"What is it?" Trixie asked as she placed the kit on the table and opened the lid. "You have this weird look on your face like you've seen a ghost."

She dug out cotton balls and peroxide from the container along with square bandages to apply over the wounds as he slammed his fist down on the table and rambled off a slew of colorful words.

"I can't believe he sold me out."

"Who?"

"Rick Jenkins." He shot up out of the seat as Trixie doused one of the cotton balls in peroxide. "He's an officer with Atlanta PD. We've fed each other info on various cases and he's given me a hand with this one as well. He's the one who told me where Vega would be. That slimy sack of shit."

"It seems like he's been playing on both teams from the sound of it. Vega probably has others in his pocket as well besides Officer Jenkins." Trixie waved her arm at Sledge to come back and sit down so she could tend to his wounds.

Sledge was floored by the realization as he aimlessly wandered about the kitchen. His hands bunched into fists. His nostrils flared in rage.

Officer Jenkins had betrayed their trust and more importantly, delayed Sledge's attempts at rescuing Kim. As he made his way back to the chair and sat down, he thought back to Trent and pondered if Rick knew whom he was up against.

A heavy silence draped over the kitchen like a shroud. The bitter taste of treachery wouldn't leave Sledge's mouth. It twisted his face into a mask of contempt for the cop that he stepped out on a limb to trust, but in return, got stabbed in the back.

"So, what are you going to do now?" Trixie asked as she dabbed the wet cotton ball on the gunshot wound first. "How do you know who else you can trust on the Atlanta police force? For all you know, there could be more moles planted in every department."

The sting of the peroxide rubbing on the damaged flesh didn't stir Sledge's thoughts away from the crooked cop. His threshold for enduring pain was higher than normal, and he was able to stomach the treatment without as much as a cringe.

"I don't know whom I can trust other than Detective Wentworth," Sledge replied as she fixed a bandage over the torn skin on his arm. "He's shot me straight so far with what he knows about Kim's case and Vega's crew. The impression I got from him was that he loathed the man and wanted to find Kim before it was too late.

"Granted, with recent developments, I could be wrong again, but his actions as of late haven't hinted at him being on the take like Rick. I'll have to get with Wentworth and let him know who has been muddying up his investigation, but not before I have a word with that slimeball Rick first thing in the morning."

Trixie tossed the bloody cotton onto the table. Sledge waved her off as he took over to dress his injuries. She backed away and put her hands on her hips as he cleaned the remaining cuts.

"You know, this rabbit hole is getting deeper by the second. Who knows how far up the chain in the police department it goes, or who else is tied to them? This is becoming far bigger than just a simple kidnapping case."

"Oh, it's much bigger than just a random human trafficking ring." Sledge splattered peroxide on each cut, then followed up with cotton pinched between his fingers. "And tomorrow, Rick is going to spill what he knows or I'm going to rip his tongue out of his mouth and shove it down his throat."

Chapter 54

WHEN DAWN BROKE EARLY the next morning, Sledge was already outside of Rick's home, waiting and watching for the officer to show his face. A fistful of vengeance and a brimming volcanic rage boiling in the pit of his gut kept him on task.

His gaze was glued to the double-dealing cop's residence and the detached garage at the end of the driveway at the back of the property. So far, no motion had been detected behind the blinds or around the house.

Sledge tried to call and message Rick, but both means of communication went unanswered. For all he knew, Vega had cut ties with the bent officer and plugged him in the middle of the night. Rick's dead body could be inside the home on the floor, butchered by the crime boss. Maybe he had fled the city after the attempt at killing Sledge failed and now he was on the run. Either scenario was plausible.

Before moving in and taking a closer look, Sledge scanned the cars parked along the street. None caught his attention as being out of place. Aside from him, no other individuals were sitting and waiting in the vehicles.

With a replacement pistol for his missing 1911 tucked in the front of his pants, Sledge opened the door to the Chevelle and got out. He roved the quiet suburb with a vigilant gaze as he gently shut the door behind him and headed for Rick's pad.

All he could think about while crossing the road to the driveway was how he wanted to strangle the man and stomp his face into the ground. He wanted to beat him to within an inch of his life for setting him up. The reason didn't matter, not to Sledge. The deed was done and now multiple lives were affected by the spineless low-life.

That was why Sledge trusted so few people– for fear of being burned. The betrayal by Rick emphasized why he kept his circle small. Trust was earned and never freely given away. It made the former assassin leery of stepping outside of his comfort zone and forced him to be extra cautious in the future, especially with Cobalt on his turf.

Sledge casually strolled across the concrete path to the front porch of Rick's house. His hands were stuffed into the pockets of his pants so he wouldn't draw any attention from the cop's neighbors. He peered at the windows but couldn't see through the slanted blinds.

The door was locked, but that didn't surprise Sledge. If it hadn't been, that would have presented a different story of the officer's fate.

Instead of knocking at the door, Sledge decided to head around back and figure out a way to sneak inside the home. Despite how much he wanted to squeeze the life from Rick, the cop was still useful and would certainly have information on Kim's whereabouts since he was aiding Vega and Cobalt to mislead and hinder the investigation.

Sledge back-tracked to the empty driveway and made the corner of the home when he caught sight of the side door leading into the detached garage closing. It happened quickly and he had caught just a brief glimpse of it shutting, but Sledge was confident in what he saw.

He pulled the pistol from his waistband and kept it down at his side while he advanced up the driveway toward the garage. The backyard was clear as was the home. Sledge hurried to the corner of the garage and then moved around the bend to the side entrance. He leaned against the door and listened while gripping the doorknob.

As Sledge twisted the knob, he picked up movement inside the building. It had to be Rick, or someone else messing about the garage. He'd find out soon enough who it was.

The door opened ever so slightly into the dimly lit building. A gray, four-door sedan was parked inside with its trunk lifted. The driver's side door hung open, waiting for its operator to get behind the wheel.

Sledge slipped through the gap of the door and moved toward the back of the sedan. His gun aimed at the raised trunk lid as he maneuvered around the edge of the open car door.

A pair of hands gripped the trunk lid and slammed it shut. Rick then made for the corner of the sedan until he realized that he wasn't alone.

"Going somewhere?" Sledge asked as he aimed the barrel at the officer.

Rick jumped and stumbled backward, frightened. The blood drained from his face in a blink. "Shit, Sledge. You startled me."

"I imagine I did, considering that I should be dead, right?"

He didn't answer.

"To be honest, I thought that maybe Vega or his employer would have beat me here to silence you. Since I survived the trap you sent me to I figured they would have shown up by now. And make no mistake. You are a huge loose end."

"Listen, Sledge. Just take it easy." Rick's voice cracked as he spoke. His body trembled. Each word muttered hinged on sheer panic as he kept his distance from Sledge. "You don't want to kill a cop, do you? That wouldn't work out too well. Cop killers don't last long, even for men like you."

Hearing Rick speak as if he was an honorable member of the police brotherhood made Sledge retch. It was laughable at best. He had lost that privilege the moment he aligned himself with Vega and Cobalt to do their dirty work from inside Atlanta's police department.

"What you are is a vile, corrupt piece of trash that has no honor and doesn't deserve to be called a cop." Sledge refused to lower the gun and kept it trained at Rick's skull. "No one is going to shed a tear for the likes of you. I can promise you that."

Rick said nothing but backed away as Sledge stalked toward him.

"Why did you sell out me and your brothers in blue?" Sledge asked. "Don't try to weave a story here. Come clean."

"I've been working with Vega since before we met, for years now. Doctoring reports and muddying investigations that involve any of his business ventures," Rick answered. "As far as the why, I'm afraid it's nothing more than plain old greed. Money makes the world go 'round, Sledge. Don't act like you don't know that. The salary of a cop in this day and age isn't squat. A man has to do what he has to do to prepare for the future. The department's retirement plan is crap. When I'm chewed up and spit out from the machine, I plan to live out my days being wealthy and not as a poor cop who can't rub two nickels together."

Sledge moved around the driver's side of the trunk as Rick stood on the passenger side with his hands visible. "I doubt that the Claymores would agree with your logic in helping the likes of Vega and his employer kidnap their daughter and sell her like a commodity. Tell me, is she even still alive and in the city?"

Rick cut his eyes to the side entrance of the garage but didn't turn his head to look. Sledge caught the brief glimpse and dared him to make the move. He wouldn't make it far before being run down.

"The girl is alive as far as I know. She's been sold to a wealthy business-man overseas."

"The girl has a name. It's Kim!" Sledge shot back as he inched around the trunk to the passenger side. "Who was she sold to? Where is Vega keeping her? Tell me and perhaps you'll be able to walk out of this garage instead of being carried out in a body bag."

"You're bluffing, Sledge," Rick said as he backed further down the sedan toward the hood. "I know you. All that talking and shit you spit out is nothing but a joke. As I said, you're not going to touch me."

"If that's the case and I'm no threat, then why do you keep making your way to the door and look as if you're about to piss yourself? Huh?"

Rick cut and ran around the front end of the car toward the side en-trance. A deafening crack of gunfire exploded from Sledge's gun. The bullet hit the cop in his right shoulder and sent him slamming into the garage door.

"You shot me, you dick!" Rick groaned and palmed the gunshot wound as Sledge bounded around the hood toward him.

"I told you I would."

"Damn, man. Shit."

"Stop your bitching. At least you're alive, for now." Sledge shoved the cop into the garage door. "Now that you know I'm not bluffing, let's try this again. Where is the girl being kept and to whom did Vega sell her? I want to know everything that you do. Spill it or the next bullet I fire is going into your skull."

"I don't know where Vega is keeping the girl or the dude's name who bought her," Rick answered through gnashed teeth. "Even if I did, Vega and his partners would do far worse to me than if I said a word to you."

"Is that a challenge?" Sledge packed his forearm under the cop's chin and applied pressure to his throat. "Do not underestimate my resolve in finding that girl and the lengths to which I will go to bring Vega and his partners down, and anyone else tied to that scumbag."

Rick gagged under the weight of Sledge choking him. Feeling the cop struggle brought a sense of justice to Sledge for the hand Rick had in Kim's disappearance, and who knew what other dealings Vega and Cobalt had been involved in.

"How about you do the right thing for a change and not act like the garbage human you are? Show me you're better than this and save a life, other than your own."

"Fine," Rick said in a garbled voice as spit spiderwebbed within his mouth.

"Good man. I guess you get to live a bit longer." Sledge lowered the gun but kept his finger on the trigger. "Now. We're going to head somewhere safe and you're going to tell me everything I want to know. Where are your keys to this junk heap you call a car?"

"They're in the ignition," Rick replied with a rasp.

Sledge wagged the pistol at him, then toward the open driver's door. "Open the garage door, and then plant your ass behind the wheel. We are heading out now, together."

Chapter 55

HE GRIMACED AND TURNED toward the garage door as Sledge stood at the ready next to the passenger door. The pistol lined up with Rick's sweaty head as he shifted down to the wall and tapped the white button mounted to the exposed stud.

The motor kicked on and the door jerked as it lifted into the air. Its chain worked around the pulley overhead. Gears whined as the wheels clacked up the rails.

Sledge kept the gun on Rick as he backed to the hood and then faced the car. The cop had a frown and a pained expression planted on his face. He wasn't pleased by how his morning had begun, and very likely he wasn't going to be pleased about how the day ended.

"There is no place that's safe in this city that we'll be able to go where they won't find us," Rick said as he lumbered to the driver's side of the vehicle. "They're connected. Eyes everywhere. I'm not the only dead man in this garage."

As the door rolled to a stop above the sedan, Sledge said, "Just get in and..."

Before he could finish, a low buzzing sound entered the garage. Rick's body pitched forward onto the hood of the car; then he fell to the floor. Sledge opened the door as additional gunshots penetrated the garage from the entrance of the driveway.

The reports were muffled, silenced even, but the damage inflicted by the incoming munitions was incredible.

Sledge took a position behind the open door and waited for his chance to look. The window above busted from the incoming bullets pelting it.

Shards of glass rained down on his head. Vega had sent his goons to remove Rick from the board.

Staying low, Sledge scurried to the trunk and made his way to the driver's side. Through the back window to the windshield, he got a distorted view of a black sedan with its passenger window rolled halfway down and an armed man heading up the driveway toward them.

Don't be dead, Sledge thought as he rushed Rick's body lying on the dusty concrete slab. Blood tainted the cop's lips and teeth. He didn't appear to be alive or conscious.

He felt for a pulse on the side of his neck. It was thready and fading quickly. Sledge knew Rick would be dead long before he could get help. It was another lead removed from the table.

One of Vega's men approached the open garage. His pistol swept the interior from right to left. He steered toward the driver's side and closed in on the hood while craning his neck at the open car door.

A semi-clear shot at the henchman presented itself to Sledge as he peered around the edge of the door. He unloaded three rounds into the gunman's side and stomach before he could return fire.

His body fell to the slab as Sledge stood and moved around the car door to the hood. The three points of impact bled and stained the man's shirt red as Sledge covered him, then he glanced at the street.

Gunshots rang out from the lowered passenger window of the black sedan. The incoming gunfire punched the grill and hood of Rick's car near Sledge as he made for cover behind the wall by the garage door. He held his position for ten seconds and popped off a string of return fire at the car.

Tires squealed. The vehicle took off down the road at a fast clip. Sledge hauled ass to the street and made for his car. He caught sight of the sedan getting further away as he got inside and fired up the Chevelle.

The engine roared to life. He shifted into first gear, punched the gas pedal, and torqued the wheel. The Chevelle pulled away from the curb and made a sharp turn in the street.

Its tires smoked white as the back end swung out from the horsepower driving the bulky muscle car forward. Sledge straightened his trajectory and gave pursuit of the fleeing occupants who had just taken out Rick, and nearly him.

His hands clutched the steering wheel and gearshift as he tried to cut the distance between him and the sedan. The black car hooked a right at the stop sign without slowing a beat.

Sledge parroted the move by slamming the Chevelle into a lower gear, increasing his torque and allowing him to accelerate through the turn while keeping the tires hugging the road.

An approaching van blared its horn from a near collision of the two vehicles. The woman behind the wheel pumped her fist at Sledge and laid on the van's horn to convey her thoughts.

Traffic was sparse but Sledge hated having a high-speed chase in the suburbs. The roads were tight with cars lining the streets, not to mention the infinite blind spots that one had to be mindful of from cars backing out into the road, or kids popping out in front of them while playing.

On the straightaway, the Chevelle gained on the sedan. Its powerful engine ate at the killer's advantage with each rotation of the tires. If all went well, Sledge would overtake them.

A car backed out into the street and almost collided with the sedan. It made a wide arc around the vehicle to avoid ramming the car and maintained its heading. Sledge drove around the car as it backed up a hair more then stopped as he flew by.

The Chevelle's engine sputtered. A rattle formed under the hood and grew louder the harder Sledge pushed the muscle car after Vega's men. Although the Chevelle ran well enough, the engine's makeover wasn't complete and old parts were still scattered throughout it. Sledge prayed it wouldn't crap out on him. He needed to take the sedan out before they slipped through his fingers.

Their chase carved a path out of the suburbs and onto the freeway during rush hour. An endless sea of cars funneled into Atlanta's downtown. The glow of red brake lights shone at them. It was bumper-to-bumper as far as Sledge could see; that proved to be in his favor. The hitmen's car would be at the mercy of gridlocked traffic that kept the sedan from crossing lanes of cars and trucks driving into the city.

They kept to the shoulder of the freeway and maintained their insane speed, which was currently over seventy miles per hour and climbing. The gridlocked traffic whipped past Sledge's window in a blur of color. The driver ahead showed no fear and dodged any obstacles put in his way with little effort.

You can run but you're not going to get away. Sledge was more determined than ever to catch the fleeing men, staying within twenty feet of the speeding sedan.

As he pushed the Chevelle after the sedan, sirens whined at his six. Sledge cut his gaze to the rearview mirror. Red flashing lights from Atlanta's finest came into view. The cruiser followed their path of reckless driving along the shoulder while trying to catch up.

Not only did Sledge have to contend with the men in the sedan, but he now had to lose the patrol car trailing him. Great! That was a development he didn't need right then.

A sign up ahead signaled that the next exit was a mile up. Sledge figured the sedan would want to get off the freeway and back to the city streets. In a long enough straightway, the Chevelle would be able to overtake the sedan, but narrow city streets added a degree of difficulty to his chances of being able to accomplish that.

The sedan veered toward the throng of cars in the far-right lane to avoid a chunk of tire that resided on the shoulder. It came within inches of swapping paint with the truck that pulled away.

From there, the pickup swerved into the throng of traffic and caused a chain reaction of drivers slamming brakes and steering clear. As Sledge skirted by the rubber chunk of the tire, a car poked its nose into his path. He jerked the wheel hard toward the barrier wall. The Chevelle responded immediately and cut around the vehicle's passenger quarter panel.

Sledge threaded the muscle car through the narrow gap as he drifted toward the concrete wall. He cringed as the passenger mirror skidded over the surface. It bent inward from the contact, but as Sledge pulled away from the wall, it remained attached to the door.

The black sedan veered toward the curved exit that climbed at an angle. Cars leaving the mess of the freeway stopped and pulled over as they raced up the ramp.

A din of horns blasting their anger charged the morning air as Sledge closed in on the sedan's back bumper. They followed the winding curve of the ramp which left little room for error. Neither Sledge nor the killers he chased refused to stop while within the dense traffic of steel around them.

Sledge ignored the trailing police cruiser's flashing lights and the whine of its siren. Additional units were undoubtedly contacted and given their positions, which meant reinforcements would be tracking them down soon.

At the approaching intersection, cars refused to advance as the signal flicked from red to green. The black sedan slowed as the gap they piloted through shrank; the barrier wall to their right and the line of vehicles on their left funneled in and reduced the opening.

It failed to deter the brazen driver who expertly threaded the sedan past the cars while swapping paint with a few of them. The contact rocked the stationary vehicles. Sledge gained on the black sedan and rammed its back bumper as they emerged onto the street.

Tires screeched as they dodged cars that tried to steer out of their way. Each vehicle hurling at them changed course and flew by, darting into the opposite lane of traffic or going off the street.

No major crashes happened because of the chase. Sledge was relieved by that fact as he didn't want innocent people hurt because of them. The reckless pursuit had to end soon, one way or another.

The sedan swerved, dodging the inbound cars that drove at them. They decided on going against the flow of traffic in every attempt to ditch Sledge and the authorities that were trailing after them. He stayed the course and followed wherever the sedan went. Neither vehicle let up, pushing along the streets that teemed with early morning commuters heading to their jobs.

Cars passed by the two vehicles on either side of them as the streets cleared a path. The cruiser trailing far behind them got blocked by the mess of vehicles that were scattered across the road during the chase.

At the approaching signal, the black sedan cut across the lanes of traffic on a dime. It was a harrowing maneuver that sent the vehicle flirting with danger. Drivers not paying close enough attention slammed their brakes and steered out of the car's way as it raced past the scattering traffic.

Sledge tried to follow suit, but he was blocked by the vehicles that the sedan had cut around. His foot crammed the brake and clutch to the floor. All four tires of the muscle car locked up. It skidded to a halt just shy of crashing into a pickup truck, leaving little room between the front bumper of the Chevelle and the pickup's cab.

"Come on! Move!" Sledge waved at the driver of the truck to move out of his way, but it was too late.

By the time Sledge managed to get through the blockade, the black sedan had vanished into the city. With the claxon of sirens converging on his position, Sledge discontinued his pursuit of the killers and disappeared before the authorities had a chance to stop him.

Chapter 56

AFTER STOPPING IN AN alley and changing out the license plates on the Chevelle in a lame attempt at evading the authorities, Sledge saddled back up in the car. Between losing Rick and every other possible lead he had, the ambush at Vega's, Cobalt breathing down his neck, Trixie being in constant danger, Kim no closer to coming home, and the adrenaline surge from the high-speed chase that ended fruitlessly, Sledge was on the verge of a meltdown. This job had been a cataclysmic failure from stem to stern. Heat coursed through Sledge's veins and culminated in his head as he gripped the steering wheel and screamed the only thing that came to his mind, *"Fuuuuck!"*

His phone buzzed from his back pants pocket, reorienting him to the present moment.

Detective Wentworth's phone number splashed onto the screen. Sledge answered the call while checking the rearview mirror for Atlanta's finest.

"You have impeccable timing. What's up?"

"Nothing good."

That was not what Sledge wanted to hear. "Where are you? Do you have time to meet? I'd rather do this in person if we can."

He said nothing at first. Then Wentworth spoke up. *"Yeah. I've got a bit of time. When and where?"*

"The West End Diner." Sledge glanced at his watch. It was 8:45 a.m. "Say, fifteen minutes?"

"That will work."

"See you then. I'll have a table in the corner of the diner."

The call ended. Sledge put the phone on the seat and rubbed his hand over his face. He had no idea what bad news Wentworth would drop in his lap, but there was no avoiding the inevitable.

Sledge rolled down the alley to the street and merged with the traffic heading west. It had thinned, but the early morning commuters were still out in force. He made his way through the city while trying to figure out what bad news the detective had. His first thought was that they had discovered Kim's dead body. Even though Rick said she was still alive, the cop couldn't be trusted given recent events. As much as Sledge wanted to discount the notion, it was rooted inside his brain and expanded into a life of its own.

No. It isn't that, Sledge thought at the stop light.

His fingers tapped the base of his chin as he sat and contemplated what else it could be. The light changed and he drove on and made a right toward the diner.

He pulled into the busy parking lot and took one of the empty slots at the back. The Chevelle whipped into the space and stopped. Sledge switched off the rattling engine which sounded rough after the intense pursuit; then he removed the keys and got out of the car.

By the time Sledge made it into the diner and took his seat at the booth in the corner of the restaurant, Wentworth was walking up the walkway to the entrance. A large party of businessmen funneling outside blocked his way, forcing the detective to wait and hold the door open for them.

"What can I get started for you, honey?" an upbeat, dirty-blonde-haired woman asked. She was young, perhaps mid-thirties. A wide, inviting smile formed on her face as she waited to scribble down Sledge's order on the notepad using the pen she clutched.

"Is Sandra not working this morning?" Sledge asked as Wentworth skirted by the remainder of the suits leaving the diner.

"She's off for the next few days," the waitress answered. "I'll take good care of you, though, don't you worry." She winked and widened her smile as Wentworth approached the table.

"I'll take coffee. Black." Sledge tipped his head at the detective who slid into the bench seat across from him.

"Anything to eat, sweetie?" the waitress asked Sledge.

He was hungry. Their meeting at the diner would kill two birds with one stone.

"A slice of apple pie will be fine."

She scribbled it down and then turned to Wentworth. "And for you, handsome?"

"Coffee will be good. Cream and sugar."

"Easy enough. I'll be back shortly, gentlemen, with those cups of Joe and pie." She stuffed the notepad and pen in the front pocket of her apron. "I'm Alice, by the way. If you need anything, let me know."

"Thank you," Sledge said as she turned and made for the counter.

Wentworth stared at Sledge from across the table. "You look like shit. Rough night?"

"Rough night and morning," Sledge replied. "Your phone call didn't help either, just so you know. We need a bit of good news here."

"Yeah, well, I hate to disappoint."

Alice marched to their table with a pot of coffee, two white mugs, and a small plate of apple pie. "Okay, gentlemen. Here we are."

They tabled their conversation as she put the mugs and pie down. Alice filled both mugs with coffee, smiling the entire time. Steam rose from the brew. The scent of the roasted beans filled the air. She dug into her apron and removed the round containers of cream and put them next to Wentworth's mug.

He said, "Thank you."

"You're welcome. The sugar is in the little holder over by the napkins." Alice turned and glanced at the tables behind Wentworth. "Enjoy, gentlemen. I'll be back by here in a bit to check on you."

When she vacated the area, Wentworth continued while adding the creamer and sugar to the coffee. "The meat packing plant you told me about didn't pan out."

"Why?" Sledge asked as his stomach sank from the response. "Did you not find anything there?"

"I never made it."

"What?"

Wentworth stirred the sugar and creamer into the coffee using a spoon from his side of the table. "The judge wouldn't give me a warrant. He said there was no probable cause and evidence to support us searching it. Plus, it doesn't help that the department has a hard-on for Vega and tries to book him on any charge that will stick. That man is toxic, to say the least."

Sledge closed his eyes and tilted his head forward in frustration. Whoever Cobalt had on the inside protecting Vega in Atlanta was super connected. It wouldn't be much of a stretch if the group had judges in their pockets in addition to the police and lawyers. It was a rigged system, but how far up the chain remained to be seen.

"So even with actionable intel from a source, the judge wasn't willing to entertain your request?"

"He heard everything I had to say, which wasn't much of anything other than I had an informant who said he spotted the drugs and guns," Wentworth replied as he sipped the coffee. "He either didn't want to risk messing with Vega, or something else is going on."

As Sledge sliced a piece of pie from the end, he said, "Speaking of, I uncovered your mole inside the department."

"Oh? Who is it?"

"Rick Jenkins?"

Wentworth said nothing and sat in silence.

"I'm not sure if he's the only one Vega and his partners have in the department. There could be more."

"How do you know it's him? What proof do you have?"

"The fact is he told me himself this morning after he tried to serve me up to Vega on a silver platter last night." Sledge swallowed the pie and chased it with coffee. "I was rather shocked when I figured it out. Rick was too when I showed my face at his home early this morning as he was trying to skip town."

"Shit." Wentworth tapped his wedding ring against the side of the mug, which he hadn't removed since the divorce. "Where is he at now? We need to take him to a secure location and question him. This could be the smoking gun we need to find Kim and take Vega down."

"That's not going to happen since he's lying dead in his garage."

With his voice low but strained, Wentworth shot forward and asked, "You killed him?"

Sledge dabbed the napkin at his food around his mouth. "Not me. Vega's goons did. Two in the back. Well, at least his employer's lackeys took him out is my best guess. I shot him in the shoulder before they arrived when he was trying to escape after I busted his ass."

"How long ago did this happen?"

"An hour, give or take." Sledge continued eating as Wentworth reeled from the revelation. "I went after the shooters after they dropped Rick. I lost them in traffic a short while later and had to split before the police tagged me."

"Christ. That was you? I heard about the chase."

"Yeah. I almost had them, but the wheelman of the sedan gave me the slip."

"Did you get the plate of the car?"

Sledge shook his head. "There wasn't a plate on the back. Come to think of it, the vehicle didn't have any branding on the trunk. It could have been a Lexus, BMW, or several other sedans."

Wentworth massaged his brow. Sledge understood his irritation. He said, "Well, hell. I'll need to call in the hit on Rick and get units to his home."

"What are you going to tell the department?" Sledge wondered if the detective was going to try and take him in. That wouldn't work out too well for Wentworth if he tried.

"I'll figure something out. You should have contacted me about Rick and let me handle it."

"I doubt that would've changed the outcome," Sledge replied. "Vega and his employers are after me now. They want me dead since I'm getting closer to their operation. You should watch your six if you don't want a bullet in your back or head."

"I'm not averse to being a target of criminals. They can come at me all they want, but it's not going to dissuade me from finding Kim. By the way, we're still sucking fumes. I've got feelers out but no one is talking, not to me, anyway."

"Keep working at it. Rick told me that she was still alive and still in the city. Vega is waiting to transfer her to the scumbag who bought her. I guess us squeezing them has messed with their timetable on completing the deal."

"Name?"

"He didn't give one." Sledge placed the fork on the side of the plate and drank from the mug. "You know as much as I do now."

Wentworth removed his phone from his coat pocket and typed away on the keys. Alice returned with the pot of coffee while flashing her smile at them.

"How are we doing over here? Do either of you want me to top off your mugs?"

"I'm good. Thank you, Alice." Sledge replied as he set his mug down.

"I'm good as well," Wentworth added.

Alice nodded at the half-eaten apple pie in front of Sledge. "Is that hitting the spot, sweetie?"

"It is. Wonderful as always." Sledge smiled back at the waitress.

"Excellent. Give me a holler if you want me to top you off."

"We will."

As Alice walked off, Wentworth glanced up from his phone and asked, "Do you have anything on this group who's backing Vega?"

Sledge swallowed and decided to answer, but didn't expand much. "Cobalt. Though you might want to tread lightly since they're well-connected and run under the radar. These are not the sort of people you want to cross."

Wentworth typed on the phone. "I've never heard of them."

"That's the point, I think." Sledge toed the line of how much to say while also trying to supply Wentworth with a lead to follow. "They work in the background, hidden by the puppets they control. That's why you haven't heard of them before."

The phone in Wentworth's hand buzzed as he opened his mouth with a follow-up question. Sledge was saved by the vibrating device that snared his attention.

"Yeah," Wentworth said into the phone.

Sledge drank from the mug while studying the detective's arched brows that rose the more he listened. It wasn't good news as Wentworth sighed and glanced at his watch.

"I'm on my way. I should be there in twenty minutes." He ended the call and took another swig of the coffee as Sledge waited for him to speak. After lowering the mug, Wentworth said, "Doesn't look like I'll need to call in about Rick. Units arrived at his place a short bit ago. Neighbors must have phoned it in. I need to head over there. See if I can find anything out about Kim before anyone else that might be on Vega's payroll decides to get rid of the evidence. That is if they haven't already."

"As I said, watch your back. We don't know how high up the chain this goes," Sledge said. "The deeper you get the more dangerous this case will become."

"Thank God for bulletproof vests, then." Wentworth pounded his chest then reached into his back pants pocket for his wallet.

"I got this. Go ahead and bounce."

"Are you sure?"

Sledge removed his wallet. "It's a cup of coffee. I think I can manage a couple of bucks."

Wentworth pulled his hand back and hiked his shoulders. "Thanks."

While the detective took one final sip and slid out of the booth, Sledge said, "If you need to report that I was at Rick's this morning, go ahead. I'm in deep already, but I don't want to get you in trouble. You seem like a good cop that's doing his best with what you've got."

"I'll handle the scene at Rick's place. Don't worry," Wentworth said, trying to reassure Sledge of his plan to keep him anonymous. "Since we have no idea who we can trust, we'll keep things low-key for now. In the meantime, can you do me a favor?"

"What's that?"

"Try not to leave a trail of dead bodies across the city. That sort of thing makes it harder to spin and hide your involvement."

Sledge pulled a twenty-dollar bill out of the wallet and stood from the booth. "Where Vega and Cobalt are concerned, all bets are off. They came after the wrong person and they have Kim. I'm going to see this through to the end."

"I was afraid you were going to say that."

Wentworth left the diner as Sledge paid their bill. Alice happily cashed him out and handed him the change, but Sledge refused to take any portion of the intended tip from her.

"Thanks, doll." Alice leaned on the counter and batted her eyes at Sledge. "See you around, hopefully sooner than later."

Sledge smirked and left the diner. As he headed down the sidewalk, an Atlanta police cruiser rocketed by with its lights flashing and siren sounding. He lowered his head and made for the back corner of the parking lot where the Chevelle was parked.

His phone pinged with a message. Sledge removed the phone from his pocket as he walked to the driver's side of the car. The message was from Mr. Claymore and it was short and to the point. He wanted him to come to their estate as quickly as he could and not delay. They had matters to discuss.

Chapter 57

SLEDGE DROVE THROUGH THE gates to the Claymore estate at 10:15 a.m. The unexpected message played through his head repeatedly for the duration of the drive. He wondered what spawned the in-person meeting versus talking over the phone, and he worried that it wasn't good.

Mr. Claymore waited outside on the porch as Sledge piloted the Chevelle around the curved drive to the entrance of the home. His arms were interlocked across his chest. A somber look of sadness painted his face that made Sledge's throat move and fashioned his stomach into knots.

After cutting the engine off and getting out, Sledge made his way to the entrance of the home. He moved with purpose toward Mr. Claymore who, upon closer inspection, appeared to have been crying, from his bloodshot eyes.

"Thank you for coming on such short notice," the father said while unfolding his arms and extending his hand out to Sledge.

"Of course. Your message sounded urgent." Sledge shook his hand and then asked, "Have you uncovered something new about Kim?"

"Not exactly. Please, follow me if you will."

The lack of details from Mr. Claymore's vague answers and responses didn't help matters. Sledge played along and followed him into the home and then to his study. Mrs. Claymore was absent from their impromptu meeting. It was just the two of them in his cavernous study for what Sledge assumed was more bad news to be dumped into his lap.

"I know you're probably asking yourself why I requested you to stop by," Mr. Claymore said as he offered Sledge a seat in one of his plush brown leather chairs.

Sledge sat down in the front of the seat. "That thought has crossed my mind."

"Drink?"

"No thank you." Sledge respectfully declined the offer with a raised hand.

Mr. Claymore stood at a small round table that had a bottle of scotch and two tumblers on it. The man was hurting. That was easy to see. He had found comfort in the arms of the expensive-looking bottle that dulled the senses and made each day without his daughter bearable.

"How is the hunt coming along for my daughter?"

"It's coming along," Sledge replied. "There are some leads I'm working on that look promising. I wish I had something more concrete to tell you at the moment, but I don't. What I can say is that I think we are getting closer. I've reached out to Detective Wentworth. Between the two of us, we're casting a wide net over this city and narrowing our search."

He didn't want to give false hope to the family. That never did a bit of good from Sledge's experience. The information he had was fluid and not rock solid. Relaying second-hand accounts without verifying them first was not how Sledge operated; it wasn't what the family needed to hear either.

Mr. Claymore sipped on the scotch as he sat in the chair across from Sledge. The tumbler never left his hand as he placed the base of the glass on the arm of the seat. "Tell me, and please be honest, do you think Kim is still alive? Will we ever see her again?"

"That's a tough question to answer, Mr. Claymore," Sledge said, knowing of the dangerous ground he was now treading. "I can't say one way or another. For me to sit here, look you in the eyes, and say yes would be irresponsible of me."

"So, you don't think that we will ever get her back then?"

"That's not what I said." Sledge understood the desperation Mr. Claymore battled. The man was at his wits' end. He was short on hope, and it showed. "You have a lot of folks working on this case and doing everything they can to bring Kim home. I can assure you that none are resting and all of us are working tirelessly to try and find her."

He took another drink, but this time, it was more of a hearty swig than a sip. "The missus and I are growing doubtful that we'll ever see Kim again. We're now over a week and a half into her abduction and no one has provided a hint of evidence that she's even alive." Claymore gulped down the remaining scotch and placed the empty glass on the table near him.

With the direction the conversation was heading, Sledge could see the torment eating at the helpless father. His resolve was still strong, but weakening as the days passed. Holding tough under such pressure was a testament to the love he had for his daughter.

"Mr. Claymore, I don't try to know what you're going through and how this must be affecting your family. This is never an easy matter to face. It would test the strongest of individuals." Sledge spoke in a caring and heartfelt way to try and appease the father and to keep that spark of hope still going in him. "We will do everything humanly possible to find Kim, and to bring those who took her to justice. Of that, I can and will promise you."

"That's why I asked you here, Mr. Sledge."

"I don't follow."

"That right there. Your response and reassurance of doing everything you can to find my daughter." Mr. Claymore inched forward on the chair and then cupped his hands together. "You see, I had to see your face. Read your eyes. Study your body language to gauge if you thought we still had a chance at finding Kim, or if this was a lost cause. One can't understand such things through a crude indifferent message. It's easy to hide the truth. I've been in countless negotiations and faced the world's toughest men.

"You'd be surprised how much can be hidden, even in a face-to-face meeting such as this. For us, my wife and I, we had to know that you were still invested in finding Kim and that we didn't waste money on someone who wasn't giving it their all and simply stringing us along."

Sledge reaffirmed his commitment. "That is not the case. I'm taking this job seriously and using every resource at my disposal to find her."

"I know that now and didn't mean to disrespect you," Mr. Claymore tipped his head and raised his hands. "We just had to know and see for ourselves that you were still in this fight. You did come highly recommended and I trust the source that brought us together. I'm afraid that during this ordeal, I've become a bit doubtful of us finding Kim. Time is not our friend."

"It never is but we are close. Hang in there a bit longer. Keep the faith."

Mr. Claymore forced a half smile. "We are trying."

"Good." Sledge was ready to leave and get back to work. Oscar crossed his mind during their conversation and he wondered if he had anything new for him. "If there isn't anything else you need or want to discuss, I should head out and get back to it."

"Yes. I don't want to keep you any longer than necessary."

Both men stood from their seats. Mr. Claymore escorted him out of the study and down the corridor to the entrance of the home.

"Please give your wife my best and tell her that we are working on bringing your daughter home," Sledge said as they neared the door.

"I will do that. She would have attended our meeting but she wasn't up for it." Mr. Claymore opened the door and continued. "It's been hard on my wife. She's not been the same since Kim was abducted. Neither of us has been."

Sledge walked outside and stood on the porch, then turned toward him. "I understand."

"If you require anything from us or need extra money to help facilitate her recovery above what we're giving you, then please, don't hesitate to let me know. I'm at your disposal, day or night, whatever you need."

"I'll keep that in mind and thank you. What you've provided already is sufficient." Sledge wasn't about to take advantage of the family. That's not why he did what he did. If money was his goal, he could make far more working as an operative for any government around the world, or for a tyrannical regime that could benefit from his decades of experience and training. "Just stay by your phone and be available. That's all I require."

"We will."

"Good. Talk soon."

As Sledge descended the steps to the driveway, Mr. Claymore closed the door. Their meeting didn't provide anything new to the case, but it was one that the father needed to mollify his fractured heart.

Sledge got behind the wheel of the Chevelle and started the engine. His phone rang before he could shift into gear and drive off. It was Oscar.

"Hey. Good timing. You were actually on my mind."

"Is that good or bad?"

"That depends on you, bud." Sledge shifted into gear and steered the muscle car around the mammoth water feature. "Tell me you have some good news. I need it. Anything will do."

"I have something, though, I'm not sure if it pertains to your case or not. I'll let you be the judge of that."

"Are you at the shop?"

"I am."

"Mind if I stop by and you fill me in? You know how I am about communicating sensitive data."

"Yeah. I haven't forgotten."

"I'll be there shortly." Sledge ended the call as he sped down the winding driveway to the street, wondering what sort of good news his friend had uncovered.

Chapter 58

OSCAR OPENED THE SIDE door to the pawn shop and let Sledge in. The door slammed shut with a heavy thump against the jamb after he entered. They headed for the secured room in the back of the building with Oscar matching Sledge's stride.

"I've got my cousin up front working the counter so I figured we'd come back here so he can tend to customers while we talk shop."

Sledge bobbed his head. "That works for me. I know you've got a business to run."

"Yeah. He's good when he shows up. It's a pain at times helping out the family, but you didn't come here to hear me bitch." They walked into the secured room at the back of the pawn shop. Lights came on as Oscar trailed Sledge inside.

"That's always a bonus."

"I'm sure it is."

"So, what's up?" Sledge asked as Oscar stood across from him. "I can do without bad news. It's been one hell of a day already."

"It's news, but I'll let you be the judge on whether it's good or bad." Oscar paused a beat and then continued. "I got contacted early this morning by a former partner of mine. I'm talking before the sun even had a chance to come up."

Sledge crossed his arms and leaned on the counter behind him. "Okay. I'm assuming about Vega."

"Yeah. It seems he's moving product of some sort later tonight and is looking for extra hands to oversee the shipments." Oscar mimed air quotes with his fingers.

"What sort of shipments?"

"Don't know. It wasn't said and I didn't ask. This is one of those jobs where you don't ask questions and just show up if you want to get paid."

"So, this could be anything." Sledge rambled off a few ideas. "Guns. Drugs. I guess it could involve Kim but the way you're phrasing it makes it sound like it isn't."

"True, but here's the thing." Oscar approached the table between them and explained. "Vega is paying big money. Like fifteen large per head that he can get on this detail to make sure it goes off without a hitch. With it being a last-minute gig, this could involve your girl since you've been applying so much heat."

"I guess it could be her." Sledge paced the open floor while thinking it over.

Vega could be transferring not only the guns and drugs he previously saw but Kim too to the piece of shit who bought her. It would make sense to complete everything in one shot, especially when you have the extra muscle to ensure that the transfer goes off without a hitch.

"It's not much to go on but it's something," Oscar said. "Anyone who's been in this business long enough knows how to read between the lines, when to ask questions and when not to. Given the short notice, lack of details, extra manpower, and a large sum of money being thrown around, this has to be huge. That's how I'm reading it."

Sledge stopped pacing. "Where do they want you to go?"

"Savannah. The docks."

"So, they didn't want you to meet them in Atlanta?"

"Nope. All I was told was the amount to be paid upfront, where to be, and at what time."

"And when will this go down?"

"I'm supposed to be on-site at 10:00 p.m.," Oscar answered.

"What did you tell them?"

"That I would think it over and let them know. I've got until noon." He checked his watch. "So, twenty-five minutes to do so."

Sledge glanced at his watch and then back to Oscar. "That's around a four-hour drive from Atlanta to Savannah in normal traffic. I wish we had better intel on what Vega was moving and from where."

"It is a gamble. I wish I had more to share or offer, but I don't."

It was a gamble, one that would remove Sledge far from the city on a scant bit of information. That didn't settle well with him and made him wonder if he should chance it, especially considering that he was recently lured into a trap by someone he trusted.

That was one aspect that gave Sledge pause. He pondered whether this so-called shipment could be yet another false trail for him. For that to be, Vega would have to know that Oscar knew him. Sledge had to ask his trusted friend to appease his curiosity.

"No one is aware that we know one another, right? As in, there's no chance that they could be using you to get to me?"

Oscar disregarded the idea immediately with a shake of his head. "No. We've kept our business on the down low. As far as my contacts are concerned, I do not know a Blake Sledge. I don't know how else they would have found out since we're careful, but stranger things have happened. I haven't said a word to anyone."

"Me neither." Sledge waved off the question with a flick of his hand. Oscar could be lying to him, of course, but he could also be telling the truth. And if he was telling the truth, Sledge didn't want to risk insulting him and losing a good asset and, to date, friend. Either way, whether it was a trap or the real deal, Sledge had no other leads to follow anyway.

"It's just me being paranoid." Sledge said. "A cop I had been working with set me up last night which made for a fun time getting shot at and stabbed. Well, cut and nearly stabbed by some of Vega's goons and a new player in town." He watched Oscar's face closely to see any sign of awareness of the situation but found only surprise thereon.

"Damn. That's crazy. Did you wear the vest?"

"I did. It didn't protect against the Karambit they had, but I'm glad I wore it."

"Shit, brother. You may need an army to take these people on."

"Perhaps." Sledge then asked, "Are you going to take the job tonight at the docks?"

It wasn't difficult to see the unease wash over Oscar from the question. His hand massaged his neck as he looked away. "I think you know the answer to your question. The money is good, but I'm not excited about getting mixed up with Vega and his crew."

"Of course. I was just wondering if there was going to be a friendly on-site for when I crash their party."

"So, you're going then?"

Sledge shrugged. "It's all I've got at the moment. The timing of every-thing hints that it could involve Kim as well as whatever drugs and guns he's unloading. It wouldn't be too hard for the buyer to pick her up at the docks and disappear into the night. If I don't go and at least look into it, I'll never forgive myself if that was the last chance for me to save her and I didn't act on it. Once she leaves the country, she's in the wind. I'm not so sure she'll ever be found."

"That is true." Oscar lowered his head and then lifted it. "I'm sorry I'm not going out there with you. You know I got you, but I have to weigh my risk tolerance carefully to protect my little girl."

"There is no need to apologize. I get it and appreciate what you've already done. I'll take it from here."

Oscar held out his arms to encompass the spread of guns surrounding them. "You'll need a bit more firepower, I imagine. Why don't you take a look around, and if you see anything you want, put it in the middle here. It's on the house."

"Are you sure?"

"If I wasn't, I wouldn't have offered."

"True."

As Oscar marched to the door leading to the stockroom, he said, "Just don't be a greedy bitch and clean me out. That's all I ask."

"See. Now you're putting limits on me. You know I love being a greedy bitch."

The two men exchanged smirks.

Oscar opened the door and stepped into the doorway. "I'll be right back. I'm going to check on my cousin and write down the details for you about the exchange."

"Thanks, brother, for everything. It's beyond helpful what you've done."

"Just find that girl and get her home. That's all I ask."

Sledge tipped his head. "That's what I plan to do."

Chapter 59

EVEN THOUGH OSCAR HAD given Sledge the run of his stockpile of weapons, he was reserved in his selection. The amount of extra weight had to be minimal so that he could move without being too bogged down.

"I don't like this, but I understand why you're going," Trixie said from the other side of the workbench. "You got away twice now by the skin of your teeth. It might not be that easy this time around."

Sledge surveyed the selection of pistols, knives, and rifles spread out before him. All were curated based on performance and how well he knew the weapons would handle in a gunfight.

"It won't be easy, but it's necessary." He slapped a fully loaded magazine into the grip of an HK45 pistol Oscar had at the shop. "Vega is connected so high up that the people who can and should throw the book at him hard are allowing him and his partners to skate on by with maybe a slap on the wrist, or they're covering it up entirely. Case in point is Rick. From what I've learned, no one in law enforcement wants to get close to this case, or others, because of the protection they have."

"Did you call Detective Wentworth?"

"I did. They're not letting him move on this since the meat packing plant was a bust. Plus, it's out of his jurisdiction. He said he'd let the local blues know so they could send some help, but I asked him not to since I don't know whom we can trust. If it's not me going after Kim tonight, then it's nobody."

"Yeah. Exactly. You'll be on your own." Trixie stood straight and squared her shoulders. "That's why I think I should come with you."

"Absolutely not." Sledge didn't have to think it over. It was an instant no for him. "It's way too dangerous for that. I won't be able to concentrate on my mission and protect you at the same time."

The response from Sledge vexed Trixie. Her lips pursed and she squinted at him while he stuffed extra magazines into the pockets of the bulletproof vest.

"Do you have a death wish? I can't tell yet if it's that or if you get off on the rush of putting your life on the line constantly."

Maybe it was a bit of both; but Sledge didn't say that out loud, only in his head.

"This has nothing to do with an adrenaline rush or whatever. It's about being capable and able to help a person who needs it." Sledge stuffed the last magazine he had prepared into the vest then leaned on the tabletop. "I am aware of the risks that are involved in going to that dock tonight alone, but it is what it is. I do appreciate your willingness to go and help, but you have zero combat training and will be nothing more than a liability out there."

He hated being so blunt with Trixie, but that moment called for it. She couldn't be anywhere around Vega or Cobalt. Bringing her with him would put her in their literal crosshairs.

"The stakes are tremendously high here. If Kim is in Savannah and I don't go, then her life is only going to get much worse real fast. She'll wish for death to avoid the sort of life she's staring down. If I can stop that from happening and bring her back to her family, then I'm going to do it, or die trying."

"What am I supposed to do, then, huh?" Trixie threw her arms up in frustration. "Just sit on my hands and wait to see if you get killed or not? I don't know what I can do to help you from here. There doesn't seem to be much."

Her desire to stand shoulder-to-shoulder with him was evident. She wasn't backing down and more than conveyed that she wanted to be useful.

Sledge liked having her invested in his crusade as much as she appeared to now enjoy being there with him. Thus far, Trixie proved herself at the keyboard of her computer, and that's where Sledge needed her to be, in the warehouse, safe and far from Cobalt.

"You'll still be useful from here."

Trixie lowered her chin and glared at Sledge. "How? Thoughts and prayers won't do much against the shit storm you'll be facing."

"See if there are any cameras around the docks in Savannah. If so, hack in and get control so that you can be an extra set of eyes out there. That's something you can do, right?"

"Yeah. I should be able to do it."

"Also, check for what ships are supposed to be docking and shipping out from the port. Try and get your hands on bills of lading, look through the shipments, and see if anything feels off about any of the paperwork. That could tie Vega to whoever is coming to get his product. If there's a string we can pull, let's pull it."

She warmed up to the idea and loosened her stiffened posture. "Okay. I'll see what I can find."

Sledge glanced at his watch. The time was almost 5:00 p.m. He'd have to leave soon for Savannah to give him time to scout the area and lay out his plan of attack.

His phone rang as Trixie started speaking. He held his finger up at her to give him a minute as he peered at the screen.

"Who is it?" Trixie asked.

"I don't know."

No number or contact was listed. It was an unknown caller. That didn't happen. Sledge's phone number wasn't easily accessible as he had given it out to a select few. Curious, he hit the answer button on the screen but didn't speak.

The call connected but no one spoke from the other end. Not at first. There was someone on the phone since Sledge was able to hear what he figured to be road noise.

"*Blake Sledge,*" a smooth, confident voice said in near-perfect English. The caller had an accent that Sledge pegged as being from the Middle East region.

"Who is this?" Sledge glanced at Trixie as he waited for a response.

"*Come now, Mr. Sledge. I think you know who this is.*"

"Marko Vega."

"*Bingo.*"

Vega spoke in a jovial tone as if his world wasn't rocked or bothered by the disruption to his business. Sledge expected him to be full of piss and vinegar considering how big a thorn he had become in his side. Vega was eerily calm and collected as if he didn't have a care in the world.

Trixie paced the floor in front of the table while keeping quiet. She peered at Sledge periodically but remained silent as the two men exchanged words.

"How did you get this number?" Sledge asked.

"Let's avoid wasting time on silly questions, shall we?"

Rick came to mind, but Sledge didn't know if that was the case or if Vega had gotten it another way.

"What do you want?"

"That's always the right question. I want to speak with the man who has made it his mission to stick his nose into my business. You have become a rather big problem, I must say. My partner is dead, thanks to you, and my scout has vanished into the wind. It has, how do you Americans say, thrown a wrench into my gears."

"I'm happy to oblige," Sledge replied, thinking of how he removed Trent and Drake from the board, weakening Vega's grip on Atlanta. "If I can help out in any way, please, let me know."

Vega chuckled. His smug laughter ate at Sledge, knowing how connected and untouchable he thought he was. He'd soon learn otherwise.

"Yes. The gruff hero who fights for justice and blah, blah, blah. It's all been fun and games, I'm sure, but now, it's time to end this. I assure you that you have no chance of winning, Mr. Sledge or, I apologize, do you prefer to be called Brad Jones?"

Sledge's heart dropped to his stomach as the room tilted. Hearing that name sent a flood of emotions coursing through him. He glanced around for Trixie but she had wandered off during the start of the conversation. She was nowhere in sight.

Cobalt had somehow connected Sledge to his former assassin persona, Brad Jones. It couldn't have been Shane, the group's instructor and now apparent liaison. As far as Sledge knew, neither Shane, nor anyone else within Cobalt, or even the world, knew of the connection.

After a bit of silence, Vega spoke up. *"Have you lost the ability to speak? I know you're still there. I can hear the unfortunate condition of your ability to still breathe, though that clock is ticking down. But tell me, what's wrong? Is your mind bombarded by so many questions that you can't form words? Yes. We know about you and your history."*

"If you're that smart, then you must know that I'm the one person you do not want to mess with. You have no idea the amount of hellfire I can, and will, bring down on you." Sledge felt his blood boiling inside his veins. His neck was flush with heat that grew hotter the longer they spoke. "You'd be foolish to underestimate my resolve in completely obliterating your empire."

"My empire is far bigger than you can imagine, thanks in part to your former employer, who I must say, is rather excited about having found you."

Sledge presented an ultimatum to the crime lord. "I'll tell you what– Return the girl, unharmed, and maybe I won't personally rip you limb-from-limb."

"Temper, temper. I can assure you the girl you've been hard at work to find is unharmed. Selling busted merchandise does not benefit my business in any way. Reputation is everything, my friend. My suggestion to you is to forget the girl and worry about yourself because you are as good as dead."

"We'll see about that. I'm closer than you realize."

"Sure you are. Good luck."

The call clicked off. Vega was gone. Sledge mashed the end call button harder than he needed to and tossed the device onto the table.

Trixie walked toward the table he was stationed at and asked, "I take it that he wanted to kiss and make up? He's deeply sorry for all of the trouble he's caused, and vows to never do it again?"

"Not exactly."

"Yeah. It was probably more along the lines of a 'you're going to die and everyone else you love' sort of thing. We'll find you and yadda, yadda, yadda."

Sledge hiked his shoulders. "Basically." As he stared at Trixie, he detected the fear in her eyes. She knew the situation was dire but didn't want to add fuel to an already burning blaze.

"Vega doesn't know where we are, does he?"

"No, he doesn't. If he did, he wouldn't have bothered calling and we would already be dead. That call was him posturing and trying to scare me off the trail because he knows I'm close. Too close. He's getting worried. If by some chance he does locate us and sends men here while I'm gone, I want you to leave."

Trixie asked, "Where do I go? My apartment?"

"No." Sledge grabbed his phone and pulled up the address of a motel he'd used before. "I'm going to send you the name of a place here in Atlanta. I know the owner. She's a former client and owes me a favor. Give her my name and she'll give you a room. Wait there until you hear from me."

"Okay." Trixie checked her phone and read the screen.

As Sledge thought about it more, he wanted her to go ahead and move to the motel. He didn't want to take the chance of her having to face Vega's men, or a Cobalt hit squad, by herself. "On second thought, why don't you go to that motel now? I'll contact Tela and let her know you'll be coming by."

"Do they have a good enough internet connection? If not, or if you're unsure, then I'd rather stay here." Trixie pocketed her phone and said, "I'll need a stable connection to hack those feeds and to watch your back."

"I don't remember if they do or not, but..."

"But nothing." Trixie put her foot down and wanted Sledge to listen. "I'm staying here until it's no longer safe. You don't know for sure if Vega knows where we are." She pointed to the walls of the warehouse. "You have plenty of surveillance all over this place. No one is going to get the jump on me before I have a chance to spot them. I'll be fine. From here, I'll do my best work. That's what you need, my best. If it comes to me having to bolt, then I will. I'm good at avoiding thugs and have spent plenty of time doing it."

Although not completely sold on the idea, Sledge didn't have the luxury of waiting around to debate it. He had to get moving to make it to Savannah before it was too late. He was confident that Vega didn't know where they were, and before he'd be able to find them, Sledge would have already taken him down.

"Fine. Just stay alert and watch the security monitors. If anything feels wrong or off, you cut and run. Okay?"

Trixie didn't scoff at the request. Instead, she bowed her head. "Deal. Now you need to get going, before it's too late. Watch your ass and save that girl. End this tonight."

"You can count on that."

Chapter 60

THE TRIP TO SAVANNAH was riddled with pockets of dense traffic and one wreck that slowed Sledge's timetable by an additional forty-five minutes. He entered the fourth-busiest seaport in the United States after 9:00 p.m. using one of the port's police vehicles he stole from the yard. Sledge cruised through the massive port at a modest speed to keep eyes off of him. Sooner or later, the missing vehicle would be reported and the search for a possible intruder would begin.

Towering walls of shipping containers dotted the landscape. It was a maze of multicolored steel that went on for miles. Massive container ships were docked in port. The vessels were offloaded by large dockside gantry cranes that hauled the containers to the dock in stacks as the sun dipped below the horizon and night took hold.

Sledge kept the headlights of the police vehicle off and steered away from the workers going about their routine. Vega's port of call was ahead, past the mass of containers that walled him in.

Glancing at each of the dented and rusted steel boxes, Sledge wondered if any of them were Vega's or even Cobalt's. Not that it mattered which one they belonged to. The two were essentially one under Cobalt's network.

As Sledge learned over the past week since taking on Kim's case, Vega was nothing more than a pawn in a much larger scheme. With Cobalt involved, they pulled Vega's strings and made him act as they wanted. He was a dancing monkey that was the face of their terrorist organization so they could keep from being brought out into the light.

For such criminals, that was their worst fear, being exposed when all they wanted was to push forth their agenda from the shadows. Part of the problem was that Sledge still didn't know what Cobalt's agenda even was. The group was so well hidden under layers of smaller factions and bureaucratic cover that it was impossible to know who pulled their strings and what they touched other than the guns, drugs, and human trafficking that Sledge recently uncovered.

Of course, those were side businesses, and in the end, Sledge was certain Cobalt's reach extended to places unknown. Either way, what he did tonight would be a tiny nail in both Vega's and Cobalt's coffins. It wasn't a death blow, but it was a step in the right direction in taking them down.

Sledge tucked the patrol car between two mountainous piles of containers. He was close enough to his destination and would go the rest of the way on foot to not alert any of Vega's men standing watch.

Trixie called. His phone was set on silent in the seat next to him. The brightness of the lit screen alerted Sledge to the inbound call. He answered.

"Are you in position?"

"Yeah. I just got here."

"Traffic?"

"Yep. I'm about to scout the area. We're running out of time." Sledge adjusted the earpiece lodged in his right ear to make sure it didn't come loose while talking to Trixie. "Have you been able to tap into the security cameras?"

"We have access to all of the cameras. Nice job by the way on stealing that patrol car. It blends in better than your Chevelle."

"That it does." Sledge got out of the vehicle and opened the door behind him. His bag of gear waited for him on the seat. "How many men are we looking at?"

"Not sure. The coverage isn't the best. I don't have a clear line of sight because of the angles of the cameras and the shipping containers all over the place. Plus, it's dark, so there's that."

Sledge unzipped the bag and quickly removed the bulletproof vest first. As he placed the armor-plated vest over his head and secured the buckles fixed to the straps, he said, "That's fine. I'll do some recon. From what my buddy said, there could be a full house of extra muscle to guard this shipment and whatever else is going down."

"Speaking of shipments, I found the shipping manifest that's tied to Vega. I had to do some digging since it was listed under some bogus name. I'm guessing he might have someone on the inside there at the port working back channels and covering this up. I'm not sure, though."

"What are the container numbers?"

"*I already sent them to your phone.*"

Sledge adjusted the vest into place and glanced at his phone. "So, four different containers?"

"*That's what I'm seeing. I'm not finding what contents are in each of them, so you'll have to check them one by one. But would he seriously transport Kim in a container?*"

"I don't know. I wouldn't put anything past him." Sledge placed the phone in his back pants pocket and finished outfitting his body with the HK45, combat knives, and the M4 rifle. All guns had suppressors affixed to the barrels to minimize sound, flash, and heat signatures. "I'll have to snoop around and see. If I had to guess where Kim is, she's probably waiting for her buyer to show so Vega can be rid of her."

"*True. I'll keep working on these cameras to see if I can pick up anything else.*"

"Sounds good." Sledge shut the door to the police vehicle quietly and left it in the shadows. "Has there been any activity around the warehouse?"

"*Nope. No movement.*"

That relieved Sledge. He hoped it stayed that way for the duration of his mission since he was four hours away. "Remember. If you do..."

"*Cut and run to your sleazy motel,*" Trixie said before Sledge could finish. "*I haven't forgotten. It sounds like a real charmer from the pictures I found online and the lovely reviews.*"

Sledge moved within the murky depths of the shipping containers. He adjusted the M4 against his shoulder while sweeping each intersection he crossed. "Yeah, well, it's only used in case of an emergency and is meant to be temporary. It doesn't need to be much or look amazing to do its job."

Neither narrow corridor within the maze of containers had guards patrolling. He advanced straight ahead at a decent clip with his finger over the trigger guard of the suppressed M4 Carbine.

"*True, but I would still prefer the Ritz-Carlton or an equally nice five-star hotel. Atlanta is full of them. A lavish penthouse suite is far more appealing than a roach motel that's been defiled by hookers.*"

"Hang on..." Sledge whispered, trying to employ some noise discipline. Working with someone unaccustomed to covert missions was proving to be a challenge. He would have to put some real time into training her when he got back to the warehouse, but for now, at least Trixie was safe.

Sledge approached the next junction when he detected footfalls and a bright white light heading toward his position from the right. His gun lowered. He released the M4 Carbine and allowed it to hang from its attached sling draped across his body. Sledge opted for the combat knife sheathed at the small of his back.

He toed the edge of the towering stack of containers as the crunching footsteps and light were less than a foot away. His gloved hand cinched down on the handle. His back was pressed flat against the exterior of the container as his target emerged from the darkness of the opening carrying a pistol in one hand and the flashlight in the other.

The gunman paused and shifted right first, presenting the vulnerability of his back to Sledge as he cleared the opening within the containers. As he pivoted to his left, Sledge attacked with deadly precision. He shot forward and grabbed the patrolling guard's wrist handling the gun to keep it trained on the ground.

Sledge forced him back into the hard edge of the container and jammed the knife upward under the gunman's chin. The tip punctured the skin with ease and hit the jawbone. Its length vanished inside his skull. A muffled gurgle sounded from his gaped mouth. The flashlight fell from the guard's hand to the concrete and rolled against the base of the container.

Yanking the blade free, a string of blood chased the weapon. Sledge gently guided the dead weight of the hired gunman to the ground to minimize noise. He then retrieved the flashlight and switched it off, erasing the intrusive light from the pathway and plunging the area back into darkness.

Sledge wiped the blood off on the man's pants and placed it back into the sheath. He then took hold of the M4 Carbine and brought the rifle to bear. "Do we have any idea where Vega's shipping containers are? There's a ton of them here. It's going to be difficult to find them quickly."

Trixie broke in over the earpiece as Sledge moved down the length of the containers. "*I don't know for sure. If they're being moved out tonight, maybe by the water so they can easily be loaded onto whatever ship is taking them.*"

"Agreed, but there is still a ton of containers around here." Sledge kept within the shadows and roved the darkening landscape of the seaport. "Too many to check without being spotted."

"*Okay. After panning around the area, I think I got eyes on our containers.*"

As Trixie finished speaking, the whine of diesel engines grumbled to life. There was more than one, maybe three or more ahead of Sledge.

Headlights came into view. The rumbling beasts funneled down the dock toward him one by one. Their flatbed trailers used for hauling what he assumed to be the containers were empty as they each left the area.

"I just had four different big rigs pass by with no containers on their trailers."

"Yeah. A few guards are patrolling around two separate containers that are not stacked." Trixie said. *"The camera angle I've got isn't the greatest, and I can't tell much more than that or where the others are."*

"No worries. I'm going to have to get a closer look. That's the only way to be sure." Sledge peered through the scope mounted on top of the Carbine. "I'm going silent. Talk soon."

"Be careful."

He advanced out of the gap between the containers and marched toward the back end of the recently delivered units that had been dropped off. His rifle swept the dock as he steered into the shadows cast by the stacks of containers that blocked portions of the lights mounted around the port.

Two guards materialized ahead from between the rows of containers. Both carried what appeared to be a rifle and a pistol that they bore at a relaxed stance instead of a ready state.

Sledge popped off two quick, silenced bursts while advancing toward them. Each carefully placed shot hit home center mass in their respective targets. Both men recoiled from the punch of the rounds that sent them to the ground.

As he closed in on the guards, Sledge put two more rounds in each of their backs and then he scanned the gap between the containers from which they emerged. His Carbine swept the space and found no additional targets moving within the murk.

Both doors of the containers had no locks on them. They had numbers listed on their fronts matching the ones Trixie had sent him. Sledge advanced on the unit to his right and worked the handle up and out of its hold; then he swung the door open far enough for him to slip inside and see what was contained within.

A musty smell greeted him as he entered. Sledge switched on the gun-mounted light and searched the container. Various-sized crates were stacked along the walls with a narrow path that sliced up the middle.

The wooden boxes looked similar to the ones back at the meat packing plant that housed drugs and guns. He checked one of the crates near the front by popping it loose from the top edge and shoving the lid upward.

Inside were a variety of guns mixed in with hay, rifles that ranged from AK-47s to M16s. This was Vega's cargo, but he was more concerned with tracking down Kim than weapons or drugs.

Sledge exited the shipping container and made for the other container. As he rotated the rusted piece of steel above the handle up and out of the way, two more men rushed him from behind.

The lights from their guns shone at Sledge's back and the face of the container's door. He stood up and turned toward the hired hands that, indisputably, had the drop on him. There was no way out of this one. He was getting tired of running these missions by himself without anyone to watch his back. There is a reason for the adage, "Two is one; one is none."

"Radio the boss and let him..." one of the gunmen said to his partner before receiving a round to the back of his skull that punched through the front of his head in an explosion of brain and bone matter.

He dropped to his knees and then crashed face-first onto the concrete. His buddy gasped and spun around with his rifle shouldered as he hunted for the shooter around the cranes and containers. Before he could complete a full rotation, another round found its home in the side of the gunman's head with a definitive splat.

Confused, Sledge brought the M4 Carbine to bear and peered through the scope. As he raked the rifle around the port, he caught a glimpse of a light flashing from an elevated position atop one of the cranes down from him. Its intermittent burst signaled in Morse code. Sledge focused the scope on the light and spotted a black-clad figure within the steelwork of the crane.

His phone rang inside his ear. He pressed the button on the outside of the earpiece. "I thought you were sitting this one out?"

"*I was, but then I remembered you don't have any friends,*" Oscar replied from his nest within the crane. "*I couldn't leave you to the wolves.*"

"Nice shooting. I don't remember your aim being that good before. Have you been practicing on your long game?" Sledge quipped back despite his heart beating a dizzying rhythm. His relief was palpable. That was too close.

"*Yep. Not bad, huh? This new scope I have makes it easier to get on target.*"

"It shows. I'm just glad you didn't hit me."

"*Funny, Sledge. What's not funny is that Vega's caravan is about one hundred yards past the containers.*"

"How many are we talking about?" Sledge peered at the four dead men around him, and then turned back to the container he was trying to get inside. "Any chance you have eyes on the girl?"

"*I'm counting around a dozen armed men standing watch around three Suburbans and two Escalades. No eyes on the girl as of yet, but Vega is here with some other folks I've never seen before.*"

"That could be Vega's partners," Sledge replied as he finally worked the rusted plate out of the handle's way and pulled the heavy door open.

"*Yeah. Maybe. You might want to move a bit faster with whatever it is that you're doing. Just a suggestion.*"

Sledge shined the gun-mounted light into the container. Much to his surprise, it wasn't stocked with crates of drugs or weapons. No. It was packed with women. "You've got to be kidding me."

Chapter 61

"*What's up? What did you find?*" Oscar asked.

"More of Vega's precious cargo." Sledge trained the light on the frightened faces of the women, all with varying ethnicities, who were huddled together within the container. "It seems he's shipping out more human cargo from the country tonight." He did a headcount of the trembling and dirty women, who collectively leaned away from him. "I've got roughly thirteen females in this container."

"*No shit. I can't believe that.*"

"Believe it because I'm looking right at them," Sledge replied as he advanced toward the scared, kidnapped women. He put one hand up in a calming gesture as he continued holding the rifle, muzzle down, with the other.

Their ages ranged from what he guessed to be sixteen to late twenties. They were haggard and dingy looking, retreating into the walls of the container as he walked toward them. All were skinny and shaken by his presence. They cowed before him as if he was going to bring about more pain.

"I'm not going to hurt you," Sledge said in a soft voice as he sifted through the women for Kim. She wasn't there within the huddled mass of bodies.

"*I've got a single contact heading your way. East side of the container you're in. Want me to take him out?*"

"Wait until he's on the backside and take the shot." Sledge examined each of the girls confined to the container and asked them, "Do any of you know a Kim Claymore?"

None offered a response to his question as he made for the last of the women, and then turned to face the cracked door of the container. Sledge walked back through toward the abducted women as a light flashed from outside of the door, then to the interior.

The hinges of the steel door creaked as it swung open. As the guard stepped on the outer edge of the container and aimed his rifle and light at Sledge and the girls, his body pitched forward and crashed into the interior wall.

"Good shot. Target down."

"You're clear at the moment. No other contacts in the area, but I'd move, brother."

"Copy that." Sledge peered at the women who were shaken to their cores. They weren't his mission, but he couldn't stand idly by and not rescue them. He waved his arm at the ladies while advancing toward the opening of the container. "Come on. You need to get up and move while we can."

They stood but were hesitant to follow him outside of the container. Their fear was strong and kept them compliant in not fleeing. It was unclear how long Vega had the women under his thumb, but given their reluctance to disobey him, it seemed as if he had driven the point home of what disobedience would get them.

"Listen, I know you're scared, but if you want to get out of this alive, you have to move now. You're going to have to trust me." His tone conveyed the urgency of the matter while he also tried to be considerate of their situation. Not knowing him from every other piece of trash that they probably encountered had them leery of his intentions at first.

One by one, the women shuffled toward the entrance of the container where he waited for them. Sledge raised his hand to stop the women momentarily. He nudged the dead guard's legs away from the opening and ducked outside to check the area.

"I'm bringing the women out of the container," Sledge said to Oscar. "Are we clear to move?"

"Yeah. You should be good. The path's all clear from what I can tell."

Sledge faced the abducted women gathered at the entrance of the container and directed their attention away from their current position. "You're going to head south. Stay together and keep to the shipping containers. Get as far away from here as you can. Don't stop and don't look back. You move until you're safe. Understand?"

The woman acknowledged the order with a single tilt of their heads. They funneled out of the container two at a time as Sledge moved down to the edge of the door and peered at the side. Finding no guards advancing on their position, he moved them onward to the dark recesses of the stacked containers.

"You've got more guards inbound, brother. Four targets are approaching from the east."

They weren't clear. Not yet. Before he could respond to Oscar, one of the kidnapped brunettes stopped and said, "Kim is with them."

"With who?" Sledge replied. "Vega?"

"Do you want me to engage?" Oscar asked through the earpiece. *"They'll be on you soon."*

"Yes. She was taken before we were put in this container and transported to wherever we are," the brunette woman answered.

As the freed women scampered off into the shadows, Sledge took the young brunette by the arm and peered around the bend. Two of the guards made for the rear of the container, but Sledge couldn't lay eyes on the other two.

With no time left to think, Sledge acted. He ducked out from around the corner of the door and fired four muffled shots at the inbound gunmen. They hit center mass. Both fell to the ground before they could get a shot off.

He waved his hand at the brunette and bobbed his head in the direction the others went and said, "Run. Now."

The woman took off in a dead sprint as Sledge killed the gun-mounted light and advanced up the side of the container with his M4 Carbine shouldered.

"I took out the other two but the cat is out of the bag. Vega's men know something's up."

Sledge fired at the scrambling men on the dock while on the move. "Get ground level and make sure those women get to safety. I'll handle it from here."

"I'm not leaving you to get your ass shot. Because we both know you will."

"Just one of those women's lives is worth twelve of mine. Thanks for the assist, brother, but we can't leave them to die." Sledge ducked down behind a container for cover.

"Dammit! Roger that. Good luck."

From his current position, Sledge couldn't see the caravan of vehicles. The dented corner of the container ahead blocked his view. He moved on down the side to the opening within the containers as a salvo of gunfire pinged off the steel sides.

None of the incoming fire found its mark on him as he dipped into the darkness. Sledge stayed on the move and wormed his way through the maze of paths that sliced between the containers. Lights from the gunmen bounced into view ahead of Sledge. He remained calm and waited for each target to emerge. No wasted gunfire.

A single mark appeared from the junction ahead of him. He turned and cast his swath of light down the corridor. Sledge popped off three rounds into the man's stomach and sternum. The gunman's rifle angled downward. He stumbled back into the corner of the container and fell to the ground.

Sledge turned and checked his six o'clock. Two men rushed the opening with rifles shouldered. They fired as Sledge fell to one knee.

Muzzle fire flashed from each of the guns. The harsh bark echoed loudly within the enclosed space. Their wild volley dinged off the sides of the steel walls of the container, missing Sledge.

He returned fire at waist level. Both men took hits below their hips. As they crashed to the ground, bellowing in pain, Sledge put one additional round in each of their heads that silenced them.

He stood and got back on the move and headed down the corridor. He scanned the intersection and continued at a good clip.

About halfway down, two rounds punched Sledge's vest from behind. It knocked him off balance and sent him staggering into the side steel wall. The armored plate stopped the bullets from going through, but he felt the impact nonetheless. Sledge fired while on the move, scattering the forces tracking him through the containers.

As he gathered his legs under him and forged ahead, Sledge was ambushed by a single contact that popped out from the blind corner he neglected to check first in his haste. The large, shadowy man rammed into Sledge before he could lock onto him. His handle on the M4 loosened as he crashed to the ground. He tried to bring the weapon up to fire it, but the shadowy figure closed in on him too fast.

The M4 discharged as a boot stomped the barrel to the ground, pinning Sledge's arm under the weapon. Unable to free his limb, the big man smashed his combat boot into Sledge's face, sliced the sling attached to the M4, and then ripped him from the flat of his back to his feet. He shoved him into the wall of a container and held his knife at Sledge's throat.

"Blake Sledge, I presume," the man said with a snarl. He leaned forward and studied him. A wry grin formed as the confirmation of who Sledge was suddenly came to light. "I didn't believe it was you at first, but look at who just proved me wrong. I never forget a face, Brad Jones. You can go by whatever name you want, but the eyes never lie."

Shane, the instructor from Cobalt, was right. Sledge was able to recognize him as his features manifested through the low light. The instructor's voice, though, was more of the catalyst that triggered Sledge's memory of the hard-nosed man who enjoyed punishing the children at their prison in the mountains of Virginia.

"Where's the girl at?" Sledge asked while carefully reaching behind his back.

"Ah, yes. The kidnapped girl, your current mission so to speak if that's what you want to call her." Shane kept the pressure on Sledge's throat taut, crushing his larynx. "She's safe and sound with Vega. Soon, though, you won't have to worry about her as she'll be off to her new life overseas and you'll be dead, but not before we know what information we need from you. I'd be willing to bet you haven't forgotten our interrogation methods."

Secondary reports were fired from the immediate area even though Shane had Sledge pinned and immobile. Whoever was shooting wouldn't be shooting at them as Sledge had no assets in the area and Vega's men would be standing down since Shane had control of him. There had to be another shooter on-site that was engaging Vega's and Cobalt's forces. Had Oscar returned? Sledge didn't know, but he took advantage of the disruption and made a harrowing move.

Shane looked away while trying to triangulate the secondary shooter's position. Sledge bent his arm enough at an unnatural angle and wiggled the combat knife free from the sheath attached at the small of his back as Shane brought his narrowed gaze back to him. Within a split second, he jacked his right arm up and drove his elbow down on Shane's arm. Then he jammed the tip of the combat knife into the base of Shane's neck.

The instructor's hold on Sledge lessened and gave him room to operate. Shane retreated with the knife buried into his body and with Sledge's hand clasped around the handle.

Clomping footfalls rushed the two men from Sledge's nine o'clock. He caught a glimpse of the figure with his weapon drawn and shouldered. Sledge yanked the blade from Shane's neck, pulled his HK45 from its holster with his free hand, and unloaded it into the charging gunman.

Both Shane and the gunman crashed to the concrete. In less than a minute, Shane would bleed out and no longer be an issue.

Sledge stowed the blade and took off in a dead sprint. His hold on the HK45's grip grew tighter as he bobbed and weaved through the remaining maze among the containers. The pang in his skull from Shane's boot throbbed, but Sledge pushed on. He emerged to an opening where the caravan of vehicles was located.

Several bodies lay motionless on the ground while several more made for the Suburbans and the sedans. Sledge fired at the men by the vehicles closest to him.

Each went down with multiple shots as they were turning his way. One of the black Suburban's tail lights flashed from near the front of the vehicles. The driver pulled out and gunned it, trying to flee the shootout.

Sledge unloaded the HK45 at the Suburban while on the run. The salvo pelted the exterior of the swerving SUV and the driver's side window. The driver lost control as it darted past a stack of shipping containers.

The sound of crunching metal sounded shortly thereafter. A horn blared, bellowing into the night sky. Sledge ejected the spent magazine. It clanged off the concrete as he sped to the blind corner of the containers. He removed a magazine from the pouch of his vest, slapped it into the grip, and released the slide before slipping around the edge.

With the HK45 raised and aimed at the back of the crashed Suburban, Sledge advanced on the smoking SUV. The hood was crumpled. The rear driver-side door hung open. Its interior light illuminated the wheelman slouched forward in the seat with his head buried in the deployed airbag. Sledge craned his neck and aimed the pistol at the rear seat; there was no one there.

A scream from close by nabbed Sledge's ear. It sounded feminine. That had to be Kim. Vega must have taken her and was now on the run.

Sledge tracked the pair by the glow of light dancing in the darkness within the maze of containers. The young woman's struggle to escape acted like an additional beacon for him to follow. He rounded the hard edge of the containers and caught sight of Vega manhandling the girl within his arm. Sledge had found Kim.

She thrashed her body and kicked, trying everything in her power to escape. Sledge trained the pistol at Vega but he couldn't get a clear shot without the risk of hitting her.

"There's nowhere to go, Vega! Let the girl go! Now!" Sledge's voice boomed like thunder.

The crime boss fired at Sledge while backing up. His aim was off. Vega missed him by a small margin as Sledge ducked and moved to his right. As much as he wanted to return fire, Sledge still didn't have a clean shot.

Vega dragged Kim away while trying to line up the barrel on Sledge. Light from the pistol brightened the corridor as he forged ahead.

One additional shot came from Vega's piece at Sledge before Kim stomped his foot and wiggled free from his arms. The single round bit into the bottom portion of Sledge's vest like a hammer. It knocked the wind out of him and sent him back on his heels, but it appeared as if the bullet hadn't penetrated his body.

With Kim mostly clear of Vega, Sledge fired at Vega's right shoulder. The bullet clipped the crime boss's arm and spun him around. His pistol fell to the ground. Vega scurried down the corridor while palming the wound, leaving Kim behind.

Sledge rushed to the teenage girl's aid as she fell to her knees. "Are you okay?"

Shaken by the ordeal, Kim trembled and peered up at him. She offered a slight tilt of her head, which bore a few bruises and cuts blemishing her young face.

"I was hired by your mom and dad to find you. You're safe now." As Sledge helped Kim stand, footfalls closed on them from behind. He pointed the HK45 at the gloom where Oscar stopped and threw his hands up.

"Whoa, brother. It's just me."

"Christ." Sledge lowered the gun. "What are you doing here? I thought you were supposed to be making sure the other women got out safely."

Oscar lowered his arms and the pistol he wielded. A sling attached to a rifle was slung across his body. "I made sure they were clear and directed them on where to go, but I wasn't about to leave you to deal with these assholes alone."

Sledge glanced in the direction Vega had scampered off and then said to Kim, "This is Oscar. He's a friend of mine. You'll be safe with him." He then looked at Oscar. "Get her out of here and call the cops."

"Where are you going?" Oscar asked as Kim shifted toward him.

"After Vega. He's not getting away this time. Not a chance."

Chapter 62

AFTER OSCAR AND KIM fled the area, Sledge went after Vega. He tracked the criminal by the blood leaking from the wound through the seaport. Sledge was getting close. He could feel it.

There would be no mercy shown. Vega was too well-connected. His partnership with Cobalt made him nearly untouchable and a menace to society. One way or another, Sledge was going to end the slippery thug that night.

The blood trail went cold after a while. It was as if Vega had vanished into thin air. As Sledge searched the immediate area with his Taclight to determine which way Vega had gone, an eerie sensation crawled up his spine.

A feeling of imminent doom sent Sledge into a defensive stance. With the HK45 trained ahead and the light's beam cast at the blackness, he raked the passageway.

Subtle footsteps sounded above Sledge and then stopped. By the time he realized what it was and looked up, a figure crashed down on him. He flew back into the hard surface of the shipping container. The HK45 and his Taclight popped out of his hand to the ground as the assassin from Vega's home launched a roundhouse kick at his head.

He ducked and slipped under the formidable killer's black combat boot that dinged off the container. Sledge hopped back with his fists raised.

His adversary wore the same black mask as before, concealing his identity. He was likely part of Cobalt's elite unit of trained hitmen based on his fighting style. There would be no reasoning with him or talking his way out of their death match. It would end only after one of them was dead.

The assassin didn't reach for the gun that was stowed in the shoulder holster. A simple pull and shoot would end the battle before it began. It confused Sledge why the assassin opted not to employ this method since it was in his interest to kill him as quickly and efficiently as possible. Either way, it was a bad and fatal decision.

They stared each other down at first. Then the assassin made his move. He threw a volley of jabs at Sledge's head then landed a roundhouse kick to his stomach. The blow caught more of the vest than his body, reducing the impact of the strike.

Sledge countered by spring-boarding forward as the assassin adjusted his footing to throw another kick. He connected a jab into the assassin's face that knocked him backward. Sledge didn't let up and continued his assault with right crosses and knees to the gut.

Bloody and bruised, Sledge pulled his combat knife from the small of his back as he flanked the assassin. He jabbed at the killer's spine but he spun out of the way and slashed Sledge's forearm with his Karambit.

The sharpened, curved knife sliced the flesh open with ease. Blood ran from the gash and dripped onto the concrete. The pair circled each other, waiting for their counterpart to make the first move.

Sledge felt the wetness on his skin. It burned and stung from the sweat hitting the damaged flesh.

He attacked Sledge with a lightning-fast upward slash near his head. Sledge ducked and sliced across the assassin's black, long-sleeve top at the midsection and below the protective vest he wore. The blade cut through the fabric, but Sledge was unsure if he struck meat.

Unfazed, the assassin spun around and brought the Karambit downward from above his head. Sledge caught his arm and threw him against the outside of the container, face first. As he directed the tip of the combat knife at the back of the man's skull, the assassin tilted his head slightly to the left.

The blade pinged off the steel and broke the tip. The assassin jabbed his elbow into Sledge's side, then he maneuvered the Karambit toward his hand wielding the combat knife.

It dislodged from Sledge's grip to the ground. He worked his arm up and over the assassin's arm, and then he bent the limb behind the killer to remove the deadly blade from the fight.

Sledge shoved the assassin forward into the container. He hammered his kidneys with four hard strikes and ripped the Karambit from the gloved hand. He grabbed the back of the killer's head and slammed it twice into the surface of the container.

The assassin slouched, his legs weakened under him. As Sledge adjusted the Karambit in his hand, the killer fell to the ground with Sledge's finger gripping the mask.

He pulled it free as the body hit the pavement. Sledge glanced at the mask, then the body that lay prone on its stomach. He straddled the assassin and flipped him over as he leveled the curved knife with the throat, but he stopped.

It wasn't a man he fought. It was a woman. In mere seconds, the light bulb dinged inside Sledge's head at her identity. He pulled the knife away and backed away from the killer that Cobalt directed to end him.

With his world shattered by the revelation of who the assassin was, Sledge muttered a single word. "Mya?"

Chapter 63

THE DEFEATED-LOOKING FROWNS THE Claymores previously wore were now replaced with wide smiles and tears of joy. They couldn't help but smother their daughter with hugs; she sat between them on the couch in their plush home two days after Sledge had brought her back to them.

Kim looked remarkably well. Her face still had hints of abuse. She moved a bit slowly as she absorbed the constant hugs from her mom and dad. Overall, she appeared to be recovering from her traumatic experience without many issues.

"We can't thank you enough," Mr. Claymore said.

"Yes. Both of you have our undying gratitude." Mrs. Claymore latched onto Kim's arm. "I don't know if we'll ever be able to repay you."

"I'm just happy that you have your daughter back," Detective Wentworth said with a wide smile. "That's all that matters."

"Indeed." Sledge stared at Kim. "Are you holding up okay?"

She moved some strands of her hair behind her ear and nodded. "I am. Thank you again for everything, Mr. Sledge."

"Of course."

Mr. Claymore motioned with his head at Sledge to stand and follow him. The two men stepped away as Detective Wentworth continued speaking with the mom and daughter. Once they were out of range of the cop, Mr. Claymore whispered to Sledge. "The remainder of the money has been wired into your account. Twenty thousand."

"Thank you. I'm just happy that she's here with you. That was my main concern."

"I know it wasn't easy and you risked much to bring our daughter back." He extended his hand to Sledge and said, "If there is anything you ever need down the road, please don't hesitate to reach out to us. We are forever in your debt."

Sledge shook his hand. "Thank you. Take care of her. That's all you need to do."

"We will do that. No question about it."

Detective Wentworth stood as did Kim and her mom. He looked to Sledge and the dad. "I need to head out. Duty calls."

"I should be going as well," Sledge shot back.

The family said their goodbyes and Kim hugged both men before Mr. Claymore escorted them to the main entrance of the home. As they headed down to their cars parked in the circle driveway, Detective Wentworth spoke up.

"You did a good thing for that family. I'm sorry I wasn't more help on the case. Damn corruption had my arms tied to the point of not being able to do much for her."

Sledge waved off the apology. "No need to thank me or to beat yourself up. That's the difference between us."

"What's that?"

"You're forced to abide by rules and regulations. I'm not. You deal with black and white. I work in the gray area." Sledge stopped on the driveway next to his Chevelle and continued. "This was a joint venture. It doesn't matter who brought Kim home. She's here and that's all that matters to me."

"Me as well." Wentworth nodded. "You have shaken things up, though, with this case. Internal Affairs is conducting a thorough investigation within the police force and into other parties in office throughout Atlanta who worked under Vega. It seems that change is coming soon because of you."

"That's good to hear. Any word on Vega's whereabouts?"

"Not yet, but we're hunting for him."

That makes two of us, Sledge thought.

As the two men shook hands and parted ways, Sledge got behind the wheel of his muscle car. Detective Wentworth drove off first.

Sledge started the Chevelle and took one final look at the Claymore home, satisfied with the outcome for the family, but he knew that his and Trixie's problems were just beginning.

Epilogue

THEY HAD LITTLE BREATHING room since completing Kim's case. A bigger threat lurked on the horizon for the duo who got back to work on tracking down Vega, but that was only part of the plan.

Trixie had overtaken Sledge's office. It was now hers to work out of. She was the genius behind the keyboard while Sledge was the ground force who hit the streets. Together, they formed a powerful alliance, one that grew stronger day by day.

"Anything new on Vega?" Sledge asked from the doorway of his former office.

"Not yet, but I'll track him down," Trixie said from her chair planted in front of her computer. "I'm not easily swayed."

"That you're not." Sledge glanced down the hall toward one of the empty back bedrooms. "If you find anything, let me know."

She gave him a thumbs-up and continued her hunt while clacking at the keys.

Sledge was headed down the hallway when his phone started to ring. He pulled it out and peered at the screen. *Unknown Caller* displayed on the device. He answered the call, figuring it was a member of Cobalt ready to throw threats his way. "Hello?"

"*Blake Sledge?*" the well-spoken man asked.

"Who is this?"

"*Someone who has been following your recent dismantling of Cobalt's hold in Atlanta. Nice work by the way.*"

Sledge stopped shy of the closed bedroom door and tried to figure out who was on the phone with him. His mind was a blank canvas of possible suspects. "What do you want?"

"A meeting, if possible. We have similar goals and enemies."

"I don't know, I'm pretty busy." Sledge said, trying to gauge with whom he was speaking.

"Yes, I've heard. Are you happy chasing the tail of the snake or are you ready to cut off its head?"

There was much to process from the few sentences the caller spouted. Who was he? How did he know about Sledge and Cobalt? Was this another trap? Sledge didn't have answers to any of the questions, but taking down Cobalt did pique his interest.

"I'm listening."

"Perfect. I'll be in touch soon with a time and place for us to meet."

"What do I call you?"

"Charles, for now. Talk soon."

The call ended. Sledge pulled the phone away from his ear, shoved it into the back pocket of his pants, and then unlocked the heavy door leading into the bedroom. He pushed it open, stepped inside the room, and stared at his guest who was restrained.

Battered and beaten, Mya glared at Sledge. Her intense gaze burned a hole through his skull. If looks could kill, her job would be complete.

Sledge was going to have his work cut out with her, that is, if she didn't kill him first.

About the Author

R.D. West is the pseudonym for writing duo Derek Shupert and Rebecca Sitton. They have combined their writing skills and life experiences to create gritty thrillers with flawed and dynamic characters.

Printed in Great Britain
by Amazon

17784222R00171